Reviews for *Eternae*

"My imagination runs wild as Carly's search for the Grail continues. In this next adventure, she encounters obstacle after obstacle. In typical Carly style, she faces these obstacles one step at a time, with bravery and her team—and in really great shoes."

— **Courtney C.**, *Lipstick Hoarder and Avid Reader*
Follow Courtney on Instagram @the_pages_within

"A novel to grow with you! I haven't been this hung on to 'what happens next' since I was a teenager. The drama and emotion draw you in and do not release you! I read it through entirely before I set it down and was engrossed from start to finish. Galib has mastered the art of 'enthrall.' The Knights of the Dagger series continues to be a work of art for inspired and hopeful young women."

— **Tiffany J.**, *Administration and Communications MVP*

"I thoroughly enjoyed reading Carly and Blane's adventures in *Etched in Stone* and couldn't wait to read *Eternae*, the second novel in The Knights of the Dagger trilogy. *Eternae* picks up where *Etched* left off, taking Carly et al., and the reader, on a breathtaking adventure into a world of darkness, deviousness, and deception. Galib's brilliant imagination weaves a tale of old grudges, family rivalries, greed, and archaeology together with the pursuit of truth and the Holy Grail. But will good triumph over evil? I was glued to the book from beginning to end to find out. Galib's spectacular ending propels *Eternae* into the ranks of great Arthurian and Nordic heroic legends."

— **Grace G.**, *Reader, Medical Practice Manager, and Healthcare Provider*

"The night after I read the preface, I dreamed about the book, imagining what would happen based on those hints. Carly and Blane are vivid enough to dream about . . . Galib's greatest strengths are writing compelling characters I care about and well-crafted mysteries. I would recommend it to my friends!"

— **Charity L.**, *Renaissance Woman, Stargazer, and Collector of Video Games*

"The story stays with me in the technicalities of how it came together, and the plot is immaculate and very distinctive . . . I'm positive I caught at least one fly in my mouth because my jaw was dropped the whole time in awe of this ending. I'd recommend to all my friends who love a good mystery."

— **Kaya S.**, *Believer in Magic, Devourer of Books, and Explorer of Worlds*

ETERNAE

THE KNIGHTS OF THE DAGGER
BOOK II

CHRISTINE GALIB

road less traveled
enterprises

Author's note: This is a work of fiction. Names, characters, places, and incidents are the product of the author's imagination or are used fictitiously.

ETERNAE

Editor: Kristen Corrects, kristencorrects.com
Typesetter & Proofreader: Kingsman Editing, kingsmanediting.com
Cover Illustrator: Giselle Harrington, giselleharrington.com

First edition published 2023
ISBN: 978-1-955824-04-0 (paperback)
ISBN: 978-1-955824-05-7 (e-book)
christinegalib.com

Published by road less traveled enterprises
roadlesstraveledenterprises.com

For Charlotte

&

*For every knight tackling her or his quest
and chasing the impossible
with a pure heart and
grace, courage, and faith . . .*

In memoriam:

Dr. MNS, RQ, and EMF

"sic transit gloria mundi"

"We are at another point of historical inflection. What hitherto seemed magical will become real. It is a time in which humanity will redefine what is possible, a time of ending the inevitable. Indeed, it is a time in which we will redefine what it means to be human, for this is not just the start of a revolution, it is the start of an evolution."

— **David Sinclair**, *Lifespan: Why We Age—and Why We Don't Have To*

"It is the magician's bargain: give up our soul, get power in return. But once our souls, that is, ourselves, have been given up, the power thus conferred will not belong to us. We shall in fact be the slaves and puppets of that to which we have given our souls . . . if man chooses to treat himself as raw material, raw material he will be: not raw material to be manipulated, as he fondly imagined, by himself, but by mere appetite, that is, mere Nature, in the person of his de-humanized Conditioners."

— **C.S. Lewis**, *The Abolition of Man*

PREFACE

In his book *Profiles of the Future: An Inquiry into the Limits of the Possible*, Arthur C. Clarke wrote, "Any sufficiently advanced technology is indistinguishable from magic."

With our incredible breakthroughs in technology and medicine, we are blurring the lines between science and magic, making real and replicable what once seemed mythical and magical. We are challenging the rules that regulate life itself, redefining what is possible and what it means to be human. As we challenge these rules, we find ourselves playing with the power to control our destiny at the press of a button or tweak of a gene. Seduced by this power, we test limits of our reality—one experiment at a time. As we do, we gain more knowledge. And with great knowledge, comes great responsibility. And with great responsibility, comes great obligation—obligation to do what is right.

How do we know what is right? And just because we *can* do something, does that mean we should? What moral obligations, if any, and to whom, do we have as we chase the impossible, claiming we act for the "greater good"—when our feigned altruism masks our own lusts and desires? When we take decisions of life and death into our own hands—in the name of science—who wins, and who loses?

In *Eternae*, Carly Stuart, Blane Henley, Lydia Kells, and Kenneth Wengaro are back. Our favorite Fearless Foursome continues their Grail quest, one step and one leap of faith at a time. In *Eternae*, the stakes are higher, the characters more conniving, the science more complicated, the technology more magical, and the magic more real. Carly takes an unexpected road less traveled, but with the Holy Grail itself on the line, I don't blame her . . . Can you? Carly has got to do what she feels is right as she lives Gran's legacy and walks in Gran's shoes—no matter how dangerous the path.

In *Eternae*, Carly makes new friends—and enemies—as she discovers what it means to keep a promise at all costs. More than that, Carly realizes that to understand her future, she must confront her past, even if she isn't ready. In *Eternae*, Carly's quest forces her to step out of her comfort zone and into a high-tech laboratory where secrets are hidden in spell books and basements . . . and where every answer leads to more and more questions.

So, as you read *Eternae*, I hope you—like Carly, Blane, Lydia, and Kenneth—keep asking questions. I hope you enjoy reading *Eternae* as much as I have enjoyed writing it, and I'd love to hear your thoughts. Send me a note at christinegalib.com— where you can also learn about the characters in The Knights of the Dagger series—or find me on Instagram @christinegalibauthor. Use the hashtags #Eternae and #TheKnightsoftheDagger and post your reactions, questions, and comments—and pictures—as you read!

ETERNAE

THE KNIGHTS OF THE DAGGER
BOOK II

I

I blinked my eyes open. Hot sweat dripped down my neck. I bolted upright and peeled my damp bedsheets off my legs. My heart was pounding like a jackhammer. *"Watch your back, Carly Stuart. When our paths cross again, you won't be as lucky."* Dr. Pritzmord's words echoed in my head.

4:04 a.m.

The digits of the clock on the nightstand cut the darkness with bright red light. Blane slept peacefully in the bed next to me, breathing with a measured, calm cadence. I lay back and closed my eyes, trying to sleep, but I saw Dr. Wengaro's hands as he strangled Dr. Pritzmord. I gasped for air in sharp, shallow inhales. My breath didn't come easily to me. My blood raced through my body as I heard Dr. Pritzmord's voice in my head: *"Watch your back. The Grail will be mine yet."* I saw Dr. Pritzmord's eyes bulging out of his head as he gasped for air.

Dr. Lydia Kells, my archaeology professor, was Gran's partner—and now was my partner in our Grail quest. J. Carmichael, Gran's closest friend, was a Knight of the Dagger who seemed to know a lot about my family. Dr. Sidney Hasserin, the professor and rising-star archaeologist, pushed Gran and stole a priceless ruby. Dr. Kenneth Wengaro, the Nassauton faculty member Lydia and I wrongly suspected of murder, was a Knight of the Dagger and our teammate. Dr. Daniel Pritzmord, who deceived us into believing he was a respectable dean, was a violent killer and our enemy. *In what other evils is Dr. Pritzmord involved?*

1

I sighed, wiping the sweat on my neck. We were in our Amesbury cottage in England. We had a box that didn't contain the Grail, but a mortar, pestle, and Nazi journal—with its cover page mysteriously written in English, not German. Blane said the Grail had been lost for centuries. Didn't King Arthur find—and hide—it? Weren't the Knights of the Dagger and the White Wave trying to locate it?

Or were the stories only legends after all—legends that led to danger? Dr. Wengaro was in the hospital. Blane was recovering from his ankle injuries. We were thousands of miles from Nassauton. It seemed like ages since I'd seen or texted Lara. And I hadn't talked to my mom in forever. *Would Gran be proud of me? Could she have guessed the Grealmæp would lead me down such a dangerous path? What else did J. Carmichael know about the Knights of the Dagger—and Gran?* Of all people, J. Carmichael—with his fluency in five languages and expertise in drug developments and regulation—might help me translate the journal. I needed to meet up with him as soon as possible.

I opened my eyes and sighed.

4:29 a.m.

The digits of the clock were blood red, like the double dagger marks tattooed on the inside of Dr. Wengaro's and J. Carmichael's left wrists. *What other secrets do the Knights of the Dagger—and the Grealmæp—have?*

I rubbed my eyes and rolled to my side, tucking my head under my arm. Closing my eyes, I took a deep breath and buried my face in the pillow. The leaps of faith I had taken to find the Grail had only led me to more mysteries—and danger.

††

I awoke to a hand tapping gently on my shoulder. Blane was sitting on my bed.

"You know you're not supposed to walk on your ankle as it's

healing," I mumbled, looking at him. His hair was tousled and his eyes bleary. He'd pulled his sweatshirt hood around his head.

"And you must be freezing!" I exclaimed, pointing at his face.

"Don't worry about me," he said, leaning closer. "And I'm not going to wheel myself from my bed to yours. It's not that far of a walk!"

"You need to listen to the doctors."

"I am!"

"Okay," I sighed. "I just want you to get better."

I instinctively opened my arms for a hug. Blane scooped me up, gently stroking my curls. I let out a deep breath.

"You were having another nightmare, weren't you?" he asked, holding me tighter. He released the hug. "You were tossing and turning and talking in your sleep."

I propped myself up on the bed. "You heard me?"

Blane nodded. "You were crying out about the Grail. What's going on?"

"I keep seeing Dr. Pritzmord when Dr. Wengaro strangled him. I can't get his bulging eyes out of my mind. That image. His threat. *'Carly Stuart, when our paths cross again, you won't be as lucky. Watch your back.'* He says that to me over and over again in my nightmares."

"Oh Carly." Blane sighed, squeezing my hand. "It's an empty threat. It's all behind us. He's in jail."

"For now. What if he escapes?" I looked at Blane with fear in my eyes.

"He's not going to escape."

I shook my head and looked at my Ailm charm, then at Blane. No matter how many sites around Amesbury we saw and happy memories we made—from taking our selfie in front of Stonehenge, to aligning the Grealmæp with the stones, to eating dinner at The Courtly Robin—I couldn't erase the memories of Dr. Pritzmord. We'd been in Amesbury for over a week, and no matter how many scenes of families playing in the park, times we'd looked the wrong way trying to cross the street, or moments we'd laughed in the grocery store filled my days, scenes of Dr. Pritzmord's terror filled my nights.

When I first told Blane and Lydia about my nightmares, they suggested we stop visiting Dr. Wengaro. Blane thought the hospital visits triggered the nightmares. But I enjoyed our visits, since seeing Dr. Wengaro's progress helped me know we were moving on. Lydia told me to focus on the evidence and not get lost in the traumatic emotion and my nightmares. I knew she was trying to help, but my nightmares were evidence—and just like any other type of evidence, they needed to be examined. Writing down my nightmares in my journal helped me get them out of my head and on paper so I could move on.

Another activity that helped me move on was Dr. Gellmane's crash course in artifact curation. Knowing we'd be in town while Dr. Wengaro and Blane recovered, Dr. Gellmane offered to teach behind-the-scenes insights into artifacts preparation and curation. Lydia joined, which made me feel like we were back at Nassauton.

In Dr. Gellmane's classes, I realized I loved cataloguing artifacts and preparing them for curation. I'd never thought about those processes before. In listening to Gran's stories, I'd focused on finding the artifacts. But learning about preparation and curation was interesting. I could see how those processes enabled new generations to experience the artifacts. And I could see how much damage I could have caused the Grealmæp by wearing it, though I had been careful. Dr. Gellmane also explained how to properly store artifacts. She taught us that each display case had to be specially made so it was climate, temperature, and sunlight controlled.

"It's like the librarian told me the first time I went to Rockfire," I whispered to Blane as we practiced preparing sample artifacts under Dr. Gellmane's supervision. "In the Rare Books Room, each book is stored in those temperature-sealed cabinets." I chuckled. "The librarian talked about those books like they had temperaments and needed maintenance—like they were people."

The more I practiced with the samples, the more I understood the importance of carefully preserving the artifacts. Each artifact had a character and a story, and the goal of preparation and curation was to preserve the artifact's character—and let the artifact tell its story. I smiled. I was developing an appreciation for curation and wanted to learn more about how to collect and maintain artifacts.

I also wanted to know more about Gran's and Lydia's archaeological adventures and the artifacts they collected. Maybe one day, I'd visit more of these artifacts—more than the burnt orange bowl I'd seen in Nassauton's display case. Maybe one day, I'd curate my own collection. *What if my first collected artifact is the Holy Grail?* Seeking the Grail was like chasing the impossible, but there was no way I was giving up on my quest. Grinning, I looked at my Ailm charm. *What will it feel like to find the Grail?*

Once Blane and I mastered preparing our samples, we were ready to tackle the mortar, pestle, and Nazi journal. Dr. Gellmane was kind enough to let us work on-site with the artifacts, explaining the only way for them to leave the museum was through a museum transfer or a private acquisition. She'd walked Lydia to a workstation in the Examination Room. I followed, pushing Blane in his wheelchair. The doctors said if he kept taking it easy and continued with his physical therapy exercises, he'd be on crutches and a boot in no time. I couldn't wait to have my teammate back to full health.

Dr. Gellmane flipped several lights on around the workstation, then set up the table, gathering towels, tools, and boxes. She pulled her long platinum hair back into a ponytail, then slid her gloves over her hands. Her fingernails were short and unpolished. Her skin was rough and strong, as though her hands held years of experience in preparing thousands of artifacts. As she placed our box and a towel on the workstation table, I noticed a small scar on the back of her right hand, like she'd had an accident with a kitchen knife.

Watching Dr. Gellmane, I wondered how Gran fell in love

with archaeology. Outside of the stories of her digs, I didn't know much about Gran's early life and career. I knew she started "I Dig It," the week-long intensive bootcamp for women, but that wasn't until later in her career. *What leaps of faith did Gran take to become a world-renowned archaeologist?*

"Dr. Gellmane," I asked as she laid a towel over the workstation table. "Do you know the name Lyle Ainsley?"

"Who doesn't?" Dr. Gellmane smiled. "She was one of the most famous archaeologists in the world. A real trailblazer, responsible for many great discoveries."

I grinned, proud to hear the director of the Amesbury Museum talk about Gran with such esteem. I was also puzzled Dr. Gellmane didn't mention Lydia. *Did she not know Gran and Lydia were partners?* I looked over at Lydia, and she smiled. She didn't seem to care that she wasn't mentioned, and she wasn't about to connect any dots. I could tell she was playing it safe. Though Dr. Gellmane arrested Dr. Pritzmord, we didn't know if she could be trusted, even if she seemed to be on our side.

"Her passing was a great loss," said Lydia, her voice trailing off. "But in the end, death always has its own plans and doesn't let any man—or woman—stop them."

Dr. Gellmane nodded, opening our box and removing the mortar, pestle, and journal. I looked at Lydia and Blane, who had wheeled himself around the table to get a better view. Dr. Gellmane arranged the artifacts on the towel. "So, you thought the Holy Grail would be in this box?" She smiled slightly, changing the subject.

I blushed, embarrassed to admit I sincerely believed we'd find the Grail on our first attempt. I nodded. Dr. Gellmane must have sensed my embarrassment, since she smiled and quickly responded, "Don't be embarrassed. Loads of people come here seeking the Grail. We are the official museum for Stonehenge artifacts, after all."

I grinned, relieved she didn't think I was too naïve. Still, I didn't want to discuss the Grail in detail around people we didn't completely trust. I pointed at our workstation table, changing the subject back to artifact preparation and curation. "If you found a box with a mortar, pestle, and journal, which one would you prepare first and why?"

"The journal," Dr. Gellmane replied. "But that's my preference. The journal looks like it's the most interesting and will take the most time, because of all the pages we need to photograph. Let's get started."

As Dr. Gellmane moved the journal to the towel's center, I took out my phone and put on my gloves.

"Oh no, don't use your phone. They make DSLRs for a reason, love." Dr. Gellmane reached into a box on the table for her camera.

"My phone camera is really good," I said. "Plus, it saves me a step in uploading the pictures and emailing them to myself."

Dr. Gellmane chuckled, rolling her eyes. "Young people and their new technology. Fine, have it your way, but remember, start with the covers before you go into the weeds of the pages." Dr. Gellmane left me with the journal and started to prepare the mortar and pestle with Lydia and Blane. Blane wheeled himself around the workstation, and Lydia adjusted her glasses.

I didn't understand what the big deal was. Pictures were pictures. It wasn't like my life depended on the details that a smartphone wouldn't pick up. And my phone camera was pretty good! As Dr. Gellmane turned around to focus on the mortar and pestle, I rolled my eyes behind her back, mouthing, "Young people and their new technology." Our new technology was better than her old technology! I centered my phone on the swastika, letting my camera focus before I snapped the picture.

"Good, now get the back, then the interior," Dr. Gellmane called from the other corner of the workstation.

After I had gotten the pictures, I carefully opened the journal to the cover page.

††

Notes and Experiments, Volume IV:
Making Grealia Eternae, Part II

By KAvG

Judging from the double dagger marks, KAvG was a Knight of the Dagger. More than that, he was a German chemist. *Why is this written in English?* I flipped through the pages of chemistry equations and notes. Sentences here and there were also in English, with the longer entries written in German. *KAvG must have been fluent in both. Why? What Nazi secrets are in his journal?* A surge of anticipation pulsed through me: J. Carmichael, and his translation expertise, couldn't come fast enough! I texted him to make sure he still planned to meet us in Amesbury as soon as he could catch a break from his cases.

Grealia Eternae. I snapped my picture of the cover page. I'd seen the word *Eternae* in only one other place. *Could Grealia Eternae be the precursor to Eternae, my dad's immunotherapy drug?* I kept taking pictures, turning the pages slowly and carefully, trying to get all the details.

"I imagine you'll want to send this residue to the lab for testing?" Dr. Gellmane asked Lydia as she and Blane examined the mortar and pestle.

Lydia nodded. "Please. What's the turnaround time?"

"A few days, a week?" Dr. Gellmane mused. "Depends on how busy the lab is."

"That's great," Blane replied. "What do you think it is?"

"Very hard to say from looking at it, love."

I chuckled at the word *love.* Dr. Gellmane's chumminess amused me. We'd heard enough people around town call us "love" in a friendly way to know it was an English term of endearment. I grinned. I liked the Britishisms I'd learned.

While Dr. Gellmane, Lydia, and Blane chatted about lab analysis techniques, I stared at the journal. To put the journal in the box, KAvG had to have had a Grealmæp. *Where is KAvG's Grealmæp now? Is it the same as mine? Or is it the other one? How did KAvG know how to use the Grealmæp to open the box? Could the box ever have contained the Grail?* I jotted down my questions in my journal, realizing that our box could still lead us to the Grail, or at least to the second Grealmæp.

"Dr. Gellmane," I asked. "Wasn't that box brought to the Amesbury Museum from a Stonehenge excavation?"

Dr. Gellmane nodded as she gathered foam padding and a crate for packing the mortar and pestle. "Yes—one of many artifacts found in the Aubrey Holes and brought here. Lots of bits and bobs have been found in those little pits. Boxes, coins, urns, utensils, bowls, and the like." She listed the artifacts, counting them with her fingers. Her scar stretched out, moving with her skin as she counted. "Lots of bits and bobs," she repeated, looking at Lydia and me, "but no Grail. Of course, at this point, it's more likely that it *isn't* at Stonehenge." She playfully shook her head, chuckling. "If I had a quid for each Grail-quester who came here, I'd be retired by now. I'd have a cottage in the Cotswolds and be tending to my garden." She kept laughing. "They're quite funny, of course, Grail-questers. They drive themselves bonkers. No one has found the Grail."

"Since it doesn't exist," said Lydia, smoothing her hair and patting her bun.

"Well, who is to know for certain?" asked Dr. Gellmane. "Tell that to the Nazis who looted our towns looking for it. One could even argue that a big reason for World War II was Hitler trying to get the Grail."

"What do you mean?" I asked, handing Dr. Gellmane a marker. I'd finished taking pictures of the journal. She wrote *Fragile, handle with care* and *This side up* on the crate after she sealed it.

"Right, Paige will ship the mortar and pestle to the lab today."

"Thank you," Lydia said. "We appreciate your help."

"It's my pleasure. It's been truly marvelous working with you all, dahlings. Carly, can you hand me the journal? I'll put it back in the box, and we'll put both in the storage room for safekeeping." Dr. Gellmane smiled.

I handled her KAvG's journal, amused by how she enunciated her words. "Wait, tell me more about Hitler and the Grail."

Dr. Gellmane looked at me as she held the journal. "Some say Hitler's whole delusional fantasy for a new world order hinged on the Grail. He desperately wanted it and its immense powers—purity, immortality—for himself and his race."

She paused, looking me in the eyes. Her penetrating gaze made me uncomfortable, like she was staring deep into my mind. "It's rooted in Hitler's quest to create a pure race. He believed the Grail could help him do that. He started the Nazi party as an occult and quasi-spiritual fraternity, modeled after secret orders of knights. He was also obsessed with King Arthur. Hitler constructed Wewelsburg Castle after Camelot, naming one room after Arthur, and calling another one the Grail Room. Bet you don't learn that on the other side of the pond."

"We sure don't," Blane said. "With all this Nazi history, my favorite archaeologist wasn't too far off in his adventures on the silver screen." He looked at Lydia. Though Lydia shot him the side-eye, I swore I saw her hide a chuckle.

Scrunching my face in disgust as I thought about Hitler, I started twirling my loose curl. "So disturbing," I whispered. "Perverting orders of knights and religion."

Dr. Gellmane nodded, pointing at the swastika on the journal's cover. "The swastika is actually an ancient Eastern religious icon relating to divinity, spirituality, and prosperity. Hitler adopted it as the Nazi symbol and an emblem of the Aryan race, thus corrupting its original association." She placed the journal in the box. "He was fascinated by the intersection of the spiritual, scientific, and supernatural realms. He believed the

Grail would help him accelerate his Aryan breeding 'program' and create a race to rule this world—and the next. He wanted supremacy, not through healing the sick, but through experimenting on—or eliminating—them. He had a whole army of chemists. He authorized unimaginably inhumane experiments across Europe—Poland, Austria, Germany, to name a few places. He piled resources into drug development, attempting to discover anything that would make his 'pure race' immortal. He ran countless pseudoscientific experiments on time travel and telekinesis, trying to push the bounds of our reality for his advantage. Simply heinous and delusional."

I shook my head, cringing as I wondered how many experiments the epitome of evil himself authorized. Hearing Dr. Gellmane describe Hitler's twisted philosophies and "scientific" pursuits made me sick to my stomach. *Was Hitler directly responsible for Grealia Eternae—and ultimately, Eternae? Did KAvG know Hitler?*

"I bet you didn't know your research project would lead you down this path," Dr. Gellmane said as she finished packing the journal. She looked at Lydia, then me. "You're lucky to have a great professor."

I smiled. I was lucky I'd met Lydia at Nassauton.

"Right, I hope your research is fruitful. It's been marvelous working with you." Dr. Gellmane paused. "Stonehenge's secrets bring so many interesting people to our museum. The ley lines, the spiritual and supernatural energy, the astrology, the Grail . . ." Her voice trailed off. "Sometimes I start to think there is truth to all of it."

Lydia glared at her. "Don't be ridiculous. You're the director of a world-renowned museum. It's all fiction. There's no evidence for any of it. Just myths." She smoothed her bun, making sure not one silver strand of hair was out of place.

"Well, fiction or not, the fact is the Grail is a relic for which people are willing to die—and to kill. To this day, I'm sure. That's got to mean something."

I sighed. Dr. Gellmane didn't know how right she was about killing and the Grail. She was a wealth of information, and our time with her stimulated much more than my interest in curating artifacts and the Grail. My head was spinning with questions about the Nazis and Eternae.

"Right then, I'll ring you when we get the lab results." Dr. Gellmane smiled. "I do hope they help your research."

Dr. Gellmane walked us out of the Examination Room, back outside, and down another hallway. This hallway had more pictures of the museum's blueprints and tour groups, as well as portraits of its board and staff. It also had a large-scale diagram of Stonehenge, with the Sarsens and Aubrey Holes numbered and mapped out. As we walked by, I paused. There wasn't even a Z8 Aubrey Hole. *It's not that the Z8 Aubrey Hole is missing—the Z8 Aubrey Hole doesn't even exist.* I shook my head, continuing down the hallway. Maybe at one point, King Arthur buried the Grail at Stonehenge, near—or somehow even under—the fallen stones. But by now, the Grail could be anywhere in the world.

As I kept walking, I noticed a portrait with AMESBURY MUSEUM DIRECTOR written on a small gold plaque on its wooden frame. Dr. Gellmane was in front of a bookcase filled with leather-bound books. She wore a black pantsuit and stood with one hand on an antique tan globe. An iridescent pearl brooch in the shape of a row of ocean waves glistened on her blazer lapel.

II

As soon as Lydia, Blane, and I got to our car and closed the doors, we stared at each other. Each of us noticed Dr. Gellmane's brooch. We needed to tell Dr. Wengaro as soon as possible.

"That white wave design—it's the same brooch as Dr. Pritzmord's. That can't be a coincidence. It's the symbol of the Knights of Vanora, which changed their name to the Knights of the White Wave," I said as we drove into town and passed the cemetery. A few people were visiting gravesites and laying wreaths by their loved ones' tombstones.

"You're thinking Dr. Pritzmord and Dr. Gellmane are Knights of the White Wave? Why would Dr. Gellmane advertise this, if we know the Knights of the White Wave are evil?" Blane asked. "Do you think she's still a knight?"

"I think once a knight, always a knight," Lydia said as we pulled into the hospital parking lot. "I don't think any order would let a member leave just like that." She parked near the entrance.

"Maybe others don't know what the brooch means," I said, opening my car door. "Maybe Dr. Gellmane thinks no one outside of the Knights of the White Wave knows the brooch's meaning. Maybe she doesn't realize the Knights of the Dagger know about the White Wave's name change."

"Let's see what Kenneth has to say. He's the expert." Lydia closed her door and locked the car. Shivering in the cold March air, I quickened my pace as we entered the hospital. We arrived in Dr. Wengaro's room as he was finishing lunch.

"I'm doing very well," he said. "My doctors said I should be out in another week." He grinned. "And thank God for that! I'm ready for a real bathroom!" He pointed at the little sink and mirror in the corner. "My sink is so far away from the toilet and shower that you wonder how this passed a design and accessibility inspection!"

"That's great news," Blane said.

Dr. Wengaro nodded. "How's your ankle?"

"It's fine. I should be on crutches soon. I'm not supposed to put pressure on it in the meantime." Blane glanced at me. "Not even to walk five steps across my room."

"Happy to hear it." Dr. Wengaro smiled. "What's the latest with our box?"

We caught up Dr. Wengaro on our curation classes and Dr. Gellmane's portrait.

"That's the symbol of the Knights of the White Wave," said Kenneth. "So, she's one of them, and so is Dr. Pritzmord. Do you think they know they're both knights?"

"They have to know. If she saw his pin, wouldn't she know? And if he saw that portrait, he'd know immediately."

"The better questions," said Lydia, exhaling before she continued, "are these: If they are both Knights of the White Wave, are they collaborating to get the Grail? They know Carly has the Grealmæp. Do they have the second one? Do they know there are two? What else does Dr. Gellmane know?"

A chill ran down my spine. The four of us stared at the floor in silence.

After a few minutes had passed, Blane looked up, puzzled. "Here's what I don't get." He paused, shaking his head. "How did Dr. Gellmane not know about that box? She's the director of the museum. If she and Dr. Pritzmord know each other, and they are working together to get the Grail, why wouldn't she give the box directly to him?" Blane mused as he stared at the foot of

Dr. Wengaro's bed. "I mean, it's right there, in her museum."

"Great questions!" I looked at Blane. He grinned.

"Maybe she didn't know about the box's contents," Dr. Wengaro said. "Till we arrived."

"That's possible," said Lydia. "Or maybe she did, and knew if the box went missing"—she paused, taking a deep breath—"it would arouse suspicion. Why would someone steal an otherwise random box, packed away in an old storage room? Someone might realize it was an inside job. Even if Dr. Gellmane followed protocol and checked out the box in her name, she would draw attention to herself. Her position would be at stake if anything fishy were to happen in her museum."

"She's too smart to check it out in her name. She'd frame a post-doc?" I asked. "Wouldn't that be believable?"

"That would still attract attention to her and the museum," Lydia said. "We're missing something here. They're both Knights of the White Wave. Assume they know each other. To get the Grail, they need the Grealmæp, which we have." She paused, staring into the room. "To get the Grail, which, for all they know, could have been in that box, they need to open that box. To open that box, they need the Grealmæp . . . What if . . . what if . . . Hmm . . ." Lydia clasped her hands. "What if they arrange the whole scene in the hallway and storage room, staging Dr. Pritzmord's arrest for battery and attempted robbery? That gets Dr. Pritzmord 'in jail' and gets them the box and our Grealmæp. It also enables Dr. Gellmane to, under the guise of teaching us about artifacts while we are stuck in Amesbury recovering, learn more about what we know about the Grealmæp—and the Grail!"

My jaw dropped. "What?" I blurted out, shocked at Lydia's speculation.

"What are you suggesting?" Blane asked.

"That with us under Dr. Gellmane's watch, Dr. Pritzmord could be back at the one place the four of us are not—"

"Nassauton!" Blane interrupted her. "Poring over Dr. Hasserin's journals, Dr. Kells' books, and Dr. Wengaro's research—searching for something we missed, without anyone there to stop him, getting one step closer to the Grail."

I listened, twirling a loose curl and staring at the mirror above Dr. Wengaro's sink. *The Knights of the White Wave. The Knights of the Dagger. The Grail. Dr. Wengaro. Dr. Pritzmord's threat and bulging eyes. His revolver . . . his revolver that he never fired? He stuck his revolver into my ribs as he marched me down the hallway to the Examination Room . . . he put his revolver on the table as he inspected the dirty microfiber towel with which Lydia had wrapped the Grealmæp . . .* I looked at Lydia's satchel. The Grealmæp, in its Tupperware container, was safely hidden inside.

"Oh my gosh," I exclaimed. "What if Dr. Pritzmord wanted the Grealmæp's ruby for himself all along—and needed me to show him how the ruby worked as the key?"

"What?" Dr. Wengaro propped himself up in his bed.

"Careful, Kenneth, relax," said Lydia as she helped him sit up.

"Think about it," I said. "Dr. Pritzmord knew we had the Grealmæp. He overheard us at Nassauton—he told us that. What if he and Dr. Gellmane staged the entire arrest, like Lydia said? They knew there could be two outcomes. Outcome one: we open the box, and the Grail is in it. If that were the case, Dr. Pritzmord walks away victorious, not only knowing how the Grealmæp works, but also possessing the ruby—and the Grail. Outcome two: we open the box, and the Grail is not in it. If that were the case, which it was, Dr. Pritzmord walks away, 'arrested'—*still knowing how the Grealmæp works and with the ruby!* Either way, Dr. Pritzmord knows how the Grealmæp works and gets the ruby. That's invaluable—"

"If he has the second Grealmæp, but doesn't know how it worked, and needed both Grealmæps and their rubies!" Blane whispered in delight. "Carly, you're amazing! How'd you come up with that?"

"Remember when Dr. Pritzmord cornered us and had his revolver? He never used it. If he really were after the Grail *at all costs*, he would have no problem firing that revolver and killing—or at least hurting—us. And remember how he wouldn't give up the ruby?"

"Yeah! I get what you're saying. He purposely didn't fire," Blane added.

"Why?" asked Dr. Wengaro.

"If someone heard a gunshot, they would have called the police—the real police! That would have been game over for Dr. Pritzmord, and it would have gotten Dr. Gellmane very unfavorable press," Lydia chimed in. "This fits with my theory that they staged the whole thing, only they didn't count on us getting our Grealmæp back."

"Or Blane and Tiffdill hobbling down the hallway and getting security," I added, grabbing Blane's hand as he beamed with pride at the recognition.

I stared at Dr. Wengaro, Lydia, and Blane. "This isn't only about getting the Grail or one Grealmæp. The Grealmæps—or their rubies—must do something else. Whatever they do, I think Dr. Pritzmord knows."

As soon as I said that, I knew in addition to finding the Grail, we had to find the second Grealmæp. If Dr. Pritzmord and Dr. Gellmane had it, we had to get it from them before they stole ours.

††

April in Amesbury meant the ground was a little softer and the rain a little less cold. The month's arrival brought not only the smallest saplings of spring, but also J. Carmichael's visit. With the hint of warmer weather, The Courtly Robin had opened its back porch, where Blane, Lydia, and I met J. Carmichael in a high-backed booth. Though J. Carmichael couldn't stay too long, I was thankful for his visit. Tucked away from the hustle and bustle of the main dining room in the pub, The Courtly Robin's back porch would be the perfect place for our conversation.

I loved The Courtly Robin's design—from the entrance's stateliness to the tiniest detail of the restroom stalls. Crests of old British families and weapons from knights of ages past lined the walls—a nod to England's rich, storied, and bloody history. A full suit of armor stood by the front door, greeting diners like a host welcoming his guests. Behind the armor was a sign that read: THE COURTLY ROBIN, RECENTLY RENOVATED IN 1776. Each time I entered, I always chuckled when I read *recently*.

The Courtly Robin was one of Amesbury's oldest buildings. Part of its foundation dated back over 1,500 years. Entering The Courtly Robin was like stepping back in time. Its walls, soaked with the sweet scent of ale, had withstood the drama played out— and the meals consumed—across the centuries. Its walls had witnessed all scenes and heard all conversations. There was no telling who had walked its wooden floors, which creaked under my boots as I made my way to the back porch. I imagined the boards creaking under the weight of a knight's armor as he strode in and walked up to the bar. I could see the scene in my head: The victorious knight, laying down his shield, taking off his helmet, triumphantly saying, "Give me your best ale!" as the barmaid swooned over him, obliging his request. He'd down the whole cup, grinning as he settled in, conversing with those around him and asking for another drink.

I smiled, closing my eyes and inhaling. The sweet scent of ale filled my nostrils. I was right there alongside the victorious knight. I could see him placing his helmet on the bar and chugging his ale. I could hear him asking for more as he beamed in triumph. I could feel the barmaid's smile brightening the room as she presented him with a full cup. Imagining this scene made me feel like I was a knight.

I opened my eyes. Seeing the armor and the swords, javelins, and shields on The Courtly Robin's walls made me remember when I'd wear Gran's boots or gladiator sandals. I'd jump off our living room couch and fight mythological monsters with Gran's cane, vanquishing whatever fiends threatened me. I smiled.

Reminiscing about this memory made me feel like I could tackle whatever adventures awaited us as we sought the Grail and uncovered the mysteries of Eternae and the mortar, pestle, and Nazi journal.

"Great to see you, Carly." J. Carmichael shook my hand, then Blane's. "You must be Blane." Then, he looked into Lydia's eyes. "Hi, Lydia."

She met his gaze. "Hi, John."

"Lydia, please don't call me that. I'm J. Carmichael now."

Lydia sighed, shifting her gaze from J. Carmichael to the table. "It's been a long time, John. I don't think I'm over—"

"Lydia, I . . ." J. Carmichael stammered as Lydia stepped back, as if preparing to walk away. "I don't think we'll ever get over it. I can't."

Lydia's lip started trembling. An awkward silence filled our booth. I tapped Blane's knee under the table.

"Do you two need a moment?" Blane blurted out. "Carly and I can look at the menus." Blane hastily handed me my menu and grabbed his. We buried our faces behind them.

"Please, Lydia," said J. Carmichael. "Stay, for Carly. You know this is important."

"Oh John." Her voice wavered. I could tell Lydia was about to cry. "Seeing you brings back too many memories. I thought I could handle it. I can't." Her coat rustled as she pulled it tighter around her. "If you'll excuse me. Carly, Blane, I'm sorry." She walked away, leaving the three of us in our booth.

"What was that all about?" I asked, lowering my menu.

"She never told you?" J. Carmichael asked.

"Told me what?"

"After Lyle and I started dating, I introduced Lydia to my brother. They started dating—"

"Wait, what?" I blurted out. "You and Gran dated?" *Was that what J. Carmichael meant when he said Lyle was his best friend and love of his life?* When we met at Winnie B.'s, I wanted to explore the unexplainable connection I'd felt with him, but when his phone rang, our time was cut short.

"We did, till the day she died."

I let out a long sigh. *How is this news to me?* Gran had never mentioned this in any of her stories. Neither had my mom. Neither had Lydia. *Why are all the important people in my life withholding information from me?*

"Seriously? I had no idea." My face flushed with anger at being kept in the dark. I'd wondered if J. Carmichael and Gran were lovers. I was right. I looked at my Ailm charm. I needed to ask the obvious question . . . "Are you my grandfather?"

J. Carmichael tilted his head and looked at me in surprise. "No, I'm not. I'd known Lyle since we were children, but we didn't start dating until fifteen or so years ago—long after she and her husband separated."

What happened to Gran's husband? She never mentioned him! I'd never seen a picture of him! *Did he die? Did they divorce? Did he cheat on her? Did he come to Gran's funeral? Is he still alive? Does he know she passed away?* My mom never talked about her dad. I shook my head in disbelief. *What other secrets does my family have?*

"So, you and Lyle, and your brother and Lydia, dated?" I thought about how Lara, Paul, Blane, and I had gone on double dates at Nassauton.

First semester seemed so long ago. For second semester, I technically was enrolled as a freshman. I'd worked it out with our deans to take my classes remotely and complete my assignments under Lydia's supervision. Joyce advocated for me, citing my strong work ethic and helping me get accommodations to stay on track. This enabled me to stay with Blane and Dr. Wengaro while they recovered, as well as work on our case. Dr. Wengaro also arranged for other faculty to cover his classes and take his students to Easter Island over spring break. Lydia was able to teach her classes remotely.

But even with my accommodations and Lydia's help, I'd fallen behind, struggling to keep up with my assignments.

Focusing on my schoolwork took a back seat to learning about curation, solving our case, and supporting Blane in his recovery. I didn't have a better solution other than to try to balance everything at Nassauton. *Does Lara even remember I'm her friend?* J. Carmichael's mention of Lydia's name brought my attention back to our conversation.

"Lydia met her match in Steve. He challenged her to be more intellectual—if that was even possible—and practical at the same time. He loved seeing her apply her intellect beyond research, to teaching. Publishing really wasn't her thing. Her biggest dream was teaching. He encouraged her to pursue it, though she was hard on herself. He taught her how to give herself grace when her path got dark and difficult." J. Carmichael got misty-eyed. He tried to discreetly wipe his eyes. "They were the perfect team. She helped him appreciate the little things, his quirks, the little details she loved about him that he didn't think were important."

"What happened?" Blane asked.

"He asked her to marry him. The night before their wedding, we went out with his friends. His bachelor party—I suppose you could call it that—minus all the things guys do in their twenties. We were in our fifties." J. Carmichael sighed. A small smile of nostalgia crossed his lips. "We smoked cigars, drank rare scotch, and went to a fancy steakhouse. But as we were heading home, a drunk driver ran a red light and—"

My face twisted in grief. "No, don't say it," I whispered, bringing my hand to my mouth. Tears filled my eyes.

"He and his friends were in the car ahead of me. All of them were killed on impact." He sighed again, wiping his tears with his napkin. "I'm sorry, Carly. I know you want to talk about the journal. But I didn't realize you don't know these stories. You need to know these things about your family and those who love you."

I nodded. J. Carmichael wasn't wrong.

"Oh man," Blane added. "I'm sorry. I know what it's like to lose a brother."

I turned to Blane, shocked. "You do?"

"I have an identical twin brother, Barrett. I really don't talk about him. It's like how I told you at Winnie B.'s. I'm not good at talking about it. I don't know how to talk about him. He's my twin. And he's missing. His absence left a huge hole in my heart. It's difficult. No one I've ever met has had that, or even a similar, experience."

"I'm so sorry," I said, my shock at not knowing a key detail in Blane's life turning to sorrow. "What happened?"

"We think he was kidnapped. It's been a few years now. We hope he's still alive."

I stared at Blane in disbelief. I was hurt that when I'd confided my struggles in him, he hadn't said anything about his brother. "You never told me that," I said, careful not to sound accusatory, but conveying my disappointment at not knowing.

"I'm sorry. I should have." Blane's face fell with sadness. "Like I said, it's hard for me to talk about it, you know? I don't know how to put my feelings into words, so most of the time I don't. My whole family has coped by avoiding it and trying to move on."

I sighed. I knew everyone managed grief differently. I couldn't stay upset at Blane for too long—for coping in the only way he knew. I slung my arm around him.

"That is so hard." I pulled him closer to me. "Is that why there aren't any family pictures around your house?"

Blane nodded.

I sighed again, then continued. "I'm always here to listen and to sit with you till you find the right words. Not talking about the difficult things isn't healthy. You end up kicking the grief further and further down the road, until it's become a huge boulder that blocks your path. I, of all people, know how tough it can be."

I thought about how challenging it was for me to talk about Gran and my dad. In high school, I had a trustworthy teacher who was also a counselor. She taught me how to discuss difficult things. Blane probably never had a therapist to talk with him about what he was facing.

Our waitress came to our booth and took our order. Blane and J. Carmichael got the dinner special: a pot roast with vegetables. I got fish and chips. As we waited, I showed J. Carmichael my pictures of the journal. He took out a pair of tortoiseshell-rimmed glasses and pulled my phone up to his face. He scrolled through the pictures, muttering, "English, German, English, hmm. Some equations, some diagrams," and skimming the pages before returning to the cover page. As he read it aloud, he gasped.

††

Notes and Experiments, Volume IV:
Making Grealia Eternae, Part II

By KAvG

"Well, I'll be! KA von Genzkensaffe's journal—with his attempts to make Grealia Eternae. Remind me, Carly, what else was in the Amesbury Museum box?"

"A mortar and pestle."

"Was there residue?"

"Yep."

"What color?"

"Pale pink."

J. Carmichael nodded, his eyes sparkling as a grin spread across his face. "That residue could be the last remnants of *Grealia* itself."

"*Grealia*?" asked Blane, leaning over our table.

"Indeed." J. Carmichael lowered his voice. "This takes me back to one of my cases, Operation GE. A few months before Lyle passed away, I was assigned to a fascinating case in Kraków, Poland." J. Carmichael paused, looking at me as I started twirling my loose curl in anticipation. He continued. "A couple was renovating their new apartment. They found a secret room behind one of the walls. The room was a laboratory, dating to the 1940s. Mostly everything was intact—except for one section. There were broken test tubes, beakers, and flasks. Someone must have been working there and got interrupted unexpectedly."

"You think there was a fight?" Blane asked. He leaned closer, propping his head on our table and looking at me and J. Carmichael.

"Yes. I was sent to inspect the lab. I found chemicals and equipment that would have been state-of-the-art at the time. I also found this."

J. Carmichael hoisted his black leather briefcase to our table and popped it open. He removed a small, midnight blue leather journal, with dozens of index cards sticking out of it.

"Whose was it?" I asked as he handed it to me. After wiping my fingers on my napkin, I took it from him. The journal had a swastika on the front. I opened the front cover and gasped.

††

Notes and Experiments, Volume IV:
Making Grealia Eternae, Part I

By KAvG

"Whoa!" I said, pointing at the title. "It's KAvG's Part One!"

"As soon as you told me you'd found a Nazi journal, I knew you'd want to see this," J. Carmichael said. "I translated the German for you. Long plane rides are good for something."

"Are some parts in English too?" I asked.

"Yes. KA wrote in both German and English."

"Why?" I asked.

"Still trying to figure that out," J. Carmichael said.

I pursed my lips and tilted my head in expectation, curiosity, and horror. Thousands of miles apart, J. Carmichael and I found two journals, which belonged to the same person: a Nazi scientist who was a Knight of the Dagger! *One journal was hidden in Kraków. How did the other journal get to Amesbury? Did Hitler know KA von Genzkensaffe was a Knight of the Dagger?* I slid the journal into my satchel, staring at our table.

"Who was KA von Genzkensaffe?" I finally asked.

As J. Carmichael started to answer, our food arrived. I'd never seen fish and chips that looked so crispy and piping hot. I lifted my fork and knife and cut a piece of fish. Steam rose into my face.

"Whoa, that's right out of the fryer!" I said, fanning my face and blowing on my food to cool it down. Our waitress set Blane's and J. Carmichael's pot roasts down, smiling as she told us to let the dishes cool and making sure we received all we ordered.

"Chef tries to make sure the food doesn't wait too long once it's prepared," she said. "Enjoy!" She flitted away, eager to keep up with tending to her other guests.

"KA von Genzkensaffe was a Knight of the Dagger, as you probably figured out, and a scientist, tasked—much against his will—by Hitler to work on experimental medicines. On one of their Grail raids, the Nazis found a stone box at Stonehenge. Hitler gave it to KA, hoping KA could use its contents to produce drugs that would give the Germans superhuman power."

I took a bite of my fish. The flaky, cooked-just-right inside melted in my mouth.

"Do you think Hitler knew KA was a knight?"

"No. We don't advertise these things," said J. Carmichael.

I sipped my water and cut another forkful of fish. As I chewed, I thought about KA's work. "Is *Grealia* the same as Grealia Eternae? Did KA succeed in making it?"

"*Grealia* is an ancient medicine with incredible healing properties. It's also believed to give whoever uses it eternal life. Grealia Eternae is the drug KA tried to make using *Grealia*. We don't think he succeeded. We think Hitler discovered KA wasn't loyal to the cause and killed him." J. Carmichael paused. "His lab was broken into."

"How do you know about *Grealia*?" I sprinkled salt on my fries and picked up a few. A whiff of hot grease filled my nostrils as my teeth crunched through their crispy exterior.

"As part of my due diligence, I asked our Knights of the Dagger team to research Grealia Eternae. After some digging, they found an old Arthurian poem that mentioned *Grealia*. It was the medicine King Arthur needed after the Battle of Camlann. He didn't need the Grail as much as he needed *Grealia*."

J. Carmichael looked at his pot roast. "This looks delicious." He placed his napkin in his lap, lifted his fork, and dug in.

I twirled my loose curl as I gazed at my plate. We'd learned about the Battle of Camlann—King Arthur's final battle—in Grail Times with Dr. Wengaro. Arthur suffered life-threatening injuries and was taken to the mystical Isle of Avalon for healing.

"But I thought the Grail gives eternal life," I said. "Unless . . ." I paused, deep in thought as I picked up another fry. "Is *Grealia* connected to the Grail?"

J. Carmichael grinned, a small twinkle glimmering in his eye as he ate another bite. He swallowed, then kept talking. "You bet! The Grail is covered in Christ's DNA, which is essential to making *Grealia*. Centuries after Joseph of Arimathea brought the Grail to Britain, Merlin and Morgan le Fay—mostly Morgan—used the Grail as a vessel in the process of creating different medicines, including *Grealia*. Merlin noticed that when Morgan gave her animals *Grealia*, they seemed to live forever, despite being very old. Morgan realized Christ's DNA was the reactant that gave *Grealia* its healing properties. Merlin was astounded by Morgan's aptitude, which was well beyond her years, and made her his apprentice right then and there. He wanted to be the one to teach her—and claim credit for her discoveries."

I nodded, enthralled. *Grealia*'s existence—and KA's writings on *Grealia* and Grealia Eternae—provided scientific evidence for the Grail's link to eternal life! "How did KA get *Grealia*?" I asked.

"That mortar and pestle," said J. Carmichael, "must have *Grealia* residue." He paused, lowering his voice to a barely audible volume. "To prevent others from stealing their work, Merlin and Morgan went to great lengths to hide their lab equipment and spell books."

"I'll bet KA was desperate to find those!" Blane exclaimed. He'd hardly said a word since his pot roast arrived.

J. Carmichael chuckled. "KA, and thousands of others. It's another reason the Knights of the Dagger exist—to find and protect not only the Grail, but also Merlin and Morgan's equipment and spell books. They contain their experiment annotations, formulas, and maps of sacred sites—and notes on which medicines can be made at each site. For example, *Grealia* can only be made in certain sacred sites. If the Knights of the White Wave find all the equipment and books before we do, they can make anything, including *Grealia*, and harness the power of eternal life for themselves. They know Celtic—so they can read the spells, they know magic, and they know about the ley lines and how they connect sacred sites around the world."

"The ley lines!" Blane blurted out in between bites of pot roast. He looked up, grinning as he quickly swallowed. "I knew Earth's energy grid was important!"

J. Carmichael nodded as I beamed at Blane.

Our waitress came by to refill our glasses. "Right, my loves, need a top-up? How is everything?"

"Thank you, everything is delicious!" Blane said.

"Right, great, enjoy!" She headed to another table.

"The ley lines are *crucial*," said J. Carmichael. "They connect sites in Europe, Asia, Africa, Australia, and North and South America—including sites of incredible energy like Glastonbury Tor and the Hill of Tara."

"What about Avalon?" I asked, thinking of where King Arthur was taken after the Battle of Camlann.

"Avalon is another name for Glastonbury Tor. It's an incredibly powerful ley line site—one of the most sacred places on Earth and portal to the land of the dead. It's where Joseph of Arimathea arrived when he brought the Grail and his rubies to Britain. Numerous miracles have occurred there, from Joseph's staff taking root and blossoming into Glastonbury's Thorn, to Excalibur's creation—the sword was forged there, through a process no one has been able to replicate. We also think Morgan made *Grealia* at Avalon, using the Grealmæps' rubies."

I listened, intensely twirling a loose curl. When we'd assembled our complete Grealmæp in Lydia's office, Dr. Wengaro mentioned Merlin made the Grealmæp using Joseph's rubies.

"How do the rubies make *Grealia*?" I asked, wondering if Morgan mentioned the rubies in her spell books.

"We're still trying to figure that out—and we hope the Knights of the White Wave don't know, either!"

I looked at my Ailm charm, taking a deep breath. *Does Dr. Pritzmord know how the rubies make Grealia?*

"We never learned this in Dr. Wengaro's class," Blane muttered.

"This is classified Knights of the Dagger information. Took us centuries to piece this together. No way Kenneth is going to teach this to college students." J. Carmichael smiled. "Good old Kenneth. As soon as my boss met him, he nominated him to be a knight. Kenneth is an expert on these sacred sites. He's one of the rare archaeologists who honors their spiritual nature. He doesn't dismiss it as superstition, but approaches its study through history, archaeology, and science."

"What do you mean?" I asked.

"There is substantial evidence these sites have supernatural secrets. Many are quick to dismiss them—many who claim to take a 'scholarly approach.'" J. Carmichael chuckled as he lowered his air quotes. "*Real* scholars have an open mind, following where the evidence leads, even if it forces them to abandon their old beliefs. *Real* scholars aren't afraid to ask questions that lead them to the truth—they don't create their desired truth and manufacture evidence that confirms it. The evidence we have from these sacred sites points to highly logical laws of higher dimensions—laws that govern *all* dimensions, not just the material ones."

I chuckled. If Lydia were here, she'd be rolling her eyes so hard, they'd be getting the best workout of their lives. "What kind of higher dimensions?"

"Dimensions in which incredible healings, superhuman strength, dark energy, dark matter, and the space-time continuum are the norm. Dimensions in which ley lines play a key role—that's why Kenneth's research is so valuable. His research provided the archaeological and scientific evidence to understand the ley lines' function and the significance of the Grealmæps. Before Kenneth, we didn't even know the Grealmæps' name. Now, we have the knowledge to study the ley lines, locate Merlin and Morgan's equipment and spell books, and find the Grail."

"Dark matter?" asked Blane. "The space-time continuum? Now you're talking straight up science fiction."

I grinned, nodding in excitement. "Science fiction is future fact."

"Not just future fact, but present reality," J. Carmichael added. He looked at Blane. "I know at first it's hard to believe, but think about Glastonbury—it's a portal to the land of the dead. That's very well established."

Blane nodded. "With what evidence?"

"Okay, Lydia," I said, rolling my eyes at Blane. "Where's that adventurous spirit?" I playfully poked Blane's shoulder.

"I'm serious," said Blane. "This isn't science. It's some quack repeating it enough times until it becomes real. Legends aren't history or science. We all know that."

"But some are," said J. Carmichael as he finished his pot roast. "Take King Arthur. The Knights of the Dagger and the White Wave. The new world order—*et in terra pax*—the restorative peace on Earth that we're so desperately wanting, the peace that will come once the Grail has been found. Archaeology and science do corroborate the stories—some of them, at least. With *these* stories, and Kenneth's research, we learn more. The stories lead us to the science, and the science substantiates the stories." He arranged his fork and knife side-by-side on his plate to signal he was finished. "Kenneth studied the Grealmæps' story. He found evidence that there are two Grealmæps. He uncovered texts that revealed the rubies are keys that unlock Merlin and Morgan's boxes. His next discoveries may help us understand how the rubies make *Grealia*."

"*Boxes*?" I asked. "There are multiple?"

J. Carmichael smiled. "Ahh. Yes. Merlin and Morgan's boxes. Some have their lab equipment—like the mortar and pestle. Some have their spell books. One might even have the Grail. All require one ruby, or both rubies, to open them. We think the boxes that require both contain special equipment and spell books—or the Grail. So without the second Grealmæp, and really the second ruby, in our possession, we risk the Knights of the White Wave finding the Grail first."

"Or getting the spell books," Blane added, nodding and lacing his fingers together. "And learning Merlin and Morgan's magic. Who knows what other evils they will unleash with *those* spells?"

I looked at Blane, thinking about the rubies and the boxes. Everything was related, like puzzle pieces that connected, one at a time, forming a larger picture . . . We needed to find the second Grealmæp and ruby, before Dr. Pritzmord, Dr. Gellmane, and the rest of the Knights of the White Wave did. I looked at my bracelet. My Ailm charm glimmered in the light of the booth.

"What's our next step?" I asked as the urgency of our new objective set in. "Any clue where the other Grealmæp is? Or do we start throwing darts at a map of the world?"

J. Carmichael chuckled. "Fortunately, no, mostly since my dart game is really rusty." He paused, taking a deep breath, and looking at one of the crests on the wall. "What I'm about to share will distress you, Carly. Are you sure you want to hear?"

I nodded, reaching for Blane's hand. He squeezed it. We looked at each other, waiting for J. Carmichael to continue.

"Carly, your dad. He was in a trial for an experimental immunotherapy drug to kill his cancer."

I nodded, squeezing Blane's hand. I wasn't mentally or emotionally prepared to discuss my dad. I closed my eyes and took a deep breath. "Yes, Phase I, I remember."

"And what happened?"

As soon as J. Carmichael asked that, the memories of my Confirmation Day, of my parents sitting on the couch, telling me my dad was pulled from the trial, hit me like a punch to my stomach. I took another deep breath. "He was removed from the trial. They didn't think he could handle a higher dosage." I paused, shaking my head. My lower lip started trembling. I opened my eyes. "J. Carmichael, I—"

"Carly, I know. You need to hear this. I'm pretty sure Eternae, the drug your dad took, had *Grealia* in it."

I stared at J. Carmichael, my shock hitting me like punches to my stomach. The noise of The Courtly Robin faded away. I squeezed Blane's hand harder. "I don't understand. *Grealia*? Merlin and Morgan's *Grealia*? Eternal life *Grealia*? How do you know? If *Grealia* provides eternal life, why did my dad die?"

"Great questions." J. Carmichael looked me in the eyes. "I'm sorry, Carly. I know this is difficult. One day when I visited Lyle, I chatted with your mom. She mentioned GE Pharmaceuticals invited your dad to participate in its Eternae trial, and that this could be your dad's lucky break. Immediately, I thought of KA von Genzkensaffe and Grealia Eternae. Under the guise of doing a facility audit, I flew to GE Pharmaceuticals' lab in Somerset, England."

"What happened when you arrived?" Blane asked.

"They weren't pleased a regulator had shown up. They said as a very early-stage startup, they couldn't have restrictions stunting their ability to be agile and scale rapidly. They said not to worry, they were following the rules. They had to, or else they'd be shut down. I remember one person got very upset. He told me countless lives were at stake, and I was slowing down their life-saving work."

"That attitude is a bit of a red flag, right?" I asked. "If they weren't hiding anything, why get upset?"

"Startups can be overly protective of their intellectual property. They think we'll steal it. But yes, it was a red flag. And I could talk to only one person, since everyone else was busy with their 'life-saving work.' I overheard a conversation between lab technicians about the boss being stressed since GE's supply of *Grealia* was running out. But the most suspicious incident was when I discovered a locked door on the lower level. I tried to get more information, but the next thing I knew, they told me my visit was over and showed me the door." J. Carmichael smiled. "But not before I took some very interesting pictures."

He pulled his phone out and started scrolling.

"What's that?" Blane asked, pointing to a little silver bar sticking out of the phone's top.

"It's a sentinel. It's an encryption device that scrambles incoming and outgoing communication so only another person with a sentinel can read it. If the message gets intercepted, the sentinel senses the interception and deletes the message."

"That's amazing!" I looked at the sentinel. "Does every knight have one?"

"Eventually. A handful of us are testing them before we roll them out across the organization." He stopped scrolling. "Does that look familiar?"

Blane and I looked at J. Carmichael's phone. "The Grealmæp!" we exclaimed in unison.

"Yep. The insignia on GE Pharmaceuticals' doors,

letterheads, lab coats—everything—was the Grealmæp. Or, as I knew it at the time, Lyle's Henge Piece. So, naturally, I needed to know how GE Pharmaceuticals, a life sciences startup, learned about the Grealmæp. At the time, we didn't have Kenneth, so I only knew about Lyle's Grealmæp. But I didn't know where hers was. When you and I met at Winnie B.'s, it clicked."

I took a deep breath.

J. Carmichael continued. "I know it's a lot to process, Carly. You need to get to GE Pharmaceuticals and find the other Grealmæp. It could be what they are hiding behind that locked door. If the Knights of the White Wave know about GE Pharmaceuticals, and get there first, you—and all of us—will be in more danger than you could possibly imagine."

III

As we discussed our dessert choices, I looked at the crests on the wall. Judging by their size and material—each looked like they were solid oak, with metal detailing—they were heavy. The vibrantly colored crests, with animals and symbols in the center and mottos at the bottom, were securely nailed into the stone wall. The crests probably hadn't been moved in centuries.

I recognized a few English surnames and names of King Arthur's knights from Grail Times. One crest in green and yellow, with beautiful gold filigree, stood out to me. The brass plaque under the crest read: MORGAN LE FAY. "Morgan," I whispered to myself, thinking about Merlin's apprentice who made *Grealia*.

Her crest featured a relief of a winged brown lion with a full mane and hollowed-out eyes, wearing a necklace, ring, and ear cuff. Written under it were the words *AUDACES FORUNA JUVAT*.

The necklace caught my eye. It was a gold chain with two pendants—a gold cross inside a silver disc and an aquamarine stone.

I knew exactly where I'd seen that pattern. I held my arm up to Morgan's crest. *The charms of my bracelet and Morgan le Fay's necklace are the Ailm!* I grinned, excitedly showing Blane and snapping a picture.

"That's neat!" Blane pointed at Morgan's crest. "That Ailm is a Celtic symbol of physical, mental, and spiritual strength. Morgan was a strong woman."

I gazed at the winged lion. "Yeah." I beamed, thrilled that

through the Ailm, I was connected to Morgan. "And it symbolizes healing, which checks out since she made *Grealia*."

J. Carmichael smiled. "Morgan was one of the greatest healers to have lived. Speaking of healers, should we get back to GE Pharmaceuticals and KA von Genzkensaffe's journals?"

"Yeah, but shouldn't we wait for Lydia?" I asked. "Maybe we can text her and she'll come back."

"Good, sweet thought, but maybe it's best if we let Lydia process things on her own tonight," said J. Carmichael. "I'm sure she needs some time to herself."

I nodded. My gut told me J. Carmichael was right. "We can catch her up later, when we talk to Dr. Wengaro."

I handed my phone to J. Carmichael. He adjusted his tortoiseshell-rimmed glasses and peered at my screen.

"I love how you named the album *Amesbury Museum, Nazi Journal*. Great file-naming system." He scrolled through the pictures, picking up where he'd left off. "That's one thing they stress for first-year knights: foolproof data collection and storage methods save hours of trouble."

"All right, my loves, what will it be?" Our waitress pulled out her notepad from her apron pocket.

J. Carmichael glanced up from my phone, smiling at our waitress. "I'll have the double-malt scotch," he said. "Thank you."

"Lovely, a splendid choice for the gentleman. And you, miss?"

"I'll have a lemon tea, with a biscuit."

"Certainly, and for the young gentleman?"

"A cappuccino, please," said Blane.

"Right, I'll get these straight away." Our waitress put her notepad back in her pocket and started to walk away.

"Wait," I said. "I have a question."

"Yes, love?"

"That crest on the wall, that's Morgan le Fay's."

"Yes dear, what about her?"

"What do you know about her?" I hoped our waitress would

know more lore about Morgan.

She smiled. "She was a brave, powerful enchantress in King Arthur's time. She was sea-born, which gave her shape-shifting powers." She pointed at the crest. "See that aquamarine jewelry on the gryphon? That was Morgan's gemstone." She smoothed her hands on her apron. "Morgan was smart and beautiful. She apprenticed with Merlin. She made all sorts of potions, ultimately becoming a better wizard than Merlin himself."

My eyes widened in wonder as I twirled my loose curl. *How could Morgan have become better than Merlin, and at his own magic?*

Noticing my interest, our waitress continued. "She was a great healer, using her powers for good. She also took our beloved King Arthur on his final journey to Avalon to rest in eternal peace. Once Arthur's greatest enemy, she wanted the throne for herself. See, as Arthur's half-sister, she was entitled to the crown. But she was a woman, which disqualified her from ruling. But she and Arthur reconciled, and she cared for him in his last hours."

I beamed, exuberant after hearing these legends. *Morgan le Fay was King Arthur's half-sister!* "How do you know so much about her?"

"She's The Courtly Robin's patron saint. Or something like it. Rumor has it she still watches over The Courtly Robin, protecting our guests." Our waitress chuckled. "She mostly protects men from wily women since she hated Guinevere. When Guinevere was exiled, Morgan didn't trust the convent walls to keep Guinevere away from the town's men. So, she cast a spell on Amesbury to protect the knights from Guinevere's guiles."

I chuckled. "Did it work?" Morgan sure had a quirky way of using her magic.

"I'd say so, yes, love." Our waitress grinned. "No Amesbury knight ever fell for Guinevere. Some even say this was one of her best healing spells—keeping men from becoming lovesick for Guinevere! Fun story, right? This place is full of these stories—and of Morgan's spirit. Sometimes I swear Morgan is with me in the kitchen. Legend has it the kitchen, and these booths, used to be her library and research room. That was, of course, centuries before the renovation."

I laughed. "The renovation in 1776, right?"

Our waitress chuckled. "That was the recent renovation. I should have said the restoration, in 1340, after the great fire. The fire destroyed most of this building. Only a few parts of the foundation and this wall and the one next to it remained. During construction, they barely set foot back here since they were afraid of rousing Morgan's spirit. They left the walls as is. That's why all these crests are here, 'cos Morgan put them here." Our waitress smiled again, staring off into the distance. "Fascinating one, that Morgan, simply fascinating. Here, let me get you your drinks."

She disappeared to the bar.

"As for the Latin," J. Carmichael added, pointing at the motto on Morgan's crest, "it means 'fortune favors the bold.' Interesting, right?"

I nodded. I wanted to be bold. Like Morgan le Fay. Like Gran. Grinning, I looked at my Ailm charm—my connection to Morgan. *Did Morgan realize Grealia would be so coveted?*

Noticing J. Carmichael finished looking at the pictures, I asked, "What do you think of KA's journal?"

J. Carmichael held my phone and looked at me. "This one seems to be mostly chemical reactions and annotations. Some English here and there, but mostly German. But there is an entry I found fascinating."

He scrolled until he found a picture of an entry that looked like a letter. Translating the German, he read:

16 August 1942

Dear Felda,

I'm sorry, my sweet child. I have failed. I couldn't make the medicine for Herr Dietrich. I know you love him, from your days teaching chemistry at Augusta Victoria College. I hope he does not die! Papa did the best he could, but he failed you. For this, I cannot forgive myself; maybe you can forgive me?

Maybe even better: Where I failed, you can succeed. Take my mortar and pestle, containing the residue of the precious Grealia particles. Do more than I could!

All my love,
KAvG

"I didn't know he had a daughter," J. Carmichael said, handing me my phone. "Felda von Genzkensaffe."

"He tried to make more *Grealia* for Felda," Blane mused. "Or use it to make more medicine to heal her lover. But he couldn't, so he gave her his journal and the mortar and pestle."

"Yes. He put them in the box—the box you found—for Felda to pick up, using Stonehenge—probably an Aubrey Hole—as their dead drop," J. Carmichael said.

"The Aubrey Hole!" I blurted out. "Felda must have had a Grealmæp—maybe Gran's Grealmæp, maybe the other one—to open the box."

"Maybe he sent her a Grealmæp?" pondered Blane.

I nodded. "Something must have happened to Felda, since she never picked up the box. Someone must have found it in that

Aubrey Hole and brought it to the Amesbury Museum." I paused, looking at my screen. "Augusta Victoria College could help us with the answers."

††

By the time we left The Courtly Robin, it had started to rain. We didn't bring an umbrella, but luckily, we didn't have too far to go.

"April in England," J. Carmichael muttered. "In all my trips here, I've never learned to bring an umbrella with me."

When we got back to our cottage, the lights were off. Lydia wasn't there. She'd left a note saying she'd gone out to dinner and not to worry about or wait up for her. J. Carmichael had to leave, so he'd walked us back and arranged for a cab to pick him up at our cottage.

"Cute little place. Love the blue door. And that big bay window! Charming!" He turned on the lights in the study, walking around and running his hand along the bookshelves. "Cozy and full of great reading material. And that chair is the perfect place to get lost in adventures on a stormy night like this."

After a few minutes, J. Carmichael's phone rang.

"That's my ride. Carly, keep me posted. Remember the locked door on the lower level and the Grealmæp. I'm always a text away. Any time I can get to you, I will."

"Thank you." I hugged him. "Thank you for everything. I really appreciate you."

I was sad to see J. Carmichael leave. I valued his wisdom. Now that I knew about his relationship with Gran, I wanted to work with him and learn more from him.

"Great to meet you, J. Carmichael," said Blane. "Thank you for your help. It means a lot to Carly, so it means a lot to me." Blane wheeled himself out of the study as we walked J. Carmichael to the door.

"We'll get to the bottom of the lab, I promise." I squeezed

Blane's hand. "We're an unstoppable team."

The cab pulled up to our cottage. "Good night, you two." J. Carmichael waved as he dashed out and hopped into the cab. In the past ten minutes, the rain had gotten worse. The wind had also picked up, causing the branches on the trees in front of our cottage to sway violently.

"Be safe in this storm!" I yelled after him.

"I'll tell the driver." J. Carmichael chuckled. "In all seriousness, it is looking pretty bad out there."

I locked the door and wiped my feet on the doormat.

"Can't wait till I'm out of this wheelchair," said Blane. "I feel fine, so maybe during tomorrow's visit, they'll let me go to crutches."

I grinned. Blane had been very good about doing his physical therapy. I was sure tomorrow's visit would go well.

"I'm so proud of you," I said as Blane wheeled himself down the hallway to the kitchen, dining room, and living room. I walked next to him. He parked himself by the couch and pushed himself up, out of his chair. He sat down, resting his leg on the coffee table.

"Hey, flip the lights off. Let's put the TV on."

A peal of thunder filled the room, rattling the windows. I jumped at the unexpected sound.

"That was huge! Hope we don't lose power," Blane added.

I looked out the window. The rain had turned to a torrential downpour. I sighed. "I hope the roads aren't too bad."

"I'm sure they get storms like this all the time." A bolt of lightning flashed across the sky. Blane patted the couch. "Perfect weather for cuddling."

I grinned. Blane was right.

"Do you want tea or anything?" I asked.

"I'm good. Just need you to relax and come cuddle with me."

I beamed, flipping the lights off. Blane turned on the TV and lowered the volume so we could talk. I plopped down next to him, resting my phone on the coffee table near some books.

"How're you feeling?" Blane asked, wrapping his arms around me. The touch of his fingertips sent shivers of anticipation all over my body. When Blane held me, I felt protected from every evil and the most ferocious of monsters.

"I'm okay," I sighed. "I learned more in that conversation than in eighteen years on this planet. My family has some pretty big secrets."

He pulled me closer. His heart beat steadily. Its measured, calm cadence made me feel safe. "Every family has secrets. That's what makes our histories interesting."

I nodded. Something told me my family's secrets went much, much deeper than what I'd learned over dinner. "I guess so. But sometimes I'd like to hear the stories, without digging for them, you know?"

Blane nodded.

"How're you feeling?" I asked.

"I'm okay. I'm ready for tomorrow. I'm pretty sure they'll upgrade me to the boot, and maybe crutches, but I probably won't need them. My Nassauton work is a lot—I'm trying to keep up. I wasn't expecting to talk about my brother. But, I'm glad I did. Talking about it helped."

I looked at Blane, kissing his cheeks and forehead. "I'm so proud of your recovery! And I'm glad you shared about your brother. One word at a time." I kissed his lips.

He smiled, then nodded. "When I start thinking about him, it takes me to a dark place."

"Would talking about him more, rather than thinking about him, help?"

"Maybe."

I held Blane's hand. "Tell me about him."

"He loved running—and chemistry and computer science. He said running helped him do his best thinking." Blane paused. "He is a genius—like you. A whole other level of intelligence."

I squeezed Blane's hand and smiled. "Thank you. You're

sweet to say that. But it's not like I'm the only smart person in the room. You're so much smarter than I am!"

"No way!"

"Yes! I could never conquer those economic problem sets like you do! The math goes way over my head!" I kissed him again. He grinned.

"Barrett won our high school science fair for his research. He designed some algorithm that predicted telomere properties based on cancer type. Very advanced. Couldn't tell you how it worked, but I could tell you his research was groundbreaking, got published, picked up by the media, and won him a scholarship to Nerz College."

"Nerz? That's one of the best science and technology colleges in the country! Wow! What got him interested in that? Cancer and how it metastasizes are fascinating to me." As I said that, I couldn't help but think of my dad and Eternae.

"I'm not sure, actually. He was always into science. Growing up, he watched medical drama TV shows. He babbled about the epigenetics of cancer to anyone who would listen. I wish I could explain it better." Blane rubbed my shoulders, moving his hands around my shoulder blades and collarbone. I reciprocated by tracing my fingers around his forearms.

"That makes the two of us. I wish I knew more about cancer. My dad told me the Eternae folks were trying to measure it—measure what they couldn't see—since they'd never seen a cancer as unique as his. He had so many questions about it. His whole cancer experience really tested—and strengthened—his faith."

Blane nodded. "Sounds like your dad was a very intelligent, thoughtful man."

I squeezed Blane's hand. "He was. He helped me realize the importance of asking questions and seeking the truth."

"Sounds a lot like my granddad. He's the archaeologist. He's on some dig in Asia. He is obsessed with ancient civilizations and their mechanisms for establishing markets and trade. He always told me the most telling sign of how civilized a society was, was their monetary and banking system. Who made the system, who had access to it, who made the rules, who had the money. 'Follow the money,' he used to say. Whoever controls the money has the power."

"That's fascinating!" I exclaimed. "It shows how archaeology points us to clues that reveal what we value and how our world works."

"Exactly," said Blane. "Grandad and Barrett discussed value a lot. Barrett saw studying chemistry and coding as a way to create something of value—something that would change the world."

Nodding, I took a deep breath and looked Blane in the eyes. "What exactly happened to him?"

"One day, he went for a run and never came back."

"What do you mean, never came back?"

"We don't know. Gone. No trace." Blane sighed. "Even the police don't know. We searched for him for months. Nothing. No body, no nothing."

I hugged Blane, caressing his back. He stared at the TV. The rain pelted the roof and the windowpanes, its sound filling the silence.

"There's no closure," he finally said. "It's an empty, open wound in my heart. I try to avoid it. But it's always there. I focus on other things and try to be goofy. I don't know. I don't know how to talk about my feelings. I'm afraid of them. I probably should see someone to help me."

I nodded. Blane's mature self-analysis impressed me. Under his goofy demeanor, he had a sensitive side. I was proud he'd recognized he needed professional help—and he'd been vulnerable and shared that with me.

"A therapist is a great idea." I squeezed Blane's hand. "Thank you for sharing that with me. I know it must be hard."

He smiled, leaning in to kiss my lips. "Thank you for listening. It feels good to talk about this with you." He started kissing me again.

Butterflies filled my stomach. I closed my eyes and kissed him hard. I barely could say "I love you" as I felt Blane's hands holding the back of my head, caressing my hair. Our lips locked with a gentle firmness as he moved his hands down my back, pulling me closer. I felt simultaneously grounded and weightless. I was safe and I was free. Nothing else mattered, other than being with Blane and feeling his body on me, his breath on mine. We paused, catching our breath. He grinned as he tilted his head back and looked at me. I could feel my curls frizzing out and becoming unruly. I tried to smooth them out.

"You're beautiful, Carly." He smiled as he stopped me. From the TV's light, I could see his hazel eyes sparkling. I blushed. "Even with unruly curls and especially when you're not wearing eye shadow that makes you look like Lara dusted a whole box of glitter on your face."

Remembering the countless hours I'd spent in Lara's makeup tutorials, I laughed so hard, I snorted. "What makes you say that?" I shifted my posture, so Blane was spooning me. His body protecting mine was the best feeling in the world.

"Because I fell in love with a girl who was so comfortable in her own skin, she wore vintage movie-poster T-shirts and didn't mind helping some helpless college freshman boy struggling with a box that he was so sure he could hold."

I ran my hands along his biceps. Feeling his bare skin sent tingles all over my body. "You remember that?"

"Of course! Your compassion, kindness, and gentleness were the first things I noticed about you."

I loved that Blane valued kindness. Even from our first moment, our relationship had been grounded in kindness and respect.

"I saw a lanky, handsome guy with a box that was getting the better of him. Helping him was the right thing to do."

Blane kissed the back of my neck. "Maybe the right thing for you. You'd be surprised how many people don't notice others around them." He ran his hands up and down my back. "Also," he said, pausing, "do you really think I'm handsome?"

I nodded. "I do. Very."

He blushed, slipping his hands under my shirt. His hands felt smooth and strong as they massaged my back.

"Thank you." He smiled. "We sure do make a good-looking team, teammate."

"And a very smart team, teammate!"

"Without a doubt. Another one of the many reasons I fell hard for you. You're the most intelligent woman I've met!"

I grinned.

Blane tugged the back of my shirt up. "May I?"

"Yes." I smiled.

He raised the back of my shirt and placed his hand on my lower back. I had always imagined what this moment would feel like. I was exhilarated and completely at ease. I felt confident and comfortable.

"Whoa, that's the coolest birthmark I've ever seen," he said.

In the moment, I'd forgotten about my star map.

"Is it? It's my star map." I grinned, telling Blane how my birthmark reminded me of a constellation of stars shaped like an infinity sign.

"That's so cool!" He tapped his fingers on the dots on my back. "One, two, three, four, five, six, seven. Yeah, you're right. It does look like an infinity sign!"

"You really think it's cool?"

"Yes," said Blane. "I do. It makes you even more unique. I bet no one else has a star map like yours."

I turned my head as my lips found their way to his. I turned my whole body around. As my eyes closed, I surrendered to the feeling of never wanting to have an adventure if Blane wasn't by my side. Just before I lost myself in the moment, I popped my eyes open.

"What if Lydia comes back?" I giggled.

He grinned. "We'll hear her, I'm sure." He gently pulled my head back toward him. Our lips locked.

I'd just closed my eyes when I heard glass shattering. Blane and I instantly jerked apart.

"What was that?" I whispered. I looked around the living room, then at Blane. His face was pale white.

"Something must have smashed through the bay window."

"I'll check," I said. "You stay here."

"Did we really have to break the window like that?" a woman's voice asked.

I froze. *Someone broke in.*

"Did you hear that?" I whispered to Blane.

Blane nodded as he flicked the TV off. "We gotta hide. Behind the curtains. Quick!"

Fight or flight immediately set in. My heart was pounding so fast, the beats were indistinguishable from each other. I grabbed Blane's hand. Careful not to hurt his ankle, but still moving fast, we crawled behind the yellow curtains. We lay down along the bottom and flattened ourselves against the glass door. I tried to take deep, long breaths, but I could only get shallow breaths. I looked at my Ailm charm. *Be brave.*

"How's your ankle?"

"It's okay. Glad we're lying down."

"Do you think they heard the TV?"

"Not with all that glass shattering."

I heard the same woman's voice. "It's obvious someone broke in, with all this glass shattered," she said.

"Is that, is that . . . ?" I could barely string my words together.

"Dr. Gellmane," said Blane. "Don't move. And try not to breathe loudly."

I closed my mouth.

"Well, don't stop breathing," Blane whispered.

"Relax, they'll think the window blew out in the storm," said a man's voice. "And when they find the branch on the floor, that will be proof."

I panicked. My heart beat even faster. Anxiety filled my

stomach. I'd recognize that voice anywhere—from Nassauton, to the hallway in the Amesbury Museum, to my nightmares. *Dr. Pritzmord. The man who murdered Dr. Hasserin. The man who masqueraded as a dean and followed us to the Amesbury Museum. The man who is a Knight of the White Wave, questing after the Grail with an insidious, insatiable bloodlust.* Chills ran up and down my arms. I gripped Blane's hand.

"You actually brought the branch with you?" asked Dr. Gellmane.

"Of course. We've got to make it look real."

I heard Dr. Pritzmord's words in my head. *"Carly Stuart, when our paths cross again, you won't be as lucky. Watch your back."*

"You think of everything. And this storm is one of the worst we've had."

"First compliment you've given me in years, wow," Dr. Pritzmord said sarcastically.

"Right, let's find that Grealmæp and get out of here."

"What do you think I'm doing? We've got to search this entire cottage."

Their footsteps echoed as they walked closer. I pressed my back against the glass door, hoping the curtains weren't moving.

The kitchen lights flicked on. I could smell Blane's sweat. He was as scared as I was. My heart pounded. I could barely breathe.

"Dammit, Daniel, it's not going to be in the kitchen. With the spoons? The teacups? Don't be ridiculous."

"It could be anywhere. I'm not leaving here without it."

I could hear them opening cabinets and moving pots and pans around.

"I should have killed them in that hallway, when I had the chance."

My hands got clammy and cold. The blood drained from my face.

"If you had, you never would have learned how it worked. I would have had to put you in jail, and the museum would have been investigated for a shooting on our property. You know I couldn't have taken that risk. Our plan worked well."

"Until I had to drop the ruby and give up the Grealmæp!"

"We'll get them back. I know we will. It had to be like that. For the museum's reputation."

"You're right. It's *all* about the museum's reputation. And yours."

"Don't be sarcastic. My reputation has saved us several times."

"So has mine!"

"Really? When? What have you done? Writing some scary double dagger notes and leaving them around that dead professor's house? That saved us? If you hadn't murdered that man, he would still be alive, and the Grail could have been ours by now. Dead men don't talk. You should know that!" She paused, then spat out, "Stop trying to make this about you. Let's find this thing and get out of here."

I heard a grunt and could only imagine Dr. Pritzmord rolling his eyes at Dr. Gellmane.

"Well then lead the way, Madame Director." Dr. Pritzmord's sarcasm was obvious.

Dr. Gellmane flipped the light off. As they headed down the hallway, I breathed a small sigh of relief. My pulse was still racing. They climbed the stairs.

"Do you think Lydia took the Grealmæp with her?" I asked Blane in a whisper.

"I'm sure of it. She won't let it out of her sight."

I heard footsteps walking across the floor as doors opened and closed. Then, footsteps on the stairs.

"Like I said, Daniel, it's not here. She probably has it."

"So, what's our next move, Madame Director?"

"Quit calling me that. I don't appreciate your sarcasm. We keep watching the cottage. When they leave, we follow them."

I froze in fear. I thought Amesbury was a safe, quaint, and charming town. *Are Dr. Gellmane and Dr. Pritzmord watching us as we walk around? At The Courtly Robin? In the stores? Crossing the street?*

"Follow them?"

"Are you afraid of them? The great Nassauton dean, afraid of a bumbling university archaeologist, a gimpy boy, and a goody-two-shoes girl?" Dr. Gellmane taunted Dr. Pritzmord. "And that other professor—that wannabe rockstar with his long hair?"

"I'm not afraid of anything," Dr. Pritzmord snapped. "But the girl is smart. She knows how to work the ruby. I saw it."

"But she probably doesn't know what else it does," Dr. Gellmane added. "Or what else she does!"

"I'm sure she doesn't know!" Dr. Pritzmord said, giddy with excitement.

"They have no idea what they're up against and how many threads this ball of yarn has. And with GE finally collaborating, we're unstoppable. We'll succeed, without question."

"I love when you say 'we,' Elyse," Dr. Pritzmord said. "You and me—"

"The Knights of the White Wave," Dr. Gellmane interrupted. "The Knights of the White Wave will succeed."

"But what about the prophecy?" Dr. Pritzmord asked. He sounded crestfallen after Dr. Gellmane's interruption.

"What about it? Their magic is great, but ours is greater. And when you combine magic and science, you get the best of both worlds—all worlds."

"Of course," Dr. Pritzmord said. "You're so sexy when you talk about science. You're so smart, it's scary sometimes."

"Only sometimes?" Dr. Gellmane teased. I shuddered at her tone.

"All the time."

"That's better. Let's get out of here before they come back."

I heard the lock click as they opened the door.

"This storm is something terrible. Too bad that branch broke their window," Dr. Pritzmord said.

The door slammed shut. I opened the curtains and looked at

Blane. Dr. Gellmane and Dr. Pritzmord were working together to get the Grealmæp and its ruby, like we had speculated! Shaking, I collapsed into Blane's arms. He pulled me close to him—the closest he'd ever held me—and tenderly stroked my curls. We both took long, deep breaths, too scared to move or say anything. The rain pelted the windowpanes as the wind howled outside.

IV

The next morning, I woke up in a panic. Thoughts swirled around my head like a vortex. I looked at Blane, who was sleeping in his bed. I'd hardly gotten any sleep. After the break-in, Blane and I discussed spending the night at a bed and breakfast, since we didn't feel safe in our cottage with the broken window. But we also didn't want Lydia to come back and not find us. Eventually, we decided to lock ourselves in our room and wait until the morning, when we'd have a chance to talk with Lydia.

We also decided to wait to talk with her before reporting the break-in. We feared if we called the police, Dr. Gellmane would use her reputation against us, saying the broken window was obviously caused by the branch in the storm. It was our word against hers—and there was a branch right in the middle of the study.

I grabbed my journal and pencil from my nightstand and propped myself up in bed. I had to get my thoughts on paper before they overwhelmed me. *Do Dr. Gellmane and Dr. Pritzmord have a box that needs two rubies to open it? Is this why they want our Grealmæp? What is the prophecy? What else does the ruby do? What do I do—and how do they know? Do KA and Felda von Genzkensaffe, Grealia, and Augusta Victoria College fit into these new mysteries?*

I heard Dr. Gellmane's words in my head. *"But she probably doesn't know what else it does. Or what else she does!"* I circled *prophecy* and scribbled my question next to it.

"What *do* I do?" I mused aloud, twirling a loose curl and staring at the carpet. Remembering J. Carmichael's letter to Gran, I pulled it out of my journal and reread the last two sentences.

Only then will the Grail—and the world—be safe.

When your young explorer is old enough, you must   . We both know she holds

*   .*

*   , till we meet again,*

J. Car

I sighed, pulling my finger out of my curl. *Too many questions and too many unknowns . . .*

I grabbed my laptop, journal, and KA's journal and quietly closed our door. It was best to let Blane rest before his checkup. I headed to the kitchen. The branch was still on the floor of the study, with glass all around it. The broken window had let in too much cold air overnight. I shivered as I passed the study and entered the kitchen.

Lydia was already up. She'd opened the yellow curtains, revealing the gray sky and mist of the cool, post-storm April morning. She'd made a fresh pot of coffee and was sitting at the dining room table, her elbows on her placemat and her nose buried behind a newspaper. Her messy bun, with strands of her silver hair uncharacteristically disheveled and out of place, poked out over the top of the newspaper.

"Good morning." I poured a cup of coffee and sat down across from her. I wanted to ask her about Steve. I wanted to ask her what she'd had for dinner and how her evening was. I wanted to tell her about the break-in. But, judging from her demeanor, she wasn't in a mood to talk. I simply said, "You were out late last night."

She peered over the newspaper, barely lowering it from in front of her face. "Some storm," she muttered. "Brought that branch right into our study."

"Well, actually"—I took a sip of coffee—"Dr. Gellmane and Dr. Pritzmord broke into our cottage. Dr. Pritzmord brought the branch so everyone would think it was the storm."

"What?" Lydia asked skeptically, still holding her newspaper up, as though she wanted to hide her face.

"I swear it. Blane and I heard them."

"Carly," said Lydia stoically as she turned the page, "there was a very bad storm last night, and there is a branch in our study. Do you expect me to believe that, in the storm, Dr. Gellmane—the director of the Amesbury Museum—and Dr. Pritzmord—whom we saw get arrested—broke into our cottage?"

I nodded, a little annoyed Lydia was questioning me. "Yes, I'm telling you, we heard them! They were here!"

"Where is the evidence?" Lydia asked, lowering her newspaper. "Did you actually see them?"

"Well, no . . . but I—"

"Carly." Lydia's tone was quiet. "I know you won't admit this since you're afraid you'll disappoint yourself—and me. But I think this case is getting too much for you. Your nightmares. Your Nassauton work, the Grail, the Grealmæp . . . You're telling me you heard a well-known museum director—Knight of the White Wave or not—and a man who is in jail break into our cottage? There is a branch on the floor. That's the evidence— evidence from the storm." She looked at me, shaking her head in concern. Her eyes filled with a gentle sternness and compassion. "I've been worried about you, and now . . . well now, maybe it's best we took a break."

I took a sip of coffee and let out a long sigh. Disappointment filled my stomach. I didn't understand how Lydia didn't believe me, and how she was asking for evidence. *Evidence?* I was telling her I heard Dr. Gellmane and Dr. Pritzmord break in! What more evidence did she need? Instead, she thought I was stressed out and imagining it. I clutched my journal.

"Lydia, this is evidence!" I flipped through my journal's pages, then picked up KA's journal. "And *this*—the journal J. Carmichael found—is evidence." I wasn't angry. I was frustrated. "And the mortar and pestle are evidence. I don't understand how you don't see that."

"I do. But I also see how your mental health has deteriorated. It's just . . ." She sighed. "You need to take care of yourself. We've all been there at some point in our lives. And the only person who can take care of yourself is you. Think about it. You're not disappointing anyone if you pause to prioritize yourself." She sighed again, turning the paper as she pulled the newspaper back over her face. A few moments later, she gasped.

"Oh my god," she whispered. "Oh my god!" She repeated her words louder as she set the newspaper on the table and pointed at a headline.

MAJOR ACCIDENT ON WINTERSLOW ROAD,
THREE KILLED IN LORRY–CAR COLLISION

I read the headline and the rest of the story. The driver tried to stop at an intersection but lost control of his truck on the slick roads. The truck crashed into the oncoming car, killing all three people instantly. I read the names of the deceased: *Termont Dustin, Peter Jarmond, and John Carmichael.*

I gasped, looking at Lydia and bursting into tears. My whole body shook as I sobbed. She got up and embraced me.

"Oh Carly," was the only thing she managed to say as she held me and let me cry.

I didn't say anything. I didn't have any words. Just when I started learning more about my family's history, when I started asking better questions and finding answers . . . J. Carmichael was taken from me. I thought about his sister and her family. I thought about my mom—and the lavender honey he'd gotten her from France. I thought about his visits to my gran. I thought about *Grealia*, GE Pharmaceuticals, and Eternae.

Still sobbing, I took a deep breath. I buried my head in my hands. Lydia walked to the sink and grabbed a paper towel. She sat next to me, handing me the towel and placing her hand on my back. I wiped my face in between tears.

"I don't believe it," I said, still sobbing. "How is he gone?"

"That storm last night was terrible." Lydia was crying too. "Accidents happen." She clasped her hands together, interlacing her fingers. She unclasped her hands and wiped her face. "I was afraid for Allister and Beth on their drive back."

"Dr. Leith? His wife? You met up with them?"

"Yes. I asked if they could meet for dinner. I couldn't handle seeing John. I really couldn't. I'm sorry. Allister and Beth know the whole story with Steve. They have been my anchors over the years. Steve's passing, Lyle's passing, they have been there for me through all of it." She paused, wiping more tears from her face. "But had I known . . . had I just known"—she sniffled in sorrow—"John's gone now too."

I looked at Lydia. The wrinkles around her eyes were more pronounced. She looked weary.

"Oh, Lydia." I scooted my chair toward hers.

We embraced, letting our tears flow. As we cried, I finally said, "I'd barely gotten to know him. Only two conversations. He was Lyle's best friend. I just learned they dated for years. I had no idea."

Lydia smiled. "She loved John so much—and he loved her more. They were good for each other. So much respect. Teamwork. They were best teammates in life, and I'm sure wherever they are now, they're together again."

"If you believe in that. But yeah, I hope so too."

Lydia didn't say anything. I sighed. I was still in shock. The break-in, J. Carmichael's fatal accident, Lydia's dinner with Allister and Beth . . . It was a lot to take in, in one morning.

Sensing I was lost in thought, Lydia put her hand on my shoulder. "Maybe we should stop the case," she said. "We're both dealing with a lot of trauma and grief."

I closed my eyes. J. Carmichael told me to remember the locked door and the Grealmæps. I sighed again, wiping more tears and blowing my nose. I looked at my Ailm charm. "I promised J. Carmichael we'd get to the bottom of the lab. A promise is a promise. We're not stopping until we find the second Grealmæp and discover what GE Pharmaceuticals is hiding. It's what J. Carmichael told us to do. The least we can do to honor his memory is not give up."

Lydia looked at me. I smoothed my hair and tucked my curls behind my ears before I continued. "Blane and I have a lot to catch you up on."

I showed her my notes, KA's journal, and J. Carmichael's translations. I told her about *Grealia*, GE Pharmaceuticals, the Grealmæp insignia, and the locked door. I told her about Felda, KA's dead drop, and Augusta Victoria College. I told her what Blane and I overheard Dr. Gellmane and Dr. Pritzmord say when they broke in.

She took notes, nodding and gazing pensively into the kitchen every now and then. When I was done, she pursed her lips and looked at her notes and KA's journal. Then, she looked straight into my eyes.

"These, and the break-in, certainly give us more evidence in our case," she said. "I owe you an apology. I'm sorry I doubted your explanation for the branch in the study. With these learnings, everything is starting to make a little more sense now."

I nodded. "Thank you. Apology accepted. I know you're

under as much pressure as I am. Maybe even more."

Lydia's lips curled in a small smile. "I am, but Nassauton will have to wait. Right now, we have to work with the facts we have."

"And we have to be more careful. No one goes anywhere in Amesbury alone," I said. "We need to find the other Grealmæp and learn more about KA and Felda. We know she never picked up her dad's journal and the mortar and pestle."

Lydia nodded, flipping to the cover page of KA's journal. "It can't be a coincidence that GE Pharmaceuticals named their drug Eternae. They must know about Grealia Eternae and they obviously know about the Grealmæp,"

"Yup," I said, writing Lydia's comments in my journal. "Maybe they have the Grealmæp and Merlin and Morgan's spell books, and are trying to manufacture *Grealia*? J. Carmichael said he believed Eternae had *Grealia* in it! What if they are hiding the Grail behind the locked door?"

Lydia nodded with renewed excitement. "Fabulous questions—write them down! Anything is possible at this point."

I scribbled my questions in my journal, then flipped through KA's journal. Every few pages, I'd study the entries, which dated from January 1941 to September 1942, and were mostly diagrams of plants and chemical equations. One was a diagram of our mortar and pestle, with the residue circled. Others were entries in German, for which I used J. Carmichael's translations.

"Wait a minute." I held a few index cards and stared at an entry—one of the few in English. "Look at this."

Lydia put her coffee cup down and picked up the journal.

Once we confirm receipt, you'll receive directions on how to sign up for fall classes. If you need assistance or have questions, please contact the registrar's office.

I looked at KA's journal, then at my email. I wasn't ready for sophomore year. I flagged the email for later and opened a new tab. I typed in *Augusta Victoria College* and was horrified by what I found.

Augusta Victoria College was a finishing school for German girls in the 1930s. Strategically located in Bexhill-on-Sea, a small town on England's southeast coast, the college's purpose was to educate the daughters of the highest-ranking Nazi officials in German ideals—and English customs. The Nazis hoped the girls would marry into English high society, cementing English-German relations. The school had closed abruptly when World War II started. Now, it was a World War II maritime and military museum. A quick search revealed Bexhill was a two-and-a-half-hour drive from Amesbury.

"Let's drive to Bexhill," I said. "Dr. Wengaro won't mind if we take a day trip."

"I don't see why he would," said Lydia. "We've got the rental car, and anything that helps us learn more about *Grealia*, the Grealmæp, and GE Pharmaceuticals is worth it." She paused, nodding pensively. "Though I suggest we tell Kenneth about the break-in after our trip, once we have more evidence. I don't want to derail his recovery process with news that will upset him unless we have a strong sense of our next steps."

††

We had a full morning before driving to Bexhill. After Blane woke up, we told him about J. Carmichael's accident. He couldn't hide his tears. "He was the only man I'd met who understood what I'm going through with my brother," Blane said.

While Blane wasn't connected to J. Carmichael in the same way I was, the fact that both suffered tragedies related to their brothers had been something Blane latched on to.

"I'll miss him," he said as we headed to his checkup. "But he's here in spirit. He would have wanted us to continue our case—and we will."

As Blane hoped, he exceeded expectations for progress. His doctors graduated him out of his wheelchair.

"I don't need these crutches!" he exclaimed as we left the doctor's office. "I feel great."

"Take them anyway," said Lydia as we started our drive. "You never know how you'll feel this afternoon."

I was glad Blane listened. I didn't want him relapsing. He stretched out in the back seat while I sat in the front, marveling at the ease with which Lydia drove stick shift on the other side of the road. She expertly navigated around fallen branches the strong winds felled in the storm. She didn't let the debris and detours faze her.

We were about an hour into our drive and had navigated past one crew tackling a downed tree when her phone rang. She put it on speaker and placed it on the console.

"Hello, Lydia? It's Dr. Gellmane. How are you?"

The three of us stared at each other. My heart started pounding. Dr. Gellmane didn't know we knew she was a Knight of the White Wave—or that she had broken into our cottage.

"We're great," Lydia said. She knew she had to keep a good rapport with Dr. Gellmane to avoid suspicion.

"Marvelous, dahlings! Right, well, I've got some news for you. The lab results for the mortar and pestle residue came back."

"And?"

"The analysis is inconclusive. The lab tried mass spec, chromatography, everything. They're not sure what it is, where it comes from, and why it won't register on any comparative element chart. They said they've never seen anything like it."

My eyes widened as I looked at Blane. We were thinking the same thing. *This is scientific evidence the residue, which we knew was Grealia from KA's journal, was made of otherworldly reactants.* My heart fluttered in excitement. A wide grin spread across my face. The science confirmed *Grealia* had supernatural qualities!

"That's very interesting," said Lydia, holding back her excitement so she didn't blow our cover. "So, there's no way to figure out what the residue is? No other tests you can run?" she asked in a matter-of-fact tone.

"I'm afraid not, not with this lab."

"I see. Is there another lab you can send it to?" Lydia asked.

"Yep." Dr. Gellmane paused. "The mortar and pestle are already on their way back to us. We'll send them to another lab that can run different tests."

"Sounds good, thank you," Lydia said. "We appreciate the call. Keep us posted."

V

With its row houses with thatched roofs and window boxes for planting flowers, Bexhill reminded me of Amesbury. Clusters of small shops and restaurants made it feel quaint, and the gray sky, greenish blues of the sea, and tan sand of the beaches gave Bexhill a chilly English spring charm. Our first stop was for lunch at The Elephant and Pen, a pub around the corner from Bexhill Maritime and Military Museum. It had a chalkboard sign outside its door that advertised a fish and chips special.

"I'm in," I announced as Lydia parked the car. "Can't get more English than fish and chips in a little seaside town." I smiled, thinking about The Courtly Robin's fish and chips. I also noticed the pub's sign: it had a smiling elephant wearing thick, black glasses and a top hat. It was sitting on a circus ball, holding a fountain pen in the air as if it were about to write something.

"That sounds delicious," said Blane as he swung his legs out of the car, testing his boot on the ground. "Especially on a blustery day like today."

I tucked an unruly curl behind my ear. "How's your ankle?"

"It's fine, but I'll bring one crutch just in case." Blane grabbed the crutch from the back seat. We walked to the door. I liked that The Elephant and Pen was whimsical, and I couldn't wait to see the decorations inside.

As we walked in and the host seated us, I chuckled at all the elephant paintings on the wall. Some were elephants at the circus; some were elephants in the wild. The owner undoubtedly wanted to celebrate these gentle, intelligent, and playful giants.

The host sat us at a booth near the window and bar, which was filled with young professionals and locals. A few families with small children were seated at tables across the pub's main room. One woman seated at the bar was having a loud conversation as she sipped her drink.

"You're full of excuses. I'm left empty-handed. You promised me you'd get it for me. Where is it?" She spat the words into her phone.

She wore a big, wide-brimmed felt hat, which covered most of her head. Her long, blonde locks tumbled down her back.

"That's the key to the whole thing! Thousands are depending on me. I work with the smartest people in Somerset. We are stuck until I have it. We're racing against time. I don't understand why this is so difficult."

She hung up.

"Froustratin' dai?" the bartender asked her. I heard a distinctly different accent in Bexhill than the ones I'd heard in Amesbury.

"Very!" She couldn't hide her displeasure from the bartender—or the patrons around her. "You'd think people could do what you hire them to do."

"Oh, muhh love, do I noowww the feelin'," said the bartender. "They say they can do enethin', and 'en when you ask 'em to do somethin' simple, all of a sudden it's like you asked 'em to move the mountains."

The lady laughed. "You get me, mate, you get me."

"I'm a barkeep, it's wot I'm 'ere for. You're almost out. Wont another?"

"No, I appreciate it. I need to head back. Drove all the way to the museum from Somerset, couldn't find what I needed, found you all, and grabbed a quick bite. But the lab is calling. What do I owe you?"

"Right, one moment please."

As soon as the lady paid, she grabbed her bag from the stool next to her. It was a rich, dark leather tote bag. It looked very durable and smooth—and expensive. I didn't recognize the brand—MvG—which was stamped on the tote's center with what must have been a five-inch by five-inch branding iron. As she adjusted the bag on her shoulder, I noticed a gold-and-silver ring with a sparkling gemstone on her right hand.

I watched as she strode to the door, wondering about her conversation. *Somerset . . . the lab is calling . . . Does this woman work at GE Pharmaceuticals?*

††

After lunch, we walked to the Bexhill Maritime and Military Museum. A lone white door stood in the center of the building, and windows dotted the ivy-covered stone walls. Beyond the building, it looked like there had been tennis courts and a patio. I cringed, picturing German girls playing tennis after their Nazi history lessons. I didn't want to spend a minute more than was necessary here.

As we entered the museum's lobby, two chipper young professionals greeted us. They looked like they were in their mid-twenties and were dressed in all black.

"Welcome to the Bexhill Maritime and Military Museum," said one, proudly pointing to her name tag and adjusting her neon-pink necklace. She had a different accent than the bartender at The Elephant and Pen. "I'm Sarah Joy. Help yourself to a map to begin your self-guided tour." Her chunky, plastic neon-colored bracelets clacked against each other. They were different shades of pink and complemented her necklace.

"There is no admissions fee, although donations are encouraged," said the other, pointing to a glass case with coins and bills in it. "I'm Clive, happy to answer any questions."

"Thank you," said Lydia, picking up a map. "We're here to learn about a teacher. We think she worked at Augusta Victoria."

"Right, you'll want to visit our special exhibit. It's on the second floor." Clive stepped out from behind the desk. He pointed down the hallway, which had a long staircase at the end of it. "Most of the rooms on this floor are maritime and military history. The special exhibit has the artifacts from the school."

"Great, we'll head up there." I motioned to Lydia and Blane to follow me. Pictures of the schoolgirls and their teachers lined the hallway walls. In some pictures, the girls were in classrooms. In others, they were walking around in a circle, balancing porcelain plates on their heads. I cringed again, feeling watched.

"Which one is Felda?" asked Blane as we headed for the staircase. He walked effortlessly in his boot, barely using his crutch.

"Look at this one," Lydia said. She pointed to a picture of thirty girls in rows practicing the Nazi salute. The image made my stomach churn.

"Do you think Hitler ever came here?" I asked, reading the caption. "Here they are preparing for his birthday celebration."

"That's creepy," said Blane. "What if he hid Nazi treasure here, in the basement?"

The queasy feeling in my stomach intensified as I thought about Hitler visiting the school. Undoubtedly, the presence of evil still lingered in the hallways,

"I don't really need the crutches," Blane said, making it up the stairs. "The boot is plenty good."

The special exhibit at the top of the stairs was partitioned into different sections, creating the effect of walking through a maze. The poster by the entrance gave an overview of the exhibit:

These are the stories of the teachers of Augusta Victoria College. The college staff were hand-selected by the highest-ranking German officials to provide the best education to their daughters. Facing imprisonment—or worst—

for disobeying official orders, the teachers could not decline the assignment. Staff followed strict rules, which included living on campus and observing strict curfews. They were prohibited from having relationships with German men—as that went against the purpose of establishing Augusta Victoria as an integration site between English and German societies. As the war broke out on 1 September 1939, the school was shut down abruptly. All personnel were evacuated.

You'll step back in time as you listen to the stories and look at the artifacts—the personal possessions of faculty that give insights into daily life at the school. They have been restored for viewing by museum staff. This restoration work was made possible by the support of Lord Breekson, who believes that to avoid repeating the evils of the past, we must learn lessons from history. We must never forget the atrocities authored by the Nazi party, which resulted in the loss of countless innocent lives.

"Lord Breekson!" I nudged Blane. "That's the guy from the Amesbury Museum."

"Interesting! Dr. Gellmane said he is a philanthropist, so I'm sure he's donated a ton of money to museums."

"Must be nice to have that much money and donate it to educational causes," I mused.

"Or to receive that much money and make wealthy people's donations matter for something!" Blane grinned. "That's the cooler part, to me at least."

"Go on." I grinned. I liked when Blane shared his interests. He had a boyish optimism and exuberance that made me feel like whatever he said was sure to come true, because he would try his hardest to make it happen. That attitude and Blane's exuberance inspired me.

"Well, imagine this," he said as we walked into the special exhibit. He leaned on his crutch with one arm and gestured with his other, as if creating the future as he spoke. "What if, after wildly successful careers as a famous archaeological duo, you and I know enough wealthy patrons that we ask them to donate money to us. We could start our own museum. You'll curate the collection; I'll run education programs."

I turned bright red, feeling my face burning as I blushed. Blane considered us partners in our careers. This made me feel like he was in our relationship for the long haul. It was April. We hadn't even been dating for a year—but in that year we'd had more adventures than most couples had in a lifetime. In every moment, Blane proved he was kind, capable, and intelligent. He challenged me in the best ways and encouraged me constantly.

"That would make me really happy," I said, standing on my tiptoes and kissing Blane's cheek. "You make me really happy."

"You make me the happiest." He wrapped his arm around my shoulder as we walked through the exhibit.

We saw sections with artifacts for Augusta Victoria's chef, tennis coach, and mathematics, history, and Latin teachers. Fräulein Musseldorf. Fräulein Himmler. Frau Stein. Frau Bellsdussel. Fräulein Schmidt.

"Whoa!" I whispered, stopping in front of Fräulein von Genzkensaffe's section.

Felda von Genzkensaffe was Augusta Victoria's chemistry teacher. Felda was interested in medicinal herbs, especially those relating to chronic pain management. She took after her father, KA von Genzkensaffe, an expert chemist who was recruited by the Nazi party.

When KA learned Augusta Victoria was hiring, he sent his daughter to teach here. Under strict orders to communicate with her in English, KA corresponded with Felda regularly, sharing his expertise so she could pass it on to her students. While the college retained some of her chemistry notes, the most intriguing of Felda's effects are the letters she shared with her clandestine German lover, Herr Dietrich. Felda met him when a group of German soldiers came to Augusta Victoria for Hitler's birthday celebration. They were inseparable from the moment they met. When Herr Dietrich, who was charged with insurrection after exposing Hitler's evils while deployed on a secret mission, fell sick, Felda tried to use her chemistry expertise to help him, but to no avail. When Augusta Victoria shut down, Felda fled to Yeovil, working in a lab there. While in Yeovil, Felda gave birth to her son, Albert von Genzkensaffe.

"Herr Dietrich was her *secret* lover," I said, walking up to the framed letters on the wall. Next to each letter was its translation. "Let's see what these say."

7 June 1939

Dear Felda,

You are brilliant! One day, I will build you your own laboratory. My love, my Felda.

Yours always,
Dietrich

17 July 1939

Dear Felda,

My love Felda! I am happy you visited Stonehenge. I will be very busy these upcoming months, on official party business. I will try to visit soon, before I'm deployed. I think about you always! My love, my Felda.

Yours always,
Dietrich

30 August 1939

Dear Herr Dietrich,

I write with exciting—and terrifying—news. I am pregnant. I had not been feeling well. I went to the college infirmary. It is confirmed! We are to be parents. I am terrified since you are not here. I know exactly what I will call him: Albert. What do you think?

All my love,
Felda

That was the last letter. Days later, World War II broke out, and the school was evacuated.

"Felda never sent Herr Dietrich that letter," Blane said. "He probably never knew she was pregnant."

"Yeah. And she never came to pick up the box from the Aubrey Hole." I stared at the wall with Felda's letters, trying to piece together her story. Noticing Lydia walking nearby, I asked her if she saw Felda's exhibit.

"Not yet." She turned around and walked toward us. "Did you and Blane see the memorial and Felda's journal entries?"

"No." Blane and I walked over to Lydia. Blane steadied himself on his crutch.

"All this standing is getting to me," he said. "I should rest soon."

I nodded as I read the text on the memorial plaque.

Augusta Victoria College Faculty lost in World War II

The Blitz of London
7 September 1940–11 May 1941
Anne Musseldorf – Elsa Bellsdussel – Annalise Sammer –
Liesel Strubenhaüs

Yeovil Air Raid
5 August 1942
Felda von Genzkensaffe

"So that's why she never picked up the box," Blane said.

"Correct," Lydia said. She pointed to the glass display case behind her. "Read Felda's journal entries."

Blane and I walked over to the case. Each entry had a card next to it, with its English translation. Next to the journals were pictures of Felda wearing long, blonde hair in braids. Lydia, Blane, and I huddled around the case.

Felda von Genzkensaffe's journals provide insights into her life. They also detail her love for Herr Dietrich. These journals were donated to the museum by Felda's son, Albert von Genzkensaffe, in memory of his mother and to celebrate her accomplishments as a female chemist.

11 June 1942

My love is still sick. Something terrible, they don't know. Hospital doctors, they don't know! I've asked Father for help—if he can send me his healing medicine, I can get some to my love!

13 June 1942

What am I supposed to do with this instrument? It looks like a horseshoe, like Stonehenge. Father says it unlocks the box he will send—the box with healing medicine. But how? He promised he will send his journal and equipment. With each passing day, Herr Dietrich gets sicker!

9 July 1942,

My love is dying! They cannot save him! I cannot save him. I wish desperately to return to Germany to be with him in his last hours. Nothing from Father—no medicine, no equipment, no journal.

"Blane, Felda *did* have the Grealmæp!" I whispered. "KA von Genzkensaffe sent it to her! But she didn't know how to use it."

"Do you think her Grealmæp—the other Grealmæp—is here?" Blane asked.

"I don't see it in these cases. It could be in storage?" Lydia mused.

"Or maybe it's with Albert," I pondered.

"Do you think Albert is still alive?" asked Lydia. "If he was born in 1940, he'd be in his late seventies now."

"Maybe Clive and Sarah Joy know," Blane said.

We headed down the stairs. Sarah Joy and Clive sat behind the information desk, scrolling on their phones. They immediately looked up when they saw us.

"Lots of history up there, yeah?" Sarah Joy asked, walking around the desk to us.

"Yes. Especially that Felda von Genzkensaffe!" I blurted out.

"Her lover died, and she was pregnant with their son!"

"Oh, Felda," said Clive. "Fascinating story! We have her journals only cos her son and Lord Breekson were best mates."

Lord Breekson's name again. "Isn't he the same guy who donated the funds to restore the artifacts?" I asked.

"Yes. Lord Breekson and Albert met in grammar school." Sarah Joy's eyes lit up as she started gesturing to enunciate her words. "Albert survived the air raid that killed Felda. I'm sure you saw the memorial plaque. After the air raid, Albert was recovered from the rubble of Felda's house. A miracle he survived. He was taken to a church orphanage in Somerset, with no real knowledge of his mother."

Somerset. That's where GE Pharmaceuticals is. I twirled two curls and listened.

"The orphanage staff collected what they could from the rubble: Albert, his baby blanket, some clothes, a few pictures of Felda, a few of her lab journals, two sealed vials of light pinkish powder, and her jewelry box."

The powder had to be Grealia!

"The box is my favorite. It had the vials and some of Felda's jewelry—one was a silver-and-gold ring with an aquamarine stone, and her pendants," Clive added. "One was this golden pendant with a brilliant red ruby. No information on how she got the vials or her jewelry. They must have been passed down in her family. No information on what was in the vials—we don't even think she knew! Fascinating, right?"

I tilted my head when I heard the words *golden pendant with a brilliant red ruby.* Goose bumps appeared on my arms.

"The pendant had some kind of dagger across it—no one knows what for," Sarah Joy added. "We think Felda's dad gave it to her when she came to teach here."

"But we don't know how he got it. Maybe the Nazis found the jewelry and vials on one of their raids, then gave the jewelry to her dad as payment—and the vials for him to use in his experiments," Clive said. "But they were sealed, so who knows if he ever opened them."

"Where's the pendant and the rest of Felda's jewelry now?" asked Lydia.

"Felda's granddaughter—Albert's daughter—has them." Sarah Joy paused. "Albert was adamant he wouldn't leave Felda's jewelry to the museum, despite Lord Breekson pleading with him. Albert said Thilda needed something to remind her of her grandmother."

Thilda. Does Thilda know her great-grandfather was a Knight of the Dagger? Is Thilda herself a Knight of the Dagger?

"Where is Thilda?" Blane asked. "She's got to be a young professional now."

"In Somerset," Clive said. "About four hours away."

"Oh yeah," Sarah Joy added. "She runs an amazing startup. She's a highly accomplished scientist and an inspiration for women in the sciences."

"What does she do?" I asked.

Sarah Joy smiled. "She's the CEO of GE Pharmaceuticals."

VI

After our visit to the Bexhill Maritime and Military Museum, we drove back to Amesbury to meet with Dr. Wengaro. Felda's pendant, which Albert, then Thilda, had inherited, had to be the Grealmæp.

"I'll bet she's hiding the Grealmæp behind that door and trying to make *Grealia*," Blane said as Lydia pulled into the hospital parking lot. "Why else would she lock the door?"

"That could be it," I mused. "Or what if she has one of Merlin and Morgan's boxes and needs both rubies to open it? That box could contain the Grail!"

"And remember what Dr. Gellmane and Dr. Pritzmord said about GE backing them? If GE is GE Pharmaceuticals, I bet all three of them are after the second Grealmæp—our Grealmæp," Lydia added.

"Go figure: a twenty-first-century laboratory making Morgan's medicine!" Blane grinned, his hazel eyes sparkling with excitement. "Thilda's whole family tried to make *Grealia*—and couldn't! I bet that's what keeps her up at night. And if she has Felda's journals, maybe she also has whatever equipment KA sent Felda. She makes *Grealia*, she patents it, and she's set."

"Neither the Knights of the Dagger, nor the White Wave, will be able to legally claim the drug that gives eternal life!" I whispered, thinking about the profit implications if Thilda patented *Grealia*.

Lydia finally found a spot. As she parked, I stared out the car window. Though we'd visited Dr. Wengaro countless times, I hadn't noticed how dated the hospital building's exterior was—like it was designed decades ago and was never renovated. *Everything deteriorates*, I thought. *Everything, eventually, dies.* The hospital was full of patients waiting for loved ones' visits—patients who might never leave, whose visits with their families tonight might be their last. No Grail, and its promise of eternal life, was available to them. No *Grealia*—Morgan's healing medicine—could be manufactured and administered to them. They would die, just like my gran and my dad . . . *Where is Christ to cure them? How can He claim to be the ultimate healer? How can God let these patients die, taking them from their loved ones, the same way He'd taken Gran and Dad from me?*

The memories of my dad hit me all at once. Our conversation by our bonfire, making s'mores. Our hikes in the park. My Confirmation Day. The day he and Mom sat next to me on the couch. The day he told me he had cancer. The day he told me they released him from the trial. *Eternae didn't work for him. He died.* I bit my lip as tears streamed down my face.

"Coming, Carly?" Lydia asked, opening the car door. Her face fell when she saw mine. "Carly, what's wrong?"

I shook my head. My bottom lip was trembling. "My dad had cancer. He was in GE Pharmaceuticals' Eternae trial. He couldn't handle a higher dosage. They dismissed him. That's what they told us. His cancer killed him."

"Oh, Carly." Lydia's tone softened. She put her hand on my shoulder.

"It was right after we buried Gran," I added, tucking my curls behind my ears.

"Not too long after our last dig," said Lydia. "I wonder if Lyle knew."

"I don't know. I didn't even know, till the very end." I sighed, then snidely added, "My family apparently excels at keeping secrets from me."

I got out of the car. Blane hobbled around to me, propping

himself up with his crutch. He reached for my hand as we walked to the entrance. Holding his hand made me feel calm and at peace.

"What happened to the rest of the Eternae participants?" Blane asked.

I shrugged. "No clue."

"All the more reason for us to get to GE Pharmaceuticals as soon as we can and figure out what Thilda is hiding."

We took the elevator up to Dr. Wengaro's room.

"Lydia! Blane! Carly! Great to see you. Tell me about your trip."

"We have a lot to share. And I'm happy to see you so chipper, Kenneth."

Dr. Wengaro's half-eaten dinner was by his bed. His ponytail was tucked behind his left shoulder. His face had much more color than it had the last time we'd seen him, and he looked animated and in very good spirits.

"I am elated. The doctors said I'll be out in a few days! They're quite pleased with my progress."

"Lemme guess, the first thing you'll want is a decent meal?" I chuckled, pointing at the dinner tray.

"At The Courtly Robin, yes please!" Dr. Wengaro replied, grinning. "And a big pint of their delicious ale."

"Maybe we could branch out and try somewhere new," said Blane. "Lots of great places here. And . . ." He paused, sitting in one of the chairs and loosening his ankle boot. "All this walking. Ankle's acting up." He took his foot out and continued. "We'll need to try a few new pubs before we leave for our next adventure!"

Dr. Wengaro looked at us. "Next adventure? What *have* you been up to?"

We told him what we'd overheard at The Elephant and Pen and learned at the museum. Dr. Wengaro's eyes lit up at the mention of Felda's jewelry and the Grealmæp. We also told him about the break-in, how GE was backing Dr. Gellmane and

Dr. Pritzmord, and the prophecy.

"Pritzmord, that devil!" Dr. Wengaro said. "In cahoots with Gellmane all along!" He shook his head. "Do you think Thilda knows about Carly's Grealmæp?" He got out of his bed and paced around the room.

I smiled. Dr. Wengaro referred to the Grealmæp as mine. This made me feel like he was taking me seriously as an archaeologist.

"Kenneth, look at you, walking!" Lydia smiled. "Wonderful progress!"

"Thank you, Lydia, I've really tried. I don't want to be here a minute longer than I need to be."

"I don't know if she knows about my Grealmæp," I finally said. "Or if she knows there are two. But I bet she has Felda's— her lab's insignia is the Grealmæp. Don't forget J. Carmichael's pictures."

"J. Carmichael." Lydia shook her head. "Kenneth, you might want to sit down."

She told Kenneth how J. Carmichael died in the car accident, the same night as the break-in. Upon hearing the news, Dr. Wengaro placed his hand over his red double dagger tattoo, closed his eyes, and whispered a short prayer. "He was a good man," Dr. Wengaro said. "And a great knight. May his soul rest in eternal peace." He sighed as he gripped his left wrist and looked at us.

Lydia, Blane, and I nodded solemnly.

"Will the knights have a funeral for him?" I asked. "I think his only family is his sister."

"I'm sure we will." Dr. Wengaro gazed pensively out his window. "But I don't know the details. There's a lot about the knights I'm still learning." He held up his left arm, pointing at his double dagger marks. "So far, I've only been to Imprint. That's the first milestone, six months into our Quest Phase. I'll go through Intake two months from now, in June." He paused and smiled as he tightened his ponytail. "A year ago, I was in a totally different place in my life. I had no idea who the Knights of the Dagger were. And now . . . well, it's hard to believe how much has happened in less than a year."

I looked at Dr. Wengaro, then glanced at the mirror above his sink. A year ago, I was finishing high school, the shadow of Gran's and my dad's deaths still long and dark across my path. I doubted everything I thought was true. The only thing I knew I wanted was to follow in Gran's footsteps and do her proud at Nassauton. I had no idea what adventures awaited me.

At Nassauton, I'd found Blane—my teammate in every sense of the word. I'd found the Grealmæp and Gran's poem in a shoebox and discovered my archaeology professor was Gran's partner. We got swept up in solving a murder and looking for the Holy Grail—a quest that had seduced knights, priests, politicians, cult leaders, archaeologists, and now two freshmen and their professors. Together, we'd persevered, ending up halfway around the world and discovering more danger than we imagined.

Now, we were wrapped up in another mystery—and a prophecy—far deeper than the Holy Grail. This new mystery was leading us to a lab with secrets hidden behind locked doors, run by a powerful CEO whose ancestors were obsessed with *Grealia*. *What other secrets is GE Pharmaceuticals hiding?*

††

I stared at the ceiling.

2:45 a.m.

How are these mysteries related? What is the prophecy? What else do I do? The Grealmæps, the rubies, Grealia, GE Pharmaceuticals, Thilda . . .

Blane was sleeping peacefully in his bed. I quietly peeled back my sheets and blankets. Slipping into my moccasins, I grabbed my phone, journal, and pencil, and walked down the stairs to the study. The bay window was boarded up, the broken glass removed. Lydia must have told the cottage owners about the damage. They must have fixed it when we went to Bexhill. *Did she say it was a branch in the storm?*

I sank into a leather armchair, kicking off my moccasins and placing my phone and journal next to the lamp on the side table. I pulled my legs up to my chest, wrapping my arms around my legs. My Ailm charm sparkled in what little light streamed in from the lamp on the landing, through the cracks of the boarded-up window. *Wisdom. Purpose. Physical, mental, spiritual strength. A clear path forward.* Our next destination was clear—GE Pharmaceuticals. But our path forward wasn't. We couldn't show up and expect a warm welcome from Thilda.

My phone lit up with alerts, their jarring notifications pinging in the darkness. *OVERDUE/INCOMPLETE: COS 201 – ASSIGNMENT #5, ENG 245 – PAPER #2, ENG 245 – REFLECTION #5, HIS 102 – PRESENTATION #4, DISCUSSION BOARD #5.*

With KA's journals, Felda, and GE Pharmaceuticals on my mind, I'd completely neglected my Nassauton work. Now, even with my accommodations, there was no way I could catch up.

I took a deep breath and looked at my Ailm charm. "Be brave," I whispered to myself, closing my eyes and inhaling and exhaling. I opened my eyes, flipping on the lamp and grabbing my journal and pencil. Writing down my thoughts always helped me understand them—and process how to take my next steps.

"Carly?"

I put down my pencil and looked up. Blane stood in the doorframe.

"Blane?"

"What are you doing here?" we asked simultaneously.

"I couldn't sleep. I'm worried about school," I replied.

Blane perched next to me on one of the armrests, taking off his boot. He opened his arms and wrapped me in a hug.

"I'll scooch over," I said. "We can both fit."

"If we snuggle," he said, sliding down into the armchair as we smushed closer.

"I can't do this. I can't balance schoolwork and our Grail

quest. I can't go to GE Pharmaceuticals, get Thilda's Grealmæp, and do my homework." I pointed at my phone as the enormous weight of the consequences of my choices sank in. "All these incomplete assignments. I can't finish the term. And if you come with me, you won't be able to finish, either. I can't have that on my mind. I can't be responsible for you failing!"

"Shh. Deep breath." He caressed my curls. "Deep breath. It's going to be okay. I'm doing everything online. Even my midterm papers and assignments. I'll be fine."

I started shaking and crying. I went to Nassauton to study archaeology, follow in Gran's footsteps, and do well academically. I tried to balance everything. *What would Joyce say if she saw me now?* In prioritizing our Grail quest, I'd let Joyce, who'd advocated for me and attested to my work ethic, and my mom, who was so proud of me for my academic accomplishments last semester, down. I had also been a bad friend to Lara, neglecting to text her and not being on campus to hang out with her. But if I didn't prioritize our Grail quest, I would have let Lydia, Blane, Dr. Wengaro, Gran, and J. Carmichael down. No matter my choice, I couldn't win.

I sighed, closing my eyes. Deep in my heart, I knew now wasn't the right time for me to be at Nassauton. Remembering when I'd reflected at the soldiers' memorial in the park, I couldn't let go of my belief that because of my knowledge, I had a moral obligation to find the Grail. With what I knew about GE Pharmaceuticals, Thilda, and the Grealmæp—and what I needed to learn about the prophecy and myself—I had an even deeper sense of obligation. If I chose Nassauton, I'd never learn about GE Pharmaceuticals and Eternae—and why it didn't work for my dad. I'd never learn if Thilda was making *Grealia* or what she was hiding behind the locked door. I opened my eyes, looking at the boarded-up window. My choice was clear.

"I need to drop out. I have to email the registrar."

Blane listened, wrapping me in his arms.

"I have a moral obligation to find the Grail," I continued.

"And to uncover Thilda's secrets. Our evidence is not leading me to Nassauton." I paused. "I can always take summer classes, but right now I need to focus on GE Pharmaceuticals."

Blane kissed the top of my head—a kiss that lingered, full of love and admiration, a kiss that told me Blane respected me and my choice. "If you've examined the evidence and you know this leap of faith is the right choice, I support you entirely."

I nodded. "I have. And I know. This is the right next step."

"Then I'll take it with you," Blane added.

I bit my lip, trying not to tremble and cry. Overwhelmed by how Blane reassured, championed, and validated me, I threw my arms around him, grasping him like I never wanted to let go. He caressed my curls, his fingers playing with their ringlets as he pulled my head toward his.

"I love you, Carly Stuart," Blane murmured as he kissed me. "You chase your dreams. You inspire me to chase mine. That's a powerful—and freeing—feeling."

I blushed, grinning at what Blane said. "I love you, Blane Henley. Thank you for being the best teammate."

"I'm all the luckier for it." Blane smiled. "And I'm here with you no matter what."

I grinned. "Even when I have to call my mom and tell her? She's not going to handle this well." I dreaded my mom's reaction to learning I was dropping out.

"Especially when you have to call your mom! We'll call her a little later today."

"We?"

"Heck yeah, I'm not letting you make that call alone!" His hazel eyes sparkled in the light. I grinned, reaching up and shutting off the lamp. In his arms, I drifted into a peaceful sleep.

VII

We woke up to the smell of coffee wafting from the kitchen. "Good morning, you two," Lydia said as Blane and I plopped ourselves on the living room couch. "I should say, good almost-afternoon."

"Morning, Lydia." I chuckled as I looked at the clock on the microwave.

11:35 a.m.

It wasn't like me to sleep in this late, but the stress of the semester and my decision had caught up with me. "I had to think through a big decision. Can I share it?"

"Of course. Here. Have some coffee." Lydia grabbed a mug from the cupboard as I got up from the couch and walked to the fridge.

"What number coffee are you on, Dr. Kells?" asked Blane. He joined me by the fridge. I grabbed some blueberries and dairy-free yogurt.

"Grab the granola from the pantry, please?" I asked Blane.

"Of course," he said, reaching to open the door.

"It's my third cup, and it's not even noon. Keeping up with everything at Nassauton is taking its toll."

I nodded. I wasn't the only one struggling. Blane and I walked to the kitchen table and sat across from Lydia. I stared at the crinkled, dying flowers in the vase on the table.

"So, what's your decision?" Peering at me inquisitively through her glasses, she wrapped her hands around her mug and took a long sip of coffee. Her bracelets and bangles clinked together. Her Ailm charm glistened in the April morning sunlight.

I looked at my Ailm charm. *Be brave.* I took a deep breath and let it out. "I'm withdrawing from Nassauton for the semester. I can't handle the workload and our Grail quest. Doing both is too much, and the only person who can take care of me is myself." I let out another breath. "I've made my choice."

I didn't know how Lydia would react, but I was surprised by how easy it was to say that to her. She took another sip of coffee. Her bangles clanged together as she lowered her mug. She looked out the window for what seemed an eternity. Then she turned to me, her gaze meeting mine.

"Carlyle Stuart. I'm surprised. I never thought I'd hear you say that."

Tears welled up in my eyes and my lips started trembling. I blew it. I'd disappointed Lydia too. I reached for Blane's hand under the table. I stared at my coffee mug and the dying flowers, looking everywhere but at Lydia.

Lydia patted her bun, smiling. "I'm surprised, since I think you're showing wisdom beyond your years," she finally said. "Making a choice of that magnitude requires wisdom—not knowledge." She smiled again. "And I think—no, I know—that's what Lyle would have done if she were in your shoes. In fact, that is what she did."

When Lydia mentioned Gran, I beamed. "What do you mean, that's what she did?"

"Our junior year, Lyle withdrew. She debated it for weeks. Her dad was livid—he was helping her with tuition. It strained their relationship for decades. Every chance he got, he'd make some snide comment about her withdrawing."

"Wait, what?" I leaned across the table in shock. "Gran dropped out of college?"

"Yes. She did go back, but it took her a while. She went back when she was ready. But she couldn't pass up her first big opportunity to work on her dream project. It fell in her lap from one of our professors, who was hired to consult on an excavation in Rome. He noticed Lyle's interest and aptitude and arranged for her to get the experience. But that meant taking the term off."

"What was the excavation?" Blane asked.

"Commercial developers were demolishing an old villa outside of Rome to make way for a new office complex. They were digging up the foundation and found human bones, which led them to speculate—"

"It was a burial site?" I blurted out.

"Yep." Lydia smiled. "You sure think like an archaeologist."

Blane beamed at me and poked my shoulder. "That's my teammate!"

I grinned, sliding my hand under the table on Blane's thigh. He winked at me.

"It wasn't just any burial site. Lyle's work, more specifically her questions—the questions of someone with an open mind and relatively little archaeological experience—led to the discoveries of one of the oldest Christian catacombs in Rome, with some of the most complex inscriptions and early wall art. This discovery was pivotal to our understanding of early Christian life."

My jaw dropped. I'd always assumed Gran went straight from college to her master's, then to her doctorate studies.

"That's amazing," I said. "Gran never shared that story with me."

"She probably was too busy telling you more exciting stories." Lydia grinned. "There were many, many others. Although that *was* a special story for Lyle. In addition to her discovery, she also met the man she'd eventually marry."

I grinned. "She did?" While Gran always shared her archaeological adventure stories with me, she never divulged anything about her romantic relationships. "I'm sure he was a very intelligent and dashingly handsome archaeologist," I mused, sipping my coffee.

"Not quite archaeologist, though he was intelligent and

dashingly handsome. He was a rising politician and philanthropist. He funded the dig. You've seen his name before."

"I have?"

"Lord Breekson."

I choked, coughing up my coffee. My jaw dropped. "What? Lord Breekson and Gran were married?"

"Yes. I'm shocked you didn't know."

"No one ever told me!" I said in anger. This was the ultimate betrayal. I thought I knew my gran, but I was learning that there was so much she and my mom hadn't told me. In Amesbury, I'd learned major revelations about Gran and my family—from J. Carmichael and Lydia. I was eighteen, almost nineteen, and only now was I learning basic facts that every granddaughter should know about her grandmother. *Why have I been kept in the dark all these years?*

"I had no idea," I finally said. "I know very little about Gran's personal life." *When did Lord Breekson and Gran get married? Why did they get divorced? Did he know about me? Did he know about my mom? Is Lord Breekson my grandfather?*

"I had no idea," I repeated, shaking my head in disbelief. "I have so many questions. What else do you know about their marriage?"

"Not much. I know their divorce was messy—and heartbreaking. They kept it very private, for professional reasons. It was a very difficult situation, and Lyle really didn't like talking about it. She channeled her energy into her research and publications."

I nodded. I could see why Gran and my mom never talked about it, but I still felt my mom owed me some answers. The gaps in my understanding of my own family were getting bigger and bigger.

"I understand keeping the divorce private," I said. "It must have been painful."

"Carly." Lydia paused, her bangles clanging as she set her coffee mug down. "It was one of the most difficult experiences in Lyle's life. She didn't have anyone to turn to, other than me. She had nowhere to go. Allister—you remember him—he'd just gotten married, and Beth wasn't having any of another woman staying with them. So, Lyle poured everything into her work— channeling her energy to ensure women had access to choices that could help them be independent and, in some cases, survive. She didn't want what happened to her to happen to others."

I nodded, finally understanding why Gran was such a champion for archaeological education for women—no matter their age or academic status. Gran's "I Dig It" week-long intensive bootcamp had even more significance. It gave women a chance to create more professional options for themselves, when they had few career paths outside the home.

"So, you're not disappointed in me because I'm dropping out?"

"Not one bit. If you've examined the evidence—and you're operating from evidence, and not emotion—then you know you're doing what's right and what's needed. And nothing, and no one, should convince you otherwise." Lydia looked at me. "If your quest is to get to GE Pharmaceuticals and get the Grealmæp and the Grail, then give it your all. Go full throttle—nothing less!"

I nodded, grinning with renewed faith in my decision.

"Thank you, Lydia. That means the world to me." I stared at the kitchen table, sighing. "I'm not sure my mom is going to have the same attitude as you."

"Do you want to talk me through what you're planning to tell her?" Lydia asked. "I'm happy to listen."

"Yes, that would help."

I grabbed my journal and flipped to my notes. As I rehearsed my talking points, Lydia gave me advice. "Bring it back to the evidence," she said. "State the evidence and help your mom understand the evidence is what makes this so urgent, not the emotion."

I nodded. *Evidence, not emotion.*

"And don't make it sound like you're dropping out completely. Tell her you have a plan for summer classes, that you've researched getting a tuition refund. I think you're still in the window for a partial refund."

"That's great advice." I scribbled Lydia's suggestions alongside my notes and looked up Nassauton's tuition refund policy. I *was* eligible for a partial refund. "I'm ready."

"Yeah? Should we FaceTime her?" Blane asked.

"Yep, let me review my notes one more time and draft the email to the registrar." I grabbed my laptop and pulled up the course registration email. As I typed my response, I thought through my talking points again. I tried to imagine how my mom would react and how I would respond. Any way I looked at it, this was going to be a very difficult conversation, even with Lydia's advice and Blane's support.

"All right." I looked at Blane. "Better now than never." I gazed at my Ailm charm. *Be brave.* I took a deep breath.

I propped up my phone against the flower vase. Blane and I pulled our chairs around the table, right in front of the screen. Lydia mouthed the words "good luck" and headed to her laptop at the other end of the table.

"Good morning, Mom!" I waved, seeing my mom's face fill the screen. She was sipping her coffee at our kitchen table.

"Good morning, sweetheart! It's been a while since we FaceTimed. I'm sure you've been busy! How is your research going?"

"It's great." No way I was going to tell my mom the whole truth.

Blane waved. "Good morning, America! Hi, Mrs. Stuart."

He was being extra goofy. He was as nervous for me as I was.

"Hi, Blane. How's it 'cross the pond?"

"Oh, it's cold. April in England is still cold—don't be fooled."

My mom smiled. "I'm amazed you two are taking everything in your stride and your research is going well. And you're keeping up with schoolwork. Great discipline. Well done!"

I gulped as anxiety filled my stomach.

"Mom, I need to tell you something." My leg started shaking. Blane put his hand on it to help calm me down.

"Yes, sweetheart?"

"I'm taking this term off from Nassauton." I spoke slowly, looking directly at my phone's camera. "There are too many urgent priorities in our case for me to continue with school now."

"You're what?" My mom's expression immediately turned from curiosity to shock. "What did you say, Carly? You've got to be kidding me!"

"I'm not. I've never been more serious. I'm taking this term off from Nassauton." I was very careful not to mention words like *dropping out* or *quitting college*.

As I let my mom process my response, I twirled my loose curls and tried to ignore the nausea in my stomach.

"How can you say that? At this time in your life, your education is your number one priority." She sounded thoroughly disappointed, like I'd let her down by telling her I wasn't interested in her plan for my life. "There is absolutely nothing more important than your education at this time, Carlyle Elizabeth."

I hated when my mom called me by my full first and middle name. She only did it when she was angry or wanted to remind me she was my mother and I was her daughter—and that relationship gave her a certain authority over me. I decided it would be best to remain silent and let her talk as she processed my decision.

"You can't wake up one day and decide to quit. What about your tuition? I'm sure Nassauton won't refund it."

"I already looked it up, and we *are* eligible for a partial refund." I tried to assuage her worries by calmly stating the facts. "And I'm not quitting college. I'm taking the term off. And I didn't just wake up one day and decide that." I tried to sound respectful but firm. I'd made up my mind. My mom was not going to convince me otherwise. "I'm an adult. I have to make my own choices—and accept the consequences. You can't make my choices for me."

"Yes, I can. I've worked too hard to be able to help you pay for school. We are blessed now with the funds I've saved, not to mention a great financial aid package. Who knows what it will be like when—or if—you wake up one day and decide school is for you after all?"

I wanted to retort with a snide comment about how Gran took the term off and eventually went back. I wanted to scream, as if that would convince my mom I was right. I wanted to accuse her of keeping family secrets from me.

I took a deep breath. For my mom, taking the term off was about money—and was a gateway to dropping out completely. She wasn't seeing the bigger picture of the urgency of our Grail quest. I needed her to understand the importance of my research, without sharing all the details. I was afraid if I did, we'd be back to square one with her telling me to drop the case because it was too dangerous. Screaming at or accusing her wouldn't convince her—maybe sharing a little bit about my plan to research summer school, and what I'd learned about Eternae, might. I took another deep breath. Blane put his arm around me. I looked at him appreciatively, then at my mom on my phone screen. *Tell her you have a plan.*

"Mom," I said slowly and gently. "I *will* go back. I'm not dropping out forever. I'll research summer classes so I can stay on track. And I can work with Nassauton on the financial aid. I respectfully disagree about needing to finish my year now. I have evidence to support my choice, and . . ." I took a deep breath before I continued. *Evidence, not emotion.* I needed to give my mom the facts in a way she would understand—and relate to them—to make our conversation easier. "I know about GE Pharmaceuticals and Eternae," I added.

My mom paused, looking straight at me. "What did you say?"

I repeated myself. "And I know Eternae's history. Blane and

I have learned a lot in the past few weeks."

Help your mom understand. We told her J. Carmichael passed away in an accident. We told her about our trip to Bexhill, and about Felda, Albert, and Thilda. We purposely didn't say anything about Dr. Gellmane, Dr. Pritzmord, and the break-in. I could tell my mom was listening and was genuinely interested. She'd lean in closer to her camera or sip her coffee and stare pensively into the distance. "Lastly, I know about Gran and Lord Breekson."

I'd laid it all—mostly all—on the table. I waited, watching my mom process what she'd heard. She stared into her coffee cup, taking deep breaths and closing her eyes. She seemed to be searching for something to say, something that would connect us despite the distance. Finally, she opened her eyes.

"Oh sweetheart. I'm so—"

"Disappointed?"

If that's what she was going to say, I might as well say it and clear the air.

"That's not the word I was going to use, no."

I bit my lip and squeezed Blane's hand.

"I was going to say, I'm so amazed by how much research you've done. I had no idea you were researching Eternae."

I half smiled. At least my mom could appreciate my sleuthing skills.

Sighing, she continued. "I'd closed the door on GE Pharmaceuticals after your dad passed away. I tried to, at least. Eternae was our last hope."

"But it didn't work."

"No."

"And you didn't tell me until the last minute. And you never told me about Gran and Lord Breekson. I thought you said there can't be more secrets in this family, and yet there are so many. I promised not to keep secrets from you. I'm upholding my promise by telling you I'm taking this term off. I need to learn more about GE Pharmaceuticals."

My mom finished her coffee, then took a deep breath. "You're right, sweetheart. I promise there won't be any more secrets." She paused, grinning cheekily. "You're so hopelessly headstrong and stubborn, like your dad and my mom. Nothing I say will convince you to change your mind, will it?"

I grinned, shaking my head.

"I need to learn to trust you, Carly. You're almost nineteen, and you've already had international adventures. I just don't want to lose you. You know this. Will Dr. Kells, Dr. Wengaro, and Blane always be with you?"

Nodding, Blane hugged me. "Yes ma'am, I'll be with her."

Lydia grinned from across the table and gave me a thumbs-up. Her bracelets clanked together down her arm.

My mom smiled. "Two more things, sweetheart."

"Yes, Mom?"

"I'll help you find summer classes and get the refund. Once you're signed up, I'll be less worried. And if you don't go, you can pay me back the money. Deal?"

I beamed. "Deal! Thank you, Mom! What's the second thing?"

"In the spirit of not keeping secrets, I have something for you. I'll ship it to you, since you won't be back here for your birthday."

"What is it?"

"It's a necklace. One of your grandmother's first wishes when you were born was that I continue the tradition of our necklace. It's been in our family for ages, passed down through generations of strong women. She got it a year and a day after her eighteenth birthday and gave it to me a year and a day after my eighteenth birthday. She made me promise to do the same for you."

I smiled. *A necklace from Gran!* Through this necklace, like through her shoes, Gran would be even more present with me as I uncovered GE Pharmaceuticals' secrets and sought the Grail.

"That's so cool! Thanks Mom!"

She grinned. "And you'll find this even cooler. Lyle used to say there was something spiritual—magical—about her necklace. Whenever she wore it, she always felt calm and connected to our ancestors—like they were reminding her of her purpose. I never felt anything, so who knows what the truth was, but she swore by it."

I grinned. "Sure sounds like Gran. Right, well! I can't wait to get it. We're heading to GE Pharmaceuticals in a few days, once Dr. Wengaro is discharged. Once we're sorted in Somerset, I'll get you our address."

My mom chuckled. "You and your Fearless Foursome. Be safe! I love you so much."

I loved that she called us the Fearless Foursome. She finally acknowledged I was part of a team of experts, and we were pursuing a real quest. I made my hands into the shape of a heart and stuck them up to my camera. Grinning, I gazed through the heart.

"I love you, too, Mom. Of course, we'll be safe. Why're you laughing?"

"Because look at you, not even a semester in England and you're picking up British phrases: Right? Sorted?"

I laughed, quipping, "I can't help it. I like them. And if I'm going to be here for the rest of the semester, picking up the Britishisms can't hurt, right?"

She smiled. "Not at all. Be safe, sweetheart!"

I hung up our FaceTime and tapped my laptop to wake it from sleep. I looked at my Ailm charm. *Be brave.* I skimmed my email to the registrar and clicked send.

VIII

The next day, the hospital called. Dr. Wengaro was ready to leave. To celebrate, Lydia, Blane, and I decided we'd cook dinner. Blane's ankle was stronger, so we walked to the farmer's market. On our way back to our cottage, Lydia's phone rang. Lydia motioned for us to stop at a nearby bench. She put down our grocery bags and sat.

"Hello, Dr. Gellmane."

Blane and I sat down next to Lydia.

"Oh, they can't? You're sure?"

Even though we couldn't hear Dr. Gellmane, we could see Lydia's expressions.

"That's interesting." Lydia got up and started pacing around the bench. "Oh wow. I appreciate it. I'll tell them. Thank you, take care!"

"Let me guess," said Blane as Lydia sat down. "The other lab can't identify it."

"Correct. But they did find something interesting."

Blane leaned closer to Lydia. She turned, facing us on the bench and calmly clasping her hands together in her lap.

"They compared the residue to elements in a database of all known elements and their properties, like melting, boiling, and freezing points. It's not exact, but this comparative analysis supposedly helps place the unknown specimen in a family with similar properties."

"What did they find?" I stood up and faced Lydia and Blane.

Amesbury townspeople. We speculated GE Pharmaceuticals was hiding something more than intellectual property. Since Dr. Gellmane told Lydia she'd sent the residue to GE Pharmaceuticals, we figured she didn't know we were on GE's—and her—case. This gave us an advantage. Once we picked up Dr. Wengaro, we needed a plan to get to Somerset and infiltrate GE Pharmaceuticals undetected.

Dr. Wengaro was in great spirits as we left his room. His doctors and nurses waved goodbye as we walked down the hallway.

"You're quite the celebrity, Kenneth," said Lydia. "Did you charm everyone here with Arthurian legends and tales of knights?"

"You know I did." Dr. Wengaro chuckled. "That's all I've been doing here—that, and aggressive physical and mental therapy. Positive thinking works wonders for physical healing."

Lydia rolled her eyes. "You know I think that's all wackadoo pseudoscience."

Dr. Wengaro chuckled again. "Think whatever you want. But here I am, with a full recovery after a crazy escapade with a murderer masquerading as a dean." He grinned, tightening his ponytail. "It sure feels good to get back to the world."

With Dr. Wengaro fully recovered and out of the hospital, the Fearless Foursome was back.

††

When we returned to our cottage, we wasted no time in devising our strategy. Huddling in our living room, we spread out KA von Genzkensaffe's journal, my journal and pencil, and our laptops on the coffee table. Lydia made tea and we snacked on biscuits from the farmer's market.

"I forgot how ugly those curtains are," Dr. Wengaro said, looking up from his laptop. "I really don't like that shade of yellow."

"Those shades saved Carly's and my lives, so don't throw shade on the . . . wait for it . . . *shades*," said Blane.

Lydia groaned, rolling her eyes at Blane. "That was terrib—"

"I know it was bad," Blane interrupted. "But at least I didn't name-drop my favorite archaeologist!" Blane laughed so hard, he snorted.

Lydia shook her head. "Old habits, like bad puns, die hard."

"Or never," added Dr. Wengaro. "Blane, keep making bad puns and keep admiring your favorite archaeologist—and don't let a woman stop you." He grinned, glaring playfully at Lydia.

"Dr. Kenneth Wengaro, how dare you." Lydia tried to be serious but couldn't help but chuckle. "I'm not just 'a woman.' I'm an archaeologist, professor, and scholar."

"Speaking of archaeologists and scholars, Carly, there's something that came in the mail for you. They sent it to me, at the hospital."

Dr. Wengaro opened his hospital bag and pulled out a small package wrapped in brown parcel paper and twine.

"For me? Who knows I'm in Amesbury?" I reached for the package.

"Look at it and see."

Carlyle S.
c/o J. C. c/o Kenneth W.

"Why was it addressed to J. Carmichael and then to you?"

"KDI prepared it for him. When they learned he passed away, they texted me they'd be sending it to my attention."

"KDI?" I asked, staring at the package.

"The Knights of the Dagger Intelligence."

"You have your own intel team?" asked Blane. "Whoa, as if the Knights of the Dagger couldn't get any cooler!"

"Yes," Dr. Wengaro replied, adjusting his chair to face Blane and me. "They're a mix of James Bond's Q and the world's smartest scientists, archaeologists, and historians. Half the time they're inventing new gadgets to keep the knights safe; half the time they're nerding out over which knight of the Round Table had the best superpowers."

"It would be really cool to be a knight!" said Blane as he pointed at my package. "Aren't you gonna open it, Carly?"

I looked at Blane, then Lydia, then Dr. Wengaro. Dr. Wengaro nodded. I carefully unknotted the twine and peeled the paper off the package. Underneath the paper was a small, sealed opaque bag. A black envelope with Kenneth's and my names in gold was taped to the bag. A shiver of excitement ran down my spine. I pulled the envelope and flipped it over. I gasped at the red wax seal with red double dagger marks. *The Knights of the Dagger are so old-fashioned in their correspondence!* I carefully broke the seal, opening the envelope.

††

Dear Kenneth and Carly: We are so sorry about J. C. We hope no foul play, and no White Waves, were behind the accident. We don't know yet; we are still analyzing the evidence.

J. put this in as a time-sensitive request. Please understand that giving a non-knight KDI tech is usually a policy violation; however, considering who she is, what she is facing, and everything J. told us about her, we are granting an exception under these special circumstances.

Kenneth: You are on track for Intake. We expect to see you on the June Solstice. This will mark the end of your year and a day Quest Phase.

Also, you should know J. nominated her. We hope you'll carry through with his nomination, as her sponsor?

Carly: We hope you'll accept your nomination. We are rooting for you! Be safe!

Both: Keep your daggers close to your heart and hand.

KDI

I started trembling. *Who she is? Exception? Special circumstances?* Looking at Dr. Wengaro quizzically, I asked, "What was J. Carmichael's time-sensitive request?"

"Open the bag," Dr. Wengaro said.

I didn't waste a moment. My jaw dropped when I saw the small, effortlessly sleek, polished silver bar. "A sentinel! How does it pair with my phone?"

"You stick it on your phone, like this." Dr. Wengaro pulled out his phone and showed me how his sentinel attached to it. Then, he helped me attach my sentinel to my phone. I grinned. Now, I could communicate securely with other knights.

"That's so cool." I ran my finger across the bar, marveling at the craftsmanship. I set my phone on the kitchen table and reread the note.

"That's awesome!" Blane picked up my phone, examining the sentinel. "You have a real sentinel!"

"You're probably also wondering what J. Carmichael nominated you for." Dr. Wengaro glanced at me as I reread the note.

I nodded. I had a hunch, but I didn't want to say anything—especially since Blane said how cool it would be to be a knight, and I was conscious of his feelings.

"He nominated you to be a Knight of the Dagger. I happily endorse this and will be your sponsor. Do you accept, Carly Stuart?"

I looked at the letter, then at the red double dagger marks on the broken wax seal. I looked at Dr. Wengaro, then Lydia, then Blane. I looked at my Ailm charm. *Be brave.* I closed my eyes.

I didn't know what to think or how to feel. *J. Carmichael nominated me to be a knight!* J. Carmichael, the man who was childhood friends with Gran, who dated her after her divorce and loved her until her death. He'd written her letters and knew my family history. I squeezed my eyes tighter, as though that would make him know how much I respected and missed him. He'd made sure my mom was okay after Gran's and Dad's deaths. He got my mom lavender honey from France. He spent time with his sister and her kids. He promised he'd always be a text away. He'd helped me start piecing together my past and believed in me enough to make me reconsider my future—and he wouldn't get to see me create my future.

My eyes still closed, I sighed. J. Carmichael nominated me to join the Knights of the Dagger! *Why? Am I worthy?* My body surged with adrenaline—and anxiety. He wouldn't have nominated me if I was unworthy. This was my chance to be part of the group that was fighting for good, that swore to protect and find the Grail and preserve Morgan's magic. As a knight, I'd have KDI. Their research and technology, like my sentinel, would keep me safe. My mom wouldn't have to worry. *What dangers—and adventures—awaited me as a knight?*

I also really didn't know a lot about the knights—only what J. Carmichael and Dr. Wengaro told me. They hadn't lied to me, and I trusted them. *But where is the rest of the evidence? What do others say about the knights?* If I accepted, I could learn more about the knights and their history. The knights didn't care that I was a college freshman—technically a dropped-out freshman. *What if I let them down? What if I didn't? What if I brought the knights honor? What would Gran advise me to do? What would my dad tell me to do?* There was only one way to find out. I had to take the leap of faith.

I opened my eyes and looked right into Dr. Wengaro's. "I accept your nomination, Dr. Wengaro."

Beaming, he jumped out of his chair to hug me. Lydia smiled, nodding.

"Fabulous, Carly! And please, call me Kenneth."

"That's amazing." Blane hugged me—a limp, half-hearted hug that hardly felt like the strong embraces I was used to. I could sense a sadness and distance in Blane's demeanor.

"Thank you, teammate! I love you so much."

"Would anyone like lunch? I can start making it." Blane headed to the fridge. He took out some carrots.

Lydia, Kenneth, and I looked at each other.

"I'm not hungry just yet," I said. "Why don't we go for a walk, Blane?"

"Oh no, I'm not hungry," chimed in Kenneth, sensing what I was trying to do.

"Yeah, I could wait at least an hour," said Lydia.

"Sure," said Blane. He left the carrots on the countertop. "I'll get my jacket."

I grabbed my jacket and followed Blane down the hallway.

IX

Crossing the street, we passed The Courtly Robin. Spring in Amesbury had sprung. The grass was greener, the sky bluer and brighter, the wind gentler. Winter's cold, sleeping earth had awakened, eager to transform into spring's warm, fertile soil. Flowers poked out of the ground and window boxes as nature's breath inspired life into the once-barren land. The sun hung high—a glowing orb suspended in the midday sky.

We walked to the church with the stone wall and cemetery. Gray and granite headstones dotted the graveyard. Some were ordered in neat, manicured rows. Others were haphazardly strewn around in clumps. Some had bouquets or poppy wreaths by the headstones. Some were tall, marble mausoleums. Others were flat, shiny plateaus that reflected the sunlight.

The path meandered aimlessly around the gravestones, taking a pensive wanderer on a journey through the stories of the deceased. I approached a tall, gray gravestone with a long, flat base. The moss grew over the base, making no distinction between the ground and the grave.

"Which dukes are buried here?" I asked, finally breaking our silence. I squatted, looking at the names and dates on the gravestone.

"Doesn't matter," Blane mumbled, staring at the ground.

"Babe." I looked at Blane. "What's wrong?"

"Nothing." He shifted his gaze to the gravestone.

"No, something's wrong. You're not even looking at me." I

stood up, opening my arms to hug Blane. He stepped back.

"Whoa." Tears filled my eyes. "What's going on?" I looked at him as tears trickled down my cheeks. He looked at me and sighed.

"Oh, Carly." He sat in front of the gravestone, crossing his legs and resting his elbows on his thighs. I sat in front of him, mirroring his posture. We looked into each other's eyes. The glints of gold that usually sparkled in the hazel of his eyes were gone. He grasped both of my hands in his, massaging my hands with his thumbs.

"No, it's nothing. It's going to sound so stupid."

"I'm sure whatever it is, it's not." I squeezed his hands. "A penny for your thoughts?"

He gave a small chuckle. "They're not that cheap."

"I'll pay whatever price you want." I squeezed his hands again.

He sighed, bringing his hands to his lap and lacing his fingers together.

"It's so stupid." He sighed again, staring at the moss around the gravestone.

"I bet you it isn't. I'm here to listen." I put my hands on his kneecaps. "I love you."

"Oh, babe." His gaze met mine. I could see tears in his eyes. "Can I hold you for a little?"

I scooted around as Blane shifted and reclined on the gravestone. I leaned back into his chest as he wrapped his arms around me. He rested his chin on my shoulder. We stared at the cemetery in silence.

"I've always wanted to be a knight," he finally said. "Ever since I was a kid. I was obsessed with King Arthur. I watched that movie. I had my book."

I nodded. "You told me! That's so cool."

He continued. "I've always wanted to be a knight, and now . . ." His voice trailed off as he paused. "I told you it's stupid."

I knew what Blane was going to say.

"You're going to be a knight, which is amazing!" He paused, his voice hardly a whisper. "I wish I could be one too."

I held his hands in mine. He took a deep breath. I didn't say anything. It was the time to listen, not talk.

"I told you it was stupid, but I feel like I'm not contributing to our team. At all. What's a team when one partner isn't contributing anything?"

"Babe. What you feel isn't stupid. Never say that. And you're wrong." I sat up and turned my head, looking Blane in the eyes.

"What do you mean?" He leaned back a little, still looking at me.

"You're wrong. You contribute so much." I beamed, tucking my curls behind my ears. "You contributed the Glastonbury and Jerusalem connection and remembered Morgan could have made *Grealia* at Glastonbury, since it's a ley line site. That was incredible!"

"You really think so?"

"I know so!" I nodded. "And you know what else I know?"

"What?"

"You're already a knight—you're *my* knight."

Blane chuckled. "That was cheesy."

"But it's true. And it made you smile." I turned my body around so I could face him. "I can't do this without you. You're the one who taught me to have the confidence to take a leap of faith—even when I am afraid. You're the one who helped me value my unique traits—and use them for good."

"You really mean that?" A small sparkle of gold flickered in the hazel of his eyes.

"Of course, I really mean that. Why would I say it if I didn't mean it?"

"I guess you wouldn't." He smiled.

"You guess I wouldn't? We need to do better than guessing!" I paused, grinning and adopting a goofy announcer's voice as I pretended to hold a microphone. I jumped up. "Step right up for this important declaration! Lady Carly has evidence! There is no guessing over here! See, look." I pointed to an imaginary board and pretended to write EVIDENCE. "Evidence—lots of evidence! Knights of the Round Table, I give you all the evidence you need! And so, it is proven, what Lady Carly says is one-hundred percent true!" I flourished my arms in the air, taking a big, theatrical bow.

Blane erupted in snorts and laughter as he stood up. "Carly, I love you, but leave the goofiness to me." He grabbed my pretend microphone from my hands.

I smiled, kissing him. "Hey, you can't just take my mic."

"I just did!" He grinned. "My goofy lines, my mic. Deal?"

"Deal, but only if—"

"If what?"

"You promise not to bottle up your emotions, and always tell me what you're feeling. We're partners. We're knights on a quest. We tell each other everything. We have to."

"I'll try. I promise I'll try." Blane paused. "It's not going to be easy."

"I know. But you have a teammate who is not going to leave you. I promise."

"Pinky promise?" He held his hand out, extending his pinky.

"Pinky promise." I linked his pinky with mine.

We gazed at each other as we kissed our hands.

††

When we returned to our cottage, Lydia and Kenneth were preparing lunch. They'd arranged the vegetables and brought out cutting boards and pots and pans. A big stockpot was bubbling on the stove. Classic rock music blasted from Lydia's laptop. Lydia and Kenneth sang along, using spatulas for air drums and ladles for air guitars. Kenneth had undone his ponytail, letting his brown curls fly around as he head-banged to the music.

"I never thought my professors would be rockstars," said Blane.

"In a former life," said Kenneth, chuckling. "I'm an old soul who likes timeless music, ancient burial sites, and sacred grounds. Can't help it." He picked up a few spatulas and began an air drum solo. "I was raised right on the classics—the classic rockstars, that is!"

Lydia and I chuckled as Kenneth continued.

"I was born in the wrong decade. I should have been born earlier, when I could experience the glory days of the 1970s." He grinned. "So, it's great to let loose a little. All good fun among friends."

"The music keeps me from losing my memories," said Lydia, holding a fork up to her mouth like a microphone as she belted out a few lines. "It helps me remember my favorite moments."

"Like what?" I asked.

"Well, there was this one song Lyle and I played when we'd study. Let me see if I can find it."

Fork in hand, Lydia walked to her laptop and typed in the song name. I didn't recognize the lyrics, but as soon as it started playing, Lydia closed her eyes. She held her fork up to her mouth and started singing.

By the time the song finished, the soup was bubbling over. Kenneth rushed to the stove to move the stockpot. Lydia didn't notice or seem to care. The song transported her to a different time and place. Watching her made me want to learn more about her and Gran's adventures.

"Lydia, that was beautiful! What memory did that song remind you of?" I asked.

She smiled, looking at her fork. "It was the first time I met Lyle. I'd skipped my freshmen pottery class since T.R.R. John—a philosopher and expert on Greek mythology—was giving one of his famous lectures at our campus. He spoke on the importance of myths, believing scholars had too much of a tendency to dissect the story instead of appreciating it as art in and of itself."

"Whoa!" exclaimed Kenneth. "You heard T.R.R. John speak? That must have been incredible. He was a legend!"

———

"I did." Lydia beamed. "It was one of his last lectures. The hall was packed. I was terrified since the only open seat was in the front, and I hate sitting in the front. But I'd skipped class, and there was no turning back." She adjusted her bun. "I'm so glad I went, because the girl I sat next to became my best friend. She had long, curly black hair—that was one of the first things I noticed about her. It was striking. She wore bell-bottoms and a flowy, tie-dye tank top, with a white peace sign. Her necklace was beautiful and had two pendants: one, the size of a small coin—a gold cross inside a plain silver disc; the other, a pale, sea-foam-green-colored stone. And she had these big, green eyes that sparkled with a magical light."

I beamed, twirling one of my long curls. I never pictured Gran as a hippie whose necklace was the Ailm. *Is there a story behind how Lydia's bracelet and Gran's pendant are both the Ailm?*

Lydia continued. "I noticed her necklace, which she said was a family heirloom. She noticed my oversized aviator sunglasses. She said with their purple tint, I looked like a movie star. I told her I wanted to get my hands dirty in the dig and didn't care to have my face touched up on the silver screen. That was when we realized we both wanted to be archaeologists. After T.R.R. John's talk, Lyle and I got lunch. I'd wanted to try this diner—famous for its milkshakes and burgers. Lyle got a burger but no milkshake since she was allergic to dairy. When the burger arrived, one of the top forty songs came on the radio. Lyle immediately started singing, using her French fries as drums. She was so happy and carefree. I loved that about her. In that moment, I knew she was going to be my best friend."

"And she was," I said as Lydia finished her story, gazing nostalgically at her fork and sighing.

She looked at me, smiling. "She was, indeed."

My phone rang with a FaceTime call from my mom. I propped my phone up against the backsplash as I cut carrots on my cutting board.

<hr>

"Hi, Mom! What's going on?"

"Hi, sweetheart!" She was in our kitchen, struggling to peel a cucumber. "Nothing too much, trying a new recipe for a smoothie. Do you have a minute? Can we chat about summer school—and Eternae?"

"Of course."

"First, summer school. Nassauton doesn't offer summer classes, so I did a quick search. A few colleges around town have classes. They start at beginning of June or right after July fourth. Tell me which classes you want and I'll sign you up."

"Sounds great, thank you, Mom. I appreciate you!" I did appreciate her. Her effort in FaceTiming me was a big step that made me feel validated. Instead of channeling her fears and anxieties toward controlling or stopping me, she directed them toward helping me. Her help made me feel like she was interested in my adventure—and had accepted I was growing up and could make my own choices.

I looked at my mom. The cucumber was getting the better of her. Her peeler wasn't doing the trick. I laughed as she tried to balance the cucumber on her cutting board. "Mom, isn't it time to get you a new peeler?" I scooped up a handful of my carrots and dumped them into the stockpot. Kenneth picked up his spatula and started stirring.

"Oh no. I'll never give this one up. Your dad got it for me. When we first started dating, he joked I was an absolute disgrace in the kitchen, that I couldn't tell a fork from a spoon if someone poked me with it." She chuckled.

"Oh yeah? But you're such a good cook now! You just need a new peeler!"

"He taught me everything I know. He loved cooking. He took it upon himself to teach me. We cooked a lot. We'd go for a hike, stop by the store afterward, and cook dinner. That was our favorite way to spend our weekends."

My mom put her peeler down, wiping her eyes with the back of her hand. "I'm sorry. I really miss him."

"It's okay, Mom. Here, hang on a second." I put my knife on the cutting board, picked up my phone, and walked to the couch. "I've been thinking a lot about Dad too. Tell me about him."

My mom smiled. "He was a physical chemistry nerd. He loved studying subatomic particles and their properties—almost as much as he loved running." She chuckled. "But I think he loved running—or to be more precise, his running group—more."

"What do you mean?" I asked.

"His running group leader set us up on our first date. The rest, as they say, was history."

Out of the corner of my eye, I saw Kenneth waving to get my attention. He pointed at the carrots on the cutting board and made a cutting motion. I heard Lydia say, "Kenneth, I'll cut them. Let her talk to her mom."

I smiled, happy to see my mom sharing a cherished memory.

"He sure loved hitting the trails. He couldn't go a day without running or hiking. And then the canc—"

"Yeah," I said. "Maybe he's running now—wherever he is."

"Absolutely." Mom grinned. "He's running in Heaven." She paused. "I can't imagine that Heaven, for him, wouldn't have running. He always believed he would get there—to that eternal, perfect place. His faith is what gave him hope as he faced his suffering. His faith was one of the things I loved most about him."

"Why's that?"

"Imagine a physical chemist thinking through faith. It wasn't blind—far from it. It was deep, yet full of doubts." She stared beyond her phone. "He'd study and search and cite and still have questions. He'd read, listen to lectures, attend discussions. Always asking questions. The questions got bigger and deeper when he was diagnosed as terminal. Why him? Why this suffering? He was an athlete, ate heathy, didn't smoke, got enough sleep. The answers didn't come so easy—if at all."

She paused and walked to the kitchen table. "Here's what I wanted to show you." She propped her phone up and held up a glossy white folder with *ETERNAE* written in red. Right below it was the Grealmæp insignia in gold. "Eternae. Clever name." She pointed at the insignia. "And cool logo. I didn't realize it was your Henge Piece, till you described your pendant."

I nodded.

She smiled. "Of course, I'm sure you already knew GE Pharmaceuticals and the Henge Piece are related."

I smiled, chuckling.

"But, I bet you don't know GE's address."

I shook my head. She held up a glossy white business card with GE's name and address written in red, black, and gold ink on the front, and the Grealmæp insignia on the back.

"I'll text you a picture," said my mom.

I loved that my mom was proactively sharing information. I also thought it was adorable that she didn't realize we could google the address.

"Thank you, Mom!" I grinned. "Your help means the world to me."

"Well, at this point, I know better than to tell you to stop. I figure I can help you instead." She smiled. "So be careful. I know you have your Fearless Foursome. But that pendant has brought you nothing but danger."

"I know. But if there's anything we've proven to ourselves, it's that as a team, we can face whatever danger it brings us."

My mom took a deep breath. "I love you, sweetheart. My mom, and your dad, would be so proud of how their young explorer is becoming such a wise adult. Be safe."

"I promise we will!"

I hung up and waited for the photo to come through.

GE Pharmaceuticals
oo End Cap Road
Middlezoy, Bridgwater, UK TATA-TTAGGG 8

As I read the address and favorited the photo, excitement and nervousness filled my stomach. I looked at my Ailm charm. We were one step closer to GE Pharmaceuticals.

We were also one step closer to my nineteenth birthday and the day after it—the day I'd receive Gran's necklace. I chuckled, shaking my head and remembering the last time I'd come across one of Gran's jewelry items.

"Soup's ready!" Kenneth lifted the stockpot's lid. The smell of steamed vegetables, chicken stock, and spices filled the kitchen.

"Mmm! Simply scrumptious, Kenneth!" said Lydia. "Where'd you learn to cook?"

"Thank you! Grad school. I taught myself how to get creative with ramen noodles—and the leftovers from the lectures when the department ordered too much."

"I'll get the bowls," said Blane as he opened one of the cupboards.

The soup was the perfect temperature. I could taste the distinct, complementary flavors of the carrots, leeks, onions, garlic, beans, and salt. With the freshly baked bread from the farmer's market, our meal was hearty and filling. As we chatted, I felt proud of our group—and our research. My stomach was full of warmth and carrots, and my heart was full of gratitude and belonging. I was with my favorite people, taking our next steps in our quest.

"So, how are we infiltrating GE Pharmaceuticals?" Lydia tipped her bowl away from her, slowly spooning the last of her soup from her bowl. "And what's our plan for getting Thilda's Grealmæp?"

"And figuring out what GE is hiding," I added.

"And making sure we stay ahead of Dr. Gellmane and Dr. Pritzmord," Blane said.

I high-fived Blane. I wanted to make more of a conscious effort to build him up in front of Lydia and Kenneth.

Blane grinned. "Go team!" He whispered in my ear, "Two knights, together on our quest."

"First things first." Kenneth pulled out his phone. "I reached out to KDI. They shared J. Carmichael's intel from a few years ago, including the name of the guy J. Carmichael spoke with, Sebastian Waugh. They also note GE's address, website, and phone number are unlisted."

"Further evidence they're hiding something," said Blane.

I beamed at Blane.

"How did John get their address in the first place?" Lydia asked.

I smiled. I knew exactly how. "My mom gave it to him. She also gave it to us." I showed Blane, Lydia, and Kenneth my photo of GE's business card.

"And there's the Grealmæp," said Blane, pointing at my screen. "Wee-hoo! What a crazy adventure that's come full circle! I never imagined that in college, I'd revisit my favorite book on King Arthur and search for the Grail with my favorite person by my side." He looked at me and slung his arm around my shoulder. "Or be solving a mystery with a killer dean, recovering from an injury, and completing my semester remotely—but what's life without a little adventure?" I scooted my chair closer to him. He grinned.

I held Blane's hand. "Two knights," I whispered in his ear. "Together on our quest."

As we looked at GE's card, the sentinels on Kenneth's and my phones gleamed. It was so subtle, I thought I imagined it. Then it gleamed again, a little brighter.

"Whoa, Kenneth, what's happening?"

"KDI is sending us info. They must have synced you to our case and synced you and me to each other."

The sentinel gleamed a third time. Four double dagger marks, two in matte gold and two on top of them in red, popped up on Kenneth's and my screens. I turned to Blane, speechless and in awe of KDI's technology.

"Tap the middle," said Kenneth. "Like this."

A blank text box with directions above it popped up.

"Input case identifier number?" I asked. "What's that?"

"One moment," said Kenneth. "Try TATA-TTAGGG 8."

"That's from their address?"

"Yep. KDI always uses something like the last bits of the address, if they can, for the case identifier. It makes it easy to remember but hard to guess."

I typed in the letters and number. The text box disappeared to reveal KDI's message.

††

Kenneth, Carly: We've got new intel. Sometime this summer, GE Pharmaceuticals (GE) wants to celebrate a major milestone for Eternae. They want it to be the party of the century and they need professional party planners to help them. They're running print and digital ads for in-person interviews. The party has got to be flawless. The world's dignitaries, leading scientists and chief medical officers, and other C-level leaders will be there.

We can't teach you how to party plan—sorry, not our skillset. But we can get you more intel, when we learn it, and help you go undercover. We'll be with you every step of the way.

Keep your daggers close to your heart and hand,
KDI

"That's perfect!" Kenneth said. "We can go undercover as their party planners!"

"Perfect?" I stared out the window at the patio. Three little brown birds hopped on the table, pecking for food. "I thought KDI would get us invitations! How on earth can we plan a party like that? It takes years for people to learn those skills. I just learned how to apply eye shadow, for goodness' sake!"

Blane laughed. "Lara." He paused. "Gotta love her. I hope she and Paul are doing well. It's been ages since we checked in with them."

I nodded, looking at Blane. With our case as my priority, I kept forgetting to text Lara. I looked back at the birds. A fourth had joined. I remembered when Lara pacified my mom after she drove up to berate me for pursuing the Grail. They'd sat in our dorm room, like old friends. I sighed. Now, with my dropout paperwork signed and submitted, I was officially no longer a freshman at Nassauton College. *Will I ever go back?* The birds flitted around an empty table, not finding any crumbs.

Kenneth got up to clear our dishes. He smiled. "So, who can throw a party? Anyone? Blane? Lydia? I mean, worst case we theme it 1970s classic rock, hire a tribute band, and call it a day."

Lydia laughed as she took our glasses to the sink. "Not everything is classic rock and air drums, Kenneth. Party planning is very difficult."

"And how would you know?" Kenneth asked, respectfully and curiously.

"I've done it." Lydia beamed. "With Lyle."

"You have?" I asked. Lydia's talents never ceased to surprise me.

"When Lyle and I threw our galas, guess who planned them?" She started washing our glasses as Kenneth brought the last few dishes to the sink. "It was one of my favorite things to do. I developed a systematic approach to ensure the process was smooth. Anything can be accomplished with a good syst—"

"Like Rockfire?" interrupted Blane. "I'm sorry to interrupt,

I just . . . That's so c—"

"Exactly like Rockfire!" Lydia grinned. "I like systems and processes. They keep me organized." Her eyes got misty. "Steve always told me it was one of my superpowers." She wiped her eyes with the back of her hand and picked up another glass. "Lyle and I hosted so many galas. Every time we came back from a dig with our artifacts, we'd throw a party." She set the glass on the drying rack. "Even major, international archaeological conferences started calling me to plan their cocktail receptions. I'd have so much fun: picking the theme, curating the VIP list, scoping out the site, managing the budget, dreaming up the details, and executing the event. And Lyle had no interest in it, only in researching and publishing. So, she loved how I had this little . . . what do you call it . . . side hustle going. The faculty also loved it, as the Archaeology Department had the best Christmas parties on campus."

I thought about the Grealmæp picture, with Gran and Lydia in their olive-green jumpsuits, gold-rimmed aviators, and Atlas heels. *Had Lydia planned that party?*

"Here's what I propose." Lydia set the last glass on the rack and started rinsing the spoons. Kenneth and Blane playfully tapped their fingers on the kitchen counter like mini drumsticks. They laughed when they realized they had the same uncoordinated reaction at the same time.

"Kenneth, tell KDI we will go undercover as professional party planners. KDI can help us apply with fake IDs and portfolios."

Kenneth nodded. "I love where this is heading!" He smiled. "If KDI can help me get a job at Nassauton, they can help us get a job as party planners!"

"Us?" asked Lydia. "Carly and me. You and Blane team up and make friends with GE Pharmaceuticals' researchers. That way, the four of us cover all our bases to get the Grealmæp, find the Grail, and discover what's behind that locked door!"

"Brilliant! And we'll have a knight"—Kenneth looked at me,

grinning—"or soon-to-be knight, on each team. This will be good experience for you in your Quest Phase. And," said Kenneth as he pointed at Blane and himself, "no one will question two men walking around a lab."

Lydia glared at Kenneth. "No one will question two women walking around a lab, either!"

Blane smiled. "The Fearless Foursome is ready for adventure!" He grabbed my pen from the kitchen table, lifting it in the air like he was lifting a sword. "For the Grail!"

"For the Grail!" Lydia raised a spoon. Kenneth raised a glass. I raised my phone.

"For the Grail!" we said in unison.

My sentinel sparkled in the sunlight.

X

With Kenneth and Blane fully recovered, we were ready to head to Somerset. Jude, Kenneth's friend who picked us up from the airport and helped us get our Amesbury cottage, found us a cottage in Somerset.

"I took care of everything. They'll have it cleaned, prepped, and move-in ready in a few days. You're going to love spending more time in the English countryside. I'm so glad you've extended your trip."

I stifled a small chuckle. Kenneth hadn't told Jude about his or Blane's injuries—or the real reason we were staying.

"Thank you, my friend," said Kenneth. He bro-hugged Jude. "As long as our cottage doesn't have ugly yellow curtains, I'll be fine." He pointed at the curtains in front of the glass door.

"Kenneth, come on, that's a beautiful pastel yellow." Lydia chuckled. "Where is your sense of design?"

Jude laughed. "You're funny. It's like you've been working together for years."

I grinned. Not missing a beat, Kenneth responded, "It feels like it! We have a great team." He smiled.

"What's your plan for your last days in Amesbury?" Jude asked.

"Carly and Lydia are going shopping, and Blane and I will get some research done."

"Oh, Jude, can you give me the address?" I asked. "My mom has to send me something."

"You bet, Carly."

I texted the address to my mom. With my birthday less than two weeks away, I eagerly anticipated receiving Gran's necklace. I also hoped Blane and I could sneak away and spend some time together for a nice dinner. During our last days in Amesbury, I wanted to find some nice outfits for party planning—and for a few date nights. I'd have to ask my mom to send me some of Gran's heels. I smiled, looking at Gran's boots. They'd served me well so far, but without question, cute heels would be better for date nights than boots.

††

Thread Head was Amesbury's famous boutique that specialized in recycled vintage clothes. As the owner explained, vintage with an edge was in. The more I looked around, the more I realized the outfits were too trendy for me. I couldn't picture myself wearing ripped bell-bottoms around Somerset, certainly not at GE Pharmaceuticals, and definitely not on a date. After thanking the owner, Lydia and I walked to the next store.

Jemison Julia's was a few doors down. Its windows were full of cute, coordinated outfits: pantsuits and long, form-fitting pencil skirts with silk blouses. But after seeing the prices, I shook my head.

"I can barely afford a button on one of those blouses," I said, converting the currency in my head. "Don't they have shops here for college students?"

Lydia shrugged, distracted by a turquoise-colored straw hat with a silk, coral ribbon.

"That's beautiful," I said as she ran her hand along the silk band.

"Isn't it? It reminds me of the colors of the Mediterranean Coast." Lydia smiled. "Whenever we weren't working, Lyle and I vacationed there. We'd get lost in these tiny Greek towns, exploring islands and hopping ferries to every little port."

"Sounds like the perfect vacation for two archaeologists." I grinned. I loved when Lydia shared stories about Gran. "You should buy it."

Lydia looked at the price tag: £79.95. "Not that affordable on a professor's salary." She sighed, putting the hat back.

"Try Act II. They might have something similar at a lower cost." I hadn't noticed anyone behind the register, but upon hearing a voice, I turned around. A tall, lanky woman with long, braided red hair smiled at us. "They're our sister store."

"Hi, I didn't even see you!" I said.

"That's no problem, love. Like I said, give Act II a go. They're just down the street. Walk out of here, turn left, keep walking a few steps, walk down the little alley on your left, and you'll see Act II's sign. Very easy to miss—and a real hidden gem."

"Thank you," said Lydia. "You mentioned they're your sister store?"

"Yes. My friend and I cofounded both brands." The lady emerged from around the counter, walking up to the long, emerald-green dress hanging next to me. She began gently smoothing out its wrinkles. "Jemison Julia is more of an upscale boutique. Act II is a secondhand store. We created Act II after noticing many of our clientele wear an item once or twice—and then it gets buried in their closets, never to see the light of day again. Or worse yet, they throw the item out. We wanted to do something about that, so we created Act II to close the loop. We give cash or points to people who bring in their outfits. They can apply their points to purchases here or at Act II." She moved the green dress to an empty rack.

"That's really cool," I said. "Sustainable fashion that benefits the buyer too."

"Yes, the circular economy has reduced a lot of waste." The lady smiled. "Well, go on, check out Act II. Hope you find something there that speaks to your soul." She grinned as she ushered us out the door. "I'll ring Sharon and tell her you're coming."

Lydia and I turned left and kept walking. We almost missed the little alley and barely saw Act II's sign. The sign was two theater masks painted onto a white wood board, one wearing a wreath made of ivy on her head, and the other a baseball cap with a club on it.

"That's adorable." I pointed at the masks. "They're wearing hats!"

Lydia looked at the sign. "You mean Thalia and Melpomene?"

"Thalia and Melpomean?"

"Melpomene," said Lydia, correcting me. "Thalia is the Ancient Greek Muse of Comedy, and Melpomene is the Muse of Tragedy. They're purposefully paired, especially in the theater, to show the extremes of our emotions. It's said everything we do can be traced to whether we want to be perceived as funny, or whether we operate from personal, unresolved tragedy or trauma."

"That's very interesting," I said as we walked in the door. I loved that as an Ancient Greek scholar, Lydia knew so many facts and sprinkled her conversation with them. One day, I'd like to spout titbits off the tip of my tongue like that. Studying the past was one skill. Sharing it so readily in conversation was another.

"Good day!" A lady in a navy-blue pantsuit with a long, pale-pink blouse was folding shirts on a table in the middle of the store. Her ice-blue eyes sparkled as she greeted us. Her long, blonde hair fell to her hips in waves. "Jemison told me you were coming. I'm Sharon. Pleasure!" She extended her right hand to shake ours. The silver bangle on her left wrist, and her bright white teeth, gleamed in the store's light. "Have a look around! Anything you're wanting?"

Act II was packed with all types of clothes. Since it didn't have any windows, it had a cozy vibe that reminded me of Gran's walk-in closet.

"I'm looking for professional clothes and date night outfits,"

I said, picking up a crushed velvet clutch. "Something affordable."

"Right this way. I know exactly where to get you started."

Lydia and I followed Sharon around the shop. Maybe it was the volume of clothes—suits, dresses, cardigans, blouses, and bell-bottoms—or maybe it was the absence of clear aisles and walkways, but the shop wasn't as big as I expected. As Sharon pulled the bell-bottoms off the rack, I turned to Lydia.

"What was Gran like when she was in college? When did you realize you'd be such great partners?"

Lydia smiled. "Very thoughtful questions. Let's see, after that lecture, we were inseparable. We must have discussed T.R.R. John for hours, and then we realized we shared a class: Foundations of Archaeology and Art. As naïve young scholars, we questioned why the professor lumped archaeology and art together. We both felt each deserved its own class and tried to petition the deans to change it."

I chuckled. "I'm sure they didn't listen to you. They probably were convinced their way—the way of the academe—was right."

Lydia laughed, sensing my sprinkle of sarcasm. "I never thought I'd hear someone like you say something like that," she said.

Sharon handed me an armload's worth of outfits. "Go ahead and try them on—the dressing room is right back here."

Lydia and I kept chatting as I walked into the dressing room.

"Why is that?" I chuckled, closing the door and hanging up my outfits. The room was very small. A tapestry of a unicorn in a wooden circular fence covered one of the walls. A pile of cardboard boxes was stacked in front of the tapestry. A floor-to-ceiling mirror covered another wall. A wooden plaque at the top of the mirror read: *TEMET NOSCE*.

"What does *temet nosce* mean?" I took off my jacket, placing it on the cardboard boxes. "There's a plaque in here with that written on it."

"It means 'know thyself.' It comes from the Greek maxim

inscribed at the Temple of Apollo at Delphi.”

I grinned. Sharon was clever to put that maxim in the dressing room, as if encouraging guests to find their identities in their outfits. *What does a professional party planner wear?* I picked up the bell-bottoms, laughing. “No way,” I whispered to myself.

“The academe,” I heard Lydia mumble from beyond the door as I stepped into a pair of pants. “You seem to appreciate the tradition and scholarliness of the academe. You’re a deeply curious person, Carly. You fit right into the university setting.”

While my chest swelled with pride, I couldn’t help but disagree. I was interested in so much more than spending time on a university campus.

“Maybe,” I mused, trying on a black pantsuit and deep-purple silk shirt. “But I’m also interested in adventures beyond the university. Traveling to faraway digs. Finding artifacts. Curating museum collections. I loved our crash course with Dr. Gellmane.”

“The two aren’t mutually exclusive. You have an open path ahead of you. You get to create your journey, choose your adventure, and make the road your own, Carly.”

I stepped out of the dressing room, modeling my pantsuit for Lydia.

“You look like you’re a professional party planner!” Lydia beamed. “All you need are some fabulous shoes.”

“I don’t think I need any help in that department.” I chuckled, heading back into the dressing room. “Now that I’ve found the outfit, I’ll text Mom to send me Gran’s shoes.”

I’d found two date night outfits and four work outfits. Sharon met us at the register. As she rang up my clothes, I took out my debit card. Before she took it, she said, “Whoops, almost forgot.” She reached under the cabinet and looked at Lydia. “This is for you.” She handed Lydia a pastel-green straw hat with a light-pink silk ribbon on it. “It’s not quite the one Jemison has, but hopefully it will do.”

Lydia grinned. "That is very thoughtful of Jemison to tell you what I was looking at. It's lovely."

I gave Sharon my debit card, but Lydia was having none of it.

"Let me get this. It's the least I can do for my best friend's granddaughter."

I smiled in gratitude. I wasn't going to argue with Lydia. Over the past month, I'd gotten to know her a lot more. Whether it was having morning coffee chats before Blane woke up, walking around town, or thinking through our case, I'd completely forgotten Lydia was my professor. Lydia didn't mind. She treated me like a partner and friend—more than a student—and shared her stories with me. She'd traveled quite extensively, loved the theater and New York, and had never gotten married or had kids. She didn't like talking about those topics, probably since they triggered memories of Steve.

Lydia fished her credit card out of her wallet. As Sharon accepted Lydia's credit card, I noticed that under her silver bangle, on the inside of her left wrist, were red double dagger marks. *Whoa*, I thought, smiling. I didn't want to get into a conversation with Sharon now, when others could walk into her store without warning. And I certainly didn't want her to ask me how I knew about the marks. But my curiosity got the better of me, and I had to ask.

"Nice tattoo." I pointed to her wrist. "Where's it from?"

She chuckled uncomfortably, flipping her wrist around to insert Lydia's card.

"This thing? I've had it for ages." She smiled, taking out a reusable bag with Thalia and Melpomene, and their headgear, on it. The credit card reader beeped as she carefully placed my clothes and Lydia's hat in the bag.

"Here's your card. Thank you for shopping at Act II! Enjoy!" Sharon walked around the counter and handed Lydia her bag. "Take care now." She ushered us to the door and closed it behind us.

———

††

Lydia and I plopped our bags on the couch in our living room. I told Kenneth and Blane about Sharon's double dagger marks. He smiled, as if to say, *Yep, we're everywhere.*

"I'm going to miss our cottage," Lydia said, looking at the yellow curtains. "Quite a charming little place."

"Sure, if you forget about the whole break-in," said Blane.

"How did Dr. Gellmane know we were staying here?" I asked, looking up from texting my mom which pairs of Gran's heels to send.

"The Amesbury Museum asked for our address when we checked in," Kenneth replied. "All she had to do was look at our file."

"She had it all along." I shook my head. "Amesbury sure has given us some crazy adventures."

"Carly," said Kenneth. "If you think these adventures are crazy, just wait." He handed me a small brown envelope. "This is for you."

I opened the envelope. Inside was a black matte envelope with my name in gold script on one side, and on the other, a red wax seal with the double daggers mark. I looked at Kenneth.

"Open it," he said, smiling.

I carefully broke the seal and slid the tri-folded, tan parchment paper out. Trembling with excitement, I began to read.

††

Dear Carly:

YES!

We are thrilled you've accepted your nomination to join the Knights of the Dagger. Your Quest Phase starts immediately and lasts a year and a day from the date of this letter. During this phase, you are explicitly prohibited from talking to any knight other than your sponsor, Kenneth. Kenneth serves in place of J. C., a dearly missed and much-respected Knight of the Dagger. We will never contact you unless it is through Kenneth. This is for your—and our—protection. We look forward to your Quest Phase.

Keep your daggers close to your heart and hand,
KDI

XI

After spending six weeks in Amesbury, I'd fallen in love with the quaint town that was home to Stonehenge. I'd miss Amesbury's beauty, history, and charm—and our meals at The Courtly Robin. I sighed, taking a final look around the cottage before getting in our car, hoping that someday I'd come back.

Our path forward was clear. With KDI's help, Lydia and I—or as we were now, Ashlyn Drew and Trinity Lewis—had our fake IDs and portfolios. We officially were party planners from the Hamptons, having worked with all types of celebrities and stars. KDI applied to GE Pharmaceuticals for us, sending our materials, headshots, and credentials and setting up our interview. They even selected a hair stylist in Somerset to meet us at our cottage and color our hair to match our fake ID pictures.

"I'll be around," Jude said as he crammed the last of our luggage in the back seat. "Don't hesitate to ring if you need anything."

"Thank you." Kenneth bro-hugged his friend and hopped in the driver's seat. "Really, really appreciate you."

"Ready to hit the road?" Kenneth asked Lydia, Blane, and me. He put his sunglasses on and tightened his ponytail. He looked like he was going to sing classic rock songs the whole drive to Somerset. I grinned. If he did, I certainly wouldn't mind.

"You bet," said Blane, the hazel in his eyes sparkling as an impish grin spread across his face. "I mostly can't wait to see Dr. Wengaro pretend to be interested in science."

Kenneth chuckled, adjusting his seat and mirror before shifting out of park. "Hey, back when I was in grad school, I was friends with the scientists. Benchies, as I called them. We loved doing nerdy things. Going to the pub. Trivia. Going to another pub. More trivia."

We drove past The Courtly Robin and the cemetery, following the road from the city center to the outskirts of town.

"That's how you're going to infiltrate the lab? Pubs and trivia?" Lydia asked.

"Yep," chuckled Kenneth. "The researchers will embrace us as friends and fellow scientists. We'll gain their trust by hanging out and chatting with them. How else do you think Thilda, or any of her staff, will let us near that locked door?"

"That's brilliant," I said, staring out at the houses dotting the countryside.

"It was Blane's idea." Kenneth smiled. "He's done some smart planning for our mission."

Blane beamed, obviously proud Kenneth acknowledged him. "I'm a nerd. They're nerds. It's the one time in my life when it's cool to be a nerd. I know how they behave. Once you get them talking, they can't stop." Blane paused. "But the best part," he went on, pausing for effect, "is Dr. Wengaro got KDI to make us fake IDs and portfolios too!"

"Oh?" Lydia turned around, surprised.

Kenneth nodded. "That was another one of Blane's ideas. And please, Blane, call me Kenneth. We're colleagues now—we've been for a while!"

Blane smiled. "What I really should call you is Frank Tepperton."

Kenneth chuckled. "Right, right, Chris Angelton."

"Those are our fake names," said Blane. "Frank and Chris, two researchers from New York. Ever since hearing Thilda von Genzkensaffe, the visionary startup CEO, speak at one of the biggest conferences in the world, Frank and Chris have wanted to work at GE Pharmaceuticals."

"Not only that," said Kenneth, "but Frank and Chris know two of the best party planners: Ashlyn Drew and Trinity Lewis. And we come as a package deal: Thilda hires you as party planners, and we share our cutting-edge research with her staff."

"Isn't that too buddy-buddy, 'I know a friend of a friend'?" Lydia asked.

"Kind of," said Kenneth. "But that's how the industry is. KDI set it up so we're your references, because you plan our lab's holiday parties."

"It still feels a little odd," said Lydia.

"Isn't our archaeology world like that?" Kenneth said, looking at her puzzled expression. "Don't we refer each other all the time and hire our friends? Plus, a startup like GE Pharmaceuticals will eat this right up. It's an efficient, four-for-one deal!"

Lydia paused, pursing her lips and pensively gazing at the console. "I guess."

I smiled, holding Blane's hand in the back seat.

"That's how the four of us get in—and get in together." Blane grinned. "When a CEO like Thilda wants a VIP party, she'll get the best VIP party! And she'll get some dang good researchers too!"

I smiled at Blane. While I wasn't sure how we would pull off posing as party planners and scientists, jumping right into GE's culture and blending in with the staff, I felt reassured that the Fearless Foursome would take our leap of faith as a team.

††

The drive from Amesbury to Somerset took us through some of the prettiest countryside I'd seen. We drove through rolling green fields dotted with clusters of sheep, and through quaint towns with thatched-roof houses, exactly like in Amesbury. As I gazed out the window, I could picture knights on horseback galloping across the emerald-green fields, their armor sparkling in the mid-April sunlight. Maybe they were setting off on their quests or maybe they were returning home. Undoubtedly, the English countryside was made for knights and their adventures.

A car heading the opposite direction whizzed by us on my right. "I don't think I'll ever get used to that," I said, grabbing Blane's forearm and staring out the window.

"I'm sure you would." Blane squeezed my hand. "If you lived here long enough."

"Maybe." I smiled, watching the oncoming cars drive by. "One way to find out, right?"

"You could study abroad here," said Kenneth. "Nassauton is very supportive of studying abroad. Once you re-enroll, ask. Your credits would transfer. Don't rule it out."

I never considered studying abroad. But if Kenneth said it was an option . . .

"I could go somewhere in England," I mused.

"Or Scotland," said Lydia. "They have great universities— and beautiful highlands with stunning hikes. You'd have a great time, being the archaeology whiz that you are!" She smiled, glancing at me in the rearview mirror. "They have centuries-old castles full of stories of kings and queens."

"That sounds amazing." I grinned. Lydia called me an archaeology whiz. "But first I have to knock out these summer classes. I promised my mom."

"And you will." Blane gave my hand a reassuring squeeze. "I know you will."

††

Our cottage was several miles from GE Pharmaceuticals. "No yellow curtains" was Kenneth's one request, which Jude had taken very seriously.

———

"Purple curtains?" Kenneth grumbled as we walked into the living room.

"You said no yellow!" Lydia chuckled. "This purple is quite lovely."

I walked up the stairs to what would be Blane's and my room. The walls were covered in floral wallpaper—little prints of flowers and bouquets—that reminded me of a Victorian dollhouse. I shook my head. It wasn't exactly my style, but I was thankful for our room and thankful it had two queen-size beds. *How did Jude find this on such short notice? How do Kenneth and Jude know each other?* I knew Kenneth did Jude a favor . . .

We'd barely had a moment to settle in when our stylist arrived with her supplies. As she transformed Lydia's and my hair to match our fake ID pictures, she didn't provide her name or ask any questions. She just smiled, flashed her double dagger tattoo, and wished us good luck.

Later that night as I plopped down on my bed, our proximity to GE Pharmaceuticals and the impending start of our next adventure finally hit me. We had clear goals: get Thilda's Grealmæp and discover what Thilda was hiding—and determine if it was the Grail. We also had to ace the interview. I was excited and nervous, and knew that whatever was ahead, the Fearless Foursome would tackle it together. I looked at my Ailm charm. *Be brave.*

††

After a surprisingly good night's rest, I woke up refreshed. We grabbed a quick breakfast and headed to GE Pharmaceuticals.

"Have everything?" Kenneth asked, donning his tweed blazer. He tightened his ponytail and threw it behind his left shoulder. "Ashlyn Drew, are you ready for your first interview in, what's it been, forty years?" He chuckled, teasing her.

Lydia smiled. "Sure am, Frank Tepperton. Don't forget, I've

been party planning my whole life."

"Good." Kenneth smiled. "With our research on *C. elegans* and how studying them helps us understand cancer, Chris Angelton and I are ready. KDI confirmed our nine thirty interview and submitted all four of our profiles, portfolios, recommendation letters, and CVs."

A surge of pride in being a knight in her Quest Phase pulsed through me. KDI was effortlessly cool and extraordinarily competent. I'd made the right choice in accepting J. Carmichael's nomination.

"*C. elegans*?" Lydia asked. "The worm?"

"Uhh, you mean the nematode," Blane pretended to chastise Lydia.

"Nematode?" I burst out laughing. "I've never heard that word before."

"Me neither," said Blane. "But this morning has been a deep dive—headfirst, and without a backward glance—into all things nematode. These tiny creatures are fascinating!"

With the Fearless Foursome in great spirits, we put GE Pharmaceuticals' address in our GPS. After a fifteen-minute drive through the Somerset countryside, we saw a gray and brown stone wall, which blocked the open fields and farmland from our view.

"We're getting close," I said, looking at the icon of our car on the GPS screen. "The driveway should be—"

"Right there!" Blane pointed at a large wrought-iron gate with two tall stone pillars on either side. Kenneth pulled up to the keypad and pressed the call button.

A woman's voice answered curtly. "State your name and reason for your visit."

"Ashlyn Drew and Trinity Lewis," Lydia said. "We're here for our interview."

"And Frank Tepperton and Chris Angelton, researchers and also their references."

The line clicked off.

I looked at Blane in suspense.

Silence.

The line clicked back on.

"Thank you for your patience. You look exactly like your IDs. But Ashlyn and Trinity, you're early. You've got another hour. Half ten. It's almost half nine now."

What does she mean, half ten, half nine?

"Shoot," said Kenneth under his breath so she didn't hear him. "Rookie mistake. Half ten is ten thirty, not nine thirty."

I looked at the keypad. Little cameras above the numbers looked back at me, undoubtedly watching us. The line clicked off.

Silence.

More silence.

The line clicked back on.

"I suppose it's quite all right. We can use the extra time to process your paperwork without being rushed. As a research facility, we do have strict security protocols. Drive on up."

The line clicked off. Seconds later, the gate opened, scraping backward as its two halves lurched apart. I looked at my Ailm charm. *Be brave.* Kenneth carefully accelerated. Our car rumbled over the grates at the mouth of the driveway. The gravel crunched under the tires as we entered. As far as I could see, the tree-lined driveway extended into the distance. I could barely see the lab facility itself—and couldn't believe it would be tucked all the way behind the wall. I looked behind me. The wrought-iron gates clanged shut, locking together.

The facility had several buildings in one compound: an old, stone four-story farmhouse; a big stone-and-wood barn that looked like it belonged in an English countryside postcard; and a building that looked like a dormitory. The farmhouse had a thick chimney at one end, and the barn stood between the farmhouse and the dormitory, towering over the other buildings and landscape. *How many researchers work here? Do they live on-site in dorms?*

As Kenneth pulled the car into a spot near the farmhouse, I noticed its red door—a pop of brightness among the stone colors.

"Here we are," he said, turning off the car. "There's no turning back now."

I opened the door and got out. The gravel crunched under my boots—the same boots Gran had worn on her archaeological adventures over the years. *Gran is with me now as I'm taking my first steps at GE Pharmaceuticals—the same place that made the drug that was supposed to save my dad.* A shiver of excitement and anxiety ran down my back.

I took a deep breath, inhaling the cool air. As I exhaled, I noticed a small flower garden outside the farmhouse's entrance where red, pink, and yellow flowers were planted neatly in precise rows. They seemed to glow with an otherworldly, vibrant brilliance, like they were fed an extra dose of the best flower food.

"Look at those flowers," I said. "Aren't they unnaturally bright?"

Blane squatted down by the garden.

"Yeah. Kinda weird. They look too luscious for springtime." He pushed himself back up. We caught up with Kenneth and Lydia in front of the farmhouse door. "Maybe Thilda discovered how to make flowers brighter. Science is cool like that."

The Grealmæp insignia, painted in the middle of the door under the wrought-iron knocker, was unmistakable. Before we could raise the knocker, the door opened. A young woman in her late twenties greeted us. She wore a fitted black jumpsuit, red heels, and pink lipstick. Her hair was jet black and stick straight. Not one hair moved out of place as she shook Lydia's and my hands.

"Good morning, Ashlyn, Trinity. Do come in."

Lydia and I nodded as the four of us walked into the foyer. The foyer was unimaginably large compared to the size of the red door. *How is a room this cavernous possible in the farmhouse?* The room had white walls, vaulted ceilings, and a spiral staircase in one corner. A large, cordless neon sign that spelled ETERNAE in crimson red script hung on one wall. The floor was made up of big, glossy black and white squares and looked like a chessboard. I hopped to one of the black squares.

"Queen to black," I whispered to Blane. "And that's checkmate."

Blane whispered back, careful not to be too overtly flirtatious so as not to draw attention to our real identities. "You've got me!"

"I'm Pippa. I'm GE Pharma's property and operations manager." She closed the door behind us and stood on a black square. It reflected her red heels. "I'm also the chef. Despite all our property, we're still a startup. Maybe ten, fifteen researchers, and a handful of staff wearing multiple hats. Let's see, your interview is at ten thirty?"

We nodded.

"Right, great."

Lydia smiled, advancing a square to shake hands with Pippa. "Hi, Pippa. I'm Ashlyn, and this is Trinity." Lydia pointed at me.

As I looked at Pippa's face, I noticed her pink lipstick made her gray eyes look a steely silver. "Nice floor," I said. "It reminds me of a chessboard."

"That's intentional. Thilda's favorite game is chess. When she's thinking, she comes here and moves from square to square. It's like her mind is calculating every possible move, every possible outcome before she makes a decision."

I looked at the floor. The more I learned about Thilda, the more she intrigued me.

"And these two gentlemen must be Frank and Chris." She pointed at Kenneth and Blane.

"Yup, they're the scientists who told us about this opportunity. We've planned their parties before," Lydia replied.

Kenneth smiled. "We love Ashlyn and Trinity's work. And, when we attended Thilda's keynote in New York, we knew we had to get to GE Pharmaceuticals. With all the chatter about her milestone party, we knew just the people to plan it—and of course wanted to meet her and collaborate with her team too."

Pippa smiled, trying to connect the dots. "Which keynote?"

My chest tightened. How would Kenneth respond?

"The one at Credenza Labs," Kenneth said, unfazed. "The papers picked it up and showered her with praise!"

"Right!" Pippa exclaimed. "That was just last month! She got a lot of good press for that, but I didn't realize she's been buzzing about the party."

A wave of relief washed over me.

Kenneth nodded. "She has—and she is one impressive CEO!"

Pippa smiled. "She *is* impressive. And she's also hard to impress. She hasn't been impressed—at all—by the other candidates' proposals."

"What do you mean?" asked Lydia.

Pippa sighed. "It's been, erm, quite a struggle. We need competent, professional party planners who can create the experience Thilda wants. She says she'll know it when she sees it. Even I don't know what she's wanting, but I do know Boss Lady hasn't been too thrill—" Pippa stopped herself. "I need to check your credentials, IDs, letters, and CVs before I say more. It's our security protocol. Right this way."

I found it funny Pippa referred to Thilda as Boss Lady. Pippa walked across the chessboard floor, her heels echoing on each tile. My boots didn't make a sound. Pippa unlocked the first door on our right and turned the light on. A fluorescent red glow filled the windowless room. I looked at the ceiling where a lattice-style grid of light tubes floated above my head.

"How does that work?" I asked. "I don't see any cords."

"Isn't it neat?" Pippa said. "Thilda designed it. It's hanging from the ceiling, but the cords are clear. Makes the whole thing seem like it's defying gravity."

Thilda, the CEO and scientist, also had a penchant for sleek design in red, black, white, and steel: the chessboard foyer floor, the red neon Eternae sign, and this room—with its floating lights, crimson carpet, and floor-to-ceiling, book-filled steel shelves.

"Take off your jackets. Have a seat." Pippa pointed to the black leather couch by one of the walls. "I'll check in each one of you individually, in my office." She pointed at a small door at the end of the room. "Ashlyn first. The others please wait here."

Pippa ushered Lydia into her office, followed her in, and closed the door behind her. I looked at the books—medical and immunology textbooks. I recognized a few titles, including some chemistry textbooks. There was an entire section on cancer and healing: *Healing with Herbs: A Botanist's Guide to Finding a Cure*, *Potions or Pills: Making Medicine that Heals*, and *From Rapamycin to Ginger Root: Creating Compounds that Cure*.

Running my finger along the spines, I remembered my first time at Rockfire, in the Archaeological Research Room. In those moments, I felt proud, knowing I belonged at Nassauton. I'd felt nervous, starting the first college project and wanting to do well since I was presenting on Gran. I'd found Gran's books and thought of all the papers that started as ideas in the Archaeology Research Room. But now as a dropout, Nassauton, my freshman year, and my academic obligations were worlds away. *Does Winnie B.'s mortarboard-wearing gargoyle ever get it wrong?*

Surrounded by Thilda's textbooks, I felt my anxiety overpower me. If Thilda was hiding the Grail, how were we going to get it? With all the security to get in, there was no way we could walk out of GE with the Grail. Had Thilda really been able to manufacture *Grealia*? Why hadn't Eternae worked for my dad? Were Dr. Gellmane, Dr. Pritzmord, and GE really collaborating—or was Dr. Gellmane manipulating Thilda? What about the prophecy? I looked at my Ailm charm. *Be brave.*

"Trinity, you're up." Pippa stuck her head out of her door as Lydia left.

I kept staring at the textbooks.

"Trinity?"

"Oh, right, yep, coming!" *You're Trinity!* I reminded myself. *Don't blow it!*

I walked to Pippa's office. My boots barely made a sound on the crimson carpet. As Lydia and I crossed paths, Lydia whispered, "Can't believe a year has gone by since I hired you after you applied." I smiled, not knowing at all what she was referring to.

Pippa sat behind her laptop, at a small desk. The desk was disorderly and cluttered, covered with boxes, books, folders, and papers. I chuckled. Lydia probably felt right at home.

"Trinity, sit down." Pippa closed the door behind me. "May I see your government-issued ID? What's your full name?"

"Trinity Lewis." I looked Pippa right in the eyes as I handed her my fake ID. She scanned it with a black-light pen, nodded, then returned it to me. *KDI thought of everything!*

"Thank you." She typed my name. "Trinity Lewis. How long have you been working with Ashlyn?"

"About a year."

"How did you meet?"

I smiled. "She needed help. I applied for the job. We clicked. I guess you could say the rest is history." Now I knew why Lydia had said what she did. Pippa was playing a prisoner's dilemma game with us, to see if our individual answers corroborated each other's. From the cameras at the entrance, to confirming our identity, Thilda took no chances with security at GE.

Pippa finished typing my response, then looked up. "Parties don't always work out the way they're planned. Tell me about a time when something went wrong, and you fixed it."

I took a deep breath, thinking of the portfolio KDI had created for us.

"There was one party Ashlyn and I planned for dignitaries and VIPs. By accident, I forgot to send the save-the-date invitation to one of the VIPs. But I caught it before it became a big deal. In the end, the VIP never knew, since Ashlyn called her and her assistant personally to ensure she knew about the party. They appreciated the white-glove touch."

Pippa smiled as she recorded my entire response. "Well done," she said. "That was quick thinking. Right, one more question. What do you like most about party planning?"

"Creating an unforgettable experience." I smiled. "What about you? Have you ever planned a party? I'd imagine as a chef, you're involved in party planning—at least the food part?"

Pippa beamed—the first big smile she'd cracked during our interview. I heard a machine under her desk rev up. "My favorite part is making the menu. A purposefully planned menu makes or breaks a party." Reaching under her desk, she handed me a label with a QR code and my name. *Trinity Lewis.* "This is your name badge for today. It must always be visible."

"What's the QR code for?" I asked, peeling off my badge and sticking it on my sweater.

"There are scanners at every door—even the bathrooms. The doors won't open if they can't read your QR code."

I nodded. "Got it."

"Right." Pippa looked at her laptop. "Your background check is almost complete, but it looks great so far. Please send in Frank or Chris."

I walked out of Pippa's office. "Frank," I said, looking at Dr. Wengaro, "your turn."

††

Pippa processed our name badges quickly. After she finished, she locked the office door.

"Right then, your background checks look good. Expert party planners! Ashlyn, how was it planning all those VIP after-parties?"

Lydia grinned. "You know NDAs mean I can't share the details. But, a lot of meetings made the whole process customized and the after-parties spectacular!"

Smiling, I sighed in relief. KDI and our fake IDs and portfolios had come through!

Pippa grinned. "And Frank and Chris. How has GE not heard of you? You'll be right at home here with the researchers. I'm sure your work on *C. elegans* will be of interest to many. Those little nematodes are fascinating."

Blane grinned. "We're in stealth mode," he said. "Our research is not public. And we can't wait to meet GE's esteemed researchers." He looked at Lydia and mouthed, "Nematodes for the win." Lydia burst out laughing.

"Chris loves those worms," Lydia said. "That's all he ever talks about. Worms."

"You mean nematodes." Blane grinned.

Pippa chuckled. "You all seem like a great bunch. Ashlyn, Trinity, I'm glad you're here. I hope Thilda likes you. And Frank and Chris, you'll fit right in." She looked at her watch. "We have some time before your interview, so we'll continue our tour. This room is GE's library. It's full of Thilda's personal books. The next room is the sitting room. Right this way, please."

Lydia, Kenneth, Blane, and I followed Pippa out of the library.

"So how do we ace our interview?" Lydia asked as we walked down the hallway.

Pippa's heels clicked on the hardwood floor. "Thilda is practical *and* highly creative. Whatever you propose, it's really got to spark her imagination."

Lydia nodded. "Trinity, are you getting this?"

"Yep," I said, jotting down Pippa's comments on my phone.

"It's got to make financial sense. Our board scrutinizes the numbers. We're still a startup. We're in desperate need of cash. Our expenses must be vett—" She stopped abruptly, covering her mouth with her hand. "I shouldn't say that—you haven't signed NDAs." She kept walking ahead, the silence punctuated by the sound of her heels on the floor. Lydia elbowed me, motioning for me to write down her comment about GE's expenses.

"Your ideas have to be wildly creative," Pippa finally said. "Thilda's sick of plain proposals. This isn't a garden party for grad students. We don't want long tables with plastic tablecloths and some fruit-filled punch bowls. This isn't Friday night at pub trivia. This isn't a birthday party for a four-year-old fairy princess. This is a VIP gala."

Lydia nodded again. "Thank you. This is very good insight."

"Pleasure. I hope these ideas inspire better ones." She unlocked another door. "Here is the sitting room—have a look. It doubles as our conference room. We have our board meetings here."

The room was big enough for fifty people. It had two long, white tables, a black tiled floor, and white walls. Two big flatscreen TVs were mounted on the side wall, each with the word ETERNAE in crimson script as a screensaver. I watched, mesmerized, as the word bounced around the screens.

A matte black marble fireplace with a sleek, black stone mantel took up one wall. The mantel was completely bare, except for a lighter, two candles in black marble candlesticks, and two photos in sterling silver frames. One photo was of a woman and man on a yacht. The woman was dancing on the deck, her back toward the camera. The other was of a beautiful woman who looked familiar to me.

"She looks like Felda, doesn't she?" Blane pointed to the picture of the woman.

I nodded.

Careful not to let Pippa see me, I snapped a picture of the photos.

"Pippa, these photos—they're beautiful. Who are they?"

Pippa joined me in front of the fireplace. "That's Thilda's mum and dad," she said, pointing to the woman and man. "And that is her grandmother."

"Beautiful family," I said, looking at Albert, Thilda's mother, and Felda.

"Yes, and smart! Thilda's dad and grandmother were chemists. Chemistry is Thilda's destiny." Pippa chuckled. "She takes it so seriously. It's her purpose and GE's purpose. Everyone who works here has to buy into her vision."

Pippa locked the door behind us as we left the room. She glanced at her watch. "The only other rooms here are the kitchen and dining room. You can see those later. I think we should head to the lab."

Lydia nodded. "Sounds good."

We walked to the end of the hallway, arriving at two locked steel doors. Pippa held her badge to the scanner on the wall. The doors clicked open, revealing a glass-enclosed walkway.

"As you can tell, we have strict security," said Pippa, motioning for us to follow her. "With our work, it must be. When Thilda and her dad converted the barn into the laboratory, they rethought everything. State-of-the-art equipment. Cutting-edge facilities. Game rooms for the researchers. On-site living quarters and dining halls, with meals prepared three times a day. I cook specifically planned, healthy meals for the whole group." She beamed, stopping in the middle of the walkway. I gazed at the barn and dormitory. GE Pharmaceuticals was impressive—and its property expansive. In the distance, beyond the rolling fields and trees, I could barely see the stone wall enclosing the property.

"Kind of like a college campus," Blane said.

"Exactly. Thilda wanted to create a campus where intellectual firepower could flourish and be applied immediately to research and development."

"How did Thilda and her dad acquire the land and fund its development?" Kenneth asked. "I thought GE is a startup."

Pippa smiled. "We are. I'm not sure of all the details. Even if I was, I couldn't disclose them to you."

"NDA, right?" Kenneth chuckled.

So did Pippa. "Right." She grinned. It seemed like she was warming up to us. "We have been very lucky to benefit from private investors."

We followed Pippa down the walkway. As we turned a corner, I saw hanging baskets of vibrant flowers, like the ones Blane and I had seen outside in the garden. A few flowers were in pots along the edges of the walkway.

"What's with the flowers?" I asked. "How are they this vibrant?"

"It's one of Thilda's cutting-edge experiments. Beautiful flowers no matter what time of year—even in winter. They don't die. It's amazing. She's always thinking and tinkering—and testing the limits of what is possible. And with that brain of hers, she never fails."

Pippa's heels clacked on the floor. "This walkway connects the farmhouse with the laboratory. We also use this section as a greenhouse, growing and studying all sorts of plants." We arrived at two steel doors, each with the Grealmæp insignia in their center. Pippa lifted her badge to the scanner. The doors unlocked, slowly opening backward.

"What's that insignia?" I was curious to hear Pippa's response.

"It's GE's logo, inspired by Thilda's family crest. Thilda has a necklace with it as a pendant. She never takes it off."

Without thinking, I gasped. I looked at Blane, trying to hide my involuntary reaction so Pippa didn't see it. *Thilda has the second Grealmæp!*

"It's beautiful," I said as the doors fully opened.

"'Tis indeed," Pippa replied, motioning for us to follow her. We walked onto a steel-floored balcony that overlooked the expanse of the entire lab. "Welcome to GE Pharmaceuticals' laboratory. This is where the magic happens." Pippa beamed, sweeping her hands in front of her to show us the level below and floors above. "And make sure you don't miss the balcony floor."

I glanced at my feet. A rainbow-colored double helix mosaic covered the entire floor. I gasped, overwhelmed by the grandeur of GE's art. My boots didn't make a sound as I walked on the mosaic up to the balcony's wall. It was a steel sheet, with a punched-out pattern of double helices and chromosomes.

I didn't know where to look first: at the level below me, the floors above me, or the roof. *How did Thilda get funding for this?* Everything—from the floor to the roof, from the lab equipment to the walls—was black, white, or stainless steel, with crimson accents. Sleek, high-tech machines and benches were arranged in long, immaculate rows on the lower level. As I gazed at the lab, I felt like I'd stepped onto a movie set.

The ground floor—the same floor as our balcony—and the floors above me had offices and conference rooms, with polished, spotless interior windows gleaming in the sunlight. I craned my neck, taking in the entire distance between the ground floor and the second floor, which was dizzyingly large. As I stood on the balcony, I felt like I was standing in a pulpit in a cathedral, overlooking the congregants in the pews. The whole place was a hive, busy with activity: gloved researchers sitting with intense, laser-like focus at their benches, technicians in white coats pushing carts around, buzzing between benches, and people in pods chit-chatting over diagrams.

A stainless-steel bridge spanned across the lab, connecting one side to the other. On either side were two staircases, each shaped like a double helix and providing access from the lower level to the bridge. One side had a glass elevator, with the Grealmæp insignia laser-cut onto its door. The barn's glass roof, supported by stainless-steel scaffolding that looked like an exoskeleton, enabled sunlight to stream through unhindered, flooding the lab with natural light.

The most impressive feature was not the lower level, light well, glass-enclosed rooms, double-helix staircases, or stainless-steel exoskeleton scaffolding. It was, without a doubt, the massive, crimson double helix dangling from a chromosome in the center of the lab's light well. The chromosome was part of the roof's scaffolding. The double helix sprouted out of the chromosome and hung in the light well's center. Propelled by a motor with a barely audible hum, the double helix spiraled around itself, into the chromosome, like an infinitely twisting tower from the lower level to the sky. As the helix spiraled, the sunlight hit it, casting a warm, crimson glow over the lab. The entire lab was a modern architecture marvel, as much as it was a functional research facility. As I gazed at the double helix, I heard Pippa's heels clack on the balcony floor.

"Impressive, right?"

I nodded, mesmerized by the helix's motion. "Who made it?"

"Our artist-in-residence, Elle Gammaday." Pippa smiled. "Thilda was adamant we have an artist-in-residence program. She loves weaving art and science together, so one of her first requests for proposals when she renovated the lab was for local artists. Her board members didn't like that. They wanted her to focus on gaining traction to show investors. But Lord Breekson shut them all down. He's a staunch supporter of the arts and sciences. He convinced the board that art brings investment into a new place, just as much as the technology!"

Lord Breekson again, this time on GE's board!

Pippa continued. "Elle wowed Thilda, and Thilda not only hired Elle to create art installations around GE's campus, but also to teach art programs here."

I grinned. I never thought about putting two different disciplines under the same roof. The concept challenged the traditional university structure, with its separately located departments and siloed disciplines. Thilda's innovative approach to creating interdisciplinary, place-based learning opportunities was visionary.

"How'd Elle make this?"

"First, the chromosome is part of the scaffolding." Pippa looked at the roof, then the double helix. "When the roof opens, steel cables suspend the chromosome and double helix in the air. They look like they're floating. Then, if you look closely, you can see all the little red gel pills. Each one has a tiny magnet holding it in place. It's supposed to symbolize the fragility and intricate beauty of life. Elle engineered the whole thing marvelously. If we see her, you can ask her more about her process." She pointed to the plaque on the balcony ledge. "You can read about it here. It's one of Thilda's favorite pieces."

The plaque, written in lowercase letters, had the artwork's title, *infinitely encoded; forever expressed*, and a few sentences describing the chromosome, double helix, nucleotides and their infinite combination of pairings, and DNA and its purpose.

"*Infinitely encoded; forever expressed* reminds researchers to reach for the heavens, aspiring to their highest potential. If DNA is possible, anything is possible. It's a matter of making it possible," I read aloud. "Very fitting for Thilda." I skimmed the rest of the plaque, adding, "Elle must love lowercase letters."

"Absolutely," said Pippa. "Yes, Elle says lowercase letters are more poetic. She only types in lowercase letters, and it drives Thilda crazy." She chuckled.

I gazed at *infinitely encoded; forever expressed*. The double helix's hypnotic spiraling, motor's soft hum, and warm crimson glow put me in a trance.

The fragility of life . . . GE Pharmaceuticals' remarkable technology. GE is a scientist's wonderland. What other experiments is Thilda running? How many researchers know about Grealia? Does Thilda's board? Does Lord Breekson?

The double helix kept spiraling, endlessly twisting around itself. *This is where Thilda made Eternae from Grealia . . . What is the status of Eternae now? Does it cure cancer? Is it on the market?* The motor kept buzzing; the double helix kept twisting. *We have to get hired. We have to get the Grealmæp. We have to discover what's beyond the locked door . . .*

Pippa tapped my elbow, jerking me out of my trance. "Ready to see where it all happens?"

I blinked, then nodded, stepping back from the balcony's edge. Pippa led us to the lower level, down the double helix-shaped stairs.

"We have the world's best scientists at GE Pharmaceuticals. When they are not in the lab, they are in their apartments. They spend their entire days at GE, tackling our world's most vexing medical challenges. Each plays a part in making medicines. Some work on the bench, some design the medicine's delivery—IV, pill, in a yogurt, in a drink—some stare into petri dishes all day. Our lab wastes nothing—every little bit of tissue, raw material, reactant, product goes back into the research. We're a sustainable operation—from our bench to our boardroom."

Pippa held her badge to the scanner by the steel doors at the bottom of the staircase. The doors clicked open, and we walked onto the lower level.

XII

As we walked around, Pippa waved to the researchers. They smiled, waving back. She also pointed out different rooms, noting each room's function and equipment. "We've got the best brain-imaging, CT-scan, and fMRI machines," Pippa said. "Whatever Thilda needs for her research, she gets."

I nodded in amazement, trying to take it all in. The more we walked around, the more I crinkled my nose. The whole floor reeked of acetone, a smell I distinctly remembered from Chemistry 101.

"That's Rania Rachel—she goes by 'RR' for short. She's a talented chromatographer. She has a master's in education and divinity too."

RR peered up from her bench, grinning. "Hey, Pippa! Hope you're well!"

Pippa nodded. "Yep! Touring more party-planning candidates before their interview. I think they could be the ones!"

"How exciting! You know I can't wait for the party!" RR smiled, refocusing on her sample. "Gotta watch this—chat later!"

"You know I can't wait for the party," said Pippa as she waved goodbye to RR. "I already have way too much on my plate as it is. But that's startup life, I suppose."

"How does Thilda have money for this incredible laboratory, yet she can't hire a few extra staff?" Kenneth asked as we passed more benches. "Didn't you say you had private investors?"

"She does," Pippa sighed. "But they specify the funds can be used only for research and development. Not for hiring help for—"

Pippa's phone rang. "Yes? Oh great! Coming right up. Yes, right now."

Pippa turned to us. "She's ready. Let's go."

We headed to the elevator. The Grealmæp insignia was exactly like my pendant, down to the double dagger marks on the ruby. *Does everyone really believe this is Thilda's family's crest?* Pippa scanned her badge, and the glass doors opened. We followed Pippa into the elevator. There were no buttons on the panel inside.

"Floor two," said Pippa as the doors closed.

Blane's mouth dropped. "It's voice activated?"

"Yep," said Pippa. "But, erm, sometimes it doesn't recognize your voice and you have to repeat yourself. And I hate repeating myself." She chuckled as our short ride ended. The doors opened. Pippa walked ahead of us, her heels clacking on the floor. She stopped at an office a few doors down. Cracking the door open, she stuck her head in, then leaned back out. "Right, come on."

Thilda's entire office was white, except for a bright crimson neon sign on one wall. ETERNAE. Written above the sign in black block capital letters was a short quotation: THOSE WHO NEVER STOP CHASING THE IMPOSSIBLE ARE THE ONES WHO MAKE IT POSSIBLE. I nodded. In our Grail quest, we were chasing the impossible.

I took a deep breath as I looked around Thilda's office. One wall had spotless floor-to-ceiling windows. *I bet she sees her whole kingdom from here . . .* Thilda's desk, made of steel and seeming to float in the air, was in front of the windows, opposite the wall with the Eternae sign. Scattered across the top were a few papers, a picture frame, and a paperweight. The paperweight was a red gel pill, with a long, gold key taped to the bottom.

A tall woman stood behind the desk, silhouetted against the sunlight in the eerie silence of her office. She gazed out the window over the property's rolling fields, her back to us, with her long, blonde locks cascading down like a waterfall. She wore a fitted black jumpsuit and crimson red heels.

"Of all the scientific forces on this planet, our infinite imagination is the most powerful," she said without turning around. "It compels us to dedicate every atom of our being to make our dreams real—no matter the cost. That's the scientist's bargain: we give up our soul, get knowledge in return. There is nothing more noble than that."

Is she reading something or quoting someone?

"With our knowledge, it is our duty—our obligation—to test the limits of what we thought possible. We must dare to dream, and *do*, the impossible, never even entertaining the idea of failure. End cancer. Eliminate pain and suffering. And why stop there? Cheat death itself." She took a deep breath. "There's a couch by the door. Sit."

I looked to my right at the white leather couch and glass coffee table. The glass was pristine—polished with the same degree of detail as the spotless floor-to-ceiling windows and the lab's interior windows. The magazines on the table had headshots of Thilda and titles that would inspire any young female scientist: "Running the World: Women in Power," "CEO OF THE YEAR: Thilda von Genzkensaffe," and "Getting to the Top—and Staying There." Not a speck of dust was on the magazines. Their glossy covers caught the sunlight, shining perfectly.

A black leather high-back chair was near the far end of the couch. The chair's steel legs and armrests reminded me of the light well ceiling's exoskeleton-like scaffolding. *Thilda's throne.* A dark leather tote bag rested on the seat, immaculately placed against an armrest. *Is GE Pharmaceuticals too perfect?*

As soon as we sat, Thilda turned around. She put her hands on her hips and walked toward us. Her big, white-rimmed sunglasses covered her eyes. Her heels struck the floor with a measured cadence, their echo filling her office. "Dare to dream the impossible. My father always told me that." She pursed her lips. A glimmer of a smile flashed across her face. "I'm Thilda, short for Mathilda von Genzkensaffe. I am the CEO of GE Pharmaceuticals. It is my job to ensure my researchers dare to dream—and do—the impossible."

She had a gold necklace and wore a gold-and-silver ring on her right pinky finger. Its aquamarine stone sparkled in the sunlight, adding elegance—and power—to her perfectly manicured crimson fingernails. Her jumpsuit hid her pendant. I heard Pippa's words in my head: *Thilda has a necklace with it as a pendant. She never takes it off.* My heart started pounding. *The second Grealmæp!*

Thilda removed her sunglasses as she sat in her chair. Her gleaming green eyes pierced through me without blinking. Her oval-shaped face was pale and angular, and her red lipstick accentuated her lips and strong jawline. She looked like she was in her mid-thirties. Without getting up, she extended her hand to shake Lydia's.

"Hello, Thilda," said Lydia. "I'm Ashlyn Drew. This is Trinity Lewis."

I stood up to shake Thilda's hand.

"No need. Sit."

I sat down as Thilda leaned toward me, shaking my hand. Despite her thin, long fingers, her grasp could have crushed a stone.

"I'm Frank. This is Chris." Kenneth extended his hand to Thilda. "We're scientists from New York. We're your biggest fans! Our research is not public yet, but it's on cancer—and worms. We're here to support the best party planners we know!"

"Great to meet you," said Blane, looking at Thilda, then Kenneth. "He means cancer and *C. elegans.*"

Thilda stared at Blane, puzzled. "Chris . . . You look familiar. Haven't I seen you before?"

I gulped, praying Thilda didn't remember seeing Blane at The Elephant and Pen.

"No, don't think so," Blane said nonchalantly, playing it cool. "We've never met."

"I see," said Thilda. She relaxed her stare. "With all the people I meet, it's hard to keep track." She paused, her mouth slightly open, as if she was about to say something else. "Let's get on with the interview," Thilda said coolly, turning to Ashlyn. If she was interested in Kenneth and Blane's research, she didn't show it. "What's your proposal for my party?"

She picked up her leather bag, turning it around as she put it on the glass table. The initials *MvG* were stamped on the bag's center. I subtly elbowed Blane.

MvG isn't a brand. It's her initials: Mathilda von Genzkensaffe. Did Thilda visit the teacher's exhibit at the museum before she went to The Elephant and Pen?

Thilda's stiletto sliced the air as she crossed her right leg over her left. A small red-black-and-white double helix was tattooed above her ankle.

"We have it right here." Lydia opened her satchel and took out her laptop. "A presentation always helps us see the party—and unleash our imagination."

I grinned, excited to see Thilda's reaction.

"Splendid," said Thilda. "You can project it on the wall."

"Great," Lydia said. "Do you have a projector?"

Thilda reached across the table, into her bag, to retrieve a small silver box. It looked like an old cigarette lighter with a lens on one side and touchscreen on the other.

"This is a beam. Any electronic device physically located on our campus recognizes it, and it can recognize any device on our campus. You don't need Wi-Fi or Bluetooth to connect your device to a beam. If you have the name of the device, you can set up the pairing through a passcode." She glanced at her beam as she turned it on. "At GE, we mastered the tech quickly. Necessity is the mother of invention, as they say. It's so much easier when researchers need to show me their work and we're on the lower level or outside, or when I'm pacing around and need to project images without having to always have larger projectors."

Lydia opened her laptop. "How do I pair with your beam?"

"Type 'Beam—Eternae HQ' into your spotlight search. Click

the first hit. Then, you and I will see a pop-up screen—you on your computer and me on my beam. Your pop-up will show the name of my beam, and my pop-up will show the name—and location—of your device."

Lydia followed Thilda's directions.

"When you see the pop-up screen, we each have one minute to enter the beam passcode on our devices."

"What's your passcode?" Lydia asked.

"I can't tell you. I'll enter it for you." Thilda smirked. "Each beam has its own passcode. We never share them. I monitor the network for additional precaution. If someone tries to guess the code, the beam locks out the device after three incorrect attempts. Only I can reset it."

"So that's how you authenticate the device pairing?" asked Blane. "The owner of the beam must authenticate the other device."

Thilda nodded. "Yep, and showing the location is another security measure. If Ashlyn's laptop were stolen, and someone tried to pair her laptop with my beam, we'd know immediately it was a malevolent pairing. And of course, we'd know where her laptop is. We can't afford breaches. Our research is our IP. No one sees what they're not supposed to."

Thilda typed her passcode on Lydia's laptop, then on her beam. Within moments, the words PAIRING SUCCESSFUL flashed across Lydia's screen. Lydia adjusted her glasses, her Ailm charm catching a red glow from the neon Eternae sign. She beamed her presentation to the white wall.

"You want a fabulous and memorable celebration. Dignitaries, C-level leaders, medical and hospital directors, ultra-high net worth individuals. You want to showcase GE Pharmaceuticals. These are my assumptions."

Thilda nodded, her eyes sparkling. Lydia clicked to her next slide. I grinned. Lydia starting with her assumptions was a very "Dr. Kells" approach. Thilda appreciated Lydia's nod to logic. She took her phone out and started jotting her notes.

"If my assumptions are accurate, then I'm proposing an interactive, themed party. We want guests to not only feel they are in the action, experiencing the story, but also creating the magic with you." Lydia arranged her bun, making sure her hair was in place. She continued. "From the moment your guests arrive at the wrought-iron gates to the moment they leave, our party is an immersive, experiential journey. Each guest is the hero in GE's story—from its beginning to this celebration."

"I love this! Experience!" exclaimed Thilda. "You're the first ones to present a themed experience. Go on!" She leaned closer to the wall, elated by Lydia's presentation.

"We could plan an experience in each room," Lydia continued. "This isn't in the presentation, but your chessboard foyer could be set up as an actual chess game. Upon arrival, guests must move chess pieces to get to the next room. We could theme everything around a world without cancer, pain, and suffering— a world in which science makes life better, and better for all. What do you think of games, food, and beverages that play off those themes? Healthy foods? Antioxidant teas? No meat?"

"No bacon, that's for sure," chimed in Blane.

Thilda laughed—the first hearty laugh I'd heard. "Absolutely no bacon. Pippa knows never to make it for our staff."

"Perfect! Pippa can oversee the menu. We'll hire caterers, of course," said Lydia. "Top grade. And professional dessert artists—think cookies in the shape of chromo—"

"Chromosomes!" Thilda interrupted her, clasping her hands together in glee. The sunlight hit her aquamarine stone, sending little green sparkles that gleamed like stars on the white walls. "Cookies in the shape of chromosomes! Elle would love that!"

Kenneth nodded. "We saw *infinitely encoded; forever expressed*. It's impressive."

Thilda smiled. "It's my favorite piece. I can't wait until she finishes her other installations."

"We'll make the whole celebration a game that culminates in

the lab, with the announcement of your milestone as the 'prize'? Each room could have clues for guests to find before moving to the next room. They can use their clues to guess your announcement. Do they get points? Maybe the guest, or team, with the most points wins a replica of *infinitely encoded; forever expressed*?"

Thilda's eyes gleamed. "Love it!" She nodded in excitement. "What else? Keep these great ideas coming!"

"The entire lab is transformed into a dance floor, with a giant disco ball. You reveal your announcement, then the celebration continues with dancing into the night."

Thilda squealed. "The disco ball, the dancing! This will be a night to remember!"

Pippa cheered. "I've never seen you this happy, Thilda!"

"These are only some ideas," said Lydia. "If hired, Trinity and I will meet with you and learn about the history of GE Pharmaceuticals—and Eternae." Lydia pointed at the neon sign. "What is Eternae? How did you start GE? What was your inspiration? How did you name it? Not the trade secrets, but the big story. What exact milestone are we celebrating? We can incorporate these into the celebration for an unforgettable experience."

I smiled at Lydia's clever tactics for getting the information on the Grealmæp and *Grealia*—and maybe even the Grail—that we needed. Her strategy was perfect.

Thilda pointed at the quotation above the neon sign. THOSE WHO NEVER STOP CHASING THE IMPOSSIBLE ARE THE ONES WHO MAKE IT POSSIBLE. "You and Trinity chase the impossible. I like that about you." She looked at us, nodding. "That was another one of my dad's quotes. He was a chemist." She took a deep breath, her steely demeanor momentarily lapsing into an uncharacteristic sadness. "Cancer is cruel. Its pain spares no one."

I took a deep breath, looking right into Thilda's green eyes. I swore I saw a few tears. "I'm sorry, Thilda. I know how difficult it is to lose your dad."

———

"Thanks, Trinly. It motivated me to dare boldly, to dream bigger, to chase harder. And in chasing the cure for cancer, GE stumbled on another incredible discovery." She beamed. "Using proprietary reactants, we've produced a drug that provides eternal life. Right here, under my—and my family's—name." She placed her hand on her chest, holding her pendant through her jumpsuit.

"It's Trinity." I corrected Thilda while trying to hide my surprise and guess as to what her proprietary reactants could be. She didn't apologize for getting my name wrong.

"GE has a lot to celebrate," she continued, beaming.

Thilda double tapped her watch. A few moments later, a hidden side door hissed open. A thin man wearing a black turtleneck and black pants walked out. The door hissed shut. He stood behind Thilda's chair.

"This is Sebastian Waugh." Thilda didn't get out of her chair and didn't invite Sebastian to sit down. "He supports Pippa. Speaking of celebrations, tell him your ideas for the party."

My eyes widened. *J. Carmichael had spoken with Sebastian Waugh.* As Lydia shared our ideas, I looked at Sebastian. He looked old and young at the same time. His hands, though well-manicured, looked weathered. But his face looked oddly boyish. His big brown eyes and smooth, soft skin glowed with an otherworldly, vibrant brilliance—like the flowers in Thilda's garden.

When Lydia finished, he smiled and whispered to Thilda. Thilda grinned, nodding excitedly. She leaped out of her chair to shake Lydia's and my hands.

"You're hired!" She beamed, hardly able to contain her exuberance.

XIII

Pippa wasted no time in setting us up in GE's systems, getting us our office keys, and printing our badges.

"Here you are," Pippa exclaimed as her machine spat out our badges. She hooked them onto red lanyards and handed them to us. "When you scan your badge, your location and time are tracked. It's for everyone's safety. We can quickly find you if there's an emergency. If you need anything, Sebastian or I can help. Our mobile numbers are printed on the back."

I nodded, looping my lanyard over my head. Sebastian smiled. I glanced at Lydia as she adjusted her lanyard. She was poised and seemed excited for her new role and our tasks ahead. I couldn't believe we'd been hired on the spot. Without KDI's thorough preparation, we never could have gone undercover as Ashlyn and Trinity.

"How do you want to be paid?" asked Pippa, turning to her laptop to complete the vendor onboarding form. Kenneth, Blane, Lydia, and I were crammed in her cluttered office, with Sebastian standing in the doorframe. "And each of you need to sign nondisclosure agreements. In planning the party, or being around the researchers, you might hear or see proprietary intellectual property. We'll hold you legally accountable to keep anything you learn confidential."

I smiled, remembering KDI's prep on nondisclosure agreements.

"A check would be great," Lydia said. "To Ashlyn Drew."

———

I peered at Kenneth. *Did KDI set up fake bank accounts?* He smiled, a small twinkle forming in his eye as if to say, *Don't worry about it!*

"Of course, we'll sign them," said Kenneth.

"Wonderful." Pippa smiled. "Anything else I'm missing?"

"We need to schedule time with Thilda to learn GE Pharmaceuticals' story. Can you help with that?"

"Sebastian can."

Sebastian tapped his watch. A hologram of a calendar popped up in the air.

"Whoa," I whispered to Blane.

Sebastian tapped one of the dates. Thilda's hourly schedule hovered above Sebastian's watch. "How's half eleven tomorrow? Right before lunch."

"Eleven thirty a.m. is perfect." Lydia smiled. "We'll be here."

††

With my nineteenth birthday a few days away, I anticipated the arrival of my present. I was also looking forward to date night. Blane and I hadn't had a night to ourselves in a long time, which was taking its toll on both of us. Since we'd arrived in Somerset, Blane took initiative to plan our date, scoping out restaurants and cute spots in town. I appreciated his thoughtfulness. His efforts showed me how much he cared about me and our relationship.

After our first day at GE, Lydia, Kenneth, Blane, and I debriefed in our cottage, over Thai food takeout. We'd set up our laptops and journals on the coffee table and sofa in our living room, sharing our observations and preparing for our meeting with Thilda.

"Thilda is KA von Genzkensaffe's great-granddaughter and Felda's granddaughter," I said. "I'm sure her pendant is the second Grealmæp. She couldn't have designed the insignia without it."

"Evidence, not emotion. What evidence do you have for that conclusion?" Lydia asked.

"Pippa said Thilda wears the Grealmæp."

"That's not evidence. That's anecdote." Lydia looked at me as she arranged her bun. Her bangles slid down her arms, clanging together. "We haven't seen the Grealmæp or heard Thilda directly mention it or share a lot about her family—beyond a little bit about her dad. So right now, it's not a conclusion but a question mark."

Kenneth nodded. "What about the photos on the mantel?" he asked. "Pippa said they're her mom, dad, and grandmom."

"I snuck pictures of them," I said. "How do we confirm their names?"

Kenneth pointed at my sentinel. "Send them to KDI."

I grinned. "How do I do that?"

"Text KDI and the case identifier: KDI-TATA-TTAGGG 8."

I followed Kenneth's instructions.

"Now we wait," he said. "Hopefully, KDI will be back to you soon."

Twenty minutes later, Kenneth's and my sentinels gleamed.

††

Dear Kenneth and Carly: The people in the photos are Felda von Genzkensaffe—Thilda's grandmother, Felda's son Albert von Genzkensaffe—Thilda's father, and his wife, Dr. Elyse Gellmane—Thilda's mother.

Also, we can confirm that J. C.'s death was no accident. As a defected Knight of the Dagger and current Knight of the White Wave, Elyse Gellmane plotted his murder.

We will do everything in our power to protect you, including alerting an insider ally. But if Gellmane and Pritzmord find you, or if Thilda realizes who you really are, you will be in even more danger. BE CAREFUL!

Keep your daggers close to your heart and hand,
KDI

My jaw dropped. I looked at Kenneth in shock. *Dr. Gellmane is Thilda's mother—and former Knight of the Dagger! Why did she defect? How did she meet Albert? If Albert and Lord Breekson were friends, is Dr. Gellmane friends with Lord Breekson too? How does Dr. Pritzmord fit in?* I scribbled my questions in my journal. The threads in the ball of yarn had just gotten much more entangled.

††

Sebastian opened Thilda's office door at 11:29 a.m. and smiled, ushering Lydia and me to the couch and sitting down next to us. He took a long, slow sip of a pink smoothie in his tall, crystal glass. Thilda sat at her desk, deep in thought and typing on her laptop. Her long, blonde locks tumbled around her face, framed by white sunglasses she wore like a headband. Her perfect, ruby-red lipstick made her lips pop against her pale skin. The sunlight flooded through her windows, surrounding her in light.

If I could only glimpse her pendant! She stared at her laptop, her fingers barely making a sound as she typed. *Was she talking to Dr. Pritzmord at The Elephant and Pen? Had she ever met him in person?* She stopped typing and looked up, clutching her pendant through her jumpsuit.

"Sebastian, I'm blanking, when's the next batch coming in?"

Sebastian tapped his watch. The hologram of the calendar appeared. "First thing next Monday."

"Great." Thilda looked at her screen and resumed typing.

Does she know her mother is a Knight of the Dagger, a Knight of the White Wave, and a murderer? Why is she collaborating with her mother and Dr. Pritzmord? Or are they manipulating her? What does she know about the Grealmæps? I looked at my Ailm charm, trying to focus on our meeting and not the questions that bombarded my attention. *Be brave.*

Thilda closed her laptop. She picked up her red gel pill paperweight. The gold key glimmered in the sunlight as she strode to the couch, her crimson stilettos echoing with each step. Paperweight in hand, she sat in her black chair and crossed her legs. My legs started shaking in my boots. Seeing Thilda walk with such power and poise made me nervous.

"Good morning, Ashlyn, Trinity. I trust you are well?"

"Good morning, Thilda." Lydia smiled, slipping her laptop out of her satchel. "We are, thank you."

Thilda nodded. "Excellent. Can Sebastian get you anything? Something to eat? Drink?" She gestured to Sebastian, who sat up at the sound of his name. "Sebastian makes a delicious smoothie. It's rejuvenating."

Sebastian smiled, taking a sip from his smoothie.

"We're fine, thank you," said Lydia. "We're ready to jump right in. Tell us about GE Pharmaceuticals' story, from the beginning." She opened her laptop.

Thilda smiled. "Sebastian, have Ashley and Trinity signed their NDAs?"

Sebastian tapped his watch, then scrolled on the screen. "Yes," he said, pointing at the hologram of our signed NDAs that appeared. "Signed and filed!" Sebastian looked at Thilda, then me, then Lydia. "You're good."

"Excellent." Thilda smiled. "My father, Albert von Genzkensaffe, laid the foundation for GE Pharmaceuticals. He was no stranger to struggle. Orphaned as a child, he had nothing but his baby blanket, a few pictures of his mother, her chemistry journals, two vials of a pinkish powder, and a jewelry box. But that was just enough for him to pursue his dream. His dream was this lab, but he passed before we took off. He'd be proud of our progress."

Thilda placed her paperweight in her lap. *Eternae* was written in white letters right above the gold key, which had a little crown stamped at one end. She pointed at her gold-and-silver ring. The aquamarine stone sparkled in the sunlight. "This ring was in the box. So was this." She took out her pendant from under her jumpsuit.

The Grealmæp!

I blurted out, "Oh my gosh, that's beautiful!"

Lydia calmly leaned over, inspecting the Grealmæp. I marveled at how she held her composure without hinting that we had the other Grealmæp safely locked away in our cottage. "That's the insignia on the doors! Is that a ruby?"

"Yes." Thilda smiled, taking off her necklace and holding the Grealmæp in her hand. "This pendant is a family heirloom, passed down from my great-grandfather to his daughter, to my father, to me. Here, hold it."

I could imagine Lydia cringing inside at holding the Grealmæp without gloves. And I, now knowing how to properly care for artifacts, cringed too. But to Thilda, it was a family heirloom. And we couldn't blow our cover. I reached for the Grealmæp. It was the same as ours: the same Stonehenge pattern, the same double dagger marks on the ruby. The ruby was the same red as Thilda's Eternae paperweight.

"It's heavy!" I said, pretending I'd never held the Grealmæp.

"It's solid gold. And that's one of the purest rubies, if not the purest, in the world. Notice those double daggers on both sides?" She popped the ruby out and pointed to the daggers etched on one side and fashioned as a relief on the other.

I nodded. "What are they for?"

"They are the keys." Thilda grinned, her green eyes sparkling. "This is Eternae's story."

Thilda reached for the Grealmæp. I handed it back to her, and she put the necklace around her neck. I pulled out my journal and pen.

"The story of Eternae starts in World War II. My great-grandfather, KA von Genzkensaffe, was a brilliant chemist. Hitler himself tricked KA into joining the Nazis, luring him with the promise of riches and fame. Hitler gave him his own lab and stolen relics from the Nazis' raids."

Lydia and I nodded, listening carefully as we took notes. Thilda picked up her Eternae paperweight.

"Hitler believed KA could extract these relics' sacred essences and manufacture drugs with supernatural properties."

I twirled a loose curl, leaning forward in anticipation.

Thilda stroked the gold key with her index finger and continued. "Two of the relics Hitler gave KA were boxes. One had this pendant. The other was sealed, with the insignia of this pendant. KA discovered the ruby's double dagger relief was a key that unlocked the box. He was so proud, and loved the pendant's design, he adopted it as our family crest."

"That's interesting," I exclaimed. I thought it was disingenuous Thilda was proud that KA adopted a stolen relic's insignia as their family crest. The Grealmæp had nothing to do with Thilda or her family. It wasn't her family's to claim as theirs.

"If you think that's cool, wait until you hear what KA found in the box!" Thilda clutched her paperweight, her eyes gleaming. "KA found my ring, two vials of pink powder, and a book."

Lydia looked up from her laptop. "Amazing! Trinity, can't you see the party coming to life? Each guest could get a small box with Thilda's family crest on it, with vials of pink powder as party favors."

I nodded. As we party planned, I loved seeing a different side of Lydia—the side that Gran knew. This made me feel more connected to Gran and my family history.

Thilda grinned. "What a great idea! Sebastian, what do you think?"

"I think you need to tell them about the book and vials." Sebastian smiled, sipping his smoothie. "That will give them plenty of wonderful ideas."

"Of course!" Thilda's green eyes sparkled more as she leaned closer to Lydia and me. "The book had instructions for complex experiments, diagrams, and maps. It belonged to Morgan le Fay, one of the greatest healers in history."

"That's fascinating! And the vials?" Lydia asked.

"The vials contained the last remnants of the greatest medicine ever created: *Grealia*. This medicine holds the key to healing—and to eternal life."

My eyes widened at hearing Thilda mention *Grealia*.

"Eternal life?" Lydia asked.

I twirled a loose curl, waiting for Thilda to respond. No matter how eager I was to learn more, we couldn't blow our cover.

"Yes. According to the book, Morgan le Fay made *Grealia* by extracting Christ's DNA from the Holy Grail." She paused. "That's where Hitler got the idea to extract sacred essences from relics. He thought if it could be done for the Grail, it could be done for all relics. I don't know the truth to that, but I do know my great-grandfather tried to make *Grealia*, using a formula in Morgan's book. He couldn't do it, Felda couldn't do it, and my father couldn't do it. But where they failed, I will succeed."

I nodded, scribbling in my journal. "So, you have the last *Grealia* remnants?"

"Yes, what little remains. They are the von Genzkensaffe family secret. Fortunately, I'm steps away from making more!" Thilda grinned.

"How would that work?" I asked, careful not to seem like I knew too much.

"Based on Morgan's work, Christ's DNA is the limiting

reagent in making *Grealia.* I don't think KA realized this, but I did."

I remembered from Chemistry 101 that limiting reagents were the reactants that got consumed first, and therefore limited the amount of product created.

"How?" Lydia looked at Thilda quizzically.

Thilda smiled. "When I was little, I saw my mom reading a beautiful book. With its notations in beautiful characters, it looked like a spell book out of a fairy tale—and like KA's book, which was passed down to my grandmother, then to my dad, then to me. When I asked my mom about it, she told me not to concern myself with adult matters. That was when I knew I wanted to be a chemist. There was something in that book that enchanted her, and I had to know. She hid the book in her bedside table, making it impossible for me to take. Years passed, and I gave up on the book. I went to uni, becoming so absorbed in my lab work, I forgot about it. But one weekend, I came home for one of her dinner parties. Lo and behold, she and her guests were clustered around her spell book! I managed to sneak some pictures and showed them to my tutors. They helped me translate the writing, and that's when I learned about *Grealia* and the Grail. I realized I needed the Grail—and only a small amount of Christ's DNA—to make *Grealia.*"

"But won't Christ's DNA run out?" I asked. "Then you won't be able to make more *Grealia.*"

Thilda grinned. "I asked the same question—and I answered it. I developed a way to replicate and amplify DNA, using the tiniest DNA fragments." She gazed at the neon Eternae sign. "Eternal life, in pill form, is here—and here to stay. I've changed science and our species forever." She pursed her lips in a coy smile that said, *I've said enough.*

Shivers ran down my spine. I desperately wanted to ask Thilda if she had the Grail. As if Lydia read my mind, she elbowed me, signaling it wasn't the right time.

"Can't you manufacture synthetic *Grealia*?" Lydia asked.

"I wish," said Thilda. "We tried. But the science doesn't work out. It's tough to replicate Christ's DNA." She chuckled, pointing to Albert's quote. "'Those who never stop chasing the impossible are the ones who make it possible.' That's exactly what I've done. I've used the *Grealia* I inherited to make Eternae. But I didn't stop there. Knowledge begets knowledge. I've transformed Eternae from the world's only cure for cancer, to a cure for mortality itself. The next phase is global distribution of Eternae—and the unimaginable profits and recognition this brings." Thilda beamed, holding up her Eternae paperweight. "Our party will celebrate this milestone."

My eyes widened as I jotted down my notes. Sebastian smiled as he sipped his smoothie. He enjoyed listening to this story as much as Thilda enjoyed telling it.

"Fascinating, right?" Thilda asked. "And it's all real. At first, I thought eternal life was a crock of pseudoscience crap. I'm a chemist. I operate from observed, scientific, chemical, and physical changes. If it can't be seen, observed, touched, and measured, it isn't real."

Lydia nodded in agreement. I knew exactly what she was thinking. *Evidence, not emotion.*

"But after studying my tutors' translations of the spell book and notes in my great-grandfather's journals, I've realized KA's science proved 'the magic.'" Thilda's long red fingernails glistened as she made air quotes. "I started GE Pharmaceuticals to bring this science to the world. I built GE's facility by staying as lean and agile as possible and wasting nothing. And with the jobs I've created, we've boosted Somerset's economy tremendously."

Sebastian chuckled. "That's true. Our scientists do keep the pubs in business." He finished his smoothie as Thilda chuckled and continued.

"Our goal is global distribution of Eternae—a pill for each person on this planet. We will eradicate cancer. We will place eternal life in the palm of people's hands. We're redefining what it means to be human. Or, really, *reclaiming* what it means to be human."

"What do you mean?" I asked. "Reclaim what?"

Thilda took a deep breath, placing one hand on her pendant and picking up her paperweight with the other. "We were created to live forever—not to die. The Bible even says that God set eternity in our hearts. With Eternae, I restore our bodies to their original state: immortality. I usher in a new world order in which death has no victory." She looked at her paperweight. The red flecks of light scattered over her white office walls.

A new world order. Is Thilda a Knight of the Dagger?

I watched as Sebastian nodded, gazing at the red flecks. "Thilda's relentless pursuit of curing cancer resulted in the creation of a much more miraculous medicine. Eternae is the only way to live forever."

Thilda looked at Sebastian, blushing. "I can't help it. It's the scientist's bargain: we give up our soul, get knowledge in return. With that knowledge, it's our obligation to act—and act for the good of mankind." She put her paperweight on the coffee table. "I'll remind you this is absolutely confidential information, not to be shared with anyone—not even Frank and Chris."

Lydia and I nodded. Sebastian smiled.

"Absolutely confidential information," he repeated. "Thilda, what you've done is amazing. You've chased the impossible—and found it. And you've saved lives—my life at least. Your family would be so proud."

I stared at Sebastian. "What do you mean?" I asked.

Sebastian grinned. "Eternae cured my cancer. And from preliminary data, my biomarkers indicate my body is developing the properties associated with immortality."

I gasped, hardly believing what I'd heard. If what Sebastian said was true, he was a modern-day scientific marvel. I looked at Lydia, shaking my head. She nodded skeptically but curiously.

"I know that's a lot," said Sebastian. "And it's isolating to be the only person in the world who can say that. I'll never fully understand the science of Eternae, but it works on telomeres. They protect our chromosomes from damage. Thilda truly has revolutionized medicine—something is definitely working for me."

Thilda smiled at her paperweight. "The science is hard—if you're not an expert. Telomeres are involved in cellular division and aging. They hold the key to curing cancer, which is unregulated cellular replication, and eternal life, which is stopping the cells' aging process."

I learned about telomeres—the endcaps of our chromosomes—in high school biology. My teacher said they were for chromosomes what aglets were for shoelaces. That analogy always stuck with me.

"All this to say, this is Eternae's and GE's story. Our party will kick off Eternae's global launch," said Thilda. "And, of course, secure the next round of necessary funds to launch. A pill in the palm of—"

"Each person on this planet!" Sebastian finished.

"Got it!" Lydia said as she typed. "We'll plan the celebration of your dreams. When is your target date?"

"Yesterday," Thilda said without cracking a smile. Sebastian laughed, and Thilda glared at him. "But since that's not possible, we'll time it for after my big interview this summer, to use the interview as a teaser. So, say end of June?"

"Wonderful." Lydia closed her laptop. "Anything else, Trinity?"

"Yes, I had another question." I stared at the crimson neon sign, twirling a loose curl. "How exactly does Eternae interact with telomeres?"

"I'm so glad you asked." Thilda smiled. "Let's head to the lower level. I'll ask one of the researchers to tell you."

††

Swiping her badge, Thilda ushered us into the lower level. The smell of acetone flooded my nostrils. We walked to a small glass-walled office near a row of benches, under the balcony where we'd first seen the lab. A gold plaque on the door spelled DR. REBECCA CAROL DEBLACK in elegant script.

As Thilda knocked on the glass, a medium-built, middle-aged woman looked up from her desk. She squinted, then pulled her glasses down to her face. Grinning, she got up and opened the door.

"Thilda, lovely to see you!" Dr. DeBlack gave Thilda a hug.

"Dr. DeBlack, meet Ashlyn and Trinity. They are planning our party. They have great ideas and were asking about telomeres. Ashlyn and Trinity, Dr. DeBlack is the world's expert on telomeres. Her research is integral to Eternae."

Dr. DeBlack swept her long brown hair behind her shoulders. "Thilda, you're too kind. Ashlyn, Trinity, come in." She moved two boxes off the chairs by her desk. A pair of lab glasses fell out of one of the boxes. Lydia bent down to pick it up, but Sebastian rushed ahead of her and picked it up first. As he handed it to Dr. DeBlack, Lydia and Sebastian chuckled as they avoided a collision. I could have sworn Sebastian put his hand on Lydia's back as he guided her to her chair, pulling it out for her as she sat down.

"Thank you," said Lydia.

He pushed her chair in and stood behind us. "I'll stay with Ashlyn and Trinity, Thilda, if that's okay?"

"Yes. Take them around after they're done with Rebecca. Introduce them to some of the other researchers."

Sebastian nodded, thanking Thilda as she left. I watched her stilettos strike the floor. Everyone seemed to love her and her work—which was noble and for the good of mankind. *Was J. Carmichael wrong?* She seemed to be exactly who she told us she was: a chemist, bringing eternal life to the world.

"As Thilda said, I'm Dr. Rebecca Carol DeBlack. I'm one of the longest-tenured GE researchers," she said. "Thilda has treated me so well. I'm obsessed with telomeres and telomerase, the enzyme that makes them, and I'm thankful I can chase my dreams here." She walked behind her desk and sat down. She picked up a squishy toy that looked like two cheese puffs in the shape of an *X*. The four ends had white caps on them. "This is a model of a chromosome," she said. "These white caps are telomeres. Telomeres protect our chromosomes, which contain our DNA, from damage." She tapped each white cap. "In normal eukaryotic cells, telomeres shorten with every round of cellular division—an evolutionary adaptation to limit cells' lifespans. You can tell a cell's age from its telomere's length."

I looked at the model, fascinated by what Dr. DeBlack was sharing. "They're like caps on the ends of the shoelace, right?"

"Exactly!" She smiled. "Someone knows her biology."

Proud a respected scientist complimented me, I grinned as I opened my satchel. I took out my journal and pencil and started doodling the model on the page.

"My dissertation was on how cellular conditions trigger telomerase to act—or not to act. I wanted to know: can we determine how to turn telomerase on or off? I've worked for some of the biggest biotech companies in the world, and when Thilda recruited me, of course I said yes."

Lydia nodded. "That's fascinating! Cookies in the shape of chromosomes, here we come!" She chuckled, explaining to Dr. DeBlack that it was one of our dessert ideas for the party. "You can help us design the cookies so they're scientifically accurate!"

Sebastian smiled at Lydia. "I love how you're weaving science and story together to plan the party."

"Thank you," Lydia said. "It's my life's work!"

Dr. DeBlack beamed as she held the chromosome model and continued. "The ability to turn telomerase on or off gives us the ability to control cell aging. If telomerase is always on, telomeres are always produced, the telomere doesn't shorten, the cell doesn't age. Because telomerase elongates the telomere by adding nucleotides—the TTAGGG sequence—to the telomere, if telomerase were always active, cells with damaged DNA could keep replicating, resulting in cancer. For good reason, telomerase is one of our most highly regulated enzymes."

I wrote down *TTAGGG: the nucleotide sequence for telomeres* and *telomerase: the most highly regulated enzyme.*

Dr. DeBlack continued. "Telomerase is found in high concentrations in cells that need to keep dividing, for example, in embryonic stem cells. These cells are three to five days old and are pluripotent, meaning they can divide into more stem cells, or become any type of cell."

"So, to study telomerase, you need embryonic stem cells?" I asked.

"Yes. You need embryos. Or cancer cells. Telomerase is active in over ninety percent of cancers. Tumors use telomerase to become immortal." She pointed to a stack of textbooks on her desk. "Tumors keep growing—dividing uncontrollably, spreading, metastasizing. Their mechanism for senescence, or cell aging and deterioration, is damaged."

"So, cancer cells don't age like a normal cell does, and keep dividing, like a normal cell doesn't?" I asked.

"Correct." Dr. DeBlack nodded, grinning as she looked at her chromosome model. "Telomerase is intriguing. It's the immortality enzyme. It's related to longevity—and cancer. Its discovery won the 2009 Nobel Prize in Physiology or Medicine, and that was just the beginning. We still have so much to learn!"

Fascinated by telomeres, I finished scribbling my notes. I gazed at the lab's lower level. The glow from *infinitely encoded; forever expressed* tinted the lab a soft crimson red. Researchers clustered around their benches, discussing their experiments. A few techs pushed carts with beakers and flasks in organized rows. As I watched them march by on their mission to get from one part of the lab to another, I thought about my dad. GE tried to measure his cancer. It had metastasized. It had very distinctive biomarkers; Eternae hadn't worked for him.

"Dr. DeBlack, may I ask a question?"

"You just did." She grinned. "But you can ask another."

I chuckled at her sense of humor. "How exactly does Eternae act on telomerase?"

Dr. DeBlack smiled. "A fabulous question. It detects and regulates hTERT with the highest degree of accuracy I have ever seen. hTERT, or human-telomerase reverse transcriptase, is a gene that directly correlates with telomerase activity and is crucial to cellular immortalization. Because of its stereochemistry and composition, Eternae not only helps us detect telomerase before it is made, but also enables us to regulate, terminate, or amplify this process."

I stared at Dr. DeBlack. "You've lost me completely."

She swiveled her chair and looked at *infinitely encoded; forever expressed*. After a few moments, she turned to us.

"Think of it this way. Say you and Ashlyn are in the car, blasting the radio. Eternae is to telomerase what you and your volume knob are to how loud the music is. So, say that knob could 'know' or 'sense' when Ashlyn wants to talk, so it automatically turns the volume down to the right level—and right level, personalized for you—before Ashlyn starts talking. And when Ashlyn is about to stop talking, the knob would know, and turn the music back up to your preferred volume. Eternae works like that, but for telomerase, enabling us to start, stop, or amplify telomerase production autonomously."

I nodded, jotting down Dr. DeBlack's analogy as I started to understand Eternae as a breakthrough in medical research.

Lydia looked at Dr. DeBlack. "So, GE would work with cancer patients to determine the correct Eternae dosage, which would autonomously detect telomerase and regulate its production for each patient. Eternae would 'know' not to just 'turn down,' but 'turn off' telomerase production to eliminate—or prevent—cancer."

"Correct!" Dr. DeBlack exclaimed.

"And if individuals don't have cancer, they could still take Eternae preventatively to pre-regulate telomerase, so they never get cancer," I added.

"You got it! For non-cancer patients, Eternae calculates the 'just right' telomerase level to keep senescence in balance. And in both cases, Eternae triggers immortality."

I shook my head in awe. I still didn't know exactly how the drug worked, but I was closer to understanding Eternae's mysteries. Beaming, Dr. DeBlack stood up and walked around her desk to us and Sebastian. "It's very complicated science, and Thilda is a genius for creating a viable, artificially intelligent drug. Eternae will change the world, right Sebastian?"

Sebastian nodded, gazing at *infinitely encoded; forever expressed* as it spiraled in the light well.

XIV

Our conversation with Dr. DeBlack yielded many answers. It also raised more questions. What had happened at GE Pharmaceuticals since my dad was in the trial? What other experiments were Thilda's researchers running?

As Sebastian led us out of Dr. DeBlack's office, he made it a point to hold the door for Lydia. "What did you think of that? Isn't your brain buzzing with ideas for the party?"

Lydia smiled. "It is," she said. "We theme the party around the story of GE. The whole party could be an interactive display of Eternae. We'd share the stories of Thilda's family, taking guests on a journey from past to present to future. We end in the lab's lower level, which will be decked out as a dance floor. Thilda will announce that Eternae, the miracle drug, is available for global distribution. Under the glow of *infinitely encoded; forever expressed*, all will revel in the future Eternae brings!"

"I love it!" Sebastian smiled at Lydia. "And talking with some other researchers, including Charles Julian and Freemont Derby, will inspire you even more."

As we walked past the benches, I saw a young woman squatting in front of a wall, surrounded by cases of paintbrushes and paint. She wore a long-sleeve black shirt and white overalls smeared with vibrant smudges. She'd pulled her long brown hair back in a ponytail.

"That's gotta be Elle!" I said to Sebastian as we walked past her.

"Yes! She's working on a new mural. I'm not quite sure what it is. Let's ask her."

As we approached, Sebastian double tapped his watch. Looking at her watch, Elle turned around and took her earbuds out.

"Hi, Sebastian! How are you?" She looked at us, smiling. "Who are your friends?"

Sebastian chuckled. "Elle, meet Ashlyn and Trinity. They're our party planners!"

"How exciting!" Elle said. "I'd shake your hands, but I have too much paint on mine." She chuckled, holding up the brushes in her right hand. A tattoo of Leonardo da Vinci's *Vitruvian Man* covered the back of her right hand.

"It's very nice to meet you, Elle," I said. "I love *infinitely encoded; forever expressed*. How'd you make it?"

"The short answer is it came to me as Thilda and I discussed her vision for GE and Eternae. It's bold, beautiful, and daring! And it's simple. Simplicity is the ultimate sophistication, after all." Elle smiled. "Or so Leonardo said."

Lydia nodded. "There's something about it that is so raw and real—and alive. The red isn't angry or hostile—it's warm, like it provides life in the light of its glow."

"Thank you," said Elle. "It's an expression of our desire to live our purpose and chase our dreams, while being authentic to who we are. Our DNA expresses our identity long before we discover who we were created to be. It's my favorite name for a piece—it's the code to everything. I like creating art that doesn't mirror reality but enhances it—art that prompts us to pursue the impossible."

I could see why Thilda liked Elle. Both were driven by chasing the impossible and translating it into everyday experiences. Thilda's medium was science; Elle's was art.

Elle smiled. "I need to get back to the mural. It was great meeting you, Ashlyn and Trinity. See you around." She waved her left hand at us. Her left ring finger had a tattoo of a paintbrush.

<hr>

"If you need anything, let me know. I'm here every day."

"Married to art?" I pointed at her finger as I grinned.

"You could say that, yes. Art certainly has my heart." She grinned, lowering her hand to grab her brush. Her wrist had a tattoo of an artist's palette. It also had another, more familiar tattoo. My eyes widened as I raised my hand to hide my gasp. Elle was a Knight of the Dagger!

††

Charles Julian and Freemont Derby weren't at their bench. Sebastian promised we'd meet them later, which was fine with Lydia and me. We wanted to get back to our office and to Kenneth and Blane. Sebastian led us to the elevator. "Great spending the morning with you." He waved goodbye. "I'm here if you need anything. Enjoy your day!"

We badged in, walking into the elevator as its doors opened. "Third floor, please," Lydia said.

"You're so polite," I said. "It's not a person."

Lydia chuckled as the elevator doors closed. "Maybe not, but it did listen to me on the first try!"

After our short elevator ride, we walked down the hallway to our office. Blane waved through the glass window and got up to open the door for us. As Lydia closed the door behind us, I hugged Blane and high-fived Kenneth.

"How's the office?" I asked, putting my satchel on the table next to Blane's laptop.

"It's great. Very quiet," said Kenneth. "And most importantly, it's not bugged."

"Yeah," said Blane. "We spent most of the morning checking the walls, table, and chairs. I wouldn't put it past Thilda to bug every room in this place."

"Smart." Lydia plopped her satchel on a chair and slid her laptop out. "She's a genius who thinks of everything."

"What else have you been up to?" I asked Blane as I sat next to him.

"I'm proud to report I'm not slacking on my Nassauton work. I completed two problem sets today. I'm still in good standing!"

I beamed at Blane. "You're managing this remote learning thing so well!"

Blane grinned, putting his arm around my shoulder. "Thank you. That means a lot." He looked at Kenneth. "Kenneth has been helping me."

Kenneth smiled. "My pleasure. I love working with dedicated students, even if it means dusting out the part of my brain that knows economics."

Blane and Kenneth chuckled. "Really couldn't do it without you, Kenneth. Thank you, man."

Kenneth nodded, turning to Lydia and looking up from his laptop. "Lydia," Kenneth began, "apparently the department is a mess. Pritzmord told them he quit. They're struggling to find a new dean. But we're not there, so not much we can do." He paused. "And honestly, I'm okay with that." He grinned, closing his laptop and standing up. "But it's a mess without you."

Lydia shook her head. "I'm sure Pritzmord omitted a few small details about why he quit," she said. "I'm sorry to hear about the department. But I have new priorities now."

"Speaking of, how was your morning?" Kenneth paced around our office in excitement. "And after you share, Blane and I have information too!"

We told Kenneth and Blane what we learned about Dr. DeBlack's research and Thilda's Eternae story. We also told them about Thilda's plan to amplify Christ's DNA, so she could have an unlimited supply of *Grealia*.

"She's got to have the Grail behind that door." I speculated.

"Only one way to prove it!" Lydia reminded me as she mouthed, "Evidence, not emotion." She added, "And that way might be closer than we think, given that Elle, Thilda's artist-in-residence, is a Knight of the Dagger." Lydia smiled at me as if to say, *I noticed her double daggers tattoo too.*

"Kenneth, can we talk to her if I'm not a knight and you haven't completed Intake?" I asked, looking at my sentinel.

"We can't. Rules are rules. If we break them, there will be consequences."

"Wait," I blurted out. "Can we ask KDI if Elle is the insider ally? There might be rules prohibiting us from talking to her, but what about rules on her talking to us?"

"Now that's out-of-the-box thinking!" Kenneth smiled. "I'll ask my sponsor."

"Now," said Blane, "wait till you hear what we learned."

"I'm all ears." I took out my journal and pen.

Blane's eyes gleamed. "So, you know Sebastian Waugh . . ."

I nodded. "Yes. He must be Thilda's personal assistant. He's always around her." I pictured Sebastian holding his smoothie glass and sharing about his biomarkers and immortality. *He looked old and young at the same time. His hands, though well-manicured, looked weathered. But his face looked oddly boyish.*

"Yes, and he's the guy J. Carmichael talked to when he was here."

I nodded again.

"Kenneth asked KDI to get some intel on him. You'll never guess what they found." Blane looked at me, then at Lydia. "Sebastian Waugh was an industrial materials manufacturer. He came to GE Pharmaceuticals a few years ago, from London. He'd developed a rare, terminal cancer from working in the factory. No doctor could cure him. He had two months to live. Desperate, he asked a friend of a friend, who referred him to Thilda. He arrived here and received an experimental treatment, which didn't just cure his cancer . . ." Blane paused for effect and took a deep breath. "It also slowed his cellular aging process. According to KDI's insider ally, Sebastian's smoothie contains the medicine that makes this possible."

††

By the end of the day, Lydia and I finished our proposal for Thilda's party. From Legend to Launch: A History of Eternae would be in the farmhouse and lab, with food and drinks themed around immortality and curing cancer. The party would culminate in the lab, with Thilda giving an inspirational speech and guests dancing into the night.

To honor Eternae's Morgan-and-Grail-inspired legends and lore, we thought the party would best take place on the summer solstice. That gave us two months. As soon as Thilda approved, we'd send the save-the-dates and start preparing. Kenneth and Blane would use the two months to befriend GE's researchers. Phrasing it as research for From Legend to Launch, they would interview GE staff for details on their contributions to Eternae—and learn more about Sebastian, his smoothies, and what Thilda was hiding.

As we packed up, Blane asked what we wanted to do for dinner.

"Pub? Or *chez nous*?" asked Lydia, locking our office door.

Blane snorted in laughter. "*Chez nous* makes our kitchen sound like a fancy French restaurant. But my vote is to cook in. We can unwind or keep brainstorming. Plus, I'll be taking Carly out for her birthday, and I want our first meal out in Somerset to be her birthday dinner." He winked at me.

"I like that," I said. "I'm in!" I grabbed Blane's hand as we headed to the elevator.

"*Chez nous* it is." Lydia smiled.

"First floor, please," said Kenneth as the elevator doors closed.

"How did Thilda program the elevator to recognize our voices?" Blane asked.

"Don't know," said Lydia. "That's too techy for me. It must be magic."

I grinned, surprised to hear Lydia—a lady of logic and evidence—compare technology to magic. The elevator doors opened on the first floor. As I stepped out, I realized I had to use the bathroom.

"Go ahead." I handed Blane my satchel. "I'll meet you at the car."

I walked down the hallway, past a few empty offices. As I opened the door, I heard Thilda's voice inside one of the closed stalls at the far end of the bathroom. With my heart pounding, I darted into the stall closest to me and locked the door.

"Daniel, I hired you to get it for me . . . I need to open that box."

Her toilet flushed.

"Damn automatic flush. The sensor is too sensitive, say that again Daniel . . . Right. It's the final step . . . Both rubies! Time is running out. My vials are almost empty! I cannot afford to delay global distribution. And the bills are piling up! I need to get home—it's late."

Her toilet flushed again. Praying I wouldn't set off my toilet's flush sensor, I pressed myself against the stall's corner so Thilda wouldn't see my boots.

Her door slammed shut. I shifted my weight, pressing myself farther away from the door.

My toilet flushed.

Trembling, I grimaced in fear.

If she investigated the flush, it was over.

She strode to the sink. "Again? That damn flush! I'll tell Pippa to fix it," Thilda muttered as she started to wash her hands.

I closed my eyes, holding my breath.

My temples throbbed as my pulse surged.

Her stilettos echoed as she left the bathroom.

The door closed behind her.

I gasped for air, taking deep breaths in relief. I opened my eyes and took a few steps forward to use the bathroom. Thilda needed the second Grealmæp so she could open a box with two rubies for keys. I knew only one Daniel who was collaborating with GE Pharmaceuticals. *Am I really prepared to face Thilda—the visionary CEO, Dr. Pritzmord—the deceitful killer, and Dr. Gellmane—J. Carmichael's heartless murderer?*

My Ailm charm gleamed in the bathroom light as I walked to the sink and washed my hands. *Be brave.*

XV

The Fearless Foursome spent most of the next week in our office. Thilda loved the "From Legend to Launch" theme. She greenlighted our proposal and summer solstice date, saying it was perfect given *Grealia*'s and Eternae's history. Lydia and I wasted no time in approving the save-the-dates, coordinating with the caterers, and designing the decorations.

After befriending most of the researchers, including Charles and Freemont, Blane and Kenneth hadn't found anything unusual. Charles' and Freemont's work focused on p53, a tumor-suppression gene that also activated DNA repair, stopped cell growth, and initiated apoptosis. Since learning that word, Blane said it every chance he got.

"It means 'programmed cell death,'" he explained, diagramming apoptosis pathways on a piece of paper. We'd wrapped up our on-site work and relocated to our cottage.

"Charles and Freemont love talking with Kenneth and me. They keep asking to read our *C. elegans* research." Blane grinned as he plopped himself on our living room couch. "We keep telling them we'll share our papers—once they're published!" He started cracking up. "That's when we beg KDI to write some papers on nematodes and cancer!"

Kenneth chuckled. "And KDI will do it while you and I conquer pub trivia!"

"Oh yeah," said Blane. "Charles and Freemont invited us to The Far Canal."

"That's awesome! You should go!" I smiled. "You'll be amazing at it!"

"We're definitely going." Blane smiled. "I'm brushing up on my useless trivia knowledge. Want to know the best part?"

"What's that?" I put my arm around Blane's shoulder.

"It doesn't conflict with my birthday dinner date with the most intelligent, beautiful girl in the world!" He kissed my hand. "Willest thouest acceptest the dinner date invitation, my fairest lady?" Blane said theatrically, pretending to be a knight speaking in made-up Arthurian English.

"The lady doth already acceptest the invitation and wouldest be delighted to acceptest her knight's invitation—again!" I giggled, gazing into Blane's eyes. "The lady can't wait."

"What else have you learned from Charles and Freemont?" Lydia asked.

"Thilda hired them to study p53's role in senescence and shortened telomeres."

"Senescence. I've heard that before." I started flipping through my journal.

"Dr. DeBlack," said Lydia. "It means cell aging, deterioration . . ."

"How'd you remember?" I was impressed by Lydia's memory.

"It comes from the Latin word *senex,* which means 'an old man.'" Lydia smiled. "Guess knowing Latin finally came in handy for something other than Roman art."

I chuckled. I liked how Lydia made jokes about herself. She was one of the most intelligent people I'd met, but she didn't take herself too seriously.

The doorbell interrupted our conversation. Kenneth answered, returning a few moments later with a big box. "Carly, it's got your name on it, and says 'Happy Birthday.'"

I grinned as I opened the box. My mom sent me two pairs of Gran's heels and her gladiator sandals.

"Nice! I know what shoes I'm wearing for date night." I grinned at Blane.

He smiled back at me. "Don't forget the card and your other box."

As I read the card, I teared up. My mom always wrote something funny or sweet, but on my nineteenth birthday, she wrote something a little different. *You're growing up to be the young lady Gran and Dad would have wanted you to be. I am so proud of you! Happy birthday sweetheart, be safe!*

I held the card, taking a deep breath before opening the other box. I knew Gran's necklace—a genuine family heirloom—was in it. I gasped as I opened the small, black velvet box. Gran's necklace was a gold chain with two pendants: one was a pale, sea-foam green stone. The other, a gold cross hammered onto a silver disc.

"It's the Ailm!" I blurted out, removing the necklace from the box.

"Cool!" Blane smiled. "Need help putting it on?"

"Please!" I got up and handed him my necklace. He slipped it over my neck and clasped it shut.

Lydia gasped. "That's the necklace Lyle wore the day I met her!"

Blane beamed at me. "Those colors really pick up the green in your eyes."

"You look like Lyle, wearing that necklace, Carly. It suits you so well."

I grinned, my chest swelling with pride as I held my pendants. They felt smooth and sturdy. As I stared more closely at the pendants, I got goose bumps. I'd seen that exact necklace before. I grabbed my phone and scrolled to the picture I'd taken of Morgan le Fay's crest at The Courtly Robin. *Is my necklace the same as the gryphon's?*

†††

For my birthday, Blane made reservations at Razz, one of Somerset's fanciest restaurants. It was part of a restored old hotel.

"One day, we'll have a weekend getaway to the hotel, for just us." Blane winked at me as our cab made its way through country roads into the city center. "Someday when we have money and aren't college kids trying to find the Grail—and uncovering a lab's hidden secrets. I promise you, Carly, I'll make it happen. Someday."

"I'd love that. Just the two of us. Someday." I sighed. I liked imagining that day, no matter how far away it seemed.

As our cab pulled into town, I clutched Gran's necklace. *How did Morgan le Fay's necklace become a family heirloom?* I wished Gran was still with me. Sometimes, all I wanted was to ask her for the answers. Our cab stopped in front of Razz. Blane walked around and opened the door for me. I blushed as he helped me get out.

"Why thank you, handsome knight." I winked at him, tilting my head up to look him in the eyes. I clutched his arm, steadying myself on the cobblestone sidewalk. I was used to walking in my boots but opted for heels to go with my strapless little black dress from Act II. Gran's hot-pink heels added the perfect pop of color to my dress, and I wore my hair down in big, wavy curls. I wasn't wearing any eye shadow.

"Of course, my lady," said Blane. He was wearing a black suit with a white shirt—and a hot-pink bow tie. When he learned that I'd be wearing hot-pink heels, he'd asked Kenneth to go shopping with him so he could find a matching tie.

Blane—my lanky, tall, and goofy boyfriend—looked so handsome in his suit. Every time I told him that, he blushed, and his hazel eyes sparkled even more. We'd held hands the entire drive, playing with each other's fingers. I still got nervous around him. It was a different type of nervousness than having a crush. It was more the type of nervousness that made me think I could spend the rest of my life with him—and our lives would be an intellectually stimulating adventure. I didn't have a name for that feeling, but it felt comforting and reassuring. In Blane, I'd found someone who appreciated me for exactly who I was—and someone who wanted to go on adventures with me no matter what.

"Shall we?" He smiled as we walked into Razz.

The restaurant was trendy, rustic, and chic. Its low lights, green and white leather couches, and blue suede booths complemented the wooden tables and bar. A wrought-iron and wood case with potted plants and little trinkets divided the front and back of the room.

"Good evening, how can I help?" the maître d' asked, smiling.

"Reservations for Henley." Blane squeezed my hand.

"Right this way." The maître d' grabbed two menus and walked us to a back booth. A pink candle flickered in a wrought-iron sconce on the wall, bathing the booth in a soft glow. The iron reminded me of GE Pharmaceuticals' wrought-iron gate and doors. Our table's centerpiece was a bouquet of red roses in a glass vase, with a card propped up against the vase and a champagne glass on either side.

"Your waiter will be with you shortly. Enjoy your meal and happy birthday!" The maître d' smiled as he headed back to his station.

I blushed as Blane clasped my hands.

"Surprised?" he asked.

"Mmhmm," I murmured, closing my eyes and kissing him on his lips.

I opened my eyes and looked at the table. "Pink champagne?" I blurted out, overwhelmed by Blane's effort to make my birthday dinner special.

"Not quite," he said. "Read the card."

———•———

I picked up the card, carefully opening the envelope and reading the handwritten message inside:

A drink for the girl
Chasing the Grail
With evidence and a leap of faith
She's not one to fail
Sparkling water—like her eyes, sparkling green
Hers are the kindest eyes I've ever seen
Cranberry juice—red, like the Grealmæp's ruby
Words could never express what she means to me
So let's toast to her birthday with "The Carly"

Elated and astounded that Blane named a drink after me, I threw my arms around him. He wrapped his arms around my waist and pulled me close, whispering, "Happy birthday, Carly Stuart. I love you so much."

"I love you!" I grinned as we grabbed our glasses and clinked them together. "Two knights, together on our quest."

We sipped our drinks, then slid into our booth.

"You got that one right!" Blane said.

The roses smelled fresh, like they had been cut only a few hours ago. I closed my eyes and inhaled their scent.

"You're so thoughtful," I said. "How did you find this place?"

"I read and I know things," Blane quipped. He smiled, reaching across the table and interlacing his fingers with mine. "Gosh, you're beautiful. That necklace really makes your eyes the most perfect shade of green. Who needs eye shadow when you have that stone?"

I sighed, remembering Lara and my makeup tutorials. I hadn't texted Lara in weeks, if not months. *How is she? Does she still consider me her friend?*

"There's something about that aquamarine color that does

something magical to your eyes. Like that necklace was made for you." Blane cocked his head and gazed at me.

"What?" I blushed.

He grinned—his big, goofy, grin.

"*What*? Silly! What's on your mind?"

"You are. How did I ever get so lucky as to get you to be my girlfriend?"

I blushed harder. "You were yourself. That was enough. More than enough." I touched my pendants. "Whatever this necklace is doing to me, it must be something special. It's been in Gran's family for ages," I said. "So, who knows, maybe it *was* made for me? Maybe it was made for me to wear in this moment, in this restaurant, with the guy of my dreams sitting across from me."

Blane and I were well past saying "I love you." Every action showed our affection for each other. The effort he put into our relationship made me feel special. I tried hard to reciprocate but always wondered if I was doing enough to show him how much I loved him.

We'd been with Lydia and Kenneth since March, living out of shared cottages and having little, if any, time to ourselves. The one night we were alone, Dr. Pritzmord and Dr. Gellmane broke into our cottage. I could tell that wore on Blane. It also wore on me. The thought of having a weekend getaway—just him and me in a cute, quaint, charming English hotel—excited me all evening.

As I looked at Blane, I started imagining taking off his suit—first his blazer, then his bow tie, then his shirt . . . Gazing at him in the candlelight electrified my entire body, leaving me craving something I'd never done before . . . *What would that feel like with Blane?*

"What will it be for dinner?" Our server's voice interrupted my thoughts.

I gazed at my menu.

"Let's get the soup, and do you want to share a few things?" I asked Blane.

"Sounds great! How about we share the Mediterranean vegetable salad bowl and a grilled salmon fillet?" Blane pointed at my menu. "I don't think the fillet has any dairy in it."

I looked at the description. "Looks delicious and dairy free!"

We placed our order and kept talking.

"We have to leave room for dessert," Blane said. "They have a rhubarb pie that has homemade granola and ginger. The reviews said it's delectable."

"Mmm," I murmured, gazing into Blane's eyes. The candlelight made the hazel in his eyes sparkle.

"How is everything going with Nassauton? I'm in awe of how you balance your Nassauton work and our case."

"You're in awe of *me*? Why? I'm doing my homework, like I would be if I was on campus." Blane finished his soup. "That minestrone was so flavorful!"

"But you're halfway around the world, doing your schoolwork—and researching GE's secrets! How do you do both at the same time? That's amazing!"

I was in awe of Blane's accomplishments during the semester, but I simultaneously felt defeated. There was no way I could have handled Nassauton and our quest, and I'd made my choice—I'd dropped out. A wave of despair washed through my stomach as I remembered my doubt when I saw my reflection in the mirror of Thilda's bathroom.

Blane smiled. "I guess it's one of my superpowers. Although . . ." His voice trailed off as he took a deep breath and looked at the candle.

"Although what?"

"I have to go back for exams in May. Nassauton is adamant I can't take them remotely."

"Oh." I looked into Blane's eyes. "When do you leave?"

"In two weeks, for a week. I've arranged to take all my exams in one week so I can come back here." Blane grinned. "Luckily, my adviser is super chill and understanding—and is one of my biggest advocates."

———— · ————

I chuckled. I knew Kenneth's help was invaluable to Blane. The two worked well together, like Lydia and me. "You're so smart, and you plan everything so well. How'd you swing that?" I reached for his hand.

"I asked. I told them I had some stuff going on and needed their support. Usually if a student has straight A's and is in good standing, they'll listen—if the student's adviser is onboard. I'll study as best I can over the next two weeks. I'll go. I'll be back before you know it."

I smiled, proud Blane had a clear path forward—and was confident in it. He was on track to finish his freshman year. Where was my clear path? Lydia was planning most of From Legend to Launch, coordinating with Pippa for catering and creating the social media campaigns. I'd worked with Elle on the save-the-dates—but she'd done most of the creative work of designing them. My biggest task for next week was mailing the invitations. What would the gargoyle with the mortarboard at Winnie B.'s think about me—a dropout with no academic accomplishments? I was so lost in my thoughts, I barely picked at our grilled salmon and salad bowl when they arrived.

Did I make the wrong decision in dropping out? Thilda didn't seem devious—just very driven. She'd introduced us to researchers and set us up with our own office. So what if she wanted our Grealmæp and hired Dr. Gellmane and Dr. Pritzmord? She probably didn't know they were murderers—why would they tell her that? She wasn't doing anything illegal. Without any concrete evidence, we didn't have a case against her. I sighed and shook my head.

"Carly?" Blane's voice brought me back to our booth. "What's going on in your big brain? It's like you're not even here." Blane sliced a piece of salmon.

I sighed again. "How do we know Thilda is even doing anything illegal? She wants our Grealmæp's ruby. We might not like that, but that's not illegal." I ate a forkful of salmon and sipped some water. "Maybe there's nothing behind the locked door. Maybe whatever J. Carmichael suspected when he visited got cleared up. Maybe I've blown a whole semester because J. Carmichael never resolved *his* case. And now *I* have to take summer classes since I pursued my emotions. I stupidly took a leap of faith. Now I've fallen. I have no friends at Nassauton. I haven't texted Lara. I've barely spoken to my mom."

"Don't say that. You didn't stupidly pursue your emotions." Blane put his silverware down. "Your leap of faith led you to pursue evidence. You have the journals. You haven't fallen. You're just on a path with many steps—and you've only taken the first ones. You know Thilda has the other Grealmæp. That's one step. You learned Elle is a Knight of the Dagger. That's another. Why would she be here if KDI wasn't monitoring GE? Think about it. Isn't her presence evidence enough? And what about Sebastian? That's another step. Doesn't his story make you want to dig a little deeper?"

I nodded, wanting to believe Blane, but finding it hard to. "There's nothing illegal about his story. Miraculous, sure—but not illegal. He came here, he got cured. He drinks some smoothies to keep him alive."

"But don't you want to learn more about him and Eternae?"

"I want to find the Grail. Even if Thilda has it, how am I going to get it undetected? She has more security in her lab than Alcatraz." I shook my head. "I'm being honest with myself."

Blane reached for my hand. "I know you're anxious since nothing concrete has turned up yet. But Kenneth and I have pub trivia with the researchers. And Lydia and you have your party. Something will turn up. We'll find a clear path to get the Grail, even if we have to make one."

I gazed at Blane and squeezed his hand.

"I guess you're right." Sighing, I took another bite of salmon. It melted in my mouth.

"No, come on, fellow knight! Guessing is not good enough!" Blane stabbed into the salmon and cut a big piece. "Come on, get the fighter spirit back, like your knight, stabbing the salmon and vanquishing it as a foe." He waved the piece of salmon in the air. I burst out laughing. Blane's goofiness always made me feel better.

"You're right. My brain knows you're right. I need to feel it in my heart."

"Well maybe splitting that rhubarb pie with your knight will help." Blane smiled. "You got this. I know you do."

I grasped Blane's hand. He squeezed it back. No matter the standstills or complexities of our quest, I had a teammate who was always my cheerleader.

XVI

Charles and Freemont knocked on our office door.

"Innit the best day of the week?" said Charles, throwing his hands in the air in celebration as he walked in.

"Can I hear you say, 'Thank God it's Friday!'" Freemont grinned as he followed Charles.

"You know it!" Kenneth smiled as he packed up his laptop. "Chris and I are ready. We've been working hard on our research. Those nematodes keep us on our toes!"

I could tell Kenneth was an academic at heart. He loved being around researchers and was at ease in their presence.

"You mean on our—wait for it—*todes*!" Blane added.

Charles, Freemont, and Kenneth simultaneously groaned. I chuckled.

"Time to head to The Far Canal!" Charles couldn't contain his excitement. "Trivia awaits!"

"The Nerdy Nerds are waiting too!" added Freemont.

"The Nerdy Nerds?" asked Lydia, peering up from her laptop as she typed an email. "You have a team name?"

"Of course," said Charles. "Come on, they're all in the van. Can't keep the Nerds waiting!"

"Have fun!" I called to Kenneth and Blane as they headed down the hallway with Charles and Freemont. "They've been so excited about this all week," I said, turning to Lydia as she finished her email. "I hope The Nerdy Nerds win."

I picked up my journal and pored over my notes. I'd hardly

skimmed a few pages when Elle knocked on our door. Her hair was pulled back in two braided pigtails. Her pockets were full of pens and brushes, and new paint smudges covered her white overalls. Her badge was clipped to her sweater, which she'd draped over her arm.

"Hi, Elle! You're here late for a Friday," I said, closing my journal and motioning for her to come in.

"Testing colors." She smiled, pointing at some of the patches on her pants. "You and Ashlyn too. How's party planning?" Elle closed the door and sat across from Lydia. She put her sweater on the table.

"It's going well!" Lydia smiled. "Pippa's been so helpful. Six weeks out and we're in good shape."

"Pippa. She's a saint." Elle smiled. "I don't know how she manages Thilda."

"What do you mean?" I asked.

"Well, Thilda—she's so . . . oh, I shouldn't be talking about my boss like this."

"It's okay, secret's safe with me." I smiled. So did Lydia.

"I mean Thilda—she's just so uptight. Some call it drive. Some call it insanity. Others call it being a psychopath. She's very intense. She's always ten steps ahead. She never lets her guard down and is obsessed with security. She achieves incredible goals, but she scares people. Rumor has it she's so laser-focused on seeing her results, she never blinks."

"Yeah, I kinda picked up on that. But you need a person like her to chase the impossible, don't you?" I asked.

"Yes, but at what cost? No matter how poised she looks, she's always paranoid." Elle traced her double dagger marks with her pointer finger. She looked around our office. "We need to talk. Fancy walking out with me?"

"Sounds good," said Lydia as she started packing up. We locked our office and headed to the elevator. The lower level was a silent, empty nest: no researchers, no technicians, no people. The benches were vacant, the carts parked neatly on one side of the lab, the pods unoccupied.

As soon as we exited, Lydia and I took our lanyards off.

"Won't be needing these till Monday," I said, placing my lanyard in my satchel. We'd parked near the entrance, so Lydia suggested leaving our bags and laptops in the car as we walked. Elle left her sweater in our car, too, given the warmth of the Somerset evening. As we approached the flower bed, Elle looked around. No one was near us.

"Right, don't share this with anyone," said Elle, pointing at her double dagger marks. "I've been given special permission to talk to you. If Thilda finds out, I could lose my job—or worse."

I looked at Elle and Lydia, my eyes wide with fear. "I understand."

"I think Thilda is hiding something. Something major. Her office is always locked. Pippa and Sebastian are the only ones with the clearance to get in."

I nodded, staring at the flowers and their otherworldly, vibrant brilliance.

"It wasn't always like this. Before Eternae's first human trial, it was different. Transparent communication. No badges. More relaxed culture." Elle paced around the flower bed, stepping over the hose and shovels. "Now, she has all these rules—down to when and with whom we can eat. She said discipline helps us focus on the vision. And if you're not in her inner circle, it's like you don't even exist. She ignores everyone except Pippa, Dr. DeBlack, Charles, and me. She likes me, for some reason. Poor Sebastian just follows her around."

"Tell me more about the trial," I asked, my pulse racing. I was sentences away from learning more about my dad. I wished I had my journal.

"She recruited twenty participants from around the world afflicted by the rarest, most aggressive cancers."

"Yes?" I blurted. My heart pounded, beating faster and faster. "Then what?"

"Thilda's mice trials finished. Eternae worked very well. It was a miracle. The cancer disappeared completely. I don't know how Thilda found human participants, but she did. She'd administered their first doses when two horrific things happened."

"What?" Lydia asked in a hushed tone. I listened intently, twirling a loose curl, sandwiching myself between Elle and Lydia as we paced around the flower bed.

"Well, first, I'm an artist. I believe seriously in magic. My playground is my palette—not a petri dish. I portray the mysteries of life and death, but I don't unravel them. Humans have no business doing that." Elle shrugged. "So I don't exactly know how it all works, but I know what happened. One day I was in Thilda's office, discussing an upcoming installation with her. She was pacing and stopped to look out her window, gazing over her property with her back to me. There was a note from Freemont on her desk: *Every single pregnant mouse is dead. ABORT ETERNAE TRIAL UNTIL WE LEARN WHY*. When I asked Freemont, he said the mice had been killed by their fellow mice— the mice who'd taken Eternae—with their uteruses gored open. He made me swear never to tell."

I gasped in horror. "Freemont warned her! She did stop the trial, didn't she?"

"No. She ignored Freemont, telling him failure was not an option—and if he knew what was best for him, he'd double down on his research."

"What was the second thing?" Lydia asked.

"Sebastian. Sebastian was Eternae's Patient Zero. He'd come from London with terminal cancer. He started earlier than Thilda's other participants. Eternae cured him."

I nodded. Elle's information validated what Blane and Kenneth told us. "How's that horrific?" I asked. "That's great!"

"It was, until one day, after Freemont told me about the mice, I noticed a terrible smell coming from one of the supply closets. I opened the door. I threw up at what I saw: the rotting remains of one of our researchers. She was pregnant, her uterus gored open like the mice. Freemont and I confronted Sebastian, since we knew he'd taken Eternae. He confessed, breaking down as he shared his battle against his overwhelming urges to kill pregnant women. He begged us not to report him, since all he remembered was waking up in the middle of the night covered in the researcher's blood. Sebastian's confession prompted Freemont and me to take matters into our own hands. We immediately dismissed a handful of trial participants and gave a placebo to the ones who were at GE. If we caught them in time, they wouldn't become killers, like the mice—and like Sebastian. We had to figure out what was happening without Thilda catching on. To confront her with no conclusive evidence would be madness. She'd use her reputation and influence to nip any rumors of wrongdoing in the bud."

The color drained from my face. I was too stunned to speak.

"Are you okay?" asked Elle. "It nauseates me too."

"I, I'll—" I mumbled.

The flower bed spun around me. Lydia grabbed my arm and tried to steady me.

"She's passing out!"

Her voice sounded far away as the flower bed kept spinning. My eyes closed.

"Carly. Carly! Stay with me, Carly!"

Darkness filled my vision.

Elle's and Lydia's voices blurred together.

"Carly? I thought you are Trinity."

"Shoot."

Darkness.

When I blinked my eyes open, my face was drenched in water. Lydia was holding the hose, a small smirk on her face. I was propped up by the farmhouse wall.

"What happened?" asked Elle.

"I must have blacked out. I'll be fine." I looked at Lydia, wiping the water out of my eyes. She looked at me and nodded as if to say, *Tell her about your dad.*

I took a deep breath. "My dad was in that trial. And I'm not Trinity Lewis. My name is Carly Stuart." I told Elle what we were really doing at GE.

Elle nodded. "KDI told me they'd send knights. Your secret is safe with me."

"I'm not a knight—yet." I pointed at my left wrist. "I'm still in my Quest Phase."

"Good. You'll go through Imprint in six months on the winter solstice." Elle smiled. "Till then, we have work to do. Thilda is dead set on distributing Eternae—and doesn't care about the side effects. We need to stop her."

I wiped the last of the water from my face. "Did Thilda realize you and Freemont stopped the trial?"

"No. We fielded participants' correspondence. When Thilda's board asked for updates, she made up data showing 'miraculous results' and 'very promising success' so she could request more funding. And she got it. But I don't know if she's ever gotten approval for Eternae. Like I said, she's always ten steps ahead. Who knows how she is covering her tracks." Elle paused. "It's late. I need to be getting home."

With Elle's information, we were one step closer to solving GE Pharmaceuticals' mysteries. If it was true that Thilda knew about Eternae's horrific side effects, refused to stop the trial, lied to her board, and proceeded to distribute Eternae without approval, she'd acted unethically—and illegally. We needed to find tangible evidence to support these claims. I looked at my Ailm charm. *Be brave.*

††

After Elle left, Lydia and I walked around GE's grounds. We needed to debrief what we'd learned and plan our next steps. Having given Elle her sweater, and with our bags safely in our car, we followed the gravel path to a line of bushes behind the lab.

As the path brought us around the back of the lab, I heard two voices behind the bushes. I motioned for Lydia to be silent. One voice I recognized as Thilda's. The other—a male's voice—sounded familiar, but I couldn't quite place it. The gravel crunched under our feet as we tried to walk more slowly.

"What was that?" asked the vaguely familiar voice.

"Probably a critter," said Thilda. "They're all out here this time of year. Spring is springing, as they say." She laughed.

I held my breath, motioning for Lydia to huddle closer to the voices, but remain behind the bushes.

"You sure no one is here?" the familiar voice asked.

"Certain. They're all at The Far Canal. Sebastian, Charles, Freemont, all of them. Even Pippa went with them. She needed the night off."

"And your party planners?" the voice asked.

Why is that voice so familiar?

"Ashlyn and Trinity? They're in their office. They're such hard workers. Ashlyn is an expert. And Trinity is smart—she's lucky to have Ashlyn as a boss. She reminds me a lot of myself when I was younger."

My breath quickened. Lydia and I looked at each other, praying Thilda and her companion wouldn't come our way. We couldn't risk being seen, but we couldn't pass up this serendipitous opportunity to learn more about Thilda and GE Pharmaceuticals, either.

"Happy to hear it, baby. And happy to spend this week with you! Long distance is so hard."

"I know. But it won't be for long. Once we begin Eternae's global distribution, open my box, and publish your research, we'll be able to get on with our lives together."

"Speaking of the box, has my dad found the pendant?"

"Your dad? The great Dr. Daniel Pritzmord?" Thilda asked sarcastically. "He's been bumbling around for who knows how long, with nothing to show for it. Absolutely nothing!"

———

Dr. Pritzmord has a son?

Thilda continued. "No pendant—and no girl. The girl has the pendant. There's no other way to open that box, other than with both rubies. I've tried everything."

I froze. My heart beat like it would punch a hole in my chest.

Dr. Pritzmord's son sighed. "I'm sorry, baby."

"It's not your fault. But it's bad. I'm running out of *Grealia*. And Sangstra is running out of patience. Without more *Grealia*, and without her supplies, our dreams will be gone."

Lydia and I stared at each other. *Sangstra's supplies?*

"Do you need to postpone the party?" Dr. Pritzmord's son asked.

"Don't be ridiculous. That party will bring in more money. That party is our chance to let everyone taste eternal life!"

"What do you mean?"

"I'm giving each guest one Eternae pill, supercharged for potent action," Thilda said. "As a little party gift."

"How neat!"

"Yes. Thankfully, we have enough *Grealia* to make these pills. And once your dad gets me the pendant, I'll open the box, extract Christ's DNA from the Grail, and make *Grealia* forever!"

She paused. I heard the gravel crunch as she started pacing. "Wait. Your research! Wait." She paused again. The gravel crunched more. "What if we—do we even need the rubies? We can use your laser to cut the box open! Rubies be damned! This is the twenty-first century. Your laser can do the job!"

"I love your spirit, and you know I'll help you. But I wouldn't mess with Morgan's magic," said Dr. Pritzmord's son. "There's a reason only the rubies open the—"

"Oh, come on, Morgan's magic?" Thilda interrupted.

"Thilda, there's something about these boxes. Think of where they were buried—sacred places with spiritual energy! You want to mess with that?"

"Spiritual energy?" Thilda paused. "Really, Elean. Magic? Magic is just science we have yet to learn. You of all people should understand. Don't be like your dad with the magic. I'm finding solutions—"

"You know I hate it when you compare me to my dad," Elean spat out. "I'm only trying to help."

Thilda sighed. "I'm sorry, I know." She sounded genuinely remorseful. "Come here, baby. I'm sorry. Between this box, these rubies, and the board meeting, I'm stressed. And I need more money. The board is not going to like that, but Sangstra doesn't like not being paid. And I'm depending on her supplies."

"You still owe her?" asked Elean. "I thought you stopped working with her."

Thilda didn't respond to Elean's question.

"I see. Does anyone know?" Elean asked.

"No way, no one!" Thilda replied. "But if I can't pay up—and pay up soon—she'll blackmail me. I'll be ruined."

"Oh baby." Elean sighed. "This is a lot, but we'll get through this. Come on, let's head back. It's been a long day. I want us to enjoy our weekend. I have some wine and cheese back home."

"Thank you, baby. I love you," Thilda said.

"I love you, Thilda. We'll find a way. We can't let small stones derail daring dreams."

"Yes, but if those small stones are in your shoes and keep disrupting your steps . . ." Thilda's voice trailed off.

"If they are, we'll pause, take our shoes off, dump the stones out, put our shoes back on, kick them out of our way, and keep marching forward!" Elean said. "You don't let anything stop you. You never have. I've always admired your drive. It's the first thing I noticed about you."

"You're sweet," Thilda said.

Their shoes crunched on the gravel. Lydia and I darted around the bushes, catching a glimpse of their backs as they disappeared to the side where we had been.

The moon hung in the starry sky, illuminating the empty stone bench. It overlooked GE Pharmaceuticals' rolling fields. The sound of Elean's and Thilda's footsteps faded, leaving Lydia's and my breaths the only sounds in the night.

"How's that for evidence of Thilda's shady dealings?" Lydia asked, stunned. "Payment? Blackmail? Sangstra? Supplies?"

I nodded, clutching the pendants of Gran's necklace and gazing at the sky in silence. The stars sparkled like diamonds in the darkness. With these new leads, we had a better case against Thilda. I glanced at Lydia, thankful she hadn't given up on our case—or on me. "I'm glad we're partners," I finally said. "Thank you for revisiting the Grail after all these years. I couldn't do this without you."

Lydia smiled, then chuckled. "You're welcome. I thought once Lyle and I closed the Henge Piece case, it was over. Look how wrong I was." She paused, a small twinkle forming in her eyes. "And Lyle wouldn't want me to do this with anyone but you."

I nodded, thinking of our meetings at Nassauton. Lydia's bracelets slid down her arms as she adjusted her bun. Our Ailm charms glistened in the moonlight.

††

I woke up Saturday to a steady rain. Blane and Kenneth were out most of the night with Charles, Freemont, and The Nerdy Nerds. Lydia and I must have been so tired that we didn't hear them when they got back.

"Do you want milk in your coffee?" I asked Blane as I poured him a cup. "Lydia, Kenneth, do you want coffee? It's ready!"

We were enjoying a late and lazy morning around our cottage. Lydia and I caught Blane and Kenneth up on what Elle shared and Thilda and Elean's conversation.

"No milk," said Blane. He'd set up his laptop at the head of the kitchen table in preparation for his study group meeting.

"I'll take a cup," said Lydia as she kept her eyes on her crossword puzzle. Her long, silver hair fell loosely past her shoulders. It was one of the few times she'd let her hair down. She was engrossed in her crossword puzzle—an activity I'd never seen her do.

"You like crossword puzzles?" I asked.

"I love them. I rarely get a chance to do them. Lyle and I loved tackling the Sunday crossword. We'd make afternoon tea and sit around our table. It was one of our things." She smiled. "Lyle was always better at it. She had a way with words."

I grinned. When our case was over, I was looking forward to sitting down with Lydia, maybe over tea, for a proper chat about her and Gran's adventures.

"How neat," I said, pouring Lydia's coffee. "Kenneth, do you want a cup?"

"I'm good. I'll take some more orange juice, though." Kenneth walked to the refrigerator. "Yesterday did a number on me. I forgot how much young researchers drink, and how much old professors like me can't keep up." He chuckled.

"But you're not old," said Blane. "You're not even in your forties."

I placed Lydia's mug down next to her. Kenneth shot Blane a sharp glance. "And I feel each one of those years. Instead of talking about aging—although maybe that's appropriate given GE Pharmaceuticals' research—let's share what we learned at trivia."

Lydia looked up from her crossword puzzle as Kenneth poured himself more orange juice. He put the container back in the refrigerator and sat down next to Lydia. Blane closed his laptop. Gripping my coffee mug, I looked at Kenneth.

"Everyone was at The Far Canal. Pippa, Charles, Sebastian, Freemont, and more. The Nerdy Nerds were out in full force!" Kenneth said.

"Wait, first, did you win?" I asked.

"We did! Of course!" Blane replied.

I smiled. "That's awesome!"

"Yeah, my knowledge of useless trivia finally came in handy," said Blane. "I got fifteen questions right!"

I rubbed Blane's thigh under the table as I beamed at him.

"After trivia ended, everyone left—except for Freemont. We hung out around the bar. Freemont got to talking. Maybe he'd had one too many, maybe he really likes Blane and me. We talked about his p53 research. Then, he started saying some interesting things. He said a few years ago, he realized something about Eternae." Kenneth took a big gulp of orange juice, glanced at Lydia, and continued.

"He said it was one of his most frightening moments. He discovered the mice that took Eternae turned into vicious murderers—but only attacked pregnant mice. He thought it had something to do with . . . what was it, Blane?"

"HURT? TERT?" Blane guessed. "I don't remember."

I stared at Kenneth and Blane. *This information corroborates what Elle shared!*

"hTERT?" I asked, remembering our conversation with Dr. DeBlack.

"hTERT, that's it." Kenneth sipped his orange juice. "He went back to his textbooks, spending unending weeks and months researching his hypothesis. He found it odd the mice only murdered pregnant mice, goring out their uterus. That gave him clues. He thought that in pre-regulating and regulating telomerase, Eternae must disrupt other biological systems or infect cells, triggering the desire to go after the fetus. He wasn't sure how but speculated it might be through phosphorylation cascades—cellular signaling pathways that amplify the smallest message in the body."

I looked at Kenneth, scrunching my face in confusion.

"He didn't really get into the details," said Blane.

"But wait till you hear what he did share," Kenneth exclaimed. "It involves our friend Sebastian—and Charles."

Lydia and I nodded, unable to take our eyes off Kenneth and Blane.

"Charles and Sebastian used to be best friends. They did

everything together. They even started The Nerdy Nerds," Kenneth said.

"What happened?" Lydia leaned in, her eyes widening.

"They had a big falling out. One day, after-hours, Sebastian saw Charles unlock a door on the lower level. As he followed him, he noticed the key Charles left in the door. It was unusual: gold, with a little crown stamped on it. Nothing could prepare Sebastian for what he saw."

I gripped my mug. *The gold key in the Eternae paperweight on Thilda's desk.* "What did he see?"

"A fake bookcase. It was open. Behind it—stairs to a hidden room. As Sebastian approached, he heard Charles talking to someone. Sebastian didn't hear the reply, since Charles started screaming about how, without these updates, his own p53 research had stalled. Charles stormed up the stairs. Sebastian confronted him, but Charles made him swear never to tell anyone—or else he'd kill him."

"Oh my gosh," I whispered. "Charles is running secret experiments in Thilda's basement. Do you think Thilda knows?"

"She must. She's probably covering up Charles' research. Remember she wouldn't let J. Carmichael near that door?" mused Lydia.

"What happened next?" I asked, sipping my coffee.

"Risking his life, and trusting Freemont since he didn't report him for murder, Sebastian confided in Freemont. He knew Charles and Freemont collaborated and feared Charles' secrets could damage Freemont's reputation. This trust opened the door for Freemont to share his hypotheses with Sebastian. That's when Sebastian told Freemont about his smoothies, saying Thilda told him he must keep drinking them as long as he's taking Eternae— for maximum benefit." Kenneth stared at Lydia and me. "Freemont put two and two together and asked if Sebastian had more urges to kill pregnant women after drinking the smoothies."

Blane continued the story. "He said no. Speculating he was onto something, Freemont studied Sebastian, taking biopsies and spending countless hours examining cell and tissue samples. His work paid off when he made a sickening discovery. He found highly contagious ancient viruses, embedded as normally dormant, unusable DNA snippets within the genome, had been 'turned on' in Sebastian's DNA, so they were no longer inactive. These infectious viruses, now activated, permanently altered Sebastian's DNA, replicating when his DNA replicated and programming his cells to crave more telomerase—no matter the cost. Since fetal tissue contains high telomerase levels, Freemont speculated this might be why only the pregnant mice were murdered—and why Sebastian had urges to kill only pregnant women. He believed Eternae must activate the viruses, and the smoothies must contain the antidote."

Lydia and I looked at each other in horror.

"Which means," I said, my face contorting in disgust as I swallowed my coffee so I didn't throw it up, "if Sebastian stops drinking his smoothies—"

"Yeah." Blane nodded, taking a deep breath. "And there are pregnant women all around Somerset."

I gasped, realizing the implications of Freemont's discovery. Thilda hadn't corrected Eternae's side effects. She'd developed an antidote—another product she could monetize. She would distribute Eternae to unsuspecting individuals, then sell them the smoothies, leaving patients with no escape from depending on GE Pharmaceuticals.

"Did Sebastian or Freemont ever discover what's going on in the basement?" Lydia asked.

"No. Freemont said no one has," Kenneth said. "There was a new researcher who came close. He turned up dead, in GE's fields. Shot in the heart. Thilda said it was a tragic loss, that he hadn't sought the mental health care he needed given the pressures of research. She sure has a grip on GE—and on this whole town. No one dares disagree with her."

"But the weird thing is," Blane added, "Freemont knew him. He swore he'd never commit suicide. Not to mention Freemont said right after that incident, Thilda mandated everyone wear badges—for their safety. Of course, safety and surveillance are different sides of the same coin, and Freemont knew Thilda's actions weren't entirely altruistic . . ."

Blane's voice trailed off as he looked at me. With Freemont's information, we now knew the horrific truth of Eternae—and the measures Thilda would take to keep it hidden.

††

The next week was a blur of party planning, working around Blane's study group schedule, and brainstorming how to get behind the locked door. On Friday, we drove Blane to the airport.

"You're gonna ace your exams!" I said, wrapping my arm around Blane's shoulder.

"Thank you. I'm ready." Blane grinned. "Our group was very helpful."

"Say hi to Lara and Paul," I added. "If only they knew we're undercover agents, in the thick of taking down a major pharmaceutical company and its evil CEO."

With Pippa's help, Lydia and I planned From Legend to Launch. With the chessboard floor, we would turn the farmhouse lobby into an immersive experience on GE Pharmaceuticals' and Eternae's history. Guests would take the tour, socializing over appetizers and cocktails. Then, they'd walk to the lab through a specially constructed wooden pergola with hundreds of red and white hanging lights.

Upon entering the lower level, they'd walk onto the dance floor, with *infinitely encoded; forever expressed* hanging majestically above them. A full bar would block access to the benches and lab equipment, containing revelers on one side of the lower level. To honor Merlin's and Morgan's legacies, Lydia, Pippa, and I designed bespoke Celtic chalices with fire in them. These chalices would set the stage for an enchanted evening, inviting guests to imagine themselves inside Morgan's laboratory. We'd line GE's driveway with the chalices, also using them to form the dance floor's perimeter.

"VIPs will feel that at any moment, they might see Morgan making healing potions," Lydia said. "When guests step through the farmhouse door, they'll think they're next to Morgan as she makes *Grealia*. When guests step into the lower level, they'll be present with Thilda as she manufactures Eternae."

"Amazing!" said Kenneth. "You're clever."

The closer we got to the airport, the more the farmhouses, fields, and cow pastures disappeared, giving way to industrial complexes, office buildings, and warehouses.

"The best part," I added, "is that it's fancy-dress. Everyone must come in costume as a wizard or witch, knight, queen, or courtly lady!"

"I love that!" Blane smiled. "Be prepared for a million Merlins. I'm definitely dressing up as him!"

"What about as a knight?" I squeezed Blane's hand.

He smiled. "Hmm, maybe!" He paused as he stared out the window. "Hey, Carly, look at that building."

He pointed to an industrial building on our right. The building's sides looked like mirrors, reflecting the clear blue sky. "Look at that neon purple sign."

I gasped. *Sangstra.*

If we wanted answers to some of our most burning questions, our next destination was staring us in the face.

††

With Blane en route to Nassauton and Lydia in full party-planning mode, Kenneth picked up Lydia's end-of-term duties.

"I appreciate it," Lydia said, ending her call with one of the caterers. "With seventy-eight VIPs registered, I've got to focus on From Legend to Launch."

"Of course!" Kenneth squinted at his laptop, tracing his finger across the screen. He sat at the head of our office table. "I have no idea how you balanced all this with your party planning."

"I don't either." Lydia laughed. "But I do know I'm getting too old for this." She arranged her bun, tucking in her stray hairs. Her bangles clanged as they slid down her arms. "When we get back to Nassauton, I'll tell them I need to scale back."

I tilted my head, looking up from my journal. If Lydia retired, the whole Archaeology Department would fall apart. "Scale back?" I asked. "What would you do with your free time?"

Lydia smiled wistfully as she sat down in front of her laptop. "Write my memoir."

I beamed. That would be a book I'd love to read.

"I've never been interested in publishing research, but I've always wanted to write my own story."

I heard a knock on our door.

"Who is it?" Lydia asked.

"Pippa."

"It's unlocked," said Kenneth. "Come in."

Pippa cracked the door open, sticking her head in. Her usually stick-straight hair was disheveled. "I need to sit for a bit," she said, closing the door and sinking into a chair. She clutched a few magazines and folders, which she placed on the floor next to her.

Her black, fitted jumpsuit was wrinkled. Her heels looked like they hadn't been polished in weeks. She wasn't wearing lipstick and had dark circles under her eyes. She looked uncharacteristically sloppy.

"Pippa! Is everything okay?" I asked. "You look like you haven't slept in days!"

She rubbed her face. "Might as well be a whole week. I'm absolutely knackered. Thilda has lost her mind over this board meeting." She buried her face in her hands and started crying. "On top of that, she's been inundated with interview requests."

Pippa pointed at the magazines. One cover featured a picture of Thilda holding her red Eternae paperweight, with the caption: "The Thrill of the Chase: Making the Impossible, Possible."

"Pippa! Oh no." Kenneth rummaged around for tissues. "I'll grab you some tissues from the bathroom. I'll be back."

"When's the meeting?" I asked. "Interviews for what?"

"It's the first week in June. It's the last one before From Legend to Launch. Thilda is stressed since she has to justify the additional party costs. And she dumped it all on me since she has an interview in London for her book. It couldn't be more ill-timed, but thankfully her boyfriend will go with her."

I leaned in, twirling a loose curl. *Thilda is an author? Is there anything she can't do?*

"Can't she reschedule the interview?" I asked.

"Oh no. It's part of her book promotion." Pippa sighed. "I guess the good part is it will lead to more revenue, which will please the board."

"Right," Lydia said. "Now what about these additional costs? I wasn't aware of any."

Pippa looked at us. "Thilda said she needed to ask the board for more funds. Maybe she omitted them the first time?"

Lydia and I looked at each other. *Had Thilda really omitted costs, or was she lying to her board—again?*

"Well, Thilda can say anything party-related is a worthy expenditure to attract more investment," Lydia said without revealing what she and I were really thinking. "The bigger the party, the bigger the check."

Pippa managed a small chuckle as she wiped a few tears. "How so?"

"VIPs love a good party. They love feeling responsible for making the vision come to life. In many ways, they are." Lydia smiled. "Their money is, at least."

"How do I tell Thilda that?" asked Pippa. "How does she say that so her board understands? She can't afford for them to reject her request. From Legend to Launch is a milestone." She wrung her hands. Kenneth returned, handing her a few tissues. She smiled in appreciation.

"It's all about ROI—return on investment. The board has got to pay to play—and to win." Lydia turned to Pippa. "Show how every dollar spent translates to five, ten, fifteen dollars returned to GE. The board needs to visualize the party's success in the language they understand—and the board is fluent in money, math, and numbers."

I loved Lydia's response. Her wealth of knowledge amazed me.

"You're brilliant," said Pippa, tossing her crumpled-up tissues in the trash bin. "That's great."

"Thank you." Lydia smiled. "We'd be happy to proof your chart. You've got this."

††

Between party planning and helping Pippa, the week flew by. I bounced out of bed on Friday, excited to pick Blane up—and even more eager to stop at Sangstra en route.

Lydia, Kenneth, and I ate a quick breakfast and hopped in our car. We'd searched for Sangstra's address but couldn't find it. We figured if we took the same route to get to the airport as before, we'd find Sangstra's building.

On the drive, Kenneth reminded us Intake was the same night as From Legend to Launch. "I'll miss the party and I'll miss the week prior. There's nothing I can do," he said. "KDI requires us to prepare seven days before Intake, in a silent retreat. I don't know much more than that."

The more I learned about the Knights of the Dagger and KDI, the more fascinated I became. KDI was always professional. Their technology was cutting-edge. They ensured their knights—and knights in their Quest Phase—were well-informed and protected. I loved learning about their traditions through

Kenneth. *What will my Imprint be like? What about Intake?* The knights were doing noble work, searching for the Grail and other sacred relics to protect the world from evil. I was proud I'd joined.

"We'll miss you." Lydia looked at Kenneth. "I'm proud of you, my friend. This is an exciting next step in your life and career."

Kenneth smiled. "Thank you. That is one of the nicest things anyone has said to me. It means a lot coming from you."

"What do you mean?" Lydia asked. "It's the truth."

"This will sound so silly." Kenneth paused as he zoomed past a car. "I've never had good friends. Take Sid. We all know how he turned out, don't we?" Kenneth focused on the road, expertly changing lanes and keeping pace with traffic. We neared the exit where Blane had spotted the Sangstra building. "It really hurt when he betrayed me. I'd lost the only friend I'd ever had. I didn't realize how much I felt that until I learned how lonely life is when you're doing it without friends—and how good it feels to have friends you trust with your life."

I spotted the neon purple sign and directed Kenneth to take the exit. "We're the Fearless Foursome!"

"And I'm so thankful for it!" Kenneth grinned.

As I looked out the window, I wondered about the history of this part of town. Industrial, 1970s-style complexes dotted the landscape. Metal scrapyards and dilapidated warehouses sat in between some of the buildings. Some buildings had gaping holes, like years of decay had eaten away at the walls. Some had unkempt gravel driveways with weeds growing out of them. Graffiti, cartoon art, and rust covered others.

"So am I," said Lydia. "I, of all people, also know how losing your best friend feels."

We entered the parking lot.

"Look at this place. It must be some massive office headquarters," said Kenneth when we found an empty spot.

Not a soul was around. As we walked to the entrance, I felt like a thousand surveillance cameras were pointed at me. I couldn't tell if it was seeing my reflection in the spotless windows, or if something—or someone—was behind the windows watching us.

Anxiety filled my stomach. *Are we being watched? Are my emotions tricking me?* There was no concrete evidence for my fear. I didn't want to say anything. I knew if I did, Lydia would tell me what she always said: *"Evidence, not emotion."* I looked at the building's exterior, searching for cameras. I didn't see any.

There was a gold plaque on the metal door that read: SANGSTRA. No address or any other information was provided, other than a small insignia. The insignia looked like a simple chalice, with an *S* stamped in the middle. The same uncomfortable feelings I had seconds ago returned. I brushed them off. My emotions were getting the better of me for no reason.

There was no bell, and the door wasn't locked. We opened it and walked in to a massive warehouse floor. As far as my eyes could see, there were rows of sealed-off booths, constructed with plexiglass paneling and curtains. In some booths, the curtains were opened. In others, they were closed. If people were talking in the booths, we couldn't hear them. The silence was pregnant— and creepy. In the distance, I saw a few women in all-white nurses' gowns walking around the floor.

"Welcome to Sangstra."

I jumped, startled by a voice behind me.

A woman in white scrubs with a clipboard approached us. "What time and with which doctor was your appointment?" She had a low, melodic—almost hypnotic—voice. The back of the clipboard had the number six and the Sangstra chalice written on it in permanent marker. The woman looked at me, then Lydia and Kenneth. "You're brave. Most women don't feel comfortable coming here with their parents. They can always wait outside if you want the privacy. We never share anything without your permission."

I stammered, "Hi, where exactly is here?"

A sobbing woman emerged from a booth. The man with her embraced her as their nurse locked the booth behind them.

"Oh dear." The woman in scrubs watched the couple walk down the aisle. Their nurse escorted them to a hallway. Finally, the woman in scrubs responded, "What's Sangstra? We're the UK's largest fertility clinic. We provide solutions from in-vitro fertilization to egg freezing." She watched the nurse and couple disappear down the hallway. "We also terminate the pregnancy if the embryo is deemed unviable."

I looked around the warehouse floor, taking in a 360-degree view of the clinic. The stages of a baby's in-utero life were printed around the walls. They started at one cell, then went through the embryonic stages, culminating in a picture of a baby, wrapped in blankets in a crib.

"The stages of fetal development." The woman in scrubs gestured to the wall as we walked to the pictures. "A journey of what happens week-by-week in utero. The in-utero environment teaches us so much."

I nodded as the woman in scrubs kept talking. Lydia was deeply engrossed in what she was saying. The plaque near the first picture gave an overview of the exhibit and details about fetal development. As I read the last paragraph, I gasped. WE ARE GRATEFUL FOR THE POLITICAL AND FINANCIAL SUPPORT OF LORD BREEKSON. HE CONTINUES TO ADVANCE OUR UNDERSTANDING OF SCIENCE AND HUMAN LIFE.

I nudged Kenneth and pointed at the plaque. *Lord Breekson's name again! Is Lord Breekson on the board of Sangstra too?*

"The womb is one of the most fascinating places on Earth. It holds untold secrets about life. It's the Holy Grail of science." The woman in scrubs gestured to the back of her clipboard. "We take the Holy Grail seriously here. It's our logo and it's in our name. Sangstra comes from *sanguine*, which means blood, and the Holy Grail, of course, is Mary Magdalene's womb and bloodline."

Lydia rolled her eyes as she shook her head. I knew exactly how she felt about Mary Magdalene's womb and the Holy Grail.

"That is intriguing," said Lydia. I could tell she was biting her tongue, unwilling to go into a lecture on the lack of scholarly—and biblical—evidence for the woman in scrubs' claims. "I could have used a place like Sangstra when I was younger. You could have helped me." She sighed, scanning the warehouse floor. "It's very difficult for a woman to choose a career over children. I always wished there was a way to have both."

I looked at Lydia, puzzled by her comment. *Did she want children and couldn't have them?*

The woman in scrubs smiled at Lydia. "That was brave of you to share. Our goal is that no woman ever must choose one over the other. Our investors share this belief, funding our research. Our proprietary algorithm analyzes each woman's blood type and endocrine system, then uses that data to design a personalized fertility plan. It tells us, to the specific time of day, when to inject which hormone so each woman can maximize, and amplify, her fertility window."

"That's incredible," I murmured.

"Yes, and our algorithm also helps us understand fetal development."

The woman pointed at one of the pictures. It looked like a bundle of marbles. "These are pluripotent stem cells, magnified thousands of times. They can become any cell in the body. They are unique since they have high levels of telomerase." She smiled. "How do these cells regulate these high levels so they don't become cancerous? This is an essential research question."

Dr. DeBlack mentioned pluripotent stem cells in our conversation . . . One of the pictures of a fetus sucking its thumb caught my eye. I thought about the sobbing woman, her partner, and the nurse.

"Who determines whether an embryo is unviable—and when?" I asked.

"I can't answer that question," said the woman in scrubs.

"So that woman . . ." I pointed down the hallway without finishing my sentence.

"It's her choice. We are here to help women make the choice that's right for them. We don't know their circumstances."

I looked at the picture of the fetus. The woman in scrubs must have felt the tension as I thought about the fetus' and the mother's lives. She quickly said, "But don't worry, we don't let anything go to waste."

The front door opened. Two women walked in. One was shaking and the other embraced her friend. The woman in scrubs glanced at them, then looked at us.

"Is there anything else I can help you with? I need to check her in."

"No," said Lydia. "We appreciate your time."

We left Sangstra in silence. As we merged onto the highway, I took out my journal, thinking about fertility, embryos, pluripotent cells, and telomerase. *The womb is the Holy Grail of science.* Sangstra's insignia was the Grail. I flipped through my journal, looking for my notes from our conversation with Dr. DeBlack. *"Telomerase is found in high concentrations in cells that need to keep dividing, for example, in embryonic stem cells. These cells are three to five days old and are pluripotent, meaning they can divide into more stem cells, or become any type of cell."*

I closed my eyes, twirling a loose curl. *Telomerase-rich, embryonic stem cells. The pregnant mice—murdered by the mice who'd had Eternae. Freemont's note to Thilda. The pregnant researcher Sebastian murdered. Sangstra's supplies. Thilda's lying, deception, and blackmail fears. Freemont's disturbing discoveries. Sebastian's smoothies.*

"Kenneth . . ." My voice trailed off as I opened my eyes. "Thilda knows Eternae's side effects. She made the smoothies as their antidote. The smoothies work for Sebastian. They satiate his telomerase addiction."

Kenneth nodded. I continued.

"If you were a ruthless, power-hungry scientist chasing profit—and telomeres—at all costs, and you knew of a clinic with pluripotent cells, what would you do to cover up your drug's horrific side effects?"

"Oh my God," Lydia blurted out. Her gaze met mine, her face contorting in disgust as she realized what I was thinking. I stared at Kenneth in the rearview mirror.

"I know what's in the smoothies," I said. "And what Thilda is hiding behind her locked door."

XVII

As Blane walked out of the arrivals gate, I ran up to him and hugged him. Though he'd been gone only a week, it felt like an eternity. I couldn't wait to hear about his exams and Nassauton—and to tell him about our conversation with Pippa and trip to Sangstra.

We celebrated Blane's return and the end of the semester at The Far Canal. After dinner, we resumed preparations for From Legend to Launch. With only a few weeks to go, Pippa, Lydia, and I were reviewing our latest run of show. Our office was bursting with boxes of decorations, which left hardly any space to walk around.

"I never thought I'd learn this new technology," Lydia said, pointing at her beam. "An old artifact like me."

Pippa laughed. "Don't say that! Ashlyn, you're doing great."

I smiled. Over the past few days, Pippa had been stopping by our office more and more, sometimes to do work, sometimes to chat. She was feeling better after taking Lydia's advice and preparing the ROI chart for the board. She was also relieved Thilda gave a successful interview and was excited about her book deal.

"That definitely spotlights From Legend to Launch," Pippa quipped. "No pressure though." She chuckled, her stick-straight hair staying in place.

"We'll be fine," said Lydia. "The run of show is airtight. We'll be all-hands-on-the-ground the day before the party. Let's review." She pointed at the wall as Pippa and I clustered around her. "We'll have food stations in the chessboard lobby and lab entrance. Our bars will be in the chessboard lobby and in the lab."

"Love it," said Pippa.

"Here is our menu." Lydia handed Pippa and me a few sheets of paper. "What do you think?"

"Appetizers: lettuce wraps with peanut sauce, breaded asparagus straws, quiche cups. Dinner: steamed salmon, baked chicken, or grilled eggplant. Desserts: make your own ice cream creation station, complete with mini-pastries, cakes, and cookies." Pippa looked at Lydia. "I love it! Sounds delicious."

"We'll also have custom-made, chromosome-shaped cookies, and red cookies shaped like the Eternae pill."

"For drinks, we'll have Celtic-themed concoctions: Druidic Droplet—an orange juice and vodka mixer, Eternael Elixir—a red cosmopolitan, and Morgan's Margarita—an aquamarine-colored margarita, served in glasses shaped like test tubes, salt-rimmed and on the rocks," I added.

"You two themed everything! The whole lab is excited. We've never had a party like this before."

"Thank you," I said. "We couldn't have done it without your help."

"Right, speaking of help, what shall we do with all these boxes?" Pippa asked, looking around our office.

"Can we move them to Thilda's office? This is a fire hazard," said Lydia. "I can barely walk around."

"Oh, we couldn't do that. She hates clutter."

"But these are the crystal goblets we've ordered for the champagne toast. I need them stored in a secure place, and our office is full. Would you rather we put them in the closet that you call your office?"

Pippa chuckled. "Good point."

"Can we ask her?" I asked. "Maybe she'll make an exception. These are the most expensive items on this campus. They're hand-designed and modeled after the Grail."

"Right," Pippa said. "I'll ask her now."

Pippa disappeared, flitting down the hallway in her heels. Lydia sat on one of the boxes marked: RED CARPET.

"So we did get the red carpet?" I smiled.

Lydia chucked. "Thilda wants a VIP party, she'll get a VIP party. Imagine that red carpet in the chessboard lobby. Stunning! And it wasn't as expensive as you'd think. We're still well under budget."

I smirked. "Must be great for Thilda. Under budget, making up numbers, lying to her board so she can pay off—"

"Sangstra. That's exactly why Thilda needs more money. We just need a way to prove it."

"And get behind that locked door," I added.

We were running out of time. After the party, we'd have no reason to stay at GE. To unlock the door, we had to get the gold key. To get the key, we had to sneak into Thilda's office—an impossible task—and get the paperweight. We also had to get Thilda's Grealmæp. And we had to find her box. There was no way we could sneak into Thilda's office, and no way Thilda would take her Grealmæp off her neck. And I had no idea where to start looking for her box. Even with more leads on Thilda's deceitful dealings, we still had no evidence, only stories and speculations.

"All our work is for nothing," I blurted in frustration as I realized how much work we had ahead of us. "Without getting into that basement, we can't prove anything!"

"Carly," Lydia sighed. "Don't say that. Think about what we already know: Thilda and Sangstra. Thilda hiring Daniel and her mother—two Knights of the White Wave. Thilda lying to her board, your dad's trial, the budget for the party. Elle and her stories. Freemont and his discoveries. Sebastian and his smoothies. Elean—he's Daniel's son, for goodness' sake. Doesn't that set off alarm bells? Isn't that a little too convenient? Father? Son? Mother? Daughter?"

"But that's not evidence—those are observations!" I stared at the floor. I could barely look Lydia in the eyes. Hopeless, I shrugged. "What does it matter anymore? We're no closer to the Grail—and without that key, no closer to the basement. I've spent the whole semester chasing stories. All I can show for it is some observations, a trip to a fertility clinic, and speculations"—I pushed one of the cardboard boxes near me—"and big boxes blocking everything in our office."

Lydia slid off her box and stood in front of me, barely fitting between me and the boxes. "Carly, what's going on? Why the change in spirit?"

I shrugged again. "I can't explain it. I'm not making any progress. Blane finished his freshman year. He's on track. Maybe my mom was right to want me to keep going. Now I have to take summer classes. What if I don't want to?" I interlaced my fingers, twirling my thumbs around each other. I felt ashamed of having to explain all my feelings to Lydia. "I expected to come here, discover what happened with my dad, and find out what Thilda is hiding. But the path hasn't been so smooth—and Blane is succeeding and I'm not."

Lydia nodded. "I see. This also isn't a college campus. This is a high-tech lab, with cunning experts spinning webs of lies." She arranged her bun. "Don't give up since the path isn't clear or the emotions are overwhelming. It's exactly in those moments we have to go back to the evidence." She pointed at my Ailm charm bracelet and necklace, and then at her bracelet. "You do know what the Ailm means, right?"

I nodded and smiled a little. "Yeah. That was one of the first things you told me when I noticed your bracelets. Surviving harsh conditions, finding your purpose, wisdom, seeing a clear path forward, blah, blah, blah." I looked at our charms and sighed. "But I don't see a clear path forward." I buried my head in my hands as tears welled up in my eyes.

"And neither did the Knights of the Dagger who came before you. And neither, for that matter, have many people—especially people I know you admire and respect. Take Lyle." Lydia chuckled as she pointed at my necklace with its aquamarine gemstone. "Take the generations of strong women she—and you—come from. Do you want to hear a story about Lyle?"

"Sure," I mumbled, still frustrated.

"Lyle and I were excavating the Sanctuary of Monte Sant'Angelo sul Gargano, Italy. The head of the Chase City Museum's Archaeology Department, Dr. Brian Timothy Staples, had arrived for a surprise visit. He'd spent the morning chastising Lyle and me for not finding anything. I'll never forget his words: 'Lord Breekson needs results. He didn't secure exclusive rights to this site for nothing. What have you and Lyle found?'" Lydia shook her head, staring wistfully at the floor. "In that moment, I realized how everything came down to the evidence. Without tangible evidence, there was nothing. After he said that, Dr. Staples stormed out of our tent, leaving us in tears."

I couldn't imagine Gran crying, upset by a man. "What'd you do?"

"Lyle fiddled with her Ailm and aquamarine pendants while I adjusted my bun. She mumbled something about being exhausted and wondering why Dr. Leith's group was finding artifact after artifact—and we weren't finding anything. She chuckled when I arranged my bun, since she knew that was how I calmed myself down. Then she went for a walk. Fifteen minutes later, she came running back, yelling she'd found something that I should see." Lydia's eyes sparkled with nostalgia. "I grabbed my gloves and field notebook. Lyle led me through trees and shrubs, to a clearing. She stood in the middle of the clearing, near a small hole, and held her aquamarine pendant. It started glowing."

I chuckled, twirling my loose curl. "Glowing?" I imagined how skeptical Lydia must have been.

"Yes. It was glowing, with a pale greenish color. I told Lyle, of course it's glowing since the sunlight is hitting it. She said, no, it's glowing with a different force. She said she'd felt it so strongly, she thought it was a sign and started digging. When I peered down the hole, lo and behold, there were bones buried there, with little beads and some type of box with a strange, half-faded insignia on it." Lydia paused. "She swore she found it because her pendant started glowing, giving her a clear sign and path forward. I told her it was a crock of crap, but she never gave it up. She swore till the day she died that her pendant's light gave her a clear path forward—and led her to find one of the most important artifacts on our dig."

I smiled, grabbing my necklace. Would Gran's pendant ever glow for me?

A knock on the door interrupted my thoughts.

"I'll get it." I slid off my box and wiggled to the door. "Pippa! Any luck?"

Pippa beamed as she pushed a dolly from behind the door. "You owe me. Come on, let's haul these to her office."

Lydia and I loaded our boxes on the dolly, taking them down to Thilda's office with Pippa's help. During our final trip, I walked up to Thilda's desk. In plain sight was Thilda's box, with its two sets of double dagger marks. I could see how both rubies were needed to open the box. I could also see the gold key taped to the bottom of the Eternae paperweight. As I gazed at the key, an idea for how to get it came to mind. I grinned. My idea gave me confidence our path ahead was getting clearer. I snapped a clandestine picture of the key and paperweight.

"Thank you for letting us store the glasses here," I said. "I know they'll be safe."

Thilda smiled at me. "My pleasure. I can't wait for the party."

††

Later that week, Blane got his last exam grades. He'd aced each of his exams.

"You amaze me, Knight Henley!" I said as we cleaned up the dishes after dinner.

"Wanna go for an evening walk?" Blane asked. "It's the right temperature, and with the breeze, it's the perfect time."

"Sure do!" I said.

The last streaks of sunlight—dusty pinks, oranges, and purples—were painted across the sky like brushstrokes on a colored canvas.

"Why do I amaze you, Knight Stuart?" Blane looked at me as we left.

"You aced your freshman year and you did it online! You don't let anything faze you. You roll with the punches and take the leaps of faith—and soar! I love that about you. You inspire me to take more leaps too."

Blane stopped under a streetlamp, grinning. He spun me toward him and kissed me. The softness of his lips on mine made me feel like I was floating.

"Stop." I giggled as we kept walking. "Would two friends kiss each other like that?"

"Maybe!" Blane laughed, brushing an unruly curl out of my face. "I can't help it. I love you!"

As we turned the street corner, we saw a little wooded trail.

"That reminds me of the trail outside my backyard. It was one of my dad's favorite trails," I said. "And it's one of mine."

"Then let's walk it. Would that make you happy?"

"Walking it with you would."

We approached the trailhead. By now, the darkness of the night sky, punctuated by bright stars and flooded by moonlight, replaced the colored canvas.

"I hope you'd never walk this alone. Not at night like this."

"No way. That was one of the first rules my dad taught me. Never walk alone."

"He was absolutely right." Blane paused. "Carly, tell me more about your dad. He seemed intelligent and caring—and a man of science and faith."

I inhaled. A plume of my breath disappeared into the air when I exhaled. I reached for Blane's hand.

"He was. He loved nature. It was his escape, the place that freed him." I looked at the trees. "When he was in nature, he felt connected to something bigger than himself. Something, or someone, bigger than what his analytical mind could comprehend. Someone who exists outside of space, time, and matter; someone who could create all these—since He existed outside of them. He saw God in nature. He knew God was real because of nature."

"That's beautiful," Blane said. "It's hard for us to grasp the magnitude of God's presence, even when He's left His fingerprints all around us."

I nodded. "I used to think those fingerprints were irrefutable proof of their owner's existence. Now, I'm not too sure. Are they even fingerprints, or is it just nature?"

"What do you mean?"

"Do we call them 'fingerprints' because we want them to belong to someone who is greater than us—because we want God to exist? I've never seen Him. He wasn't there when Gran and Dad died. How can I even know He is real?"

Blane looked at me. "I don't know how to answer that."

"It's okay." I gave a half smile. "I know those are big questions. Maybe right now I don't need answers—maybe just someone to listen to me."

"I'll always listen to you." Blane kissed my hand. "I promise."

"One of my dad's and my last walks was that trail by our backyard." I changed the subject, following the trail as it curved around a few trees. "We spent the day hiking. We discussed everything on our hike: the mathematics of the universe, Fibonacci sequences . . . the precise timing of nature, from the microscopic processes in our cell, to meiosis and mitosis, to the tides turning, to the seasons' sequence, to the complex interactions that govern life on its most fundamental level . . ."

Blane and I kept walking. The trail had a wealth of flora and fauna, making it feel like we were in an enchanted forest. I took a deep breath, remembering how on our walks, my dad would always point out each plant and share a random fact about it.

"When my dad died, I couldn't see how there was a god. If

that god were good—like all the church ladies said—how could a good god take my dad away from me? One of the ladies told me, 'Everything happens for a reason. It's all part of God's plan.' What 'plan' would take my dad away from me? What god would make it part of any plan to do that?"

I brushed my tears with the back of my hand.

"Carly, that's awful. And that's not what you needed to hear. I don't have a good answer to suffering. It's something I can't wrap my head around, either, when I think about my brother."

"Do you think you'll see him again?"

"I don't know. I still have faith I will, but it's getting harder to hold on to that faith. We haven't heard anything about him. No leads. No evidence, only emotions: anger, grief, confusion, rage."

I hugged Blane. "I'm proud of you for sharing that with me. That takes bravery. Remember in the Amesbury cemetery?" I looked into his eyes. The moonlight made his hazel eyes sparkle.

"Yeah. I'm trying, Carly, and you're helping me share."

"Teammates." I smiled.

"Two knights, together on our quest." Blane grinned.

"Two knights, together on our quest," I repeated. "Even if the emotions are difficult, it's exactly in those moments we have to go back to the evidence." I remembered Lydia's advice. "Sometimes emotions push us to search even more for the evidence—to make us ask more questions, to make us take that leap of faith."

"Leap of faith, eh?" Blane winked. "That's the spirit! Let's keep asking our questions and taking our leaps of faith. You with the Grealmæp and Thilda's locked door, and me with my brother. One step at a time."

Arm in arm, Blane and I continued our walk, ending back at our cottage with Kenneth and Lydia.

†††

Thilda's board meeting occurred without a hitch.

"I don't know how she did it, but she did! She convinced them she needed the funding!" Pippa exclaimed. "She's incredible when she gets in the zone and negotiates. She always gets what she wants but makes everyone else feel like it was their idea."

"It was your ROI chart, Pippa," said Lydia.

Pippa grinned. "Which you helped me make, Ashlyn. Thank you! You've saved GE Pharmaceuticals."

†††

I found Elle sitting by her mural on the lower level, staring at one spot as if in a trance. Elle's laptop and beam were next to her, projecting different molecules on the wall. The sunlight illuminated *infinitely encoded; forever expressed*, casting a red glow over the wall.

"Hi, Elle!"

She jolted out of her trance and bounced up from the floor.

"Hey, Car—Trinity, what's up?" She glanced around the floor. "Sorry! I don't think anyone heard. I'm trying to draw these molecules with a voice-activated paint. It's not coming together."

"What are you talking about? The mural looks great!"

We both stepped back as I blurted out, "Oh my gosh! It's a 3D chromosome!"

Elle grinned. "I'm trying to make it look like it's coming out of the wall. Watch this." She adjusted her beam, which projected the chromosome onto the wall, then said, "Telomere, wiggle!" In response, the telomeres on the chromosome tips started to wiggle. She grinned.

"Nice job!" I exclaimed. "Tech and art!"

Elle smiled. "Thank you! Do you want to try?"

"Yeah!" I grinned. "How?"

"On your phone, pull up the image you want. Pair your phone with my beam, which will project the image on the wall—and pick up your voice. Say what you want the image to do." She smiled.

"Cool!" I pulled up an image. "What's your beam name and code?"

"Look for 'Beam—Elle.'"

I found Elle's beam and clicked it. The pop-up screen appeared on her beam and my phone.

"I'll type in my code," Elle said, reaching for my phone, then her beam.

The words PAIRING SUCCESSFUL flashed across my phone.

"That was the easy part," said Elle. "Now, walk up to the wall and say what you want the image to do."

"Stars, sparkle!"

The stars started to twinkle on the wall.

"That's SO cool!" I gasped. "It's like I'm looking at diamonds in the night sky! How do the beam and paint know what the words mean?"

Elle grinned. "Smart tech. Smart paint. Want to see something cool?"

I nodded. "Of course!"

"I'm teaching the paint to change colors by voice activation. Let's try it. Say a color."

I glanced at my pendants. "Aquamarine."

An aquamarine tint covered the wall. I grinned, amazed.

"Neat, right? I call it *speak art into being*." Elle smiled. "Now, what brings you here?"

I leaned closer to Elle and whispered, "The key to the locked door is taped to the bottom of a paperweight in Thilda's office. I need you to help me get it."

"I can't sneak into Thilda's office. Don't be crazy!"

If Elle wasn't okay with my plan, there was no other way. "Elle, wait. I'm not asking you to do that."

Elle paused, taking a deep breath as she looked up at Thilda's office, then back at me. "What exactly did you have in mind?"

I showed her the picture on my phone. "Make me a copy of the paperweight—and a copy of the key. I'll swap one for the other when Lydia and I are there for our final meeting for the party."

Elle's eyes sparkled. "Now that is bold—and I love it. I'll make it. Give me a few days."

††

That night, I drifted in and out of a fitful sleep. In fewer than two weeks, From Legend to Launch would wow the medical and scientific communities, setting Thilda's plan to globally distribute Eternae—and her smoothies—into motion.

We had fewer than two weeks to get her Grealmæp and box. Without getting into the basement, we had no evidence. And without evidence, we didn't have a case. Thilda was a hometown heroine and global celebrity. Nobody would believe us if we didn't have tangible proof of her illegal, devilish scheme to profit from turning her unsuspecting guests into telomerase-addicted killers.

I held my pendants, as if they would glow and connect me to Gran's—or Morgan le Fay's—wisdom.

But there was no green glow.

Just darkness.

XVIII

Eighty-five global medical and health care VIPs would be at *From Legend to Launch*—and would leave with personalized swag bags. Each red velvet bag with a gold drawstring held cases of red jelly beans labeled ETERNAE, mini champagne bottles, and GE pens shaped like magic wands with red LED lights. Each bag also had one Eternae pill. "It's their sample-size starter pill on their journey to eternal life—just enough to hook them so they have no choice but to come back for more!" Thilda gushed.

I'd kept KDI updated with our learnings and speculations. They said they'd prioritize the case. In the meantime, Lydia and I focused on the party and mapped out the chalices' locations along the driveway, the valet lot, and the dance floor. Guests would drive up to the valet. As their cars were whisked away, they would be too, walking the red carpet to arrive at a Celtic castle and Morgan le Fay's potions laboratory. Near the farmhouse and lab, we'd constructed photo-booth-size castles with turrets and laboratories, enabling guests to snap pictures and tag themselves using #eternaeforever.

With ten days to go, Lydia and I were setting up the chalices and high-top cocktail tables in the chessboard lobby. A cool evening breeze blew through the windows as the sun set on GE's property.

"We've accomplished a lot today!" Lydia gazed across the lobby, grinning. "What do you say to unpacking a few more, then calling it for the evening?" She pointed toward Pippa's dolly. "Hand me that chalice."

As I started to unpack the chalice, Thilda walked in. She was completely lost in thought. Her red stilettos echoed on the chessboard floor as she walked square by square to the middle of the lobby. *Red heel, red heel, white square, black square. Red heel, red heel, white square, black square.* Her double-helix ankle tattoo contrasted so sharply against the white and black tiles, it looked like it was written in blood.

"Ashlyn! Trinity! You surprised me." She snapped out of her trance. "Didn't expect you to be here this late."

"Good evening." Lydia smiled, pushing the chalice into position. "We're almost done."

Thilda looked around the lobby, gushing at our work. "This room looks amazing. Thank you!"

"Of course," I said. "Will we bother you as we finish?"

"Not one bit," said Thilda. She started pacing again, moving from one square to the next with intense, laser-like focus. *Red heel, red heel, white square, black square. Red heel, red heel, white square, black square.*

I unpacked another chalice and carried it to Lydia. As Lydia positioned it, the farmhouse door flung open. A woman burst in and marched up to Thilda, not even noticing us. *The woman in scrubs from Sangstra!* I nudged Lydia, gasping.

"MATHILDA VON GENZKENSAFFE! Stop right there. Turn around and face me like a woman."

Thilda jerked out of her trance, almost slipping as she tottered on her stilettos. She quickly steadied herself, bellowing at her unexpected visitor.

"Sangstra, I TOLD you to never show your face here! NEVER MEANS NEVER."

I swore sparks shot out of Thilda's eyes as she glared at Sangstra.

"Where is my money? I'm running out of patience. What do you think Dad would say if he knew you hadn't paid a debt?"

"Ashlyn, Trinity, leave!" Thilda spat her words out with such force that if enunciation could kill, we'd have been dead.

"Ashlyn? Trinity? You're afraid your staff will learn the truth?" Sangstra didn't take her eyes off Thilda.

"Leave!" Thilda screamed.

I desperately wanted to stay, but my fear of Thilda trumped my curiosity about Sangstra. Lydia and I dropped everything and darted out the farmhouse door. As soon as we closed it, Lydia motioned for me to be quiet. We ducked out of sight and crawled around the farmhouse wall, hiding ourselves under one of the open windows.

"Leave Dad out of this. He doesn't deserve to be mentioned in this conversation."

"He doesn't deserve to have you for a daughter, Mathilda. You're putting our family reputation at stake with your delusional ambitions."

"You watch your mouth, you bitch. You're the one who left to start your own clinic. I cared for Dad. I stayed with him through his cancer. I took him to his appointments. What did you do? Saw your patients, studied fertility. Long hours this, excuses that."

"If that's how you *really* feel about my clinic, why did you come running to me when you were in trouble? 'Sangstra, *please, help me for Dad's sake*?'" Sangstra's disdain dripped off her tongue. "Begging me to help you fix some problem with your medicine, to give you fetal tissue. Begging me to pile women with experimental drugs to produce more embryonic cells—even after I told you the drugs caused infertility and cancer. Threatening to expose me for unethical conduct if I stopped helping you, when I'm the one who sounded the alarm!"

Sangstra lowered her voice but didn't waver.

"I'm done covering up for you. I'm done watching my patients' greatest dream of having children die. You can't destroy life to create it. I'm done hearing women tell me they have cancer. I won't cover for you anymore. I should never have put my family over ethics—bloodlines be damned! Pay me what you owe me, then I never want to see or hear from you again."

Silence.

"I'm sorry you feel that way, Sangstra." Thilda's voice was chilling. "But your patients' deaths are not in vain. I'm making the impossible, possible, like Dad used to say. I've discovered how to cheat death, once and for all. And I'm one step away from giving immortality to the world. I will go down in history for this achievement."

"You? It's all about you?" Sangstra laughed. "Pay me, or I'm calling the police—and the newspaper. They'll push you off your pedestal faster than you can mock me with a 'Sangstra, I'm so sorry!' And I hope your fall from glory hurts as much as you've hurt these innocent, unsuspecting women."

More silence.

My heart was pounding, but I didn't dare lift my head above the sill.

"Sangstra, sweet Sangstra." Thilda's tone was eerily calm. "You're upset. I'm upset. We've had heated words. Let's put this behind us. Let's hug it out, talk it out, sister to sister."

Thilda's voice nauseated me and sent chills up and down my spine. Feeling lightheaded, I clutched my stomach.

The silence was pregnant—and creepy.

Then, the echo of Thilda's heels filled the air.

"Checkmate, Sangstra."

I couldn't stand not being able to see inside. I popped my head over the sill to see Thilda ram her red stiletto heel into Sangstra's throat.

††

I blinked my eyes open. Everything around me slowly stopped spinning. Lydia cradled my head in her hands. We were outside of the farmhouse.

"What happened?" I whispered, looking up at Lydia as the

color returned to my face. "Where's Thilda?"

"You passed out. She loaded Sangstra's body onto Pippa's dolly, then hauled the body to her car."

I tried to sit up, but my stomach was turning.

"Did she see us?" I asked.

"No."

I groaned, closing my eyes, feeling queasy picturing Thilda dumping her sister's body in her car. "She's pure evil," I finally murmured. "And that murder is our evidence. Should *we* call the police?"

"If we do, it will be her word against ours. And it will put us in unnecessary danger," Lydia said. "We'll keep preparing for the party. We'll tell KDI, Kenneth, and Blane, and wait for KDI's direction."

††

"Congratulations, Kenneth," Lydia said, smiling. "We're proud of you. We'll miss you."

"I'll miss you all too." Kenneth stared at the purple curtains. His cab was parked outside. "Carly, you won't be able to text me. Seven days of silence means seven days of silence—no talking, no texting. It's part of preparing our hearts and minds to become a Knight of the Dagger." He gave me a hug. "Come this time next year, you'll be going to your own retreat and Intake ceremony."

He moved to Blane. "My friend," he said as they shook hands. "You've been an awesome partner-in-crime and trivia team member. See you back on campus! We'll start our version of The Nerdy Nerds. Tell Freemont I said bye!"

"You bet. The Nassauton Nematode Nerds has a nice ring to it!" Blane laughed.

"Safe drive," I said, hugging Kenneth again. "You're gonna be an awesome knight."

As Kenneth headed out the door, I couldn't help but think

about my own Intake ceremony. First, I had Imprint, at the end of this year. And long before Imprint, in just a few short days, we had From Legend to Launch.

After I told KDI about Sangstra's murder, they advised us to lay low and focus on party planning. They said Thilda would manipulate everyone into believing it was self-defense, a claim that couldn't be refuted in the absence of other witnesses. They also said they'd try to send knights to our party, but with everyone focusing on Intake, they couldn't promise anything.

††

From Legend to Launch was in three days. We'd put all the chalices in their locations, and Lydia, Pippa, and I had tested each one. We'd decorated the lab's lower level like Morgan's potions laboratory, placing the high-top tables around the dance floor. Each table had long black, white, silver, gold, or aquamarine tablecloths and tea candles and a Celtic candelabra as centerpieces. We'd set up the deejay's table right below the balcony, framed by two ten-feet-tall, silver Celtic candelabras. We'd also installed the disco ball below the balcony. In the daylight, it sent red flecks from *infinitely encoded; forever expressed* dancing around the lower level.

To complete our theme, we'd placed steel trenches around the dance floor. The trenches had rows of fire in them, with a remote control to adjust the height of the fire. To further partition the foyer and lower-level lab, we'd installed black velvet curtains with rhinestones. With the lights off, and the fire in the trenches on, the lab looked like the summer solstice night sky, surrounded by flames. With the moonlight streaming in through the open ceiling, illuminating *infinitely encoded; forever expressed*, the lab would look enchanted. If guests blinked, they'd miss a Celtic fairy casting a magic spell.

Even with the decorations, I couldn't get into the party spirit.

Every time I closed my eyes, I saw Thilda murdering Sangstra. While I knew I could confide in Lydia, I needed a professional therapist to help me. I didn't know where to find one, or what I would say. Lydia suggested asking Joyce to recommend someone from Nassauton's health services. I hoped whoever Joyce recommended would consider me a student on temporary leave and not charge me.

Elle was still working on the Eternae paperweight replica. She'd run out of resin, and her order for more hadn't arrived. In two days, Lydia and I would have our final check-in and walk-through with Thilda. From Legend to Launch would be here before we knew it.

We were at a standstill and running out of time.

††

The day before From Legend to Launch.

I had my first session with the therapist Joyce recommended, who was able to see me for free. I didn't know how Joyce worked it out, but I was grateful to her. Our first meeting went well, and I learned a few helpful breathing exercises.

After making our final notes and adjustments from our walk-through, Lydia, Blane, and I went to the farmer's market. A short walk from our cottage, the market was in a church's parking lot. As we walked through Somerset's neighborhoods, we saw couples and families sauntering down the streets or biking around town. Almost everyone smiled and wished us a good day. I loved the local, small-town charm of Somerset. *Studying abroad here could be a lot of fun*, I thought as we turned the corner and entered the market.

Farmers and small business owners set up rows of stalls and tables, each with different-colored tablecloths and signs. Some stalls were tables. Others were under tents. Some sold vegetables and others tea, pastries, mead, meats, cheeses, honey, soap, or spices.

In the middle of the parking lot was a long wooden table with benches. A group of teenage girls sat at one end and few families sat at the other, eating sandwiches and sipping from disposable cups. The teenagers chatted, passing around the soap they'd bought. They giggled as they took turns comparing their scents and textures. A mom wiped her baby's mouth with a napkin as her husband smiled adoringly at them. The whole market was bustling with life.

Noticing a stall with lavender, Lydia left Blane and me to wander around. As we walked by the tables, the full, wheaty scent of freshly made bread filled my nose.

"Made fresh this morning!" the man behind the table said, noticing me smiling at the scent. He pointed to a plate in front of him. "Care for a taste?"

"Please!" I grabbed two slices and handed one to Blane. As I chewed, the savory taste of grains I never knew existed filled my mouth.

"Try it with the olive oil." The man picked up a small ceramic bowl with olive oil and herbs in it. "Let me know how you like it."

Blane dipped his bread in the bowl. As soon as he put it in his mouth, he grinned. "It's so flavorful! Where's it from?"

"We import the olive oil from Greece. We grow the herbs in our garden. My wife makes the bread." The man pointed past the church. "We've got a small place in town. Family business for three generations. We're about to launch our new website, with online ordering!"

I smiled, chuckling at how he pronounced "herb" with an *h*. I loved the Britishisms and was going to miss England after we left Somerset.

"Congrats on the website! We'll take a loaf of the sunflower wheat." I reached for my wallet. "And some of that olive oil, please!"

After we paid, Blane and I strolled around the market. Lydia was still at the lavender stall, chatting with the owner. As we meandered over to her, an all-too-familiar face caught my eye.

I froze, gripping Blane's arm in fear.

"Blane! Look!" My heart pounded. I gripped Blane's arm tighter, my knuckles turning white.

"Owwww, you're hurting me!"

I loosened my grip. "I'm sorry. But look! Is that—" I pointed at a man sitting at the long wooden table. He took a bite out of his sandwich, unaware we were watching him. As he chewed, a woman holding two plastic cups sat down next to him. He offered her his sandwich. She waved her hand to decline, handing him one of the cups. They smiled at each other, clicking their cups together.

"Oh snap!" The color drained from Blane's face as he recognized the couple.

Instinctively, we darted behind some shoppers, hiding in the crowd as we scurried away from the table.

"Do you think they saw us?" I asked when we were safely away from the table.

"I don't think so," Blane said. "What are they doing here?"

"Probably meeting with Thilda."

"We gotta get Lydia and leave. It's game over if Dr. Gellmane and Dr. Pritzmord see us!"

††

We were back safely in our cottage, making dinner.

"That was a close call!" said Lydia. "Are you sure they didn't see you?"

"Pretty sure. We got out of there fast!" said Blane.

"We were lucky." Lydia took the chicken out of the oven, placing it on the hot pads on the counter. "Let that sit for a bit, then I'll cut it."

"I'll set the table." Blane opened the cupboard and reached

for three pale yellow plates. "Yellow." He chuckled. "Kenneth hated yellow. I hope he's doing okay." He arranged the plates on the table. "I miss him and his classic rock songs. Eating without him doesn't feel right."

The chicken hardly had a few minutes to cool when we heard a knock on the door.

"Did you invite any of The Nerdy Nerds?" Lydia wiped her hands on her apron. She smoothed her hair and patted her bun into shape.

Blane shook his head.

"Maybe Kenneth forgot something?" I asked.

"One way to find out," said Blane as the three of us walked to the door.

Nothing could have prepared us for what we saw.

"Good evening, Dr. Kells, Ms. Stuart, Mr. Henley." Dr. Pritzmord's feigned politeness sent waves of anxiety crashing into my body. Nauseated, I clutched my stomach. He wore khaki pants, a button-down shirt, a green-and-white-striped tie, and a black blazer. His broken, pearl-colored, ocean-wave brooch gleamed in the light by the front door. He gestured to Dr. Gellmane and Thilda. Dr. Gellmane wore her pearl-colored, ocean-wave brooch. Thilda wore her Grealmæp over her black jumpsuit and had slung her MvG tote bag over her shoulder. Her aquamarine ring sparkled on her right pinky finger. She looked at Blane, shocked.

"What the—" She spat. "You're supposed to be at GE prioritizing your research!"

Blane started to mumble a response, but Dr. Pritzmord cut him off.

"Last time our paths crossed, we were a few towns over, throwing a few punches and opening a little box. This time, I'm delighted it's over something more sociable." Dr. Pritzmord chuckled as he glanced at Dr. Gellmane and Thilda. "Forgive me— I took the liberty of inviting two friends. Inviting strangers wouldn't have been proper."

My heart started pounding. Fear filled my stomach, bubbling up through my chest. I tried to swallow, but my mouth was too dry. I squeezed Blane's hand and grabbed Lydia's arm. I tried to focus on controlling my breath the way my therapist taught me. *"Carly Stuart, when our paths cross again, you won't be as lucky. Watch your back."*

"Aren't you going to invite us in?" He sneered. "It would be rude not to."

"Daniel, what are you doing here?" Lydia asked.

"Same thing I was doing at the Amesbury Museum, when our reunion was cut short," Dr. Pritzmord said calmly. "Only this time, I'm finishing what I started. Hand over the Grealmæp."

I froze, swallowing the fear in my throat. I tried to find words, but none came out.

"Ms. Stuart, I see you're speechless. Must be with delight." Dr. Pritzmord stepped closer, putting his face up to mine. He whispered, "I warned you to watch your back."

My temples throbbed. My armpits dripped with sweat. My nightmares were real.

"Don't come near her," said Blane, thrusting himself between me and Dr. Pritzmord. "We don't want your company! Leave!"

"Leave?" Dr. Pritzmord turned toward Dr. Gellmane. "They want us to leave!"

Dr. Gellmane laughed. "Not tonight. We've been looking forward to this for quite some time."

The three of them walked in, closing the door behind them.

"Give us the Grealmæp," Thilda said.

"How do you know we have it?" I asked. "And if we did, why would we give it to you?"

"Don't ask questions, child!" Thilda spat. "Trinity Lewis, or should I say, Carly Stuart? Daniel told me about you. And between him, and listening to your conversations, I know everything. Don't mess with things you don't understand."

"What is it I don't understand?" I asked. "And what do you

mean, listening to our conversations?"

"*Grealia*. The Grail. Eternal life." Thilda smiled, clutching her Grealmæp. "With both rubies, I will be unstoppable. Two Grealmæps! One Grail! Unlimited *Grealia*! I'll be the only one who can control immortality." Her lips curled into a devilish smile. "Oh, if you're wondering how I learned everything, know that bugging your office was too obvious. But bugging your badges?" She smirked, tapping her head. "Now that's evidence of a mastermind."

"Control immortality?" I scoffed. "By conning Sangstra into selling you embryos and giving them to Eternae patients in smoothies? Eternae activates contagious viruses in our genome, causing permanent damage. It creates murderers. And you know it!" I paused, catching my breath. "Instead of fixing Eternae, you manufactured another product to monetize. You made a deal with Sangstra, giving innocent women carcinogenic drugs so you could get their embryos. And when your sister called you out, you murdered her! How can you look yourself in the mirror and not see a monster? These women don't get eternal life—they get cancer. Sangstra didn't get eternal life—she got death!"

Thilda cackled. "Obviously you don't understand, child. They are sacrificing their bodies—and their children—for science. Each of us has a moral obligation to our fellow humans to help our species live forever. There is no goal more noble. And to live forever, there is always a trade-off. But, the good of the species must prevail!"

"You're delusional." I spat out my words, surprised by my bravery. "And evil!"

"Pardon? I created a pill that cures cancer and offers immortality. It happened to have a teeny, tiny, itsy-bitsy adverse side effect—nothing an embryo cocktail couldn't fix." Thilda's eyes gleamed. "It's sad the women get cancer, but guess what Eternae does? Cures cancer! It works like magic. Only it's not magic, it's science—my science! I control the drug—and the cure for its side effects. And now that I control Sangstra's lab after what the papers are calling 'her tragic and unexpected demise,' I have complete and total market domination!"

My face flushed with rage. Emboldened by a desire for justice as I grasped the truth of Thilda's brazenly masterminded, immoral plan, I spoke each word slowly.

"Innocent women are unknowingly trading their fertility and bodies for eternal enslavement to you. And anyone who takes Eternae will need its antidote. It's an unending cycle of evil."

Thilda smiled, her eyes narrowing as she hissed her words. "It's an unending cycle of profit. And it's science. And there is always a trade-off. It's for the good of the species." She shrugged. "Now, where's the Grealmæp?"

"We're not giving it to you," said Lydia.

"We'll ask you nicely, one more time," said Dr. Pritzmord. He glared at Lydia, locking his eyes on hers. "Where's the Grealmæp?"

Lydia stood her ground. "You'll never have it."

"Fine. If you won't play nice," Dr. Pritzmord snarled, "we won't either."

He whipped his revolver out of his blazer pocket, pointing it at me. Instinctively, I raised my hands. Simultaneously, Dr. Gellmane lunged at Blane, pinning him to the floor. Thilda brandished a handgun with a silencer from her tote bag. She rested her perfectly manicured finger on the trigger and butted her gun against Lydia's right temple. "Give me the Grealmæp."

If Thilda could kill her sister with her stiletto, there was nothing stopping her from putting a bullet in Lydia's brain. I'd already lost Gran, my dad, and J. Carmichael. The thought of losing Lydia was unbearable. I closed my eyes and took a deep breath.

"No," said Lydia.

I opened my eyes, looking straight at Thilda as I trembled in fear.

"What was that?" Thilda asked.

Thilda pressed her gun deeper into Lydia's temple.

Lydia clenched her jaw and closed her eyes.

"I can't let you manufacture Eternae and exploit helpless women who desperately seek motherhood. If my death is the trade-off between your wicked plan and their lives, so be it. The Grealmæp's location dies with me." Lydia opened her eyes.

"Fine." Thilda looked at Lydia, then at me, then back at Lydia. "As you wish. We'll kill you, then we'll find the Grealmæp. It's got to be here. Some bumbling academics can't stop me. Your death, like the deaths of so many others, will be collateral damage."

I couldn't watch Lydia die. Still trembling, I looked at my aquamarine stone. I knew I had to take a leap of faith.

"NO! STOP!" I yelled. "It's in Lydia's room. Wrapped in microfiber towels, in a clear Tupperware in her satchel, which is locked in a dresser drawer. The key is in her nightstand drawer."

Dr. Pritzmord looked at me, smiling. "Now that's a good girl!"

I felt like I'd been punched in the stomach.

"Excellent," said Thilda. "Daniel will escort you to get it."

Dr. Pritzmord kept his gun on me as we walked up the stairs. A few minutes later, we returned with the satchel. He handed it to Thilda.

"Here you go." Dr. Pritzmord smiled.

"You sure it's in there?" Dr. Gellmane asked.

"Yes. Wrapped up in its microfiber towel. I rattled it around in that stupid Tupperware to be sure."

"Excellent," said Thilda. "Let's head back to GE. Guess we'll have to take our dinner to-go."

Held at gunpoint, we followed Dr. Pritzmord, Dr. Gellmane, and Thilda out of our cottage and into their van.

XIX

The light well's ceiling had been opened. Its stainless-steel, exoskeleton-like scaffolding reached for the stars like an overturned spider with its legs in the air. The chromosome top of *infinitely encoded; forever expressed* was split open, leaving the double helix suspended by its steel cables. Moonlight passed through the gel pills of the double helix, casting an eerie red glow over the empty lower level. I knew exactly where we were headed. As hostages, we'd finally learn what Thilda was hiding in her basement.

"Hope you like your new home." Thilda unlocked the door with her gold key.

"It's not as nice as your cottage, but until the Knights of the White Wave come, it's GE's most secure place." Dr. Gellmane sneered.

Thilda ushered us into the room, her red stilettos echoing as she strode to the bookcase on the far wall.

"Here." She plucked a book off the shelf, handing it to me. "Maybe you'd like to brush up on your chemistry."

I glanced at the cover of the book.

††

Notes and Experiments, Volume IV: Making Grealia Eternae, Part III

By KAvG

Thilda pressed a button on the shelf. The bookcase rolled into the wall, revealing another door. She unlocked it, then swung it open. She pointed to the stairs beyond.

"All right, you lot. Give me your mobiles. You won't need them—and it's not like there's any service down there." Thilda cackled.

I put my hand on my pocket.

"Mobile please, Carly," Thilda hissed. "We don't have all night."

"No way," I said, watching Lydia hand her phone to Thilda.

"Excuse me?" asked Thilda.

Dr. Pritzmord patted his revolver. "She'll cooperate."

"No," I repeated.

"We can't use them down there, Carly." Blane shook his head, handing Thilda his phone. "No service. We're trapped."

"Listen to your boyfriend. One of the few times he's right," Dr. Pritzmord jeered. "Teamwork sure does make the dream work. Even if that dream means our favorite two archaeologists end up in the dungeon."

"We're wasting time," said Dr. Gellmane. "The Grail is almost ours. Thilda's ring glowed green near that box. Get the mobile."

"Almost ours?" Thilda looked at her mother. "It's almost *mine*. The box is mine. Elean and I found it. You're not taking the Grail for some museum collection, Elyse."

"Careful how you speak to your mother. Show some respect."

"Elean helped you?" Dr. Pritzmord cackled. "That good-for-nothing college dropout son of mine managed to do one thing right." He shook his head.

Thilda glared at Dr. Pritzmord, mouthing "*My box,*" as he approached me. His ridicule changed to a threat as he held his revolver to my chest. "Give it up, Carly."

Defeated, I looked at Blane. He nodded. As I pulled my phone out, I grabbed my sentinel, slipping it off and stuffing it in my pocket.

"Good girl," said Dr. Pritzmord, handing Thilda my phone.

I cringed at Dr. Pritzmord's words.

"Right," said Thilda, gesturing down the stairs with her gun. "Try not to trip. And happy reading!"

She slammed the door behind us. The lock clicked. The bookcase rolled back into place. The sound of Thilda's stilettos faded away as she, Dr. Gellmane, and Dr. Pritzmord left us imprisoned in the basement.

††

I fumbled around, grasping at the air in the cold, complete darkness. Finally, my hand hit the railing.

"There's gotta be a light switch somewhere." My teeth chattered as I talked.

"Do you feel anything?" Blane sighed. "I don't!"

"We'll find it. Stay calm," said Lydia. "I'm making it down the stairs. The switch must be around here."

"Lydia, where are you?" I clung to the railing, taking one step at a time. Gran's boots couldn't fail me now.

"Down here. Keep walking. Easy does it."

The steps creaked under my weight.

"Good, one step at a time."

I was approaching Lydia's voice. I took another step and bumped into her. We linked arms. Water dripped in the darkness ahead of us.

"Great, leaky pipes," I mumbled.

"And unending darkness," added Blane as he grasped my hand.

"Who are you?" a shaky voice called from the distance. "Thilda? Charles? I told you I needed more starter. Please don't hurt me again."

"BLANE!" I gripped Blane's hand so hard, my knuckles were about to pop off my hands. "Did you hear that?"

"Blane?" the voice asked. "Who's there? Will you hurt me?"

"No! Unless you're on Thilda's side."

"I'm not!"

Fluorescent light filled the basement. I blinked. In the far doorway was Blane. But holding my hand, right next to me, was also Blane.

I jumped back, staring at Blane, then at the boy in the doorway.

"Barrett!? Is that you?" Blane ran to the doorway. "Oh my gosh, Barrett!" Blane started crying as he hugged his twin brother. "I thought I would never ever see you again. What have they done to you? You're so pale. And look at your hair! When was the last time you had a haircut?"

The two of them stood in the doorway, sobbing, their arms around each other.

"What are *you* doing here?" Barrett wiped his tears. "Is it really you?"

Blane nodded. "How did you get here?"

"I don't know where to begin! How are you? How are Mom and Dad? And Mardsen?"

"They're fine. I finished my first year of college. I have a girlfriend too." Blane grinned, pointing at me, then at Lydia. "This is our archaeology professor, turned teammate."

Barrett smiled. "We have a lot to catch up on." He gestured behind him. "Follow me."

We entered a small, unfinished room with a low ceiling. Exposed pipes and air ducts hung from the ceiling. Cracked plastic covers encased the fluorescent light bulbs, reminding me of the broken plastic cover in Rockfire's Archaeology Research Room. One wall had a whiteboard, computer, and desk with a rolling chair. Books, a molecule kit, and stacks of papers were spread across a desk. A twin-size mattress with a few bedsheets was pushed against another wall. Its steel frame looked like it was about to collapse. Against the third wall was a refrigerator and wooden table. The fourth wall had a door, which led to the bathroom.

"Sorry, I'm not really set up for guests." Barrett motioned for Lydia to take the rolling chair, while he sat on top of his mattress. It creaked as he sat. "Not exactly the five-star hotel they promised me."

"They promised you what?" Blane asked as we joined him, sitting in the middle of the mattress. A metal spring snapped in the frame. "To think, right above us is cutting-edge technology."

Barrett sighed. "Yeah. Some days I still can't believe it. It all started when I went for my run. I don't remember how long ago that was. I've lost track of time. While I was on my run, a car honked at me. I stopped, and Granddad and a well-dressed gentleman in a suit and bow tie got out. He had a beautiful pearl brooch. It was a row of waves, like Granddad's brooch from his archaeological society."

I'd forgotten about the brooch in the display case at Blane's house. Blane and I stared at each other as the realization hit us.

Blane took a deep breath. "That's no archaeological society. Granddad's a Knight of the White Wave. I'll tell you about it later. Keep going."

"Granddad and this man—his name was funny, Breakon or Breekton or something—were interested in my research on the telomere algorithm, TTAGGG."

Lord Breekson, again! Lord Breekson kidnapped Barrett—and is a Knight of the White Wave!

"Your algorithm has a name?" Blane asked.

"You bet. It's the genetic code for the telomere sequence.

Thymine, thymine, adenine, guanine, guanine, guanine." He smiled, getting up and pointing to his whiteboard. He'd drawn different molecules and formulas. "I live and breathe this stuff. You know that."

Barrett continued. "Granddad said Breekton was interested in funding my research and asked if I could explain it. I said sure, after my run. But Granddad said it needed to be now. I remember trying to answer, but before I knew it, I felt a towel over my face." Barrett picked up a molecule kit and started playing with its pieces. "I woke up in a private jet. Granddad reassured me everything would be fine, and I believed him. When we landed here, this beautiful woman, towering over me in red shoes, greeted us and showed us her lab. I was starstruck. She promised I could use her equipment and I'd have the finest meals and accommodations. She even promised she'd help me publish as first author on a paper! Then she took us to her office. Some other guy was here. The three of them—the woman, the guy, and Granddad—started talking to Breekton."

"I think it's Breekson," I finally said. "Lord Breekson."

"Oh." Barrett continued. "The woman, Thilda, kept praising Lord Breekson, saying how he saved Eternae. Lord Breekson kept saying how I would save Eternae. Then he said if they hadn't needed to punish Granddad for botching up the 'ruby deal with the professor,' they would never have found me. 'We don't tolerate mediocrity—or fools,' Breekson said. I remember that so clearly." Barrett paused, wrapping his arm around his brother's shoulder. "Man, it's so good to see you."

Blane hugged Barrett as if he'd never let his twin go.

"What happened next?" asked Lydia, wheeling her chair closer to the bed.

"Thilda chuckled, in a laugh that sounded more devilish than delightful. 'The universe helps you when you're chasing the impossible,'" Barrett said. "I realized I'd been kidnapped since Granddad botched a deal—and Thilda would never divulge what deal. She snapped at me, threatening me, hitting me, and telling me to stop asking questions and focus on the telomerase experiments."

Dr. Pritzmord, Dr. Gellmane, Blane's granddad, and Lord Breekson are all Knights of the White Wave! And Blane's granddad made the deal with Dr. Hasserin! I remembered Dr. Gellmane's words from the night of the break-in: "*They have no idea what they're up against and how many threads this ball of yarn has . . .*"

All these threads were tied to the Grealmæps, their rubies, and the Grail. I took a deep breath. Now that Thilda, Dr. Pritzmord, and Dr. Gellmane had both Grealmæps, all they had to do was unlock Thilda's box and the Grail was theirs. The Knights of the Dagger had lost. I'd failed Gran. I'd failed Lydia. I'd failed J. Carmichael and Kenneth. I'd failed the knights! I wasn't even a full knight, and I'd failed the knights! I'd failed myself—I'd dropped out of college and failed myself.

"Earth to Carly. Earth to Carly!" Blane tapped my shoulder. "Is everything okay? You're worlds away."

"I'm fine." I sighed. "Don't want to talk." I stood up, stretching my arms up, over, and around me.

"Okay," Blane said. "I'll be here when you're ready."

Misjudging how low the ceiling was, I hit the plastic cover of the lights as I stretched, causing the cover to fall and smash on the floor.

"Of course, you'll be here!" I snapped, kicking the pieces. "*We'll all be here!* We're hostages! No one knows we're here, other than the Knights of the White Wave!" I started shaking and sobbing.

"Carly!" Blane hugged me, caressing my hair. "It's going to be okay."

"No. No it's not. Thilda has both Grealmæps. She'll get the Grail. It's over. We've failed."

"No. Come on. Two knights. We'll figure something out. It's not over till it's over." Blane kept hugging me. "We've got a scientist, an archaeologist, and a knight whose intuition and intelligence can troubleshoot anything. And a goofy Nerdy Nerd."

In hearing Blane call me "a knight," I forced a small smile.

Blane wiped my eyes and kissed my forehead. "Don't give up. What would your gran do?"

I took a deep breath and nodded, thinking about the many adventures Gran had where she could have quit—but didn't. Blane always found a way to reassure me. I sighed. "Gran wouldn't give up. She'd find the evidence and take her leap of faith."

"You bet!" Blane exclaimed, walking over to Barrett's whiteboard. "And speaking of evidence, let's keep listening to Barrett."

"Speaking of evidence," Lydia said, "I have a small confession." She grinned as a whimsical twinkle formed in her eyes. "Thilda doesn't have both Grealmæps." She reached into her pocket, pulling out a microfiber-towel-covered lump.

"Lydia, how on earth?" I gasped, elated to see our Grealmæp as Lydia peeled the towel off the lump. "It wasn't in your satchel?"

"Of course not," said Lydia. "After you saw Elyse and Daniel, I decided the best place for the Grealmæp would be in my pocket, not my satchel. Daniel knows I keep things in Tupperwares. My satchel, with the Tupperware, is the first place they'd look. But my pocket? Not even over my dead body would they get it."

I grinned, amazed at Lydia's cleverness. Barrett got up, glancing at the Grealmæp before walking to his whiteboard. I sat down on Barrett's bed and twirled my loose curl.

"That design is all over her lab!" Barrett said. "That's crazy!"

"Yeah," said Blane. "We'll tell you everything, after you finish your story."

"Once Thilda realized I was a risk, she locked me in this room, telling me to focus on my research and test this pink powder with my algorithm. She hasn't come down here since. I doubt she'd even recognize me if she saw me. She sends Charles to do her dirty work for her. She was elated when I reported that her pink powder had incredible properties, like it was sentient and could initiate and regulate telomerase production—autonomously." Barrett walked to his desk and turned on his computer. "She gave me this computer. It's a number-crunching machine, but it has no external network connection. And she gave me these samples," he said, pointing at the refrigerator, "and made me test them too."

I walked over to the refrigerator and opened the door. My jaw dropped as I jumped back in shock. "Something, something find the evidence!" I opened the door wider, gesturing to the red bags with Sangstra's insignia that were neatly stacked on the shelves. Blane and Lydia shook their heads as I told Barrett about Thilda's dealings with Sangstra.

"No kidding," Barrett said, horrified. "No wonder she wanted those samples tested for telomerase concentration." Barrett's computer beeped. "Ahh, here we are," he said, opening a folder labeled ETERNAE TEST BATCH 6. I walked back to Barrett's desk. Blane, Lydia, and I clustered around his computer. The folder contained subfolders with individuals' names.

There it was.

TEST BATCH 6 – Subject #3: S, JACK.

I clutched Blane's arm, trying to steady myself as the room spun around me. I felt like I'd been punched in my stomach. I closed my eyes and bit my lip, unable to control my tears at seeing the folder with my dad's name.

"What's going on?" Barrett's voice sounded far away.

I took a deep breath and opened my eyes. Blane pointed at the folder. "That was Carly's dad."

"What?" Barrett asked, shocked. "Was? I don't understand." He looked at Blane, then at me.

Blane walked me back to Barrett's bed and helped me sit down. I told Barrett everything: about my poem, the Grealmæps and their rubies, the Knights of the Dagger and White Wave, KA's journal, and the mortar and pestle. About Phase I, J. Carmichael, and his GE audit. About Morgan, Merlin, and *Grealia*—and Thilda and her evil plan for Eternae and the smoothies.

"That's insane!" Barrett shook his head. "She's insane! I didn't know any of this, I swear!" Barrett sighed as he stared at his computer screen. "I just ran my algorithm, doing what I was told and testing her pink powder and these samples for her experiments."

"Thilda's pink powder—*Grealia*—must be what makes Eternae sentient," Lydia said. "Without *Grealia*, Eternae is nothing."

"But Eternae also activates that horrible virus," said Barrett. "Didn't your friend Freemont discover that? If *Grealia* were that miraculous, why does it do that?"

"A great question for after we escape," said Blane.

"You mean *if* we escape." Barrett sighed. "That woman is a cruel, calculating monster."

"She's the devil's daughter," I said. "And instead of red horns, she has red stilettos. She doesn't care about people; she only wants to make a profit."

"And she's giving Eternae to all her guests," Blane added. "Seducing them with the promise of eternal life but sentencing them to enslavement to her."

Lydia nodded. "It's sickening. But how do we stop her? At this point, she's probably realized she doesn't have the second Grealmæp. If she has Elean's laser, she's ignored his warnings, opened the box, and gotten the Grail. She's already won."

"No!" Barrett exclaimed. "There's got to be a way to stop her."

"How? We're trapped. She took our phones, and there is nothing down here—only your computer," I said. "With no network connection."

"If only Elle knew we were here!" Lydia sighed. "She'd get KDI involved!"

"Who's Elle?" Barrett asked.

"She's GE's artist-in-residence," I replied. "And she's our friend—and a knight." I paced around Barrett's desk, holding my pendants in my palm. As I rolled them around, the fluorescent lights hit the aquamarine stone, causing it to gleam green. As it gleamed, it illuminated a familiar pattern on the back of the Ailm disc. *Is Gran trying to show me something?*

"I don't believe it!" I shook my head, grinning.

"What?" Blane put his arms around me. "What's going on?"

"Blane! Look at the back of the Ailm disc!"

Blane gasped. "The pattern looks like an infinity sign, like—" He looked at me. "No way. How's that possible?"

"Share with the class?" Lydia asked, craning her neck.

"The back of my Ailm pendant has the same seven-star pattern as my birthmark—my star map. That can't be a coincidence."

"It's like the green light is revealing the star pattern and telling the stars to sparkle," Blane said.

Stars, sparkle. Stars, sparkle! Elle and speak art into being—her voice-activated installation! What if there were a way to alert Elle we were trapped?

"Blane, you're a genius!" I blurted out.

"Why, what did I say?"

"Stars, sparkle!" I replied. "Stars, sparkle!"

"I don't get it," Barrett said. "How does that help us?"

"What if we link Barrett's computer to Elle's beam? It doesn't need a network connection or Wi-Fi!" Elated, I grasped Blane's hands. "We can tell her to get us out of here!"

"What's a beam?" Barrett asked.

"It's a handheld, cordless projector. You can pair the beam with another device and display information from the device through the beam," said Lydia. "And it's a great thought, but we don't know her beam's passcode. And Thilda monitors the beams, remember?"

I sighed, defeated. Lydia was right.

"Back to square one," said Barrett, shaking his head.

"I hope not. Let me think." I stared at my Ailm charm and the infinity sign pattern.

Wisdom. Purpose. Physical, mental, spiritual strength. A

clear path forward. I closed my eyes and took a deep breath. My thoughts swirled around my head like reactants in a cauldron. *The passcode. A clear path forward. Aquamarine. My infinity sign star map. Stars, sparkle!* Speak art into being. *GE Pharmaceuticals. Tech and art.* Infinitely encoded; forever expressed. *Our DNA. Our purpose. Elle's beam.* Infinitely encoded; forever expressed. Speak art into being.

"Oh my gosh," I blurted out. "Barrett, I need your computer!"

"What, what?" asked Blane.

"This is the biggest leap of faith. If it works, we're free. If it doesn't, Thilda will be in here faster than we can say Eternae."

I typed in "Beam—Elle," selecting the name when it appeared and praying Elle would see that a device was trying to pair with her beam. Barrett's computer prompted me with a pop-up screen for a passcode. We had one minute. Trembling, I typed: *Speak Art Into Being.*

Nothing happened.

A message flashed across Barrett's computer.

Pairing Unsuccessful. You have two more attempts.

Two more attempts and fifty-five seconds to guess her password. I took a deep breath, closing my eyes again. It wasn't her new installation. I heard Elle when she first described *infinitely encoded; forever expressed:* "*Our desire to live our purpose and chase our dreams . . . our DNA . . . it's my favorite name for a piece—it's the code to everything.*" I opened my eyes.

Forty seconds.

I typed: *InfinitelyEncoded;ForeverExpressed*

A message flashed on the screen. *Pairing Unsuccessful. You have one more attempt.*

"It didn't work!" Barrett blurted out.

"Blane, what do I do?"

"I don't know!"

My hands were shaking.

Lydia looked at me.

I looked at Blane.

Thirty seconds.

"I have to get this right." I took another deep breath. My pulse was racing. I closed my eyes. *Be brave.* "What am I missing?" I opened my eyes.

"I don't know!" Blane paced.

Lydia sighed. "One more guess."

Twenty seconds.

I closed my eyes. I thought about Elle. *The artist who blends technology and art. The artist with the tattoo of a paintbrush on her left ring finger, with the Vitruvian Man tattoo on the back of her right hand. The artist who thinks it's more poetic to type in only lowercase letters. Lowercase letters!* I opened my eyes.

Ten seconds.

Blane put his arms around my shoulder. Lydia leaned in. Barrett clutched his brother's forearm. I took a deep breath. *Be brave.* All I could hear was my heartbeat.

Five seconds.

I typed in the passcode: *infinitelyencoded;foreverexpressed*

The words PAIRING SUCCESSFUL flashed across Barrett's screen.

XX

Elle perched on Barrett's bed, holding her paintbrush like a wand. We told her how Dr. Gellmane, Dr. Pritzmord, and Thilda showed up at our door and how we discovered Sangstra's supplies in the basement.

"How'd you guess my passcode?" Elle grinned. "That was genius!"

I smiled. "I have a penchant for memorable art installations." I looked at Lydia, Blane, and Barrett. "And I have a genius team. How'd you realize something was wrong?"

"When the resin finally arrived, I made the paperweight. I went to your office to give it to you, but you weren't there. Pippa told me Thilda caught you stealing GE's funds and fired you. She put Sebastian in charge of the party."

Shocked, Lydia and I looked at each other, shaking our heads.

"I thought that was suspicious. I texted KDI to trace your phone through your sentinel. But your sentinel must not be connected to your phone since that returned a null signal."

I grasped my sentinel, nodding.

"So making sure sentinels have their own tracking system, independent of the phone's, is something KDI is fixing before the knight-wide rollout."

I grinned, proud to help KDI improve its technology.

"Then, when I got a beam request from a computer that wasn't mine, but was located where *speak art into being* is, I started to connect the dots. The beam request must be from *under* my mural, in Thilda's basement."

"How'd you unlock the door?" asked Barrett. "Only Thilda has the key."

Elle grinned. "I scheduled an emergency meeting with her. I told her I'd found a structural instability in *infinitely encoded; forever expressed*, and we couldn't give VIP lab tours that went underneath it unless we fixed it. She said we weren't giving tours, so fixing it could wait. I insisted, telling her she couldn't afford to say no if a VIP asked. As she stared out of her giant glass window, deep in thought, I swapped the paperweights and got the key."

"Weren't you terrified?" Barrett asked. "I'd have been!"

"Maybe a little, but I was on a rescue mission," said Elle in a matter-of-fact tone as she looked at me. "Oh, by the way, the mortar and pestle—and her box—are on her desk. Her box isn't opened, thankfully. She must still need both rubies."

"You're amazing!" Barrett looked at Elle in awe. "Wow."

I giggled at Barrett's attempts to flirt with Elle. I couldn't tell if she was playing hard to get.

"Thanks to Lydia's clever thinking, Thilda doesn't have my Grealmæp, only hers. But that won't stop her. She wants to cut her box open with her boyfriend's laser," I said.

Elle shook her head. "We can't let her. Morgan's spells protect those boxes. If they're opened by anything other than the Grealmæps' rubies, there is no telling what evil they will unleash." Elle paused, clasping her hands together and bringing her index fingers to her lips. "It's not surprising Thilda can't see how real magic is—her faith in science blinds her to anything else."

Barrett looked at Elle's hands. "I like your tattoo. Leonardo was a genius. He's my inspiration," he stammered.

"Thank you. Yes he was." Elle hopped off Barrett's bed and started pacing around the room.

"Maybe we can talk about him sometime," said Barrett as he gazed at Elle.

Elle didn't react to Barrett. "We need to focus. We don't have much time until the party starts."

Barrett looked at Blane. Blane shrugged, as if to say, *I don't know, compliment her intelligence or her eyes. Girls love it when guys compliment their eyes.*

"KDI is trying to send knights here from Intake, but they can't guarantee anything," Elle said. "Intake is one of the most sacred nights of the year. Knights can't just miss it."

"Great," said Lydia. "Knights or no knights, we need to get Thilda's Grealmæp, her box, and the mortar and pestle."

"And stop the guests from taking Eternae," Blane added. "And we can't be seen."

"We won't be. Once we have a plan, we'll change into our costumes." Elle glanced at her phone. "You know all those guests will show up in full costume: Merlins, Celtic fairies, and witches. Once they do, Thilda, Pippa, and Sebastian will be preoccupied with entertaining them. In our costumes, we'll blend right in."

"And what about Dr. Pritzmord and Dr. Gellmane?" asked Blane. "Do you think they'll be here too?"

Elle nodded, pacing around Barrett's room. "I'm sure. But KDI has been onto them. They've been tracking Elyse since she defected. She's especially dangerous since we don't know what exactly she knows. She's been involved in many crimes: artifact heists, bribing officials, embezzling funds, forging art, and murders. Countless murders, including her husband—Albert von Genzkensaffe. And she's done time and assumed fake identities. She's elusive—and always miles ahead of KDI. When I realized she shipped the mortar and pestle to GE, I alerted KDI after I saw them on Thilda's desk."

"Like mother, like daughter," Lydia said, disgusted.

"And we know Dr. Gellmane is after the Grail," I added. "She and Pritzmord."

"She murdered her husband?" I asked, shocked. "I thought his cancer took him."

"That's what Elyse wants everyone to think. Albert *was* dying from cancer. But Elyse knew he'd left his estate to Thilda, which left her with nothing. Elyse established power of attorney over Albert's affairs and cut Thilda out."

"How did she get away with that?" Barrett asked Elle.

"She's the director of the Amesbury Museum. Her reputation carries a lot of weight. She convinced Albert's lawyers Thilda wasn't fit to steward his assets. They wouldn't give them directly to Elyse, but they set up a trust, run by the board of the Amesbury Museum."

"Which she's probably been skimming from over the years?" Barrett asked, spellbound by Elle.

"Yep." Elle smiled at Barrett. "Smart guess—and one for which KDI has evidence."

Barrett grinned at Blane, as if to say, *She thinks I'm smart!* Blane gave his brother a thumbs-up. I stared at the floor, thinking about KDI and Dr. Gellmane's nefarious actions. The threads in the ball of yarn were getting more and more entangled.

"So how do we get into Thilda's office and get her box and the mortar and pestle?" asked Barrett.

"Sebastian," Elle said. "He'll help us if I ask."

"You're so cool," Barrett blurted out. "You know everyone!"

Elle cracked a small smile at Barrett, as if to say, *You're cute, but you're going to have to try much harder for me to be interested.*

"So, are we ready to plan our escape?" Barrett asked.

Elle looked at her phone. "Yep, let's do this!"

††

With our plan in place and Elle leading the way, we slipped out of the basement undetected, darting right into Elle's supply closet. She closed the door and flipped on the light. A box of granola bars and ten purple velvet Merlin costumes hung on the wall, complete with full gray-haired beards, gold and red wizard hats, and wands.

"Ten?" I asked, noticing the extra costumes.

"Yes, in case the knights need some." Elle grinned. "Got to be prepared."

I chuckled as I slipped into my Merlin robe. I never imagined I'd be wearing a wizard costume and crashing a VIP gala in Gran's boots. As we changed, Elle handed each of us a pair of earbuds.

"These link up to mine, so we can communicate with each other over a private network. When you want to talk, tap them, speak, and tap again when you're done." She paused, a small twinkle forming in her eyes. "Try to hide them under your beard."

Barrett murmured in awe, "You're so smart, Elle. I can see it in your eyes."

Blane facepalmed himself. I shook my head. Lydia chuckled uncontrollably. Even she noticed Barrett's attempts to flirt with Elle. Blane whispered to Barrett, "Next time say something about how pretty her eyes are. You can do this, my dude."

Ten minutes later, having eaten our snack and armed with our wands, we were ready. Thilda, Dr. Pritzmord, and Dr. Gellmane had no idea we were about to infiltrate their party. From Legend to Launch would be a night to remember.

††

Thilda stood near the podium on the stage, her red stilettos poking out from under her dress. Pippa dimmed the lights. The disco ball flashed over the lower level. Fires blazed in the chalices stationed around the dance floor. The spotlight bounced around, illuminating Thilda and *infinitely encoded; forever expressed.* Merlins, witches, fairies, and Celtic princesses packed closer to the podium, eager to hear Thilda.

Thilda placed her box on the podium, moving in a dazzling white dress with long, flowy red velvet sleeves. I gazed in awe at her outfit. The corset-style top featured gold lacing, set off by a slim pencil-cut skirt with a white satin train. Little crystals were strewn on the train, like diamonds.

Thilda held a silver wand in her right hand. Over her chest, she wore her Grealmæp, the ruby gleaming, complementing her blood-red lipstick. Her immaculate outfit made her look regal and ruthless. A tall figure stood next to her, dressed in head-to-toe black armor with a helmet and metal gloves.

"I bet that's Elean," I said. "Keep an eye on him."

Blane nodded. The spotlight stopped on Thilda.

"Ladies and gentlemen, wizards, witches, knights, Celtic spirits, and fairies, welcome to From Legend to Launch!"

The guests cheered. Thilda beamed. "Welcome to the longest day—and shortest night—of the year. On this night, you get the first glimpse of Eternae—and the future of the human race."

Thilda gesticulated her wand at the projector, and the screen behind her descended. Pippa turned on the gas in the trench beds behind the bar. The flames sprang up, creating a magical and mysterious ambiance. ETERNAE flashed on the screen in neon red script.

"Distinguished guests, it is my honor to share a few words! I'll keep my remarks short. I know I'm standing between you and dancing!"

The crowd hooted and hollered. Blane and I made our way closer to the podium, smiling at the other Merlins and witches as we thanked them for letting us pass.

"Manufactured right here at GE Pharmaceuticals, Eternae is not just any medicine—it is a miracle. It cures cancer—and does so much more! Would you like to know what else it does?"

The crowd gasped in delight, applauding.

"YES!"

"Tell us more!"

"What does it do?"

The chant, "TELL US MORE! TELL US MORE! TELL US MORE!" filled the air.

Thilda beamed. "Are you ready?" She waved her wand as if she were a magician enthralling the audience. "Are you sure?" Grinning, she threw both her hands in the air and pointed her wand at the disco ball.

"YES!" screamed the crowd.

Thilda beamed. "Eternae not only prevents and cures cancer, it also gives eternal life!" She pointed her wand at the screen. "Let's see for ourselves."

The crowd fell silent as scenes of war, violence, sickness, and death appeared. ALL OUR PROBLEMS STEM FROM OUR FEAR OF DEATH scrolled across the screen. SO OUR GREATEST CHALLENGE, OUR MORAL OBLIGATION—IF WE HAVE THE KNOWLEDGE—IS TO DESTROY DEATH ITSELF.

The graphic pictures of suffering faded to clips of high-tech images and chemical equations, inspirational shots of GE Pharmaceuticals' lower level, researchers engaged in conversations, Sebastian sipping his smoothie, flowers blooming, and mortars and pestles on marble tables. There was even a clip of The Nerdy Nerds at trivia.

THROUGHOUT THE AGES, WE HAVE CHASED THE IMPOSSIBLE appeared in white cursive writing against a background of Thilda's flower bed. TODAY, WE HAVE FOUND IT. The video cut to a scene of Dr. DeBlack drawing telomeres on whiteboards and talking to technicians. TODAY, GE PHARMACEUTICALS BRINGS ETERNAL LIFE BACK TO THE PEOPLE.

A clip of Sebastian tending to the flowers in the glass hallway appeared. "I've regained my life," he said, smiling as he sipped his smoothie. I felt queasy and repulsed, knowing what was in Sebastian's drink. I cringed and closed my eyes, wishing I could unsee the scene.

I opened them to see Thilda on the screen, walking on her chessboard floor, joined by Sebastian. Her red stilettos echoed as the two of them exited the farmhouse, then entered the lab and walked through the lower level. She held a little red pill between her index finger and thumb. The camera focused on the pill and her perfectly manicured crimson nails.

"Imagine living in a world where you don't have to die." She smiled, dropping the pill into the palm of her other hand. "Now imagine you don't have to dream of this world, since it's here. Right in the palm of your hand. The new world order is here."

She shot a sultry gaze at the camera as she extended her palm. With her other hand, she beckoned to Sebastian and put her arm around him, smiling at the camera. "Immortality never tasted so good. Do you want to try it?"

The video ended with Thilda in her office, sitting in her black leather chair. She held her red pill in the palm of her outstretched hand, offering it to the viewers. Her office faded into bright white light, leaving only her hand and the Eternae pill. The scene cut to an entirely black background, with *infinitely encoded; forever expressed* spiraling on one side of the shot. The words ETERNAE NOW appeared on the other side as the credits rolled.

The crowd broke out in thunderous applause, chanting, "YES!"

Thilda beamed. "To thank you for your support during Eternae's journey, from legend to its launch, I've given each of you something special."

The crowd gasped as Thilda pointed to her left at a table. The spotlight followed her gesture, illuminating the swag bags.

"Each of those bags has one Eternae pill. One for each of you." She beamed.

The crowd went wild, cheering. I gasped in horror as chills ran up and down my spine. *The guests cannot leave with those pills!*

Thilda grinned. "We made the impossible possible. Tonight, you get the world's first taste of eternity. A bite of forbidden fruit may have robbed this right from us. But tonight, one little red pill puts that privilege back in our palms."

"ETERNAL LIFE IS OURS!"

"NO MORE DEATH!"

"WE CAN'T WAIT TO LIVE FOREVER!"

She smiled, invigorated by the crowd's cheers. She glanced at Elean, then waved her wand to quiet the crowd.

"Tonight, GE Pharmaceuticals writes our own story. We tilt history in our favor, once and for all!" Thilda paused, letting the applause die down, then continued. "We start a new chapter. A chapter in which nothing is impossible—not even living forever. As my late father loved to say, 'Those who never stop chasing the impossible are the ones who actually make it possible.' Thank you for making the impossible, possible! Now, I'd like to turn the mic over to someone whose generous support has truly made this all possible: Lord Breekson!"

I gasped. *Lord Breekson is here!* Anxiety filled my stomach; dizziness filled my head. I hoped I wouldn't throw up my granola bar. Gran's ex-husband was about to come on stage.

"BREEKSON, BREEKSON!" the crowd chanted as a lanky, elderly man stepped up to the podium. His royal-blue velvet cape billowed around his wizard robe as he faced the crowd. He held a crystal ball in one hand and a wooden staff in his other.

"What a magnificent evening." His English accent oozed old money and high society as he placed his crystal ball on the podium. "I'm so proud of Thilda for carrying her family legacy to bring Eternae to fruition. Family. Family is everything, isn't it? What Thilda has done in creating the GE Pharmaceuticals family—all the researchers, all the people who made Eternae come to life—is amazing."

How can Lord Breekson talk about the importance of family when he divorced Gran and left my family?

"I applaud Thilda for serving—and saving—humanity through science. I look forward to her continued success! Thank you all for being here. Let the dancing begin!"

Lord Breekson stepped back. Thilda teetered up to him, embracing him as the crowd cheered. Thilda grabbed her box, and when she, Elean, and Lord Breekson walked offstage, the lights dimmed, leaving only the glowing fire from the chalices, trenches, and candles on each high-top table.

I grabbed Blane's arm, fixing my gaze on Thilda. "We can't lose them."

"What about the guests? Not one of them can walk away with that poison pill!" Blane whispered.

We tapped our earbuds. Elle, Lydia, and Barrett came in. "We're following Thilda, Elean, and Breekson. We'll get the Grealmæp and Thilda's box. You three destroy those pills and find the mortar and pestle."

"Sounds good," said Lydia.

"On it," said Barrett.

"Copy," said Elle. "And standby for the knights. They're almost here. They can't stay long, though."

"Awesome news!" I said as we tapped our earbuds again to disconnect from the others.

Thilda and Elean were at the bar. Lord Breekson wasn't in sight. Blending in with the other Merlins, Blane and I made our way closer. My heart pounded. I took a deep breath, clutching Gran's necklace through my robe. *Be brave. They think we're still locked in the basement.*

"I'll have a Druidic Droplet," said Elean. "Easy on the OJ and double the vodka. The lady will have an Eternael Elixir, heavy pour. We're celebrating this amazing woman tonight!" Elean wrapped his armor-clad arm around Thilda's lower back. "Tonight is ours, my love!"

Thilda smiled. "Tonight *is* ours. And with Eternae, the future is ours. And with your work, the past will be ours. Talk about a power couple! No kids. Profits rolling in. We'll be unstoppable!" Thilda recentered her Grealmæp. "And soon, the Grail will be ours. Did your laser arrive?"

"Yep, been tracking the shipment."

"Perfect. And my mother is ready to help."

"So is my dad. For once he'll see the power of my research and take me seriously."

"After we finish making the rounds, we'll meet them in my office to cut the box."

The bartender handed Elean and Thilda their drinks.

"Thank you." She picked up her glass, turning to Elean. "I love you. To us."

Elean removed his armored glove and picked up his drink. "To us." He raised his glass and kissed Thilda. They linked arms as they chatted with guests.

Blane and I followed Thilda and Elean as they headed to the dessert station. With each step, my heart pounded more. I clutched my pendants to keep me focused. I felt as if Gran and Dad were with me, silently cheering for me.

At one of the dance floor's corners, Pippa set up the dessert station, which featured chromosome cookies, parfaits, and chocolate, vanilla, and strawberry pastries. I tapped my earbud. "They got drinks. Now they're getting dessert."

"Copy that, Carly. We've got this. We're headed to the Eternae pills. Barrett is leading the way. He's a pro at being stealthy. And the knights have arrived."

We tapped our earbuds off. Hearing how Elle described Barrett, Blane fist-pumped in the air. "Good man, Barrett! Show Elle what you got!"

Thilda picked up a chromosome cookie and bit off a telomere. "These are delicious! Very good idea. Pity that lot couldn't enjoy their party."

Elean chuckled. "Pity indeed, although that's what they get for stealing from you." He smiled at Thilda as he sipped his drink.

Thilda lied to Elean, too, about why we aren't here! What else has she lied to him about?

"My dear, that was brilliant!" Lord Breekson approached Thilda. He held two test-tube-shaped glasses brimming with Morgan's Margaritas. Accompanying him were two women, one on each arm, dressed as fairies in tight bodices and skirts that left nothing to the imagination. They wore fishnet tights and sparkling silver heels. The candlelight from the dessert station illuminated the group in a soft glow. "What a phenomenal party! You sure can make evenings—and drinks—magical." He sipped his margarita and eyed the parfaits. "These desserts look delicious!"

Thilda grinned. "Thank you, Lord Breekson; I'm thrilled you could attend." She flirted with him, unzipping his wizard robe. She stopped at his cummerbund underneath and hooked her finger around it, pulling him closer to her. He smiled in pleasure.

"Wouldn't miss it for the world." He unlinked his arms from the women and handed one a drink. "Emmaline and Caroline are the perfect accessories, aren't they?" He playfully squeezed their bottoms, then took another sip of his margarita before setting his drink on the table.

Emmaline and Caroline grinned, twirling their hair. They kissed Lord Breekson's cheeks. He giggled like a schoolboy on a first date. I cringed. *Lord Breekson is a sleazy, hypersexual womanizer.*

Lord Breekson picked up a parfait and spooned some into his mouth. "Mmm." He playfully fed Emmaline and Caroline, teasing them between bites. Emmaline stuck her tongue out and licked the spoon clean. "And with these Celtic candelabras and fire trenches, the mood is perfect. It's like we're in a hidden laboratory of a powerful enchantress."

"Thilda, can we get a picture with you?" Emmaline squeaked excitedly, opening her clutch to retrieve her phone.

Lord Breekson nodded. "That's a wonderful idea!"

"Of course," Thilda said, smiling at Emmaline and Lord Breekson. "Anything for Lord Breekson's ladies! Let's find someone to take it. We'll need some more light. Ladies, bring those candelabras here." She pointed to a few nearby tables.

Still holding her phone, Emmaline followed Caroline to get the candelabras, navigating through clusters of witches and warlocks.

"I'll help you with that, ladies." Lord Breekson patted their bottoms as he followed them.

Thilda looked around her and pointed at me. "Merlin, will you take our picture?"

I glanced behind me.

Thilda walked up to me. My stomach jumped into my mouth. I gulped, nodding, too terrified to talk. I was afraid Thilda would see my face or recognize my voice.

Thilda's eyes narrowed, her expression conniving. "Merlin, are you scared? It's okay, we don't bite." Thilda gnashed her bleached-white teeth together playfully, pulling at my costume beard flirtatiously. "Come on."

As I backed away, she tugged my beard, revealing my face. With my disguise removed, my cover was blown.

"Trinity? Carly?" Thilda spat out in shock as she recognized me. I jerked my head back and tried to run, but she deftly lunged at me, grabbing my wrist. Her nail scraped my skin, leaving a blood-red scratch. "You little rat! How did you get here? Where are your sidekicks? You're supposed to be locked up in the basement," she hissed as she pulled me by my wrist. "And as soon as we take this picture, that's exactly where you'll be headed."

"Don't you dare talk to or touch her like that!" Blane bellowed, yanking my arm so Thilda lost her grip on my wrist.

I froze, caught between wanting to expose Thilda and her evil scheme in front of her guests, and fearing no one would believe me if I accused the respected and celebrated CEO of any wrongdoing. Realizing Thilda had the upper hand at her party, I looked at Blane as if to say, *Don't draw attention to us! If it's us against Thilda, she'll win!*

"Merlin?" Thilda snarled. "Surely you're not defending the little rat?"

"Apologize to her!" Blane wasn't backing down.

"For what?" Thilda retorted.

Blane's eyes blazed with anger. He lunged at Thilda. "Don't you dare call my girl a rat, you bitch!"

"Don't you dare call my girl a bitch!" Elean bashed his armored glove into Blane's face, sending Blane reeling to the floor. He fell backward, moaning in pain.

"Blane! Are you okay?" I rushed to his side. Several guests gasped. Blane murmured incoherently.

"Come on, let's not make a scene in front of all our guests. They're here to enjoy themselves!" Thilda spat her words out as she grabbed my arm and pulled me to my feet.

"Nothing to see here," Elean said, following Thilda's direction and waving away the fairies who'd crowded around at the sight of the commotion. "Poor Merlin is a little drunk! And with the dim lights, he walked right into my armor! He'll be okay."

Thilda smiled at Elean as the fairies flitted away. "Thank you, sweet knight, for keeping the peace at our party," said Thilda. "Unlike the little rat and her boyfriend, who always manage to cause trouble." She turned to me, her face inches away from mine.

"As soon as the ladies return, you'll take our picture," said Thilda, pulling out her gun from a hidden pocket. It had a silencer on it. She held it up to my stomach, concealing it in her red velvet sleeves as she stepped back. She kept her gun trained on my stomach. "Lord Breekson is invaluable to me and my research. His wish—and his ladies' wishes—is my command. So, if they want a picture, Lord Breekson's ladies will get a picture. Once they come back, if you want to live, you will smile, accommodate their request, and take our picture. Don't try to run. Don't try anything funny." She motioned for Elean to stand next to me. He gripped my shoulder.

Emmaline, Caroline, and Lord Breekson returned with their candelabras and placed them on the high-top table near Thilda.

"I've found someone to take our picture," purred Thilda, pointing at me.

Emmaline handed me her phone. "Thank you! No need to unlock it, just swipe to the left for the camera."

"Just take the picture," Thilda mouthed to me, pointing at Elean. He tightened his grip on my shoulder.

Trembling, I tried to find the best angle. I knew it was useless to try to escape—and I didn't even know Emmaline's passcode to unlock her phone and text someone for help. I needed to talk to Lydia, Elle, and Barrett, but I couldn't let Thilda hear me. I needed time to think and time for Elle to alert the knights. *Time. Time!* Pretending I was twirling a curl, I tapped my earbud.

"It's about time for the Riddle of the Ages!" I muttered. "And it's great standing here near these yummy desserts!"

"Copy that, Carly." Lydia's voice came in through my earbud.

"I'll activate the knights," Elle added. "Sir Gawain, do you copy? Sir Kay, do you copy? Sir Percival, do you copy? Sir Lamorak, do you copy? She's by the desserts."

A wave of pride swept over me, awakening every cell in my body. *The Knights of the Dagger are named after King Arthur's knights.*

"We copy!" the knights responded in unison. "We're heading to you."

I stalled for time. "Now a serious picture!" *Click.* "A fun one!" *Click.* "A sexy one!" *Click.* Emmaline and Caroline kept gyrating, kicking their legs up or kissing Lord Breekson. Lord Breekson giggled as he grabbed their hands and arms, directing Emmaline and Caroline to pose seductively.

"Perfect!" Thilda smiled and said to the crowd that had gathered around them, "Now we must take care of this poor drunk Merlin and his lady. Elean and I will be back!"

Elean scooped Blane off the floor as Emmaline retrieved her phone from my shaking hands. Thilda sidled up to me, holding her gun to my side under her sleeves. Lord Breekson, Emmaline, and Caroline waved goodbye, disappearing to the middle of the dance floor. *Where are the knights?* The guests were drinking and dancing—pulsating to the deejay's beats, hypnotized by the music's spell and the disco ball's lights.

A dark, shadowy figure wearing a black spandex suit and a black knight's helmet snuck up behind Thilda. He held a dagger in each hand as he approached her.

"Perchance, a dance with a knight tonight?" His deep, mystical voice and rhyming words reverberated in my earbud.

She gasped, turning around to see his daggers, their silver blades glistening in the candlelight.

"ELEAN!" Her shriek pierced the air, prompting several guests to look at her. Elean dropped Blane and ran toward the knight. But the knight was too quick. Without taking his eyes off Thilda, the knight kicked Elean, causing him to trip. He crashed to the floor, knocking over a guest as he fell.

Out of the darkness, another knight in black emerged.

"Don't worry about him," said the second knight to the guests who'd congregated around Elean. "Worry about why Thilda won't dance with us." He gestured to Thilda with his daggers. "We've been waiting a long time for the honor." His daggers' silver blades gleaming, he started gliding around her. The first knight joined, trapping Thilda in a circle as their four daggers sliced the air. The guests watched, enthralled.

"So agile and precise! Simply stunning!"

"Are they professionals?"

"Let me go!" Thilda spat, trying to break through their movements. "I don't have time to dance now!"

"No time for dancing? But this is a party!" The second knight enunciated his words as he motioned behind him. Two more knights in black emerged. As all four encircled Thilda, nimbly moving around the cocktail tables, their daggers created silver streaks that made the guests cheer in delight.

Out of the corner of my eye, I saw Elean sit up. "Watch out!" I blurted out, praying the knights would hear me through their earbuds. "Elean is—"

"This is Sir Kay. I copy," the third knight said, without interrupting his dance.

I grinned as I adjusted my earbud. The knights didn't miss a beat!

One turned around, saying as if on cue, "All good things must come to an end, so better things can begin." He gestured to another knight in black, who was standing with the deejay.

"Let's get this next song started!" The knight near the deejay took the microphone, changing the song and directing guests to move closer to the deejay's table.

With guests dancing to the new song, their attention away from Thilda, the four knights closed in on her. Elean rubbed his head, then pushed himself up off the floor.

"He's getting up!" I whispered.

"This is Sir Percival. I got him," the fourth knight said.

"You're not the only one who can play this game," the first knight said to Thilda. "Do as we say and no one will get hurt. We don't like the spotlight, and you don't want a PR nightmare."

"What do you want from me?" Thilda narrowed her eyes as she stood her ground. "I'm already giving you a taste of Eternae!"

Lurking around the knights, Elean prepared to strike Sir Kay from behind.

"Eternal life in this world is a curse," said the second knight. "We want peace—"

"And justice," said Sir Percival. "Which means making sure people like you and your henchmen surrender now and forever."

He spun around, punching Elean in the stomach. Elean stumbled backward into the high-top cocktail table, sending him, the table, and the candelabras crashing to the floor. Nearby guests jumped back in terror as the tablecloth caught fire.

"GET BACK!"

"Someone ring nine-nine-nine!"

Chaotic cries rang out as nearby guests tried to stamp out the flames. A witch tore her cape off. Each time she beat the flames, they spread more. Others rushed to help, but the fire caught another woman's gown. The woman shrieked, flailing her arms in the air. Two men threw her to the ground to put out the flames.

Out of the corner of my eye, I saw two knights lunge after Thilda, the silver blades of their daggers glistening in the flames.

"They've got knives and they're going for Thilda!" a Merlin

exclaimed, dropping his drink. "Stop them!"

A warlock lunged at one of the knights, wrestling him to the ground.

"NO, HE'S GOOD! GET THILDA!" I yelled, but nobody reacted to me. I knew at Thilda's party, no one would believe me.

The warlock wound his right arm back and swung at the knight. The knight rolled to the side, missing the punch. The knight bounced up, with the warlock on his heels.

The knight swung.

The warlock ducked.

The warlock swung.

The knight stepped back, evading the punch by a split second.

Trying to catch the knight off guard, the warlock swung from his left arm. Sir Percival intercepted the punch, throwing the warlock off to the side. He tumbled into the trench behind the bar, which toppled over into the black velvet curtains.

I stared in horror as flames engulfed the curtains, turning them into a wall of fire. Guests' screams filled the air. The deejay stopped, abandoning his booth. Partygoers scrambled over each other, dropping their half-eaten desserts as they ran to the exit.

"We need to get out of here," Blane said, holding his injured face. His cheekbone had started to swell.

"Not without the Grealmæp and that box!"

"Carly, are you crazy? This is your life! The Grail isn't worth your life!"

A strange, powerful force came over me. I heard my voice, but I couldn't feel my brain telling my lips to move. "I have a moral obligation to get the Grail. I can do this. I'm a knight!"

"What are you talking about? This is beyond the knights! And you're not a knight yet! Come on, let's get out of here!"

I looked at Blane. "Not until I have the Grail!"

As he looked at me in disbelief, a masked warlock rushed from behind him and grabbed him.

———

"CARLY!" Blane screamed as he tried to elbow and kick his way free.

The warlock gripped Blane's throat, hissing, "Quiet! This time you won't be as lucky."

The voice that haunted my nightmares. Dr. Pritzmord!

A witch holding the mortar and pestle took the pestle and struck it across Blane's face. "Gimpy boy, you're coming with us." She and the warlock caught Blane's limp body, dumping it on Pippa's dolly, next to an unconscious Barrett.

"Two for the price of one," Dr. Gellmane snarled. "The smart one—"

"And the ultra-nerdy archaeologist." Dr. Pritzmord laughed. "Let's leave before this place goes up in flames."

I froze. I'd lost Thilda and Elean, and with them, the Grealmæp and Thilda's box. I'd lost the mortar and pestle. I'd lost Blane and Barrett.

I tapped my earbud. "Elle! Pritzmord and Gellmane have Blane, Barrett, and the mortar and pestle!"

"Copy that. The knights are on it."

Hot, angry tears flowed down my face. Blane was gone.

"The knights will find him. You need to get the Grealmæp and Thilda's box," Elle instructed. "Leave your earbud on."

I heard Elle activate the knights, telling them about Blane, Barrett, and the mortar and pestle.

"This is Sir Percival, copy that. Thilda and Elean are on the stairs, heading for the bridge. I'll find Pritzmord and Gellmane."

I darted to the bridge, pushing past the guests running for the door.

"Thilda, stop!" My chest heaved up and down. "Stop!" I yelled up at her.

She turned around, looking down at me. "You don't give up, do you?"

I ran up the double-helix stairs, my heart pounding. "This whole place is surrounded by knights," I lied. "They know all your secrets! It's over, Thilda. Give me the Grealmæp and your box and the knights will go easy on you."

"Never!" Thilda spat. "That box, *and* the Grail inside of it, belongs to me!"

Baa-bump.

Baa-bump.

Baa-bump.

All I could hear were my heartbeats.

"I don't have time for this, Carly Stuart. Quit meddling in things you don't understand." Thilda grasped her box. Her gold-and-silver aquamarine ring glowed, the same color as Gran's necklace.

Elean moved closer to Thilda. She handed him the box and took out her gun.

"Look at her robe! Her necklace is glowing!" Elean said, pointing at my chest. My aquamarine pendant must have popped out when I was running.

Thilda gasped. Her eyes gleamed as they fixated on my pendant. "The necklace! Hand it over. It belongs with my ring."

"Your ring belongs with my necklace," I retorted.

Lydia and Elle ran up the stairs on the other side of the bridge, blocking Thilda and Elean's escape.

"You're trapped, Thilda," said Lydia. "Give it up."

"Don't tell me what to do, you imposter. You ruined this whole party." Thilda aimed her gun at Lydia. "But you won't ruin my chance at leaving my legacy. The Grail is mine. Move!"

Lydia planted both feet, standing defiantly on the bridge. She took a deep breath and looked Thilda right in the eyes. "No."

The instant Thilda pulled the trigger, I lunged at her, knocking her over. Her bullet missed Lydia, hitting *infinitely encoded; forever expressed.* Like a waterfall of blood, red pills crashed to the floor, scattering everywhere. The fire roared as a material in the pills fueled the flames. Thilda repositioned her gun, training it on Lydia.

I tackled Thilda, knocking her on her back. Surprised by my own strength, I punched her face. I didn't care that she had a gun.

I didn't care if I got trapped in her lab. I didn't care about the Grail. I had to fight Thilda.

I punched her again and again. Blood spurted from her nose, spattering her white dress.

Elean grabbed my waist, ripping me off Thilda.

My head hit the floor.

The fractured remnants of *infinitely encoded; forever expressed* hanging in the light well became blurry.

"Carly!" Elle's voice was far away. Her hand patted my face. "Stay with me!"

Red dots. Smoky air. All I could see were red dots. All I could smell was smoke. I kept blinking. Red, blurry dots . . .

I blinked again.

My eyes closed.

Darkness.

"CARLY!" Elle screamed. "CARLY, STAY WITH ME!"

Darkness.

Pain spread from my toes to my fingertips.

My body began to go numb.

Is this what dying feels like?

A gunshot.

My eyes popped open. I jolted my head up.

Lydia clutched her stomach, crumpling as blood spurted from it. Elle rushed to her side.

"LYDIA!" I screamed. My head throbbed.

I tried to get up but couldn't. My brain was telling my body to move, but my body didn't respond.

"LYDIA, NO!" I started sobbing.

Lydia's face twisted in pain.

Thilda sneered, taunting us. "The great party planner, archaeologist, ha! It hurts, doesn't it?"

Elle patted Lydia's face. "Lydia! Stay with me, stay with me!"

"Two down . . ." Elean smirked. "One to go!"

"Forget her. Time to open our box." Hiking up her skirt, Thilda lifted one leg at a time, trampling over Lydia's body with her stilettos. "Rest in peace, bitch," she sneered.

Elean kicked Lydia as he followed Thilda. They descended the stairs on the other side of the bridge.

Elle tapped her earbud. "Sir Kay, do you copy? We need your heat generating power to help Carly and heal Lydia. We're on the bridge. Come quickly!"

"Don't lose Thilda," Lydia's fading voice came in over my earbuds. She gasped for air. "Don't lose her Grealmæp or the box." Her breathing was shallow and labored.

"I won't." Tears poured from my eyes. "I promise."

Red dots. Smoky air. All I could see were red dots. All I could smell was smoke. I kept blinking. Red, blurry dots . . .

Lydia's voice faded more. "Don't lose Thilda. Get the Grealmæp and the box. Sir Kay is coming . . ."

My eyes closed.

Darkness.

Then, hands. Warm palms on my cheeks. Strong fingers on my temples.

I blinked my eyes open. A helmet-clad knight crouched next to me. He cradled my head in his hands.

"Sir Kay?"

Warmth flowed through my temples, as if transferring energy to my brain.

"Healing hands with heat," I mumbled, remembering Grail Times. "Your superpower." I blinked again. "How's that possible? You're not really Sir Kay, are you?"

Sir Kay pressed his thumbs into my temples.

"Now is the time for healing," he said in a low, melodious voice. "Answers will come later."

My strength was returning, like nothing had happened to me.

"Get Thilda's Grealmæp and that box," Sir Kay said. "We're depending on you."

As soon as I got up, I darted to Lydia. "I'm not opening the box without you. I promise." I squeezed her hand.

She lifted her fingers to my face. "Godspeed, Carly," she said, handing me our microfiber-wrapped Grealmæp. "You'll need this. Make Lyle proud."

Thilda and Elean were nowhere in sight. I tapped my earbud, glancing down at the flames leaping up from the lower level. "Anyone know the location of Thilda and Elean?"

There was a pause, then a voice. "They're on the second floor, heading to an office."

"Right," I said. "I'm heading there!"

"I'm coming with you," said Elle. She turned to Sir Kay. "All good?"

Sir Kay looked at Lydia, then Elle. "I'll do my best. Her wound is deep."

I looked at Lydia one last time. She smiled at me, as if to say, *Do Lyle proud!*

We ran to Thilda's office, leaving Sir Kay and Lydia on the bridge. Through the cracked-open door, I saw Elean's metal gloves and suit of armor and the box on Thilda's desk, opposite a long, silver tube.

"The Holy Grail is in this box?" squealed Pippa as she hugged Sebastian. "That's wild!"

"Yes! And we're a few nucleotides away from an unending supply of pure, potent *Grealia*! Unlimited Eternae is ours!" Thilda cackled, apathetic to the fire burning down her lab. "How's that laser?" She adjusted her Grealmæp around her neck.

Careful not to be seen, I opened the door a little more. Elean stood behind the laser, aiming it at the box. *Do Dr. Gellmane and Dr. Pritzmord know Thilda is opening the box without them?*

Elean glanced up from the console. "Two minutes to showtime. Full intensity, here we come!"

"We're outnumbered. We need backup." I heard Elle's voice in my earbud. "Second floor, Thilda's office. Sir Gawain, do you copy?"

"I copy. I'll be there soon. Wait for me!"

"How long till Sir Gawain arrives?" I whispered, careful not to be too loud.

"Don't know. Never rush a knight," Elle whispered.

"But we don't have time!" I retorted.

"We cannot go in there without backup!" said Elle. "She has a gun."

"And you are a knight. You have your knives."

"We can't risk it. We need to wait for Sir Gawain."

The laser revved up to maximum intensity, its hum filling the air.

"Forty-five seconds!" Elean exclaimed.

"Elle—" I opened the door.

"Carly, no!"

Ignoring Elle, I ran to Thilda's desk. Thilda jerked her head, shocked. "You!"

"Sebastian, take over!" Elean abandoned the console and the laser and ran to stop me. I pushed Thilda's desk chair into him. He crashed to the floor, hitting the back of his head. Thilda didn't take her eyes off the laser as Sebastian guided it. Pippa rushed to Elean, tottering in her heels.

"Aren't you going to help your boyfriend?" I asked Thilda, gesturing at Elean. "Or is it only about the Grail?"

Thilda glared at me. "He's a big boy. He'll be fine."

Elean yelped in pain. "My knees!"

The laser beeped. Sebastian didn't flinch as he kept his eyes on the box. Thilda's eyes gleamed as Sebastian prepared to fire the laser.

"Ready?" she spat. "Science always beats magic."

"Not if that magic is Morgan's," said Elle, standing in the doorway.

I turned around, looking at Elle. A knight in shining silver armor stood next to her. A green *G* with gold and aquamarine detailing glistened on his breastplate.

"Don't even think of firing that laser. Thilda, we have enough evidence on you to shut this lab down and lock you in jail forever." Sir Gawain's voice boomed across Thilda's office.

Sebastian released his hand, stepping away from the console as the laser abruptly powered down.

"Who are you?" asked Thilda. "Some Somerset constable here for the party?"

Sir Gawain held a dagger in each hand. "Nobody move. Thilda von Genzkensaffe, put your hands where I can see them."

"What do you want from me?" Thilda hissed without moving her hands.

"Give it up. Give up the Grealmæp, the Grail, the lab, eternal life—everything. The new world order is not yours to usher in. You cannot write your own story to right all of history's wrongs. It's over, Thilda."

Sir Gawain is quoting the notes the Knights of the Dagger sent Lydia and Gran when they found the Grealmæp!

"That's no way to talk to a lady," Thilda said sarcastically, lifting her hands slowly.

Sir Gawain stared at her, his tone intensifying when he saw her pinky finger. "Not even wearing Morgan's ring can give you Morgan's powers."

Thilda whipped out her gun, wasting no time in firing it at Sir Gawain.

The bullet hit Sir Gawain's breastplate—then bounced off, clinking on the floor.

Thilda blinked, clearly surprised. She panicked. "What the hell?"

Sir Gawain looked at his breastplate, brushing off the spot where the bullet hit. "Amazing! Not even a dent! Gotta love Morgan's magic and KDI's technology."

"Don't just stand there, finish him!" Thilda yelled at Sebastian.

Sebastian lunged at Sir Gawain, who swatted him down in one smooth swing. Sebastian landed on the console, his body pressing several buttons as he slumped over. The laser revved up.

Thilda aimed her gun at Sir Gawain. "I'll finish him myself." As she fired, the laser beeped—a series of quick, high-pitched sounds. Startled, Thilda missed her target, hitting the red neon Eternae sign instead.

"What's the laser doing?" I asked.

"I don't know," Elle said.

The beeping accelerated and got louder.

"It's about to fire!"

I lunged at Thilda's box, clutching it to my chest. A single red line started cutting through Thilda's desk.

"Elle, get Thilda's Grealmæp!" I screamed.

Elle lunged at Thilda, grabbing the Grealmæp as Thilda tried to swat her away. But Elle was too strong. She wrestled Thilda's gun out of her hand, throwing it to the floor. Having disarmed Thilda, she yanked the Grealmæp off Thilda's neck, snapping her chain. Elle slipped the Grealmæp into her pocket and ran toward me. "Sir Gawain can handle the rest. We need to get you out of here."

The laser kept cutting Thilda's desk.

Pippa rushed to the console, supporting Sebastian as he tried to lift himself. "How do I stop this?" she asked.

"Not so fast!" Thilda screamed from behind me. She pulled my hair, twisting my curls together as she yanked my head back.

I screamed in pain.

"Give me my box!" Thilda snarled.

Elle yelled, "Carly, throw me the box!"

I heaved the box to Elle. My hands free, I spun around, pinning Thilda to the floor. I clasped my hands around her throat, feeling a sense of justice as Thilda's eyes bulged and she gasped for air. I grasped Thilda's throat tighter, trying to control my own breathing. I heard Pippa cheer as she and Sebastian shut off the laser.

"Please," wheezed Thilda, her eyes desperate. "Woman to woman. *Please.*"

I looked in her eyes. "Do you promise to give up the Grail?"

Our gazes locked.

"I promise. Just don't kill me."

I closed my eyes, my hands still on Thilda's throat.

I took a deep breath. We got the Grealmæps and Thilda's box. But we'd lost Blane, Barrett, and the mortar and pestle. *What did we really win?*

I exhaled.

I opened my eyes, taking my hands off Thilda's throat. I stood up, stepping back from Thilda.

"I knew you would do the right thing," she said as she sat up.

"The knights' punishment for you will be worse than death," I spat as I turned around and walked away, leaving Thilda sitting on her office floor.

As I did, I heard Elle scream, "CARLY, LOOK OUT!"

Before I could react, Thilda grabbed the back of my boot. I fell headfirst on the floor. My head throbbing, I rolled over to see Thilda spring up. She sneered as she towered above me.

"Good night, Carly Stuart!" She slipped one of her stilettos off her foot. Pointing its heel at my neck, she lunged forward, preparing to ram her stiletto into my throat. At the same time, Sir Gawain charged at Thilda with his daggers out. He thrusted them into her stomach, hurling her into the glass window. The glass shattered, showering shards onto the ground below. For a split second, Thilda teetered as a last look of fear filled her eyes. Sir Gawain jerked his daggers out of her body. She fell backward through the window, grasping in vain at the air.

When she landed on the ground far below, her neck snapped.

Sir Gawain looked out at GE Pharmaceuticals' property, the broken window framing his figure as he bowed his head, as though in prayer. "The two daggers are sharp and ready. Their blades are forged in steel. Bloodshed will be upon us. The world must purge so it can heal." He lifted his head. "Magic, or science, we shouldn't dabble in what we don't understand. Mathilda von Genzkensaffe, may God rest your wicked soul."

———•———

Elean screamed, "What have you done?" He crawled to the window, crying and sobbing. "THILDA! THILDA, NO!"

Pippa, Sebastian, Elle, Sir Gawain, and I bowed our heads as Elean's anguished wails filled the air.

The faraway sirens of emergency vehicles mixed with his cries, creating a cacophony of distressed, dissonant noise.

XXI

I blinked my eyes open. Hot sweat dripped down my neck. I wrapped my tattered Merlin robe around me, hoping for warmth in the cold, early morning hours.

My heart was pounding like a jackhammer.

The flashing lights of the fire trucks, police cars, and ambulances sharply contrasted with the darkness of the starless Somerset sky. I was spread out on my back, on the ground by the flower bed. *Beautiful flowers in reds, pinks, and yellows, planted neatly in precise rows* . . . Elle and Sir Gawain sat beside me.

I sat upright, pushing myself up by my elbows and palms. "Where's Lydia?"

Elle looked at me. Her lower lip trembled. She embraced me with a tenderness I'd experienced only twice before—the tenderness with which the church ladies, and J. Carmichael, embraced me when Gran, and then my dad, passed away. "Carly . . ." Elle's voice trailed off as she released her hug, gently holding the back of my head.

"No." I shook my head. "NO!" I yelled. I couldn't control my tears. "NO!" I grasped my Ailm and aquamarine pendants. Elle placed her hand on my back.

"NO!" I clenched my fists, shaking them at the flashing lights and the starless sky as I wept. Elle kept her hand on my back, silently letting me sob.

"Sir Kay couldn't save her?" I looked at Sir Gawain, hoping he'd say something to make Lydia come back.

———

"The bullet caused irreversible stomach bleeding." He sighed. "Even magic has its limits."

Sobs escaped me and I kept my eyes to the ground, looking at my Ailm charm bracelet. Lydia had an Ailm charm bracelet too. Her bracelet was one of the first things we'd talked about.

Nassauton would never be the same without her. Our office hours. Our conversations. Her lectures. Her stories of her and Gran's adventures. Evidence, not emotion! Walking to Dr. Hasserin's house. Working with Kenneth. Party planning. She'd given me advice and supported me, permitting me to prioritize the Grail. She'd conquered technology, learning how to use her beam. She'd finally learned to call the *C. elegans* a nematode. She wanted to see strong partnerships, teams, and trailblazer female archaeologists immortalized on the silver screen. Even if Kenneth and I found Blane, our Fearless Foursome would never be complete again. *How will I tell Kenneth? Or Lydia's brother and his family?*

"I know she meant a lot to you," said Elle. "And I know she'd want you not to give up now."

I nodded absentmindedly, hearing Elle's voice but not processing her words. With Lydia dead, Blane and Barrett kidnapped, and Kenneth at Intake, I didn't know how I'd be able to continue anything. I didn't even have my phone! I stood up. Elle and Sir Gawain got up too.

"I'm sorry, Carly. Your path ahead is going to be very difficult. Your quest is not yet over." Sir Gawain paused. "I hope that in me, you know you always have a steadfast ally and lifelong friend." He removed his helmet.

I gasped. *Lord Breekson!*

"The quest you're on is one of the most dangerous ones any knight has ever undergone, Carly. You're doing the best you can. Lyle would be so proud of you."

I stammered, unable to speak. *Sir Gawain is Lord Breekson? What does he know about my quest?*

"I wish we could talk more, but I need to round up the

knights. We need to get back to Intake. I'll tell Kenneth about Lydia."

Elle and Lord Breekson embraced. "Take care of her, Elle. She means the world to me."

Lord Breekson hugged me. "Carly, be careful, and recover well. If you need anything, just say the word." He pointed at my earbud, then to his. "Oh, and before I forget, this belongs to you." He handed me Thilda's gold-and-silver aquamarine ring. "Wear it, hide it, keep it safe, and in your sight. Love you, you fearless young explorer. Be safe."

"Wait!" I said. "What did you call me?"

"Young explorer. It's the nickname Lyle gave you. She always thought it was perfect for our spunky granddaughter."

I gasped again. *Lord Breekson is my grandfather!*

Lord Breekson put his helmet back on. He tapped his earbud. "Ready, knights?"

"Ready!" they responded in unison.

"He must have swiped it off Thilda's finger," Elle said as Lord Breekson walked away. "He's one of our most clever knights."

I slid Thilda's ring on my right pinky finger. It fit perfectly.

"Now all you need is the ear cuff." Elle smiled.

"What ear cuff?"

"Morgan le Fay's ear cuff. It's part of her jewelry set."

"I don't understand."

"Morgan's jewelry. It's infamous. Her spirit animal, the gryphon, is always depicted wearing it: the necklace, ring, and ear cuff. Gold, silver, and aquamarine." Elle pointed at my necklace and ring.

The gryphon in Morgan's crest in The Courtly Robin!

"Where is the ear cuff?" I asked.

"No clue, but I'm sure KDI can help us find it. In the meantime, we have a box to open."

I looked at Thilda's box. It looked like a solid cube, with no openings or cracks. There was no lock on it, only two sets of double daggers etched in stone on the top.

"I think you know what to do, Carly."

I nodded, positioning the box on the ground and squatting next to it. I wiped my hands on my Merlin sleeves, trying to clean them since I didn't have gloves. I hoped Lydia would have approved, given the circumstances. I popped the rubies out of the Grealmæps and placed them in the double dagger marks. I tried to turn both rubies to the right, searching for the click like I'd done with the box in the Amesbury Museum. But the rubies didn't move. There was no click.

"They're not working."

Elle smiled. "Just watch."

The rubies began to glow like deep red eyes, backlit from inside the box. A line of red light zigzagged from the rubies, around the box, forming a lid. I clutched Elle's arm, breathless as I watched the red light.

"Morgan's magic?" I whispered in awe.

Elle nodded.

When the red light finished zigzagging, the box hissed as the lid popped up. It hovered over the box, waiting to be opened.

"Go ahead," said Elle.

I lifted the lid. A black leather book, with red double dagger marks and the initial *M* in gold, silver, and aquamarine, rested in the center.

My eyes widened in wonder. "Is this one of Morgan's spell books?" I picked it up, flipping through the pages.

Elle pointed back to the title page, nodding. Morgan had signed, inscribed, and dated her spell book. I could make out only a few words: *Morgan le Fay, King Arthur, the Grail, Camlann,* and *Glastonbury.*

The last page caught my eye. It was a sketch of a girl, from the back. She had long, curly black hair and rosy skin. She was wearing Morgan's necklace, with her pendants—an Ailm charm and aquamarine stone—floating in front of her. She was also wearing Morgan's ear cuff and ring. Green light emanated from her jewelry, forming a bubble around her. Her outstretched arms reached for a chalice just beyond her hands.

Goose bumps appeared on my arms. "That's got to be the Grail," I whispered.

As I looked more closely at the girl, I trembled. She had seven dots scattered on her lower back, like a constellation of stars in the shape of an infinity sign. *My star map!*

I put Morgan's book in my lap and pulled up the back of my shirt. "Elle, you need to see something."

"Cool birthmark! Looks like an infinity sign." Elle smiled.

The aquamarine stones in my necklace and on my ring glowed green. *It's a sign.* I lifted the book to Elle's face. "Look closely at her back."

Elle gasped. "Whoa." She pointed to my birthmark, then to the book, then back to my birthmark. She studied my birthmark, counting each of the seven dots. Then, she stared at me, beaming as her eyes sparkled. "By Lady Morgan's magic! I never thought I'd see this day." Elle shook her head. "If I wasn't seeing this with my own eyes, I wouldn't believe this."

"What?" I asked.

"Carly, you're the girl in the prophecy."

††

As the paramedics approached us, I put Morgan's spell book back in the box, sealing the lid so it locked in place.

"You okay, love?" one asked.

"I'll be fine."

"She passed out earlier. She could have a concussion." Elle spoke firmly to the paramedic. "She'll need the full workup of brain scans and monitoring. Don't worry about the cost. We'll pay for it."

The paramedics hoisted me onto the gurney. I clutched Thilda's box.

"They won't let me come with you, unfortunately," said Elle. She handed me a card. "Take this. Kenneth and I will meet you there in December."

"For what?"

"For Imprint!"

The paramedics loaded me into the ambulance. I peered at my boots sticking over the edge of the gurney.

"Be safe, Carly. Many knights have been waiting many years for this day."

"My Imprint?"

Elle nodded, smoothing her Merlin robe and making sure her daggers were securely locked in their sheaths on her leg. "You need to recover. I'll see you soon. In the meantime, I'll work with KDI to find Blane, Barrett, Dr. Gellmane, and Dr. Pritzmord. We need to learn what they're doing with the mortar and pestle." She paused. "And I owe Barrett a chat on da Vinci's genius." Her cheeks flamed in a blush as she said his name.

As the paramedics shut the ambulance door, I looked at the card Elle gave me. It had two theater masks printed on the front. One was wearing a wreath made of ivy on her head, and the other a baseball cap with a club on it. The words *Act II* and its address were written on the back.

The ambulance lurched forward. I held Thilda's box tighter. As we headed down the driveway, GE Pharmaceuticals became a burnt shell in the darkness of the Somerset sky.

ACKNOWLEDGMENTS

I owe a debt of gratitude to my family, friends, and *Etched in Stone* readers. Thank you for your enthusiastic support, for joining our Fearless Foursome as the adventure to get the Grail continues, and for sharing Carly's story with the world. Each one of you is absolutely amazing, and Carly and I couldn't do this without you!

To MNS, who inspired countless female students to know the chemistry lab was a place for them and to pursue science with the highest standards of ethics and integrity.

To Giselle Harrington, Kristen Hamilton, Cayce Berryman, and Crystal MM Burton: You rock! Thank you for everything, especially the care and intentionality that you have given to Carly's story!

To every fearless woman who has gone before me as a trailblazer and role model . . . thank you.

292

ABOUT THE AUTHOR

Archaeology, the Holy Grail, and Arthurian legends have always fascinated Christine Galib. Christine writes to empower the knight in each of us to pursue our quests with grace, courage, and faith. She loves getting lost in a good book and can be found at christinegalib.com.

www.ingramcontent.com/pod-product-compliance
Lightning Source LLC
Chambersburg PA
CBHW061520210726
48287CB00006B/1753